W9-ACS-597

BISON
BOOKS

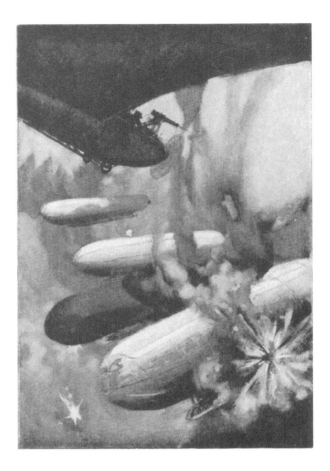

The War in the Air

H. G. Wells

INTRODUCTION TO THE BISON BOOKS EDITION BY
Dave Duncan

University of Nebraska Press
Lincoln and London

Library of Congress Cataloging-in-Publication Data
Wells, H. G. (Herbert George), 1866–1946.
The war in the air / H. G. Wells; introduction to the Bison Books edition by
Dave Duncan.
p. cm.—(Bison frontiers of imagination)
ISBN 0-8032-9831-5 (pa.: alk paper)
1. Air warfare—Fiction. I. Title. II. Series.
PR5774.W28 2002
823.'912—dc21 2002075250

Contents

Introduction

The main thing I have to tell you is that this book is still a rollicking good read. Yes, it was published almost a hundred years ago, and yes, it contains the worst blunder Wells ever made in his fiction, but his unsurpassed storytelling sweeps the reader along as well as it ever did. Furthermore, the point he made in 1908 has resumed a horrible relevance in this, our brave new twenty-first century.

I confess to being a Wells disciple. He and Jules Verne were the meat and drink of my adolescence, for back on that fog-shrouded Scottish shore the only other science fiction available to me was anonymous hackwork in boys' magazines. I now possess only one book I owned back in those days—a 1948 printing of Wells's collected short stories. My bias is declared; you have been warned.

Herbert George Wells was born into poverty—not quite the "Third World" under-swamp of Victorian society but something very close to it. By brilliance and brutal hard work he clawed his way up the social ladder, gaining an education and ruining his health. He became a teacher, and then a writer of textbooks, short stories, and transient "filler" pieces for magazines. He was probably the first literary genius with scientific training, a rare combination even now.

His first novel, *The Time Machine*, published in 1895 when he was twenty-nine, made his name and launched a new genre of fiction.

A cavalcade of masterpieces followed: *The Island of Doctor Moreau*, *The First Men in the Moon*, *The Invisible Man*, and *The War of the Worlds*, to name only the most memorable. Although his futuristic adventure stories were popular and successful, Jules Verne was a literary lightweight compared to Wells, who was acknowledged to be a first-class novelist and one of the most original thinkers of his time. The lowly draper's son eventually became a world figure hobnobbing with the great—Lenin and Franklin D. Roosevelt, among others. No science fiction writer has risen higher.

Even as a novelist Wells was always a teacher. *The Time Machine* makes a serious point about the division of society into Eloi and Morlocks. *The Invisible Man* condemns alienation. When he wrote *The War in the Air*, in 1907, Wells was veering away from what he called "scientific romances" into what we now call "mainstream" fiction, and the lecturing within the work became quite overt. He saw the future and pulled no punches. His denunciation of excessive nationalism at the beginning of chapter four seems preachy and didactic to us, but it must have been thundering heresy to the average Edwardian.

The world then was ruled by a handful of great powers, all of them except the United States being empires either ancient or upstart. The Spanish, Chinese, and Turkish empires were senile and crumbling; the Germans aggressively expansionist; Russia, Britain, France, and Austria-Hungary more or less satisfied with their status. War was a constant danger because the powers squabbled and blustered like children. An argument over an insignificant African flyspeck called Fashoda had swept France and Britain to the brink of war in 1898.

Nonetheless, by and large the English were smugly confident that the Royal Navy would always deliver them from evil. They thought of war as something done to or by foreigners on the distant South African veldt or in the snowy Crimea. No truly foreign army had set foot in England in almost seven hundred years. Even the Scots had been thrashed into submission in 1746 and had not rattled a claymore since.

Wells saw things more clearly. He may not have been alone in his insight, but he could command an audience as few others could. *The War in the Air* is a sermon on the text that flying was an infant destined to grow up rapidly, and there are no fences in the sky. Soon war would bring death and destruction to the homeland, no matter whose homeland that might be—an extraordinary perception for its day.

He erred, of course, in casting airships and not airplanes in the starring role. When writing many years later he called this an "extraordinary bad guess" and blamed bad advice from a "distinguished mathematician." Nowadays the mistake seems ludicrous, but it was not so farfetched then. By 1915 zeppelins were dropping bombs on London, and airships were not completely discredited until the *Hindenburg* disaster of 1937. In 1907 heavier-than-air machines had not yet proved their worth. Wells certainly knew of the Wright brothers (although few of his contemporary readers may have appreciated why Grub and Bert had to run a bicycle shop), but the Wrights did not become famous until 1908 when they made record-breaking flights in both the United States and Europe. In 1909 the U.S. Army adopted the Wright model and Louis Bleriot made the first aerial crossing of the English Channel. Wells was just too far ahead of his time.

Besides, if I may dare to second-guess him, I suspect he had artistic motives he does not mention. The story would not have worked without the airships' ability to stay aloft for many days, allowing time for events to unfold. Wells could make his readers believe anything he wanted but to have invented a powered aircraft of the size and range he attributed to the *Vaterland* dirigible would have laid himself open to charges of plagiarizing the incredible flying ship in Jules Verne's *Robur le Conquérant* (1886), an unthinkable choice. Airships it had to be.

It is easy to poke fun at some of Wells's details. He grossly overestimated the ability of bombing alone to win a battle, but he was not alone there. That delusion of irresistible aerial destruction haunted the century, terrifying the thirties and surviving the horrors of London, Dresden, and Tokyo. Vietnam finally laid it to rest. His description of the sea battle is short on detail, but he implies that the fight occurs at close range, with ships of the line hurling broadsides into each other like the British and French fleets at Trafalgar. The HMS *Dreadnought*, which introduced a new generation of "ironclads," had not yet been commissioned when Wells wrote this book, but even back in 1904 the Japanese defeat of the Russian fleet at Tsushina had seen both sides effectively hitting targets from a range of four miles. Wells should have attributed much better guns to the navies of his futuristic story. The fact that he did not do so shows how ignorant of military affairs civilians in general must have been. (But then, even the military were ignorant of military affairs, as the First World War demonstrated.)

No matter. On a larger scale *The War in the Air* is an amazingly accurate Jeremiad. The story is set in "the year 191–" and ends with the general collapse of governments. So it was to be. Before 1920 dawned the great empires strutted no more. China, Russia, Germany, and Austria-Hungary were gone, with Turkey crumbling in the aftershocks. Pandemic (influenza) and social chaos followed, just as Wells had prophesied. The British and French empires survived until the next round, but both had been fatally weakened, so much so that France collapsed like a soufflé in 1940 and Britain was quickly bankrupted, propped up only by American gold. The world did not end, of course, but *The War in the Air* scores much higher as successful prophecy than, say, *2001, A Space Odyssey* or *1984*.

So it sort-of came to pass; why should we care now? Well, if vision does not impress you, read the book simply for itself. Notice how the curtain rises on an ironic paean to progress. Do not overlook the humor. For example, read the excitement of the burning motorbike that starts the action of the story: "Grubb arrived, riding hard. He was shouting something. He sprang off and threw his bicycle into the hedge. 'Don't throw water on it!' he said—'don't throw water on it!' He displayed commanding presence of mind. He became captain of the occasion. Others were glad to repeat the things he said and imitate his actions. 'Don't throw water on it!' they cried. Also there was no water."

That is a jewel of pithy writing, and Wells was undoubtedly the "best" writer ever to take science fiction seriously. In the whole genre you will find no character more skillfully drawn than this ignorant but not stupid, stubborn but not heroic, honorable but not totally resistant to a promising opportunity, Albert Peter Smallways, known as Bert. The nostalgic transformations at work in his hometown of Bun Hill (Bromley, Kent) are so vividly drawn that Wells's door to the future becomes our window on the past.

Above all, marvel at the clinical prose describing cold-blooded atrocities that foreshadow at least half of all the horror movies ever made. Especially read the fate of New York at the end of chapter six: "That catastrophe was the logical outcome of the situation created by the application of science to warfare. It was unavoidable that great cities should be destroyed. In spite of his intense exasperation with his dilemma, the Prince sought to be moderate even in massacre. He tried to give a memorable lesson with the minimum waste of life and the minimum expenditure of explosives."

In those few words Wells captures the evil soul of Ares: when the foe will not yield, use harsher measures. Warriors begin with scruples, but scruples can never withstand the need to win: "If the Schlieffen Plan does not work, we must bomb London (just the docks at first, of course, not the houses) . . . If conventional assaults cannot break through the enemy's lines we are forced to use poison gas . . . They started the bombing" . . . and so it goes until a new sun shines on Hiroshima.

Wells saw this.

Inevitably his words will remind you of the fall of the World Trade Center. The resemblance is eerie. Notice how some of the aircraft in the battle scenes deliberately ram their targets. Yes, he foresaw even that.

Wells wrote to warn his contemporaries that *it can happen here*, and he was right. Nowhere will be safe, he maintained. He was proved correct in England in 1915, in Hawaii in 1941, and in New York in 2001. He wrote about the great powers, but small countries can abuse technology too. Strangely, *The War in the Air* is not even counted among H. G. Wells's best, but coming from anyone else it would be called a masterpiece. It deserves to be better remembered, and the University of Nebraska Press is to be congratulated on making it available again.

The War in the Air

ONE

Of Progress and the Smallways Family

I

"This here Progress," said Mr. Tom Smallways, "it keeps on."

"You'd hardly think it *could* keep on," said Mr. Tom Smallways.

It was long before the War in the Air began that Mr. Smallways made this remark. He was sitting on the fence at the end of his garden and surveying the great Bun Hill gas-works with an eye that neither praised nor blamed. Above the clustering gasometers three unfamiliar shapes appeared, thin, wallowing bladders that flapped and rolled about, and grew bigger and bigger and rounder and rounder—balloons in course of inflation for the South of England Aero Club's Saturday-afternoon ascent.

"They goes up every Saturday," said his neighbour, Mr. Stringer, the milkman, "It's only yesterday, so to speak, when all London turned out to see a balloon go over, and now every little place in the country has its weekly outings—uppings, rather. It's been the salvation of them gas companies."

"Larst Satiday I got three barrer-loads of gravel off my petaters," said Mr. Tom Smallways. "Three barrer-loads! What they dropped as ballase. Some of the plants was broke, and some was buried."

"Ladies, they say, goes up!"

"I suppose we got to call 'em ladies," said Mr. Tom Smallways. "Still, it ain't hardly my idea of a lady—flying about in the air, and throwing gravel at people. It ain't what I been accustomed to consider lady-like, whether or no."

Mr. Stringer nodded his head approvingly, and for a time they continued to regard the swelling bulks with expressions that had changed from indifference to disapproval.

Mr. Tom Smallways was a greengrocer by trade and a gardener by disposition; his little wife Jessica saw to the shop, and Heaven had planned him for a peaceful world. Unfortunately Heaven had not planned a peaceful world for him. He lived in a world of obstinate and incessant change, and in parts where its operations were unsparingly conspicuous. Vicissitude was in the very soil he tilled; even his garden was upon a yearly tenancy, and overshadowed by a huge board that proclaimed it not so much a garden as an eligible building-site. He was horticulture under notice to quit, the last patch of country in a district flooded by new and urban things. He did his best to console himself, to imagine matters near the turn of the tide.

"You'd hardly think it could keep on," he said.

Mr. Smallways' aged father could remember Bun Hill as an idyllic Kentish village. He had driven Sir Peter Bone until he was fifty, and then he took to drink a little and driving the station 'bus, which lasted him until he was seventy-eight. Then he retired. He sat by the fireside, a shrivelled, very, very old coachman, full charged with reminiscences and ready for any careless stranger. He could tell you of the vanished estate of Sir Peter Bone, long since cut up for building, and how that magnate ruled the countryside when it was countryside, of shooting and hunting and of coaches along the high road, of how "where the gas-works is, was a cricket-field, and of the coming of the Crystal Palace. The Crystal Palace was six miles away from Bun Hill, a great façade that glittered in the morning and was a clear blue outline against the sky in the afternoon, and at night a source of gratuitous fireworks for all the population of Bun Hill. And then had come the railway, and then villas and villas, and then the gas-works and the water-works and a great, ugly sea of workmen's houses, and then drainage, and the water vanished out of the Otterbourne and left it a dreadful ditch, and then a second railway station, Bun Hill South, and more houses and more, more shops, more competition, plate-glass shops, a board-school, rates, omnibuses, tramcars—going right away into London itself— bicycles, motor-cars, and then more motor-cars, a Carnegie library.

"You'd hardly think it could keep on," said Mr. Tom Smallways, growing up among these marvels.

But it kept on. Even from the first the greengrocer's shop which he had set up in one of the smallest of the old surviving village houses in the tail of the High Street had a submerged air, an air of hiding from something that was looking for it. When they had made up the pavement of the High Street, they levelled that up so that one had to go down three steps into the shop. Tom did his best to sell only his own excellent but limited range of produce; but Progress came shoving things into his window, French artichokes and aubergines, foreign apples—apples from the State of New York, apples from California, apples from Canada, apples from New Zealand, "pretty lookin' fruit, but not what I should call English apples," said Tom—bananas, unfamiliar nuts, grape fruits, mangoes.

The motor-cars that went by northward and southward grew more and more powerful and efficient, whizzed faster and smelt worse; there appeared great clangorous petrol trolleys delivering coal and parcels in the place of vanishing horse-vans; motor-omnibuses ousted the horse-omnibuses, even the Kentish strawberries going Londonward in the night took to machinery and clattered instead of creaking, and became affected in flavour by progress and petrol.

And then young Bert Smallways got a motorbicycle. . . .

2

Bert, it is necessary to explain, was a progressive Smallways.

Nothing speaks more eloquently of the pitiless insistence of progress and expansion in our time than that it should get into the Smallways blood. But there was something advanced and enterprising about young Smallways before he was out of short frocks. He was lost for a whole day when he was five, and nearly drowned in the reservoir of the new water-works before he was seven. He had a real pistol taken away from him by a real policeman when he was ten. And he learnt to smoke, not with pipes and brown paper and cane as Tom had done, but with a penny packet of Boys of England American cigarettes. His language shocked his father before he was twelve, and by that age, what with touting for parcels at the station and selling the Bun Hill "Weekly

Express," he was making three shillings a week or more, and spending it on "Chips," "Comic Cuts," "Ally Sloper's Half-Holiday," cigarettes, and all the concomitants of a life of pleasure and enlightenment. All of this without hindrance to his literary studies, which carried him up to the seventh standard at an exceptionally early age. I mention these things so that you may have no doubt at all concerning the sort of stuff Bert had in him.

He was six years younger than Tom, and for a time there was an attempt to utilize him in the greengrocer's shop when Tom at twenty-one married Jessica—who was thirty, and had saved a little money in service. But it was not Bert's *forte* to be utilized. He hated digging, and when he was given a basket of stuff to deliver, a nomadic instinct arose irresistibly, it became his pack, and he did not seem to care how heavy it was nor where he took it, so long as he did not take it to its destination. Glamour filled the world, and he strayed after it, basket and all. So Tom took his goods out himself, and sought employers for Bert who did not know of this strain of poetry in his nature. Bert touched the fringe of a number of trades in succession—draper's porter, chemist's boy, doctor's page, junior assistant gasfitter, envelope addresser, milk-cart assistant, golf-caddie, and at last helper in a bicycle shop. Here, apparently, he found the progressive quality his nature had craved. His employer was a pirate-souled young man named Grubb, with a black-smeared face by day and a music-hall side in the evening, who dreamt of a patent lever chain; and it seemed to Bert that he was the perfect model of a gentleman of spirit. He hired out quite the dirtiest and unsafest bicycles in the whole south of England, and conducted the subsequent discussions with astonishing verve. Bert and he settled down very well together. Bert lived in, became almost a trick rider—he could ride bicycles for miles that would have come to pieces instantly under you or me—took to washing his face after business and sometimes even his neck, and spent his surplus money upon remarkable ties and collars, cigarettes, and shorthand classes at the Bun Hill Institute.

He would go round to Tom at times and look and talk so brilliantly that Tom and Jessica, who both had a natural tendency to be respectful to anybody or anything, looked up to him immensely.

"He's a go-ahead chap, is Bert," said Tom. "He knows a thing or two."

"Let's hope he don't know too much," said Jessica, who had a fine sense of limitations.

"It's go-ahead Times," said Tom. "Noo petaters, and English at that; we'll be having 'em in March if things go on as they do go. I never see such Times. See his tie last night?"

"It wasn't suited to him, Tom. It was a gentleman's tie. He wasn't up to it—not the rest of him. It wasn't becoming. . . ."

Then presently Bert got a cyclist's suit, cap, badge and all; and to see him and Grubb going down to Brighton (and back)—heads down, handlebars down, backbones curved—was a revelation in the possibilities of the Smallways blood.

Go-ahead Times!

Old Smallways would sit over the fire mumbling of the greatness of other days, of old Sir Peter, who drove his coach to Brighton and back in eight-and-twenty hours, of old Sir Peter's white top-hats, of Lady Bone, who never set foot to ground except to walk in the garden, of the great prize-fights at Crawley. He talked of pink and pig-skin breeches, of foxes at Ring's Bottom, where now the County Council pauper lunatics were enclosed, of Lady Bone's chintzes and crinolines. Nobody heeded him. The world had thrown up a new type of gentleman altogether—a gentleman of most ungentlemanly energy, a gentleman in dusty oilskins and motor goggles and a wonderful cap, a stinkmaking gentleman, a swift, high-class badger, who fled perpetually along high roads from the dust and stink he perpetually made. And his lady, as they were able to see her at Bun Hill, was a weatherbeaten goddess as free from refinement as a gipsy—not so much dressed as packed for transit at a high velocity.

So Bert grew up, filled with ideals of speed and enterprise, and became, so far as he became anything, a kind of bicycle engineer of the let's-'ave-a-look-at-it and enamel-chipping variety. Even a road-racer, geared to a hundred and twenty, failed to satisfy him, and for a time he pined in vain at twenty miles an hour along roads that were continually more dusty and more crowded with mechanical traffic. But at last his savings accumulated, and his chance came. The hire purchase system bridged a financial gap, and one bright and memorable Sunday morning

he wheeled his new possession through the shop into the road, got on
to it with the advice and assistance of Grubb, and teufteuffed off into
the haze of the traffic-tortured high road, to add himself as one more
voluntary public danger to the amenities of the south of England.

"Orf to Brighton!" said old Smallways, regarding his youngest son
from the sitting-room window over the greengrocer's shop with something between pride and reprobation. "When I was 'is age, I'd never
been to London, never bin south of Crawley—never bin anywhere on
my own where I couldn't walk. And nobody didn't go. Not unless they
was gentry. Now everybody's orf everywhere; the whole dratted country
sims flying to pieces. Wonder they all get back. Orf to Brighton indeed!
Anybody want to buy 'orses?"

"You can't say _I_ bin to Brighton, father," said Tom.

"Nor don't want to go," said Jessica sharply; c'reering about and
spendin' your money."

3

For a time the possibilities of the motor-bicycle so occupied Bert's mind
that he remained regardless of the new direction in which the striving
soul of man was finding exercise and refreshment. He failed to observe
that the type of motor-car, like the type of bicycle, was settling down and
losing its adventurous quality. Indeed, it is as true as it is remarkable that
Tom was the first to observe the new development. But his gardening
made him attentive to the heavens and the proximity of the Bun Hill
gas-works and the Crystal Palace, from which ascents were continually
being made, and presently the descent of ballast upon his potatoes
conspired to bear in upon his unwilling mind the fact that the Goddess
of Change was turning her disturbing attention to the sky. The first
great boom in aeronautics was beginning.

Grubb and Bert heard of it in a music-hall, then it was driven
home to their minds by the cinematograph, then Bert's imagination
was stimulated by a sixpenny edition of that aeronautic classic, Mr.
George Griffith's "The Outlaws of the Air," and so the thing really got
hold of them.

At first the most obvious aspect was the multiplication of balloons.
The sky of Bun Hill began to be infested by balloons! On Wednesday

and Saturday afternoons particularly you could scarcely look skyward for a quarter of an hour without discovering a balloon somewhere. And then one bright day Bert, motoring towards Croydon, was arrested by the insurgence of a huge, bolster-shaped monster from the Crystal Palace grounds, and obliged to dismount and watch it. It was like a bolster with a broken nose, and below it, and comparatively small, was a stiff framework bearing a man and an engine with a screw that whizzed round in front and a sort of canvas rudder behind. The framework had an air of dragging the reluctant gas-cylinder after it like a brisk little terrier towing a shy, gas-distended elephant into society. The combined monster certainly travelled and steered. It went overhead perhaps a thousand feet up (Bert heard the engine), sailed away southward, vanished over the hills, reappeared a little blue outline far off in the east, going now very fast before a gentle south-west gale, returned above the Crystal Palace towers, circled round them, chose a position for descent, and sank down out of sight.

Bert sighed deeply, and turned to his motor-bicycle again.

And that was only the beginning of a succession of strange phenomena in the heavens—cylinders, cones, pear-shaped monsters, even at last a thing of aluminium that glittered wonderfully, and that Grubb, through some confusion of ideas about armour plates, was inclined to consider a war machine.

There followed actual flight.

This, however, was not an affair that was visible from Bun Hill; it was something that occurred in private grounds or other enclosed places and under favourable conditions, and it was brought home to Grubb and Bert Smallways only by means of the magazine page of the halfpenny newspapers or by cinematograph records. But it was brought home very insistently, and in those days if ever one heard a man saying in a public place in a loud, reassuring confident tone, "It's bound to come," the chances were ten to one he was talking of flying. And Bert got a box lid and wrote out in correct window-ticket style, and Grubb put in the window this inscription, "Aeroplanes made and repaired." It quite upset Tom—it seemed taking one's shop so lightly; but most of the neighbours, and all the sporting ones, approved of it as being very good indeed.

Everybody talked of flying, everybody repeated over and over again, "Bound to come." and then you know it didn't come. There was a hitch. They flew—that was all right; they flew in machines heavier than air. But they smashed. Sometimes they smashed the engine, sometimes they smashed the aeronaut, usually they smashed both. Machines that made flights of three or four miles and came down safely, went up the next time to headlong disaster. There seemed no possible trusting to them. The breeze upset them, the eddies near the ground upset them, a passing thought in the mind of the aeronaut upset them. Also they upset—simply.

"It's this 'stability' does 'em," said Grubb, repeating his newspaper. "They pitch and they pitch, till they pitch themselves to pieces."

Experiments fell away after two expectant years of this sort of success, the public and then the newspapers tired of the expensive photographic reproductions, the optimistic reports, the perpetual sequence of triumph and disaster and silence. Flying slumped, even ballooning fell away to some extent, though it remained a fairly popular sport, and continued to lift gravel from the wharf of the Bun Hill gas-works and drop it upon deserving people's lawns and gardens. There were half a dozen reassuring years for Tom—at least so far as flying was concerned. But that was the great time of mono-rail development, and his anxiety was only diverted from the high heavens by the most urgent threats and symptoms of change in the lower sky.

There had been talk of mono-rails for several years. But the real mischief began when Brennan sprang his gyroscopic mono-rail car upon the Royal Society. It was the leading sensation of the 1907 soirées; that celebrated demonstration-room was all too small for its exhibition. Brave soldiers, leading Zionists, deserving novelists, noble ladies, congested the narrow passage, and thrust distinguished elbows into ribs the world would not willingly let break, deeming themselves fortunate if they could see "just a little bit of the rail." Inaudible but convincing, the great inventor expounded his discovery and sent his obedient model of the trains of the future up gradients, round curves and across a sagging wire. It ran along on its single rail, on its single wheels, simple and sufficient; it stopped, reversed, stood still, balancing perfectly. It maintained its astounding equilibrium amidst a thunder of applause.

The audience dispersed at last, discussing how far they would enjoy crossing an abyss on a wire cable. "Suppose the gyroscope stopped!" Few of them anticipated a tithe of what the Brennan mono-rail would do for their railway securities and the face of the world.

In a few years they realized better. In a little while no one thought anything of crossing an abyss on a wire, and the mono-rail was superseding the tram-lines, railways, and indeed every form of track for mechanical locomotion. Where land was cheap the rail ran along the ground, where it was dear the rail lifted up on iron standards and passed overhead; its swift, convenient cars went everywhere and did everything that had once been done along made tracks upon the ground.

When old Smallways died, Tom could think of nothing more striking to say of him than that, "When he was a boy, there wasn't nothing higher than your chimbleys—there wasn't a wire nor a cable in the sky!"

Old Smallways went to his grave under an intricate network of wires and cables, for Bun Hill became not only a sort of minor centre of power distribution—the Home Counties Power Distribution Company set up transformers and a generating station close beside the old gas-works—but also a junction on the suburban mono-rail system. Moreover, every tradesman in the place, and indeed nearly every house, had its own telephone.

The mono-rail cable standards became a striking fact in urban landscape, for the most part stout iron erections rather like tapering trestles, and painted a bright bluish green. One, it happened, bestrode Tom's house, which looked still more retiring and apologetic beneath its immensity; and another giant stood just inside the corner of his garden, which was still not built upon and unchanged except for a couple of advertisement boards, one recommending a two-and-sixpenny watch, and one a nerve restorer. These, by the bye, were placed almost horizontally to catch the eye of the passing mono-rail passengers above, and so served admirably to roof over a tool-shed and a mushroom-shed for Tom. All day and all night the fast cars from Brighton and Hastings went murmuring by overhead—long, broad, comfortable-looking cars, that were brightly lit after dusk. As they flew by at night, transient flares of light and a rumbling sound of passage, they kept up a perpetual summer lightning and thunderstorm in the street below.

Presently the English Channel was bridged—a series of great iron Eiffel Tower pillars carrying mono-rail cables at a height of a hundred and fifty feet above the water, except near the middle, where they rose higher to allow the passage of the London and Antwerp shipping and the Hamburg-America liners.

Then heavy motor-cars began to run about on only a couple of wheels, one behind the other, which for some reason upset Tom dreadfully, and made him gloomy for days after the first one passed the shop. . . .

All this gyroscopic and mono-rail development naturally absorbed a vast amount of public attention, and there was also a huge excitement consequent upon the amazing gold discoveries off the coast of Anglesea made by a submarine prospector, Miss Patricia Giddy. She had taken her degree in geology and mineralogy in the University of London, and while working upon the auriferous rocks of North Wales after a brief holiday spent in agitating for women's suffrage, she had been struck by the possibility of these reefs cropping up again under water. She had set herself to verify this supposition by the use of the submarine crawler invented by Doctor Alberto Cassini. By a happy mingling of reasoning and intuition peculiar to her sex she found gold at her first descent, and emerged after three hours' submersion with about two hundredweight of ore containing gold in the unparalleled quantity of seventeen ounces to the ton. But the whole story of her submarine mining, intensely interesting as it is, must be told at some other time; suffice it now to remark simply that it was during the consequent great rise of prices, confidence, and enterprise that the revival of interest in flying occurred.

4

It is curious how the final boom of flying began. It was like the coming of a breeze on a quiet day, nothing started it, it came. People began to talk of flying with an air of never having for one moment dropped the subject. Pictures of flying and flying machines returned to the newspapers, articles and allusions increased and multiplied in the serious magazines. People asked in mono-rail trains, "When are we going to fly?" A new crop of inventors sprang up in a night or so like fungi. The Aero Club announced the project of a great Flying Exhibition in a large area of ground that the removal of slums in Whitechapel had rendered available.

The advancing wave soon produced a sympathetic ripple in the Bun Hill establishment. Grubb routed out his flying-machine model again, tried it in the yard behind the shop, got a kind of flight out of it, and broke seventeen panes of glass and nine flower-pots in the greenhouse that occupied the next yard but one.

And then, springing from nowhere, sustained one knew not how, came a persistent, disturbing rumour that the problem had been solved, that the secret was known. Bert met it one early-closing afternoon as he refreshed himself in an inn near Nutfield, whither his motor-bicycle had brought him. There smoked and meditated a person in khaki, an engineer, who presently took an interest in Bert's machine. It was a sturdy piece of apparatus, and it had acquired a kind of documentary value in these quick-changing times; it was now nearly eight years old. Its points discussed, the soldier broke into a new topic with, "My next's going to be an aeroplane, so far as I can see. I've had enough of roads and ways."

"They *tork*," said Bert.

"They talk—and they do," said the soldier. The thing's coming.

"It keeps *on* coming," said Bert; "I shall believe when I see it."

"That won't be long," said the soldier.

The conversation seemed degenerating into an amiable wrangle of contradiction.

"I tell you they *are* flying," the soldier insisted. "I see it myself."

"We've all seen it," said Bert.

"I don't mean flap up and smash up; I mean real, safe, steady, controlled flying, against the wind, good and right."

"You ain't seen that!"

"I '*ave*! Aldershot. They try to keep it a secret. They got it right enough. You bet—our War Office isn't going to be caught napping this time."

Bert's incredulity was shaken. He asked questions, and the soldier expanded.

"I tell you they got nearly a square mile fenced in—a sort of valley. Fences of barbed wire ten feet high, and inside that they do things. Chaps about the camp—now and then we get a peep. It isn't only us neither. There's the Japanese; you bet they got it too—and the Germans! And I never knowed anything of this sort yet that the Frencheys didn't get ahead with—after their manner! They started ironclads, they started submarines, they started navigables, and you bet they won't be far be'ind at this."

The soldier stood with his legs very wide apart, and filled his pipe thoughtfully. Bert sat on the low wall against which his motor-bicycle was leaning.

"Funny thing fighting'll be," he said.

"Flying's going to break out," said the soldier. "When it *does* come, when the curtain does go up, I tell you you'll find every one on the stage—busy. . . . Such fighting, too! . . . I suppose you don't read the papers about this sort of thing?"

"I read 'em a bit," said Bert.

"Well, have you noticed what one might call the remarkable case of the disappearing inventor—the inventor who turns up in a blaze of publicity, fires off a few successful experiments, and vanishes?"

"Can't say I 'ave," said Bert.

"Well, I 'ave, anyhow. You get anybody come along who does anything striking in this line, and, you bet, he vanishes. Just goes off quietly out of sight. After a bit, you don't hear anything more of 'em at all. See? They disappear. Gone—no address. First—oh! it's an old story now—there was those Wright brothers out in America. They glided—they glided miles and miles. Finally they glided off stage. Why, it must be nineteen hundred and four, or five, *they* vanished! Then there was those people in Ireland—no, I forget their names. Everybody said they could fly. *They* went. They ain't dead that I've heard tell; but you can't say they're alive. Not a feather of 'em can you see. Then that chap who flew round Paris and upset in the Seine. De Booley, was it? I forget. That was a grand fly in spite of the accident; but where's he got to? The accident didn't hurt him. Eh? 'E's gone to cover."

The soldier prepared to light his pipe.

"Looks like a secret society got hold of them," said Bert.

"Secret society! *Naw!*"

The soldier lit his match, and drew. "Secret society," he repeated, in response to these words, with his pipe between his teeth and the match flaring. "War Departments; that's more like it." He threw his match aside, and walked to his machine. "I tell you, sir," he said, "there isn't a big Power in Europe *or* Asia, *or* America, *or* Africa, that hasn't got at least one or two flying machines hidden up its sleeve at the present time. Not one. Real, workable, flying machines. And the spying! The spying and manœuvring to find out what the others have got. I tell you, sir, a foreigner, or, for the matter of that, an unaccredited native, can't get within four miles of Lydd nowadays—not to mention our little circus at Aldershot and the experimental camp in Galway. No!"

"Well," said Bert, "I'd like to see one of them, anyhow. Jest to help believing. I'll believe when I see, that I'll promise you."

"You'll see 'em, fast enough," said the soldier, and led his machine out into the road.

He left Bert on his wall, grave and pensive, with his cap on the back of his head, and a cigarette smouldering in the corner of his mouth.

"If what he says is true," said Bert, "me and Grubb, we been wasting our blessed old time. Besides incurring expense with thet green'ouse."

5

It was while this mysterious talk with the soldier still stirred in Bert Smallways' imagination that the most astounding incident in the whole of that dramatic chapter of human history, the coming of flying, occurred. People talk glibly enough of epoch-making events; this *was* an epoch-making event. It was the unanticipated and entirely successful flight of Mr. Alfred Butteridge from the Crystal Palace to Glasgow and back in a small business-like-looking machine heavier than air—an entirely manageable and controllable machine that could fly as well as a pigeon.

It wasn't, one felt, a fresh step forward in the matter so much as a giant stride, a leap. Mr. Butteridge remained in the air altogether for about nine hours, and during that time he flew with the ease and assurance of a bird. His machine was, however, neither bird-like nor butterfly-like, nor had it the wide, lateral expansion of the ordinary aeroplane. The effect upon the observer was rather something in the nature of a bee or wasp. Parts of the apparatus were spinning very rapidly, and gave one a hazy effect of transparent wings; but parts, including two peculiarly curved

"wing-cases"—if one may borrow a figure from the flying beetles—
remained expanded stiffly. In the middle was a long rounded body like
the body of a moth, and on this Mr. Butteridge could be seen sitting
astride, much as a man bestrides a horse. The wasp-like resemblance
was increased by the fact that the apparatus flew with a deep booming
hum, exactly the sound made by a wasp at a window-pane.

Mr. Butteridge took the world by surprise. He was one of those
gentlemen from nowhere Fate still succeeds in producing for the stim-
ulation of mankind. He came, it was variously said, from Australia
and America and the South of France. He was also described quite
incorrectly as the son of a man who had amassed a comfortable fortune
in the manufacture of gold nibs and the Butteridge fountain pens. But
this was an entirely different strain of Butteridges. For some years, in
spite of a loud voice, a large presence, an aggressive swagger, and an
implacable manner, he had been an undistinguished member of most
of the existing aeronautical associations. Then one day he wrote to all
the London papers to announce that he had made arrangements for an
ascent from the Crystal Palace of a machine that would demonstrate
satisfactorily that the outstanding difficulties in the way of flying were
finally solved. Few of the papers printed this letter, still fewer were the
people who believed in his claim. No one was excited even when a fracas
on the steps of a leading hotel in Piccadilly, in which he tried to horse-
whip a prominent German musician upon some personal account,
delayed his promised ascent. The quarrel was inadequately reported,
and his name spelt variously Betteridge and Betridge. Until his flight,
indeed, he did not and could not contrive to exist in the public mind.
There were scarcely thirty people on the look-out for him, in spite of
all his clamour, when about six o'clock one summer morning the doors
of the big shed in which he had been putting together his apparatus
opened—it was near the big model of a megatherium in the Crystal
Palace grounds—and his giant insect came droning out into a negligent
and incredulous world.

But before he had made his second circuit of the Crystal Palace
towers, Fame was lifting her trumpet, she drew a deep breath as the
startled tramps who sleep on the streets of Trafalgar Square were aroused
by his buzz, and awoke to discover him circling the Nelson column, and

by the time he had got to Birmingham, which place he crossed about half-past ten, her deafening blast was echoing throughout the country. The despaired-of thing was done. A man was flying securely and well.

Scotland was agape for his coming. Glasgow he reached by one o'clock, and it is related that scarcely a ship-yard or factory in that busy hive of industry resumed work before half-past two. The public mind was just sufficiently educated in the impossibility of flying to appreciate Mr. Butteridge at his proper value. He circled the University buildings, and dropped to within shouting distance of the crowds in West End Park and on the slope of Gilmour Hill. The thing flew quite steadily at a pace of about three miles an hour, in a wide circle, making a deep hum that would have drowned his full, rich voice completely had he not provided himself with a megaphone. He avoided churches, buildings, and mono-rail cables with consummate ease as he conversed.

"Me name's Butteridge," he shouted; "B-U-T-T-E-R-I-D-G-E. Got it? Me mother was Scotch."

And having assured himself that he had been understood, he rose amidst cheers and shouting and patriotic cries, and then flew up very swiftly and easily into the south-eastern sky, rising and falling with long, easy undulations in an extraordinary wasp-like manner.

His return to London—he visited and hovered over Manchester and Liverpool and Oxford on his way, and spelt his name out to each place—was an occasion of unparalleled excitement. Everyone was staring heavenward. More people were run over in the streets upon that one day than in the previous three months, and a County Council steamboat, the Isaac Walton, collided with a pier of Westminster Bridge, and narrowly escaped disaster by running ashore—it was low water— on the mud on the south side. He returned to the Crystal Palace grounds, that classic starting-point of aeronautical adventure, about sunset, re-entered his shed without disaster, and had the doors locked immediately upon the photographers and journalists who had been waiting his return.

"Look here, you chaps," he said, as his assistant did so, "I'm tired to death, and saddle sore. I can't give you a word of talk. I'm too—done. My name's Butteridge. B-U-T-T-E-R-I-D-G-E. Get that right. I'm an Imperial Englishman. I'll talk to you all to-morrow."

Foggy snapshots still survive to record that incident. His assistant struggles in a sea of aggressive young men carrying note-books or upholding cameras and wearing bowler hats and enterprising ties. He himself towers up in the doorway, a big figure with a mouth—an eloquent cavity beneath a vast black moustache—distorted by his shout to those relentless agents of publicity. He towers there, the most famous man in the country. Almost symbolically he holds and gesticulates with a megaphone in his left hand.

6

Tom and Bert Smallways both saw that return. They watched from the crest of Bun Hill, from which they had so often surveyed the pyrotechnics of the Crystal Palace. Bert was excited, Tom kept calm and lumpish, but neither of them realized how their own lives were to be invaded by the fruits of that beginning. "P'raps old Grubb'll mind the shop a bit now," he said, "and put his blessed model in the fire. Not that that can save us, if we don't tide over with Steinhart's account."

Bert knew enough of things and the problem of aeronautics to realize that this gigantic imitation of a bee would, to use his own idiom, "give the newspapers fits." The next day it was clear the fits had been given even as he said, their magazine pages were black with hasty photographs, their prose was convulsive, they foamed at the headline. The next day they were worse. Before the week was out they were not so much published as carried screaming into the street.

The dominant fact in the uproar was the exceptional personality of Mr. Butteridge, and the extraordinary terms he demanded for the secret of his machine.

For it was a secret, and he kept it secret in the most elaborate fashion. He built his apparatus himself, in the safe privacy of the great Crystal Palace sheds, with the assistance of inattentive workmen, and the day next following his flight he took it to pieces single-handed, packed certain portions, and then secured unintelligent assistance in packing and dispersing the rest. Sealed packing-cases went north and east and west to various pantechnicons, and the engines were boxed with peculiar care. It became evident these precautions were not inadvisable, in view of the violent demand for any sort of photograph or impressions of his machine. But Mr. Butteridge, having once made his demonstration, intended to keep his secret safe from any further risk of leakage. He faced the British public now with the question whether they wanted his secret or not; he was, he said perpetually, an "Imperial Englishman," and his first wish and his last was to see his invention the privilege and monopoly of the Empire. Only——

It was there the difficulty began.

Mr. Butteridge, it became evident, was a man singularly free from any false modesty—indeed, from any modesty of any kind—singularly willing to see interviewers, answer questions upon any topic except aeronautics, volunteer opinions, criticisms, and autobiography, supply portraits and photographs of himself, and generally spread his personality across the terrestrial sky. The published portraits insisted primarily upon an immense black moustache, and secondarily upon a fierceness behind the moustache. The general impression upon the public was that Butteridge was a small man. No one big, it was felt, could have so virulently aggressive an expression, though, as a matter of fact, Butteridge had a height of six feet two inches, and a weight altogether proportionate to that. Moreover, he had a love affair of large and unusual dimensions and irregular circumstances, and the still largely decorous British public learnt with reluctance and alarm that a sympathetic treatment of this affair was inseparable from the exclusive acquisition of the priceless secret of aerial stability by the British Empire. The exact particulars of the irregularity never came to light, but apparently the lady had, in a fit of high-minded inadverence, gone through the ceremony of marriage with—one quotes the unpublished discourse of Mr. Butteridge—"a white-livered skunk," and this zoological aberration did in some legal and vexatious manner mar her social happiness. He wanted to talk about the business, to show the splendour of her nature in the light of its complications. It was really most embarrassing to a press that has always possessed a considerable turn for reticence, that wanted things personal indeed in the modern fashion, but not too personal. It was embarrassing, I say, to be inexorably confronted with Mr. Butteridge's great heart, to see it laid open in relentless self-vivisection, and its pulsating dissepiments adorned with emphatic flag labels.

Confronted they were, and there was no getting away from it. He would make this appalling viscus beat and throb before the shrinking journalists—no uncle with a big watch and a little baby ever harped upon it so relentlessly; whatever evasion they attempted he set aside. He "gloried in his love," he said, and compelled them to write it down.

"That's, of course, a private affair, Mr. Butteridge," they would object.

"The injustice, sorr, is public. I do not care whether I am up against institutions or individuals. I do not care if I am up against the Universal All. I am pleading the cause of a woman, a woman I lurve, sorr—a noble woman—misunderstood. I intend to vindicate her, sorr, to the four winds of heaven!

"I lurve England," he used to say—"I lurve England, but Puritanism, sorr, I abhor. It fills me with loathing. It raises my gorge. Take my own case. . . ."

He insisted relentlessly upon his heart, and upon seeing proofs of the interview. If they had not done justice to his erotic bellowings and gesticulations, he stuck in, in a large inky scrawl, all and more than they had omitted.

It was a strangely embarrassing thing for British journalism. Never was there a more obvious or uninteresting affair; never had the world heard the story of erratic affection with less appetite or sympathy. On the other hand, it was extremely curious about Mr. Butteridge's invention. But when Mr. Butteridge could be deflected for a moment from the cause of the lady he championed, then he talked chiefly, and usually with tears of tenderness in his voice, about his mother and his childhood—his mother who crowned a complete encyclopædia of maternal virtue by being "largely Scotch." She was not quite neat, but nearly so. "I owe everything in me to me mother," he asserted—"everything. Eh!" and—"ask any man who's done anything. You'll hear the same story. All we have we owe to women. They are the species, sorr. Man is but a dream. He comes and goes. The woman's soul leadeth us upward and on!"

He was always going on like that.

What in particular he wanted from the Government for his secret did not appear, nor what beyond a money payment could be expected from a modern State in such an affair. The general effect upon judicious observers, indeed, was not that he was treating for anything, but that he was using an unexampled opportunity to bellow and show off to an attentive world. Rumours of his real identity spread abroad. It was said that he had been the landlord of an ambiguous hotel in Cape Town, and had there given shelter to, and witnessed the experiments, and finally stolen the papers and plans of an extremely shy and friendless young inventor named Palliser, who had come to South Africa from England in an advanced stage of consumption, and died there. This at any rate was the allegation of the more outspoken American press. But the proof or disproof of that never reached the public.

Mr. Butteridge also involved himself passionately in a tangle of disputes for the possession of a great number of valuable money prizes. Some of these had been offered so long ago as 1906 for successful mechanical flight. By the time of Mr. Butteridge's success a really very considerable number of newspapers, tempted by the impunity of the pioneers in this direction, had pledged themselves to pay in some cases quite overwhelming sums to the first person to fly from Manchester to Glasgow, from London to Manchester, one hundred miles, two hundred miles in England, and the like. Most had hedged a little with ambiguous conditions, and now offered resistance; one or two paid at once, and vehemently called attention to the fact; and Mr. Butteridge plunged into litigation with the more recalcitrant, while at the same time sustaining a vigorous agitation and canvass to induce the Government to purchase his invention.

One fact, however, remained permanent throughout all the developments of this affair behind Butteridge's preposterous love interest, his politics, and personality, and all his shouting and boasting, and that was that, so far as the mass of people knew, he was in sole possession of the secret of the practicable aeroplane in which, for all one could tell to the contrary, the key of the future empire of the world resided. And presently, to the great consternation of innumerable people, including among others Mr. Bert Smallways, it became apparent that whatever negotiations were in progress for the acquisition of this precious secret by the British Government were in danger of falling through. The London "Daily Requiem" first voiced the universal alarm, and published an interview under the terrific caption of, "Mr. Butteridge Speaks his Mind."

Therein the inventor—if he was an inventor—poured out his heart. "I came from the end of the earth," he said, which rather seemed to confirm the Cape Town story, "bringing me Motherland the secret that would give her the empire of the world. And what do I get?" He paused. "I am sniffed at by elderly mandarins! . . . And the woman I love is treated like a leper!

"I am an Imperial Englishman," he went on in a splendid outburst, subsequently written into the interview by his own hand; "but there are limits to the human heart! There are younger nations—living nations! Nations that do not snore and gurgle helplessly in paroxysms of plethora upon beds of formality and red tape! There are nations that will not fling away the empire of the earth in order to slight an unknown man and insult a noble woman whose boots they are not fitted to unlatch. There are nations not blinded to science, not given over hand and foot to effete snobocracies and Degenerate Decadents. In short, mark my words—*there are other nations*! . . ."

This speech it was that particularly impressed Bert Smallways. "If them Germans or them Americans get hold of this," he said impressively to his brother, "the British Empire's done. It's U.P. The Union Jack, so to speak, won't be worth the paper it's written on, Tom."

"I suppose you couldn't lend us a hand this morning," said Jessica, in his impressive pause. "Everybody in Bun Hill seems wanting early potatoes at once. Tom can't carry half of them."

"We're living on a volcano," said Bert, disregarding the suggestion. "At any moment war may come—such a war!"

He shook his head portentously.

"You'd better take this lot first, Tom," said Jessica. She turned briskly on Bert. "Can you spare us a morning?" she asked.

"I dessay I can," said Bert. "The shop's very quiet s'morning. Though all this danger to the Empire worries me something frightful."

"Work'll take it off your mind," said Jessica.

And presently he too was going out into a world of change and wonder, bowed beneath a load of potatoes and patriotic insecurity, that merged at last into a very definite irritation at the weight and want of style of the potatoes and a very clear conception of the entire detestableness of Jessica.

TWO

How Bert Smallways Got into Difficulties

I

It did not occur to either Tom or Bert Smallways that this remarkable aerial performance of Mr. Butteridge was likely to affect either of their lives in any special manner, that it would in any way single them out from the millions about them; and when they had witnessed it from the crest of Bun Hill, and seen the fly-like mechanism, its rotating planes a golden haze in the sunset, sink humming to the harbour of its shed again, they turned back towards the sunken greengrocery beneath the great iron standard of the London to Brighton monorail, and their minds reverted to the discussion that had engaged them before Mr. Butteridge's triumph had come in sight out of the London haze.

It was a difficult and unsuccessful discussion. They had to carry it on in shouts because of the moaning and roaring of the gyroscopic motorcars that traversed the High Street, and in its nature it was contentious and private. The Grubb business was in difficulties, and Grubb in a moment of financial eloquence had given a half share in it to Bert, whose relations with his employer had been for some time unsalaried and pallish and informal.

Bert was trying to impress Tom with the idea that the reconstructed Grubb and Smallways offered unprecedented and unparalleled opportunities to the judicious small investor. It was coming home to Bert, as though it were an entirely new fact, that Tom was entirely impervious to ideas. In the end he put the financial issues on one side, and, making the thing entirely a matter of fraternal affections succeeded in borrowing a sovereign on the security of his word of honour.

The firm of Grubb and Smallways, formerly Grubb, had indeed been persistently unlucky in the last year or so. For many years the business had struggled along with a flavour of romantic insecurity in a small, dissolute-looking shop in the High Street, adorned with brilliantly coloured advertisements of cycles, a display of bells, trouser-clips, oil-cans, pump-clips, frame-cases, wallets, and other accessories, and the announcement of "Bicycles on Hire," "Repairs," "Free Inflation," "Petrol," and similar attractions. They were agents for several obscure makes of bicycle, two samples constituted the stock, and occasionally they effected a sale; they also repaired punctures and did their best— though luck was not always on their side—with any other repairing that was brought to them. They handled a line of cheap gramophones, and did a little with musical boxes. The staple of their business was, however, the letting of bicycles on hire. It was a singular trade, obeying no known commercial or economic principles—indeed, no principles. There was a stock of ladies' and gentlemen's bicycles in a state of disrepair that passes description; the hiring stock and these were let to unexacting and reckless people, inexpert in the things of this world, at a nominal rate of one shilling for the first hour and sixpence per hour afterwards. But really there were no fixed prices, and insistent boys could get bicycles and the thrill of danger for an hour for so low a sum as threepence, provided they would convince Grubb that that was all they had. The saddle and handle-bar were then sketchily adjusted by Grubb, a deposit exacted, except in the case of familiar boys, the machine lubricated, and the adventurer started upon his career. Usually he or she came back, but at times, when the accident was serious, Bert or Grubb had to go out and fetch the machine home. Hire was always charged up to the hour of return to the shop and deducted from the deposit. It was rare that a bicycle started out from their hands in a state of pedantic efficiency. Romantic possibilities of accident lurked in the worn thread of the screw that adjusted the saddle, in the precarious pedals, in the loose-knit chain, in the handle-bars, above all in the brakes and tyres. Tappings and clankings and strange rhythmic creakings awoke as the intrepid hirer pedalled out into the country. Then perhaps the bell would jam or a

brake fail to act on a hill; or the seat pillar would get loose, and the saddle
drop three or four inches with a disconcerting bump; or the loose and
rattling chain would jump the cogs of the chain-wheel as the machine
ran down hill, and so bring the mechanism to an abrupt and disastrous
stop without at the same time arresting the forward momentum of the
rider; or a tyre would bang, or sigh quietly, and give up the struggle and
scrabble in the dust.

When the hirer returned, a heated pedestrian, Grubb would ignore
all verbal complaints, and examine the machine gravely.

"This ain't 'ad fair usage," he used to begin.

He became a mild embodiment of the spirit of reason. "You can't
expect a bicycle to take you up all in its arms and carry you," he used
to say. "You got to show intelligence. After all—it's machinery."

Sometimes the process of liquidating the consequent claims bor-
dered on violence. It was always a very rhetorical and often a trying
affair, but in these progressive times you have to make a noise to get a
living. It was often hard work, but nevertheless this hiring was a fairly
steady source of profit, until one day all the panes in the window and
door were broken and the stock on sale in the window greatly damaged
and disordered by two over-critical hirers with no sense of rhetorical
irrelevance. They were big, coarse stokers from Gravesend—one was
annoyed because his left pedal had come off, and the other because
his tyre had become deflated, small and indeed negligible accidents
by Bun Hill standards, due entirely to the ungentle handling of the
delicate machines entrusted to them, and they failed to see clearly how
they put themselves in the wrong by this method of argument. It is a
poor way of convincing a man that he has let you a defective machine
to throw his foot-pump about his shop, and take his stock of gongs
outside in order to return them through the window-panes. It carried
no real conviction to the minds of either Grubb or Bert; it only irritated
and vexed them. One quarrel makes many, and this unpleasantness led
to a violent dispute between Grubb and the landlord upon the moral
aspects and legal responsibility for the consequent re-glazing. Matters
came to a climax upon the eve of the Whitsuntide Holidays.

In the end Grubb and Smallways were put to the expense of a
strategic nocturnal removal to another position.

It was a position they had long considered. It was a small, shed-like shop with plate-glass window and one room behind, just at the sharp bend in the road at the bottom of Bun Hill, and here they struggled along bravely in spite of persistent annoyance from their former landlord, hoping for certain eventualities the peculiar situation of the shop seemed to promise. Here, too, they were doomed to disappointment.

The High Road from London to Brighton that ran through Bun Hill was like the British Empire or the British Constitution—a thing that had grown to its present importance. Unlike any other roads in Europe the British high roads have never been subjected to any organized attempts to grade or straighten them out, and to that no doubt their peculiar picturesqueness is to be ascribed. The old Bun Hill High Street drops at its end for perhaps eighty or a hundred feet of descent at an angle of one in five, turns at right angles to the left, runs in a curve for about thirty yards, to a brick bridge over the dry ditch that had once been the Otterbourne, and then bends sharply to the right again round a dense clump of trees and goes on, a simple, straightforward, peaceful high road. There had been one or two horse and van and bicycle accidents in the place before the shop Bert and Grubb took was built, and, to be frank, it was the probability of others that attracted them to it.

Its possibilities had come to them first with a humorous flavour.

"Here's one of the places where a chap might get a living by keeping hens," said Grubb.

"You can't get a living by keeping hens," said Bert.

"You'd keep the hen and have it spatch-cocked," said Grubb. "The motor chaps would pay for it."

When they really came to take the place they remembered this conversation. Hens, however, were out of the question; there was no place for a run unless they had it in the shop. It would have been obviously out of place there. The shop was much more modern than their former one, and had a plate-glass front. "Sooner or later," said Bert, "we shall get a motor-car through this."

"That's all right," said Grubb. "Compensation. I don't mind *when* that motor-car comes along. I don't mind even if it gives me a shock to the system."

"And meanwhile," said Bert, with great artfulness, "*I'm* going to buy myself a dog."

He did. He bought three in succession. He surprised the people at the Dog's Home in Battersea by demanding a deaf retriever, and rejecting every candidate that pricked up its ears. "I want a good, deaf, slow-moving dog," he said. "A dog that doesn't put himself out for things."

They displayed inconvenient curiosity; they declared a great scarcity of deaf dogs.

"You see," they said, "dogs aren't deaf."

"Mine's got to be," said Bert. "I've *had* dogs that aren't deaf. All I want. It's like this, you see—I sell gramophones. Naturally I got to make 'em talk and tootle a bit to show 'em orf. Well, a dog that isn't deaf doesn't like it—gets excited, smells round, barks, growls. That upsets the customer. See? Then a dog that has his hearing fancies things. Makes burglars out of passing tramps. Wants to fight every motor that makes a whizz. All very well if you want livening up, but our place is lively enough. I don't want a dog of that sort. I want a quiet dog."

In the end he got three in succession, but none of them turned out well. The first strayed off into the infinite, heeding no appeals; the second was killed in the night by a fruit motor-waggon which fled before Grubb could get down; the third got itself entangled in the front wheel of a passing cyclist, who came through the plate glass, and proved to be an actor out of work and an undischarged bankrupt. He demanded compensation for some fancied injury, would hear nothing of the valuable dog he had killed or the window he had broken, obliged Grubb by sheer physical obduracy to straighten his buckled front wheel, and pestered the struggling firm with a series of inhumanly worded solicitor's letters. Grubb answered them—stingingly, and put himself, Bert thought, in the wrong.

Affairs got more and more exasperating and strained under these pressures. The window was boarded up, and an unpleasant altercation about their delay in repairing it with the new landlord, a Bun Hill butcher—and a loud, bellowing, unreasonable person at that—served to remind them of their unsettled troubles with the old. Things were at this pitch when Bert bethought himself of creating a sort of debenture capital in the business for the benefit of Tom. But as I have said, Tom had no enterprise in his composition. His idea of investment was the stocking; he bribed his brother not to keep the offer open.

And then ill-luck made its last lunge at their crumbling business and brought it to the ground.

2

It is a poor heart that never rejoices, and Whitsuntide had an air of coming as an agreeable break in the business complications of Grubb and Smallways. Encouraged by the practical outcome of Bert's negotiations with his brother, and by the fact that half the hiring stock was out from Sunday to Monday, they decided to ignore the residuum of hiring-trade on Sunday and devote that day to much-needed relaxation and refreshment—to have, in fact, an unstinted good time, a beano on Whit Sunday, and return invigorated to grapple with their difficulties and the Bank Holiday repairs on the Monday. No good thing was ever done by exhausted and dispirited men. It happened that they had made the acquaintance of two young ladies in employment in Clapham, Miss Flossie Bright and Miss Edna Bunthorne, and it was resolved therefore to make a cheerful little cyclist party of four into the heart of Kent, and to picnic and spend an indolent afternoon and evening among the trees and bracken between Ashford and Maidstone,

Miss Bright could ride a bicycle, and a machine was found for her, not among the hiring stock, but specially, in the sample held for sale. Miss Bunthorne, whom Bert particularly affected, could not ride, and so with some difficulty he hired a basketwork trailer from the big business of Wray's in the Clapham Road. To see our young men, brightly dressed and cigarettes alight, wheeling off to the rendezvous, Grubb guiding the lady's machine beside him with one skilful hand, and Bert teuf-teuffing steadily, was to realize how pluck may triumph even over insolvency. Their landlord, the butcher, said "Gurr!" as they passed, and shouted, "Go it!" in a loud, savage tone to their receding backs.

Much they cared.

The weather was fine, and though they were on their way southward before nine o'clock, there was already a great multitude of holiday people abroad upon the roads. There were quantities of young men and women on bicycles and motor-bicycles, and a majority of gyroscopic motor-cars, running bicycle-fashion on two wheels, mingled with old-fashioned four-wheeled traffic. Bank Holiday times always bring out old stored-away vehicles and odd people; one saw tri-cars and electric broughams and dilapidated old racing motors with huge pneumatic tyres. Once our holiday-makers saw a horse and cart, and once a youth riding a black horse amidst the badinage of the passers-by. And there were several navigable gas air-ships, not to mention balloons, in the air. It was all immensely interesting and refreshing after the dark anxieties of the shop. Edna wore a brown straw hat with poppies, that suited her admirably, and sat in the trailer like a queen, and the eight-year-old motor-bicycle ran like a thing of yesterday.

Little it seemed to matter to Bert Smallways that a newspaper placard proclaimed:

GERMANY DENOUNCES THE
MONROE DOCTRINE.

AMBIGUOUS ATTITUDE OF
JAPAN.

WHAT WILL BRITAIN DO?

IS IT WAR?

This sort of thing was always going on, and on holidays one disregarded it as a matter of course. Week-days, in the slack time after the midday meal, then perhaps one might worry about the Empire and international politics; but not on a sunny Sunday, with a pretty girl trailing behind one, and envious cyclists trying to race you. Nor did our young people attach any great importance to the flitting suggestions of military activity they glimpsed ever and again. Near Maidstone they came on a string of eleven motor-guns of peculiar construction halted by the roadside, with a number of business-like engineers grouped about them watching through field-glasses some sort of entrenchment that was going on near the crest of the downs. It signified nothing to Bert.

"What's up?" said Edna.

"Oh!—manœuvres," said Bert.

"Oh! I thought they did them at Easter," said Edna, and troubled no more.

The last great British war, the Boer war, was over and forgotten, and the public had lost the fashion of expert military criticism.

Our four young people picnicked cheerfully, and were happy in the manner of a happiness that was an ancient mode in Nineveh. Eyes were bright, Grubb was funny and almost witty, and Bert achieved epigrams; the hedges were full of honeysuckle and dog-roses: in the woods the distant toot-toot-toot of the traffic on the dust-hazy high road might have been no more than the horns of elf-land. They laughed and gossiped and picked flowers and made love and talked, and the girls smoked cigarettes. Also they scuffled playfully. Among other things they talked aeronautics, and how they would come for a picnic together in Bert's flying-machine before ten years were out. The world seemed full of amusing possibilities that afternoon. They wondered what their great-grandparents would have thought of aeronautics. In the evening, about seven, the party turned homeward, expecting no disaster, and it was only on the crest of the downs, between Wrotham and Kingsdown, that disaster came.

They had come up the hill in the twilight, Bert was anxious to get as far as possible before he lit—or attempted to light, for the issue was a doubtful one—his lamps, and they had scorched past a number of cyclists, and by a four-wheeled motor-car of the old style lamed by a deflated tyre. Some dust had penetrated Bert's horn, and the result was a curious, amusing, wheezing sound had got into his "honk, honk." For the sake of merriment and glory he was making this sound as much as possible, and Edna was in fits of laughter in the trailer. They made a sort of rushing cheerfulness along the road that affected their fellow travellers variously, according to their temperaments. She did notice a good lot of bluish, evil-smelling smoke coming from about the bearings between his feet, but she thought this was one of the natural concomitants of motor-traction, and troubled no more about it until abruptly it burst into a little yellow-tipped flame.

"Bert!" she screamed.

But Bert had put on the brakes with such suddenness that she found herself involved with his leg as he dismounted. She got to the side of the road and hastily readjusted her hat, which had suffered.

"Gaw!" said Bert.

He stood for some fatal seconds watching the petrol drip and catch, and the flame, which was now beginning to smell of enamel as well as oil, spread and grew. His chief idea was the sorrowful one that he had not sold the machine second-hand a year ago, and that he ought to have done so—a good idea in its way, but not immediately helpful. He turned upon Edna sharply. "Get a lot of wet sand," he said. Then he wheeled the machine a little towards the side of the roadway and laid it down and looked about for a supply of wet sand. The flames received this as a helpful attention, and made the most of it. They seemed to brighten, and the twilight to deepen about them. The road was a flinty road in the chalk country, and ill-provided with sand.

Edna accosted a short, fat cyclist. "We want wet sand," she said, and added, "our motor's on fire." The short, fat cyclist stared blankly for a moment, then with a helpful cry began to scrabble in the road-grit. Whereupon Bert and Edna also scrabbled in the road-grit. Other cyclists arrived, dismounted and stood about, and their flame-lit faces expressed satisfaction, interest, curiosity. "Wet sand," said the short, fat man, scrabbling terribly—"wet sand." One joined him. They threw hard-earned handfuls of road-grit upon the flames, which accepted them with enthusiasm.

Grubb arrived, riding hard. He was shouting something. He sprang off and threw his bicycle into the hedge. "Don't throw water on it!" he said—"don't throw water on it!" He displayed commanding presence of mind. He became captain of the occasion. Others were glad to repeat the things he said and imitate his actions. "Don't throw water on it!" they cried. Also there was no water.

"Beat it out, you fools!" he said.

He seized a rug from the trailer (it was an Austrian blanket, and Bert's winter coverlet), and began to beat at the burning petrol. For a wonderful minute he seemed to succeed. But he scattered burning pools of petrol on the road, and others, fired by his enthusiasm, imitated his action. Bert caught up a trailer-cushion and began to beat, there was another cushion and a table-cloth, and these also were seized. A young hero pulled off his jacket and joined the beating. For a moment there was less talking than hard breathing, and a tremendous flapping. Flossie, arriving on the outskirts of the crowd, cried, "Oh, my God," and burst loudly into tears. "Help!" she said, and "Fire!"

The lame motor-car arrived, and stopped in consternation. A tall, goggled, grey-haired man who was driving inquired with an Oxford intonation and a clear, careful enunciation, "Can *we* help at all?"

It became manifest that the rug, the table-cloth, the cushions, the jacket, were getting smeared with petrol and burning. The soul seemed to go out of the cushion Bert was swaying, and the air was full of feathers, like a snow-storm in the still twilight.

Bert had got very dusty and sweaty and strenuous. It seemed to him his weapon had been wrested from him at the moment of victory. The fire lay like a dying thing, close to the ground and wicked, it gave a leap of anguish at every whack of the beaters. But now Grubb had gone off to stamp out the burning blanket; the others were slacking just at the moment of victory. One was running to the motor-car. " *'Ere!*" cried Bert, "keep on."

He flung the deflated burning rags of cushion aside, whipped off his jacket and sprang at the flames with a shout. He stamped into the ruin until flames ran up his boots. Edna saw him, a red-lit hero, and thought it was good to be a man.

A bystander was hit by a hot halfpenny flying out of the air. Then Bert thought of the papers in his pockets, and staggered back, trying to extinguish his burning jacket—checked, repulsed, dismayed.

Edna was struck by the benevolent appearance of an elderly spectator in a silk hat and Sabbatical garments. "Oh!" she cried to him. "Help this young man! How can you stand and see it?"

A cry of "The tarpauling!" arose.

An earnest-looking man in a very light grey cycling-suit had suddenly appeared at the side of the lame motor-car and addressed the owner. "Have you a tarpauling?" he said.

"Yes," said the gentlemanly man. "Yes. We've got a tarpauling."

"That's it," said the earnest-looking man, suddenly shouting. "Let's have it, quick!"

The gentlemanly man, with feeble and deprecatory gestures, and in a manner of a hypnotized person, produced an excellent large tarpauling.

"Here!" cried the earnest-looking man to Grubb. "Ketch holt!"

Then everybody realized that a new method was to be tried. A number of willing hands seized upon the Oxford gentleman's tarpauling. The others stood away with approving noises. The tarpauling was held over the burning bicycle like a canopy, and then smothered down upon it.

"We ought to have done this before," panted Grubb.

There was a moment of triumph. The flames vanished. Everyone who could contrive to do so touched the edge of the tarpauling. Bert held down a corner with two hands and a foot. The tarpauling, bulged up in the centre, seemed to be suppressing triumphal exaltation. Then its self-approval became too much for it; it burst into a bright red smile in the centre. It was exactly like the opening of a mouth. It laughed with a gust of flames. They were reflected redly in the observant goggles of the gentleman who owned the tarpauling. Everybody recoiled.

"Save the trailer!" cried someone, and that was the last round in the battle. But the trailer could not be detached; its wicker work had caught, and it was the last thing to burn. A sort of hush fell upon the gathering. The petrol burnt low, the wicker-work trailer banged and crackled. The crowd divided itself into an outer circle of critics, advisers, and secondary characters, who had played undistinguished parts or no parts at all in the affair, and a central group of heated and distressed principals. A young man with an inquiring mind and a considerable knowledge of motor-bicycles fixed on to Grubb and wanted to argue that the thing could not have happened. Grubb was short and inattentive with him, and the young man withdrew to the back of the crowd, and there told the benevolent old gentleman in the silk hat that people who went out with machines they didn't understand had only themselves to blame if things went wrong.

The old gentleman let him talk for some time, and then remarked in a tone of rapturous enjoyment:

"Stone deaf," and added, "Nasty things."

A rosy-faced man in a straw hat claimed attention. "I *did* save the front wheel," he said; "you'd have had that tyre catch, too, if I hadn't kept turning it round." It became manifest that this was so. The front wheel had retained its tyre, was intact, was still rotating slowly among the blackened and twisted ruins of the rest of the machine. It had something of that air of conscious virtue, of unimpeachable respectability, that distinguishes a rent collector in a low neighbourhood. "That wheel's worth a pound," said the rosy-faced man, making a song of it. "I kep' turning it round."

New-comers kept arriving from the south with the question, "What's up?" until it got on Grubb's nerves. Londonward the crowd was constantly losing people; they would mount their various wheels with the satisfied manner of spectators who have had the best. Their voices would recede into the twilight; one would hear a laugh at the memory of this particularly salient incident or that.

"I'm afraid," said the gentleman of the motor-car, my tarpauling's a bit done for."

Grubb admitted that the owner was the best judge of that.

"Nothing else I can do for you?" said the gentleman of the motor-car, it may be, with a suspicion of irony.

Bert was roused to action. "Look here," he said. "There's my young lady. If she ain't 'ome by ten they lock her out. See? Well, all the money was in my jacket pocket, and it's all mixed up with the burnt stuff, and that's too 'ot to touch. *Is* Clapham out of your way?"

"All in the day's work," said the gentleman with the motor-car, and turned to Edna. "Very pleased indeed," he said, "if you'll come with us. We're late for dinner as it is, so it won't make much difference for us to go home by way of Clapham. We've got to get to Surbiton, anyhow. I'm afraid you'll find us a little slow."

"But what's Bert going to do?" said Edna.

"I don't know that we can accommodate Bert," said the motor-car gentleman, "though we're tremendously anxious to oblige."

"You couldn't take the whole lot?" said Bert waving his hand at the deboshed and blackened ruins on the ground.

"I'm awfully afraid I can't," said the Oxford man. "Awfully sorry, you know."

"Then I'll have to stick 'ere for a bit," said Bert. "I got to see the thing through. You go on, Edna."

"Don't like leavin' you, Bert."

"You can't 'elp it, Edna."

The last Edna saw of Bert was his figure, in charred and blackened shirt-sleeves, standing in the dusk. He was musing deeply by the mixed ironwork and ashes of his vanished motor-bicycle, a melancholy figure. His retinue of spectators had shrunk now to half a dozen figures. Flossie and Grubb were preparing to follow her desertion.

"Cheer up, old Bert," cried Edna, with artificial cheerfulness. "So long."

"So long, Edna," said Bert.

"See you to-morrer."

"See you to-morrer," said Bert, though he was destined, as a matter of fact, to see much of the habitable globe before he saw her again.

Bert began to light matches from a borrowed boxful, and search for a half-crown that still eluded him among the charred remains. His face was grave and melancholy.

"I *wish* that 'adn't 'appened," said Flossie, riding on with Grubb. . . .

And at last Bert was left almost alone, a sad, blackened Promethean figure, cursed by the gift of fire. He had entertained vague ideas of hiring a cart, of achieving miraculous repairs, of still snatching some residual value from his one chief possession. Now, in the darkening night, he perceived the vanity of such intentions. Truth came to him bleakly, and laid her chill conviction upon him. He took hold of the handle-bar, stood the thing up, tried to push it forward. The tyreless hind-wheel was jammed hopelessly, even as he feared. For a minute or so he stood upholding his machine, a motionless despair. Then with a great effort he thrust the ruins from him into the ditch, kicked at it once, regarded it for a moment, and turned his face resolutely Londonward.

He did not once look back.

"That's the end of *that* game," said Bert. "No more teuf-teuf-teuf for Bert Smallways for a year or two. Good-bye 'Olidays! . . . Oh! I ought to 'ave sold the blasted thing when I had a chance three years ago."

3

The next morning found the firm of Grubb and Smallways in a state of profound despondency. It seemed a small matter to them that the newspaper and cigarette shop opposite displayed such placards as this:

REPORTED AMERICAN ULTIMATUM.

BRITAIN MUST FIGHT.

OUR INFATUATED WAR OFFICE STILL
REFUSES TO LISTEN TO MR. BUTTERIDGE.

GREAT MONO-RAIL DISASTER AT
TIMBUCTOO.

or this:

WAR A QUESTION OF HOURS.

NEW YORK CALM.

EXCITEMENT IN BERLIN.

or again:

WASHINGTON STILL SILENT.

WHAT WILL PARIS DO?

THE PANIC ON THE BOURSE.

THE KING'S GARDEN PARTY TO THE MASKED TWAREGS.

MR. BUTTERIDGE MAKES AN OFFER.

LATEST BETTING FROM TEHERAN.

or this:

WILL AMERICA FIGHT?

ANTI-GERMAN RIOT IN BAGDAD.

THE MUNICIPAL SCANDALS AT DAMASCUS.

MR. BUTTERIDGE'S INVENTION FOR AMERICA.

Bert stared at these over the card of pump-clips in the pane in the door with unseeing eyes. He wore a blackened flannel shirt and the jacketless ruins of the holiday suit of yesterday. The boarded-up shop was dark and depressing beyond words, and the few scandalous hiring machines had never looked so hopelessly disreputable. He thought of their fellows who were "out," and of the approaching disputations of the afternoon. He thought of their new landlord and of their old landlord, and of bills and claims. Life presented itself for the first time as a hopeless fight against fate. . . .

"Grubb, O' man," he said, distilling the quintessence, "I'm fair sick of this shop."

"So'm I," said Grubb.

"I'm out of conceit with it. I don't seem to care even to speak to a customer again."

"There's that trailer," said Grubb, after a pause.

"Blow the trailer," said Bert, "Anyhow, I didn't leave a deposit on it. I didn't do that. Still—Look 'ere," he said, "we aren't gettin' on here. We been losing money hand over fist. We got things tied up in fifty knots."

"What can we do?" said Grubb.

"Clear out. Sell what we can for what it will fetch, and quit. See? It's no good 'anging on to a losing concern. No sort of good. Jest foolishness."

"That's all right," said Grubb—"that's all right; but it ain't your capital been sunk in it."

"No need for us to sink after our capital," said Bert, ignoring the point.

"I'm not going to be held responsible for that trailer, anyhow. That ain't my affair."

"Nobody arst you to make it your affair. If you like to stick on here, well and good. I'm quitting. I'll see the Bank Holiday through, and then I'm O.R.P.H. See?"

"Leavin' me?"

"Leavin' you. If you must be left."

Grubb looked round the shop. It certainly had become distasteful. Once upon a time it had been bright with hope and new beginnings and stock and the prospect of credit. Now—now it was a failure and dust. Very likely the landlord would be round presently to go on with the row about the window. . . . "Where d'you think of going, Bert?" Grubb asked.

Bert turned round and regarded him. "I thought it out as I was walking 'ome, and in bed. I couldn't sleep a wink."

"What did you think out?"

"Plans."

"What plans?"

"Oh! you're for sticking here."

"Not if anything better was to offer."

"It's only an ideer," said Bert.

"Let's 'ear it."

"You made the girls laugh yestiday, that song you sang."

"Seems a long time ago now," said Grubb.

"And old Edna nearly cried—over that bit of mine."

"She got a fly in her eye," said Grubb; "I saw it. But what's this got to do with your plan?"

"No end," said Bert.

" 'Ow?"

"Don't you see?"

"Not singing in the streets?"

"Streets! No fear! But 'ow about the Tour of the Waterin' Places of England, Grubb? Singing! Young men of family doing it for a lark? You ain't got a bad voice, you know, and mine's all right. I never see a chap singing on the beach yet that I couldn't 'ave sung into a cocked hat. And we both know how to put on the toff a bit. Eh? Well, that's my ideer. Me and you. Grubb, with a refined song and a break-down. Like we was doing for foolery yestiday. That was what put it into my 'ead. Easy make up a programme—easy. Six choice items, and one or two for encores and patter. I'm all right for the patter—anyhow."

Grubb remained regarding his darkened and disheartening shop; he thought of his former landlord and his present landlord, and of the general disgustingness of business in an age which re-echoes to The Bitter Cry of the Middle Class; and then it seemed to him that afar off he heard the twankle, twankle of a banjo, and the voice of a stranded siren singing. He had a sense of hot sunshine upon sand, of the children of at least transiently opulent holiday makers in a circle round about him, of the whisper, "They are really gentlemen," and then dollop, dollop came the coppers in the hat. Sometimes even silver. It was all income; no outgoings, no bills. "I'm on, Bert," he said.

"Right O!" said Bert, and, "Now we shan't be long."

"We needn't start without capital, neither," said Grubb. "If we take the best of these machines up to the Bicycle Mart in Finsbury we'd raise six or seven pounds on 'em. We could easy do that to-morrow before anybody much was about. . . ."

"Nice to think of old Suet-and-Bones coming round to make his usual row with us, and finding a card up, 'Closed for Repairs.'"

"We'll do that," said Grubb with zest—"we'll do that. And we'll put up another notice, and jest arst all inquirers to go round to 'im and inquire. See? Then they'll know all about us."

Before the day was out the whole enterprise was planned. They decided at first that they would call themselves the Naval Mr. O's, a plagiarism, and not perhaps a very good one, from the "Scarlet Mr. E's," and Bert rather clung to the idea of a uniform of bright blue serge, with a lot of gold lace and cord ornamentation, rather like a naval officer's, but more so. But that had to be abandoned as impracticable, it would have taken too much time and money to prepare. They perceived they must wear some cheaper and more readily prepared costume, and Grubb fell back on white dominoes. They entertained the notion for a time of selecting the two worst machines from the hiring-stock, painting them over with crimson enamel paint, replacing the bells by the loudest sort of motor horn, and doing a ride about to begin and end the entertainment. They doubted the advisability of this step.

"There's people in the world," said Bert, "who wouldn't recognize us, who'd know them bicycles again like a shot, and we don't want to go on with no old stories. We want a fresh start."

"*I* do," said Grubb, "badly."

"We want to forget things—and cut all these rotten old worries. They ain't doin' us good."

Nevertheless, they decided to take the risk of these bicycles, and they decided their costumes should be brown stockings and sandals, and cheap unbleached sheets with a hole cut in the middle, and wigs and beards of tow. The rest their normal selves! "The Desert Dervishes," they would call themselves, and their chief songs would be those popular ditties, "In my Trailer," and "What Price Hairpins Now?"

They decided to begin with small seaside places, and gradually, as they gained confidence, attack larger centres. To begin with they selected Littlestone, in Kent, chiefly because of its unassuming name.

So they planned, and it seemed a small and Unimportant thing to them that as they chattered the governments of half the world and more were drifting to war. About midday they became aware of the in first of the evening-paper placards shouting to them across the street:

THE WAR-CLOUD DARKENS.

Nothing else but that.

"Always rottin' about war now," said Bert. "They'll get it in the neck in real earnest one of these days, if they ain't precious careful."

4

So you will understand the sudden apparition that surprised rather than delighted the quiet informality of Dymchurch sands. Dymchurch was one of the last places on the coast of England to be reached by the mono-rail, and so its spacious sands were still, at the time of this story, the secret and delight of quite a limited number of people. They went there to flee vulgarity and extravagances, and to bathe and sit and talk and play with their children in peace, and the Desert Dervishes did not please them at all.

The two white figures on scarlet wheels came upon them out of the infinite along the sands of Littlestone, grew nearer and larger and more audible, honk-honking and emitting weird cries, and generally threatening liveliness of the most aggressive type. "Good heavens!" said Dymchurch, "what's this?"

Then our young men, according to a preconcerted plan, wheeled round from file to line, dismounted and stood at attention. "Ladies and gentlemen," they said, "we beg to present ourselves—the Desert Dervishes." They bowed profoundly.

The few scattered groups upon the beach regarded them with horror for the most part, but some of the children were interested, and drew nearer. "There ain't a bob on the beach," said Grubb in an undertone, and the Desert Dervishes piled their bicycles with comic "business" that got a laugh from one very unsophisticated little boy. Then they took a deep breath and struck into the cheerful strain of "What Price Hair-pins Now?" Grubb sang the song. Bert did his best to make the chorus a rousing one, and at the end of each verse they danced certain steps, skirts in hand, that they had carefully rehearsed.

Ting-a-ling-a-ting-a-ling-a-ting-a-ling-a-tang.
What Price Hair-pins Now?

So they chanted and danced their steps in the sunshine of Dymchurch beach, and the children drew near these foolish young men, marvelling that they should behave in this way, and the older people looked cold and unfriendly.

All round the coasts of Europe that morning banjos were ringing, voices were bawling and singing, children were playing in the sun, pleasure boats went to and fro; the common abundant life of the time, unsuspicious of all the dangers that gathered darkly against it flowed on its cheerful, aimless way. In the cities men fussed about their businesses and engagements. The newspaper placards that had cried "wolf!" so often, cried "wolf!" now in vain.

5

Now as Bert and Grubb bawled their chorus for the third time, they became aware of a very big, golden-brown balloon low in the sky to the north-west, and coming rapidly towards them. "Jest as we're gettin' hold of 'em," muttered Grubb, "up comes a counter-attraction. Go it, Bert!"

Ting-a-ling-a-ting-a-ling-a-ting-a-ling-a-tang.
What Price Hair-pins Now?

The balloon rose and fell, went out of sight—"landed, thank goodness," said Grubb—reappeared with a leap. *"Eng!"* said Grubb. "Step it, Bert, or they'll see it!"

They finished their dance, and then stood frankly staring.

"There's something wrong with that balloon," said Bert.

Everybody now was looking at the balloon drawing rapidly nearer before a brisk north-westerly breeze. The song and dance were a "dead frost." Nobody thought any more about it. Even Bert and Grubb forgot it, and ignored the next item on the programme altogether. The balloon was bumping as though its occupants were trying to land; it would approach, sinking slowly, touch the ground, and instantly jump fifty feet or so in the air and immediately begin to fall again. Its car touched a clump of trees, and the black figure that had been struggling in the ropes fell back, or jumped back, into the car. In another moment it was close. It seemed a huge affair, as big as a house, and it floated down swiftly towards the sands; a long rope trailed behind it, and enormous shouts came from the man in the car. He seemed to be taking off his clothes, then his head came over the side of the car. "Catch hold of the rope!" they heard, quite plain.

"Salvage, Bert!" cried Grubb, and started to head off the rope.

Bert followed him, and collided, without upsetting, with a fisherman bent upon a similar errand. A woman carrying a baby in her arms, two small boys with toy spades, and a stout gentleman in flannels all got to the trailing rope at about the same time, and began to dance over it in their attempts to secure it. Bert came up to this wriggling, elusive serpent and got his foot on it, went down on all fours and achieved a grip. In half a dozen seconds the whole diffused population of the beach had, as it were, crystallised on the rope, and was pulling against the balloon under the vehement and stimulating directions of the man in the car. "Pull, I tell you," said the man in the car. "Pull!"

For a second or so the balloon obeyed its momentum and the wind and tugged its human anchor seaward. It dropped, touched the water, and made a flat, silvery splash, and recoiled as one's finger recoils when one touches anything hot. "Pull her in," said the man in the car. "*She's fainted!*"

He occupied himself with some unseen object while the people on the rope pulled him in. Bert was nearest the balloon, and much excited and interested. He kept stumbling over the tail of the Dervish costume in his zeal. He had never imagined before what a big, light, wallowing thing a balloon was. The car was of brown coarse wicker-work, and comparatively small. The rope he tugged at was fastened to a stout looking ring, four or five feet above the car. At each tug he drew in a yard or so of rope, and the waggling wicker-work was drawn so much nearer. Out of the car came wrathful bellowings: "Fainted she has!" and then: "It's her heart—broken with all she's had to go through."

The balloon ceased to struggle, and sank downward. Bert dropped the rope, and ran forward to catch it in a new place. In another moment he had his hand on the car. "Lay hold of it," said the man in the car, and his face appeared close to Bert's—a strangely familiar face, fierce eyebrows, a flattish nose, a huge black moustache. He had discarded coat and waistcoat—perhaps with some idea of presently having to swim for his life—and his black hair was extraordinarily disordered. "Will all you people get hold round the car," he said. "There's a lady here fainted—or got failure of the heart. Heaven alone knows which! My name is Butteridge. Butteridge, my name is—in a balloon. Now, please, all on to the edge. This is the last time I trust myself to one of these paleolithic contrivances. The ripping-cord failed, and the valve wouldn't act. If ever I meet the scoundrel who ought to have seen—"

He stuck his head out between the ropes abruptly, and said, in a note of earnest expostulation: "Get some brandy!—some neat brandy!" Someone went up the beach for it.

In the car, sprawling upon a sort of bed-bench, in an attitude of elaborate self-abandonment, was a large, blond lady, wearing a fur coat and a big floriferous hat. Her head lolled back against the padded corner of the car, and her eyes were shut and her mouth open. "Me dear!" said Mr. Butteridge, in a common loud voice, "we're safe!"

She gave no sign.

"Me dear!" said Mr. Butteridge, in a greatly intensified loud voice, "we're safe!"

She was still quite impassive.

Then Mr. Butteridge showed the fiery cord of his soul. "If she is dead," he said, slowly lifting a fist towards the balloon above him, and speaking in an immense tremulous bellow—"if she is dead, I will r-r-rend the heavens like a garment! I must get her out," he cried, his nostrils dilated with emotion. "I must get her out. I cannot have her die in a wicker-work basket nine feet square—she who was made for kings' palaces! Keep hold of this car! Is there a strong man among ye to take her if I hand her out?"

He swept the lady together by a powerful movement of his arms, and lifted her. "Keep the car from jumping," he said to those who clustered about him. "Keep your weight on it. She is no light woman, and when she is out of—it will be relieved."

Bert leapt lightly into a sitting position on the edge of the car. The others took a firmer grip upon the ropes and ring.

"Are you ready?" said Mr. Butteridge.

He stood upon the bed-bench and lifted the lady carefully. Then he sat down on the wicker edge opposite to Bert, and put one leg over to dangle outside. A rope or so seemed to incommode him. "Will someone assist me?" he said. "If they would take this lady?"

It was just at this moment, with Mr. Butteridge and the lady balanced finely on the basket brim, that she came to. She came to suddenly and violently with a loud, heart-rending cry of "Alfred! Save me!" And she waved her arms searchingly, and then clasped Mr. Butteridge about.

It seemed to Bert that the car swayed for a moment and then buck-jumped and kicked him. Also he saw the boots of the lady and the right leg of the gentleman describing arcs through the air, preparatory to vanishing over the side of the car. His impressions were complex, but they also comprehended the fact that he had lost his balance, and was going to stand on his head inside this creaking basket. He spread out clutching arms. He did stand on his head, more or less, his tow beard came off and got in his mouth, and his cheek slid along against padding. His nose buried itself in a bag of sand. The car gave a violent lurch, and became still.

"Confound it!" he said.

He had an impression he must be stunned, because of a surging in his ears, and because all the voices of the people about him had become small and remote. They were shouting like elves inside a hill.

He found it a little difficult to get on his feet. His limbs were mixed up with the garments Mr. Butteridge had discarded when that gentleman had thought he must needs plunge into the sea. Bert bawled out half angry, half rueful, "You might have said you were going to tip the basket." Then he stood up and clutched the ropes of the car convulsively.

Below him, far below him, shining blue, were the waters of the English Channel. Far off, a little thing in the sunshine, and rushing down as if some one was bending it hollow, was the beach and the irregular cluster of houses that constituted Dymchurch. He could see the little crowd of people he had so abruptly left. Grubb, in the white wrapper of a Desert Dervish, was running along the edge of the sea. Mr. Butteridge was knee-deep in the water, bawling immensely. The lady was sitting up with her floriferous hat in her lap, shockingly neglected. The beach, east and west, was dotted with little people—they seemed all heads and feet—looking up. And the balloon, released from the twenty-five stone or so of Mr. Butteridge and his lady, was rushing up into the sky at the pace of a racing motor-car. "My crikey!" said Bert; "here's a go!"

He looked down with a pinched face at the receding beach, and reflected that he wasn't giddy; then he made a superficial survey of the cords and ropes about him with a vague idea of "doing something." "I'm not going to mess about with the thing," he said at last, and sat down upon the mattress. "I'm not going to touch it. . . . I wonder what one ought to do?"

Soon he got up again and stared for a long time at the sinking world below, at white cliffs to the east and flattening marsh to the left at a minute wide prospect of weald and downland, at dim towns and harbours, and rivers and ribbon-like roads, at ships and ships, decks and foreshortened funnels upon the ever-widening sea, and at the great mono-rail bridge that straddled the Channel from Folkestone to Boulogne, until at length, first little wisps and then a veil of filmy cloud hid the prospect from his eyes. He wasn't at all giddy nor very much frightened, only in a state of enormous consternation.

THREE

The Balloon

I

Bert Smallways was a vulgar little creature, the sort of pert, limited soul that the old civilisation of the early twentieth century produced by the million in every country of the world. He had lived all his life in narrow streets, and between mean houses he could not look over, and in a narrow circle of ideas from which there was no escape. He thought the whole duty of man was to be smarter than his fellows, get his hands, as he put it, "on the dibs," and have a good time. He was, in fact, the sort of man who had made England and America what they were. The luck had been against him so far, but that was by the way. He was a mere aggressive and acquisitive individual with no sense of the State, no habitual loyalty, no devotion, no code of honour, no code even of courage. Now by a curious accident he found himself lifted out of his marvellous modern world for a time, out of all the rush and confused appeals of it, and floating like a thing dead and disembodied between sea and sky. It was as if Heaven was experimenting with him, had picked him out as a sample from the English millions to look at him more nearly and to see what was happening to the soul of man. But what Heaven made of him in that case I cannot profess to imagine, for I have long since abandoned all theories about the ideals and satisfactions of Heaven.

To be alone in a balloon at a height of fourteen or fifteen thousand feet—and to that height Bert Smallways presently rose—is like nothing else in human experience. It is one of the supreme things possible to man. No flying-machine can ever better it. It is to pass extraordinarily out of human things. It is to be still and alone to an unprecedented degree. It is solitude without the suggestion of intervention; it is calm without a single irrelevant murmur. It is to see the sky.

No sound reaches one of all the roar and jar of humanity, the air is clear and sweet beyond the thought of defilement. No bird, no insect comes so high. No wind blows ever in a balloon, no breeze rustles, for it moves with the wind and is itself a part of the atmosphere. Once started it does not rock nor sway; you cannot feel whether it rises or falls. Bert felt acutely cold, but he wasn't mountain sick; he put on the coat and overcoat and gloves Butteridge had discarded—put them over the "Desert Dervish" sheet that covered his cheap best suit—and sat very still for a long time overawed by the new-found quiet of the world. Above him was the light, translucent, billowing globe of shining brown oiled silk and the blazing sunlight and the great deep blue dome of the sky. Below, far below, was a torn floor of sunlit cloud, slashed by enormous rents, through which he saw the sea.

If you had been watching him from below you would have seen his head, a motionless little black knob, sticking out from the car first of all for a long time on one side, and then vanishing to reappear after a time at some other point.

He wasn't in the least degree uncomfortable or afraid. He did not think that as this uncontrollable thing had thus rushed up the sky with him it might presently rush down again, but this consideration did not trouble him very much. Essentially his state was wonder. There is no fear nor trouble in balloons—until they descend.

"Gollys!" he said at last, feeling a need for talking; "it's better than a motor-bike.

"It's all right!

"I suppose they're telegraphing about, about me. . . ."

The second hour found him examining the equipment of the car with great particularity. Above him was the throat of the balloon bunched and tied together, but with an open lumen, through which Bert could peer up into a vast, empty quiet interior, and out of which descended two fine cords of unknown import, one white, one crimson, to pockets below the ring. The netting about the balloon ended in cords attached to the ring, a big steel-bound hoop to which the car was slung by ropes. From it depended the trail rope and grapnel, and over the sides of the car were a number of canvas bags that Bert decided must be ballast to "chuck down" if the balloon fell. ("Not much falling just yet," said Bert.)

There were an aneroid and another box-shaped instrument hanging from the ring. The latter had an ivory plate bearing "statoscope" and other words in French, and a little indicator quivered and waggled between *Montée* and *Descente*. "That's all right," said Bert. "That tells if you're going up or down." On the crimson padded seat of the balloon there lay a couple of rugs and a kodak, and in opposite corners of the bottom of the car were an empty champagne bottle and a glass. "Refreshments," said Bert meditatively, tilting the empty bottle. Then he had a brilliant idea. The two padded bed-like seats, each with blankets and mattress, he perceived, were boxes, and within he found Mr. Butteridge's conception of an adequate equipment for a balloon ascent; a hamper which included a game pie, a Roman pie, a cold fowl, tomatoes, lettuce, ham sandwiches, shrimp sandwiches, a large cake, knives and forks and paper plates, self-heating tins of coffee and cocoa, bread, butter, and marmalade, several carefully packed bottles of champagne, bottles of Perrier water, and a big jar of water for washing, a portfolio, maps, and a compass, a rücksack containing a number of conveniences, including curling-tongs and hairpins, a cap with ear-flaps, and so forth.

"A 'ome from 'ome," said Bert, surveying this provision as he tied the ear-flaps under his chin.

He looked over the side of the car. Far below were the shining clouds. They had thickened so that the whole world was hidden. Southward they were piled in great snowy masses; he was half disposed to think them mountains; northward and eastward they were in wavelike levels, and blindingly sunlit.

"Wonder how long a balloon keeps up," he said.

He imagined he was not moving, so insensibly did the monster drift with the air about it. "No good coming down till we shift a bit," he said.

He consulted the statoscope.

"Still monty," he said.

"Wonder what would happen if you pulled a cord?"

"No," he decided. "I ain't going to mess it about."

Afterwards he did pull both the ripping- and the valve-cords, but, as Mr. Butteridge had already discovered, they had fouled a fold of silk in the throat. Nothing happened. But for that little hitch the ripping-cord would have torn the balloon open as though it had been slashed by a sword, and hurled Mr. Smallways to eternity at the rate of some thousand feet a second. "No go!" he said, giving it a final tug. Then he lunched.

He opened a bottle of champagne, which, as soon as he cut the wire, blew its cork out with incredible violence, and for the most part followed it into space. Bert, however, got about a tumblerful. "Atmospheric pressure," said Bert, finding an application at last for the elementary physiography of his seventh-standard days. "I'll have to be more careful next time. No good wastin' drink."

Then he routed about for matches to utilize Mr. Butteridge's cigars; but here again luck was on his side, and he couldn't find any wherewith to set light to the gas above him. Or else he would have dropped in a flare, a splendid but transitory pyrotechnic display. "Eng old Grubb!" said Bert, slapping unproductive pockets. " 'E didn't ought to 'ave kep' my box, 'E's always sneaking matches."

He reposed for a time. Then he got up, paddled about, rearranged the ballast bags on the floor, watched the clouds for a time, and turned over the maps on the locker. Bert liked maps, and he spent some time in trying to find one of France or the Channel; but they were all British ordnance maps of English counties. That set him thinking about languages and trying to recall his seventh-standard French. "Je suis Anglais. C'est une méprise. Je suis arrivé par accident ici," he decided upon as convenient phrases. Then it occurred to him that he would entertain himself by reading Mr. Butteridge's letters and examining his pocket-book, and in this manner he whiled away the afternoon.

2

He sat upon the padded locker, wrapped about very carefully, for the air, though calm, was exhilaratingly cold and clear. He was wearing first a modest suit of blue serge and all the unpretending underwear of a suburban young man of fashion, with sandal-like cycling-shoes and brown stockings drawn over his trouser ends; then the perforated sheet proper to a Desert Dervish; then the coat and waistcoat and big fur-trimmed overcoat of Mr. Butteridge; then a lady's large fur cloak, and round his knees a blanket. Over his head was a tow wig, surmounted by a large cap of Mr. Butteridge's with the flaps down over his ears. And some fur sleeping-boots of Mr. Butteridge's warmed his feet. The car of the balloon was small and neat, some bags of ballast the untidiest of its contents, and he had found a light folding-table and put it at his elbow, and on that was a glass with champagne. And about him, above and below, was space—such a clear emptiness and silence of space as only the aeronaut can experience.

He did not know where he might be drifting, or what might happen next. He accepted this state of affairs with a serenity creditable to the Smallways' courage, which one might reasonably have expected to be of a more degenerate and contemptible quality altogether. His impression was that he was bound to come down somewhere, and that then, if he wasn't smashed, some one, some "society" perhaps, would probably pack him and the balloon back to England. If not, he would ask very firmly for the British Consul. "Le consuelo Britannique," he decided this would be. "Apportez moi à le consuelo Britannique s'il vous plait," he would say, for he was by no means ignorant of French. In the meanwhile he found the intimate aspects of Mr. Butteridge an interesting study.

There were letters of an entirely private character addressed to Mr. Butteridge, and among others several love-letters of a devouring sort in a large feminine hand. These are no business of ours, and one remarks with regret that Bert read them.

When he had read them he remarked, "Gollys!" in an awe-stricken tone, and then, after a long interval, "I wonder if that was her?"

"Lord!"

He mused for a time.

He resumed his exploration of the Butteridge interior. It included a number of press cuttings of interviews and also several letters in German, then some in the same German handwriting, but in English. "Hul-*lo*!" said Bert.

One of the latter, the first he took, began with an apology to Butteridge for not writing to him in English before, and for the inconvenience and delay that had been caused him by that, and went on to matter that Bert found exciting in the highest degree. "We can understand entirely the difficulties of your position, and that you shall possibly be watched at the present juncture. But, sir, we do not believe that any serious obstacles will be put in your way if you wished to endeavour to leave the country and come to us with your plans by the customary routes—either via Dover, Ostend, Boulogne, or Dieppe. We find it difficult to think you are right in supposing yourself to be in danger of murder for your invaluable invention."

"Funny!" said Bert, and meditated.

Then he went through the other letters.

"They seem to want him to come," said Bert; "but they don't seem hurting themselves to get 'im. Or else they're shamming don't care to get his prices down.

"They don't quite seem to be the gov'ment," he reflected after an interval. "It's more like some firm's paper. All this printed stuff at the top. *Drachenflieger. Drachenballons. Ballonstoffe. Kugelballons.* Greek to me.

"But he was trying to sell his blessed secret abroad. That's all right. No Greek about that! Gollys! Here *is* the secret!"

He tumbled off the seat, opened the locker, and had the portfolio open before him on the folding-table. It was full of drawings done in the peculiar flat style and conventional colours engineers adopt. And, in addition, there were some rather under-exposed photographs, obviously done by an amateur at close quarters, of the actual machine Butteridge had made, in its shed near the Crystal Palace. Bert found he was trembling. "Lord!" he said, "here am I and the whole blessed secret flying—lost up here on the roof of everywhere.

"Let's see!" He fell studying the drawings and comparing them with the photographs. They puzzled him. Half of them seemed to be missing. He tried to imagine how they fitted together, and found the effort too great for his mind.

"It's tryin'," said Bert. "I wish I'd been brought up to the engineering. If I could only make it out!"

He went to the side of the car and remained for a time staring with unseeing eyes at a huge cluster of great clouds—a cluster of slowly dissolving Monte Rosas, sunlit below. His attention was arrested by a strange black spot that moved over them. It alarmed him. It was a black spot moving slowly with him far below, following him down there, indefatigably over the cloud mountains. Why should such a thing follow him? What could it be? . . .

He had an inspiration. "Uv course!" he said. It was the shadow of the balloon. But he still watched it dubiously for a time.

He returned to the plans on the table.

He spent a long afternoon between his struggles to understand them and fits of meditation. He evolved a remarkable new sentence in French. "Voici Mossoo!—Je suis un inventeur Anglais. Mon nom est Butteridge. Beh. oo. teh. teh. eh. arr. E. deh. ghe. eh. J'avais ici pour vendre le secret de le *flying-machine*. Comprenez? Vendre pour l'argent tout suite, l'argent en main. Comprenez? C'est le machine à jouer dans l'air. Comprenez? C'est le machine a faire l'oiseau. Comprenez? Balancer? Oui exactement! Battir l'oiseau en fait, à son propre jeu. Je désire de vendre ceci à votre government national. Voulez vous me directer la?

"Bit rummy, I expect, from the point of view of grammar," said Bert, "but they ought to get the hang of it all right.

"But then, if they arst me to explain the blessed thing?"

He returned in a worried way to the plans. "I don't believe it's all here!" he said. . . .

He got more and more perplexed up there among the clouds as to what he should do with this wonderful find of his. At any moment, so far as he could tell, he might descend among he knew not what foreign people.

"It's the chance of my life!" he said.

It became more and more manifest to him that it wasn't. "Directly I come down they'll telegraph—put it in the papers. Butteridge'll know of it and come along—on my track."

Butteridge would be a terrible person to be on any one's track. Bert thought of the great black moustaches, the triangular nose, the searching bellow and the glare. His afternoon's dream of a marvellous seizure and sale of the great Butteridge secret crumpled up in his mind, dissolved, and vanished. He awoke to sanity again.

"Wouldn't do. What's the good of thinking of it?" He proceeded slowly and reluctantly to replace the Butteridge papers in pockets and portfolio as he had found them. He became aware of a splendid golden light upon the balloon above him, and of a new warmth in the blue dome of the sky. He stood up and beheld the sun, a great ball of blinding gold, setting upon a tumbled sea of gold-edged crimson and purple clouds, strange and wonderful beyond imagining. Eastward cloudland stretched for ever, darkling blue, and it seemed to Bert the whole round hemisphere of the world was under his eyes.

Then far away over the blue he caught sight of three long, dark shapes like hurrying fish that drove one after the other, as porpoises follow one another in the water. They were very fish-like indeed—with tails. It was an unconvincing impression in that light. He blinked his eyes, stared again, and they had vanished. For a long time he scrutinized those remote blue levels and saw no more. . . .

"Wonder if I ever saw anything," he said, and then: "There ain't such things. . . ."

Down went the sun and down, not diving steeply, but passing northward as it sank, and then suddenly daylight and the expansive warmth of daylight had gone altogether, and the index of the statoscope quivered over to *Descente*.

3

"Now what's going to 'appen?" said Bert.

He found the cold, grey cloud wilderness rising towards him with a wide, slow steadiness As he sank down among them the clouds ceased to seem the snow-clad mountain-slopes they had resembled heretofore, became unsubstantial, confessed an immense silent drift and eddy in their substance. For a moment, when he was nearly among their twilight masses, his descent was checked. Then abruptly the sky was hidden, the last vestiges of daylight gone, and he was falling rapidly in an evening twilight through a whirl of fine snowflakes that streamed past him towards the zenith, that drifted in upon the things about him and melted, that touched his face with ghostly fingers. He shivered. His breath came smoking from his lips, and everything was instantly bedewed and wet.

He had an impression of a snowstorm pouring with unexampled and increasing fury *upward;* then he realized that he was falling faster and faster.

Imperceptibly a sound grew upon his ears. The great silence of the world was at an end.

What was this confused sound?

He craned his head over the side, concerned, perplexed.

First he seemed to see, and then not to see. Then he saw clearly little edges of foam pursuing each other, and a wide waste of weltering waters below him. Far away was a pilot boat with a big sail bearing dim black letters, and a little pinkish-yellow light, and it was rolling and pitching—rolling and pitching in a gale, while he could feel no wind at all. Soon the sound of waters was loud and near. He was dropping, dropping—into the sea!

He became convulsively active.

"Ballast!" he cried, and seized a little sack from the floor, and heaved it overboard. He did not wait for the effect of that, but sent another after it. He looked over in time to see a minute white splash in the dim waters below him, and then he was back in the snow and clouds again.

He sent out quite needlessly a third sack of ballast and a fourth, and presently had the immense satisfaction of soaring up out of the damp and chill into the clear, cold upper air in which the day still lingered. "Thang-God!" he said, with all his heart.

A few stars now had pierced the blue, and in the east there shone brightly a prolate moon.

4

That first downward plunge filled Bert with a haunting sense of boundless waters below. It was a summer's night, but it seemed to him, nevertheless, extraordinarily long. He had a feeling of insecurity that he fancied quite irrationally the sunrise would dispel. Also he was hungry. He felt in the dark in the locker, put his fingers in the Roman pie, and got some sandwiches, and he also opened rather successfully a half-bottle of champagne. That warmed and restored him, he grumbled at Grubb about the matches, wrapped himself up warmly on the locker, and dozed for a time. He got up once or twice to make sure that he was still securely high above the sea. The first time the moonlit clouds were white and dense, and the shadow of the balloon ran athwart them like a dog that followed; afterwards they seemed thinner. As he lay still, staring up at the huge dark balloon above, he made a discovery. His—or rather Mr. Butteridge's—waistcoat rustled as he breathed. It was lined with papers. But Bert could not see to get them out or examine them, much as he wished to do so. . . .

He was awakened by the crowing of cocks, the barking of dogs, and a clamour of birds. He was driving slowly at a low level over a broad land lit golden by sunrise under a clear sky. He stared out upon hedgeless, well-cultivated fields intersected by roads, each lined with cable-bearing red poles. He had just passed over a compact, whitewashed village with a straight church tower and steep red-tiled roofs. A number of peasants, men and women, in shiny blouses and lumpish footwear, stood regarding him, arrested on their way to work. He was so low that the end of his rope was trailing.

He stared out at these people. "I wonder how you land," he thought. "S'pose I *ought* to land?"

He found himself drifting down towards a monorail line, and hastily flung out two or three handsful of ballast to clear it.

"Lemme see! One might say just 'Prenez'! Wish I knew the French for take hold of the rope! . . . I suppose they are French?"

He surveyed the country again. "Might be Holland. Or Luxembourg. Or Lorraine's far as *I* know. Wonder what those big affairs over there are. Some sort of kiln? Prosperous-looking country. . . ."

The respectability of the country's appearance awakened answering chords in his nature.

"Make myself a bit shipshape first," he said.

He resolved to rise a little and get rid of his wig (which now felt hot on his head), and so forth. He threw out a bag of ballast, and was astonished to find himself careering up through the air very rapidly.

"Blow!" said Mr. Smallways. "I've overdone the ballast trick. . . . Wonder when I shall get down again? . . . Brekfus' on board, anyhow."

He removed his cap and wig, for the air was warm, and an improvident impulse made him cast the latter object overboard. The statoscope responded with a vigorous swing to "Montée."

"The blessed thing goes up if you only *look* overboard," he remarked, and assailed the locker. He found, among other items, several tins of liquid cocoa containing explicit directions for opening that he followed with minute care. He pierced the bottom with the key provided in the holes indicated, and forthwith the can grew from cold to hotter and hotter, until at last he could scarcely touch it, and then he opened the can at the other end, and there was his cocoa smoking, without the use of match or flame of any sort. It was an old invention, but new to Bert. There was also ham and marmalade and bread, so that he had a really very tolerable breakfast indeed.

Then he took off his overcoat, for the sunshine was now inclined to be hot, and that reminded him of the rustling he had heard in the night. He took off the waistcoat and examined it. "Old Butteridge won't like me unpicking this." He hesitated, and finally proceeded to unpick it. He found the missing drawings of the lateral rotating planes, on which the whole stability of the flying machine depended.

An observant angel would have seen Bert sitting for a long time after this discovery in a state of intense meditation. Then at last he rose with an air of inspiration, took Mr. Butteridge's ripped, demolished, and ransacked waistcoat, and hurled it from the balloon, whence it fluttered down slowly and eddyingly until at last it came to rest with a contented flop upon the face of a German tourist sleeping peacefully beside the Höhenweg, near Wildbad. Also this sent the balloon higher, and so into a position still more convenient for observation by our imaginary angel, who would next have seen Mr. Smallways tear open his own jacket and waistcoat, remove his collar, open his shirt, thrust his hand into his bosom, and tear his heart out—or at least, if not his heart, some large bright scarlet object. If the observer, overcoming a thrill of celestial horror, had scrutinized this scarlet object more narrowly, one of Bert's most cherished secrets, one of his essential weaknesses, would have been laid bare. It was a red flannel chest protector, one of those large quasi-hygienic objects that with pills and medicines take the place of beneficial relics and images among the Protestant peoples of

Christendom. Always Bert wore this thing; it was his cherished illusion, based on the advice of a shilling fortune-teller at Margate, that he was weak in the lungs.

He now proceeded to unbutton his fetish, to attack it with a pen-knife, and to thrust the new-found plans between the two layers of imitation Saxony flannel of which it was made. Then with the help of Mr. Butteridge's small shaving-mirror and his folding canvas basin, he readjusted his costume with the gravity of a man who has taken an irrevocable step in life, buttoned up his jacket, cast the white sheet of the Desert Dervish on one side, washed temperately, shaved, resumed the big cap and the fur overcoat, and, much refreshed by these exercises, surveyed the country below him.

It was indeed a spectacle of incredible magnificence. If perhaps it was not so strange and magnificent as the sunlit cloudland of the previous day, it was at any rate infinitely more interesting. The air was at its utmost clearness, and, except to the south and south-west, there was not a cloud in the sky. The country was hilly, with occasional fir plantations and bleak upland spaces, but also with numerous farms, and the hills were deeply intersected by the gorges of several winding rivers, interrupted at intervals by the banked-up ponds and weirs of electric generating wheels. It was dotted with bright-looking, steep-roofed villages, and each showed a distinctive and interesting church beside its wireless telegraph steeple; here and there were large châteaux and parks and white roads, and paths lined with red and white cable posts were extremely conspicuous in the landscape. There were walled enclosures like gardens and rickyards, and great roofs of barns and many electric dairy centres. The uplands were populous with cattle. At places he would see the track of one of the old tail-roads (converted now to mono-rails) dodging through tunnels and crossing embankments, and a rushing hum would mark the passing of a train. Everything was extraordinarily clear as well as minute. Once or twice he saw guns and soldiers, and was reminded of the stir of military preparations he had witnessed on the Bank Holiday in England; but there was nothing to tell him that these military preparations were abnormal, or to explain an occasional faint irregular firing of guns that drifted up to him.

"Wish I knew how to get down," said Bert, ten thousand feet or so above it all, and gave himself to much futile tugging at the red and white cords. Afterwards he made a sort of inventory of the provisions. Life in the high air was giving him an appalling appetite, and it seemed to him discreet at this stage to portion out his supply into rations. So far as he could see, he might pass a week in the air.

At first all the vast panorama below had been as silent as a painted picture. But as the day wore on, and the gas diffused slowly from the balloon, it sank earthward again, details increased, men became more visible, and he began to hear the whistle and moan of trains and cars, sounds of cattle, bugles and kettle-drums, and presently even men's voices. And at last his guide-rope was trailing again, and he found it possible to attempt a landing. Once or twice, as the rope dragged over cables, he found his hair erect with electricity, and once he had a slight shock, and sparks snapped about the car. He took these things among the chances of the voyage. He had one idea now very clear in his mind, and that was to drop the iron grapnel that hung from the ring.

From the first this attempt was unfortunate, perhaps because the place for descent was ill-chosen. A balloon should come in an empty open space, and he chose a crowd. He made his decision suddenly, and without proper reflection. As he trailed, Bert saw ahead of him one of the most attractive little towns in the world—a cluster of steep gables surmounted by a high church tower and diversified with trees, walled, and with a fine, large gateway opening out upon a tree-lined high road. All the wires and cables of the countryside converged upon it like guests to entertainment. It had a most homelike and comfortable quality, and it was made gayer by abundant flags. Along the road a quantity of peasant folk, in big pair-wheeled carts and afoot, were coming and going, beside an occasional mono-rail car; and at the car-junction, under the trees outside the town, was a busy little fair of booths. It seemed a warm, human, well-rooted, and altogether delightful place to Bert. He came low over the tree-tops, with his grapnel ready to throw, and so anchor him—a curious, interested and interesting guest, so his imagination figured it, in the very middle of it all.

He thought of himself performing feats with the sign language, and chance linguistics amidst a circle of admiring rustics. . . .

And then the chapter of adverse accidents began.

The rope made itself unpopular long before the crowd had fully realized his advent over the trees. An elderly and apparently intoxicated peasant in a shiny black hat, and carrying a large crimson umbrella, caught sight of it first as it trailed past him, and was seized with a discreditable ambition to kill it. He pursued it briskly with unpleasant cries. It crossed the road obliquely, splashed into a pan of milk upon a stall, and slapped its milky tail athwart a motor-car load of factory girls halted outside the town gates. They screamed loudly. People looked up and saw Bert making what he meant to be genial salutations, but what they considered, in view of the feminine outcry, to be insulting gestures. Then the car hit the roof of the gate-house smartly, snapped a flagstaff, played a tune upon some telegraph wires, and sent a broken wire like a whip-lash to do its share in accumulating unpopularity. Bert, by clutching convulsively, just escaped being pitched headlong. Two young soldiers and several peasants shouted things up to him, and shook fists at him, and began to run in pursuit as he disappeared over the wall into the town. Admiring rustics, indeed!

The balloon leapt at once, in the manner of balloons when part of their weight is released by touching down, with a sort of flippancy, and in another moment Bert was over a street crowded with peasants and soldiers, that opened into a busy market-square. The wave of unfriendliness pursued him.

"Grapnel," said Bert, and then, with an afterthought shouted, "*Têtes,* there, you! I say! I say! *Têtes.* Eng it!"

The grapnel clattered down a steeply sloping roof, followed by an avalanche of broken tiles, jumped the street amidst shrieks and cries, and smashed into a plate-glass window with an immense and sickening impact. The balloon rolled nauseatingly and the car pitched. But the grapnel had not held. It emerged at once bearing on one fluke, with a ridiculous air of fastidious selection, a small child's chair, and pursued by a maddened shopman. It lifted its catch, swung about with an appearance of painful indecision amidst a roar of wrath, and dropped it at last neatly, and as if by inspiration, over the head of a peasant woman in charge of an assortment of cabbages in the market-place.

Everybody now was aware of the balloon. Everybody was either trying to dodge the grapnel, or catch the trail rope. With a pendulum-like swoop through the crowd, that sent people flying right and left, the grapnel came to earth again, tried for and missed a stout gentleman in a blue suit and a straw hat, smacked away the trestle from under a stall of haberdashery, made a cyclist soldier in knickerbockers leap like a chamois, and secured itself uncertainly among the hind-legs of a sheep—which made convulsive, ungracious efforts to free itself, and was dragged into a position of rest against a stone cross in the middle of the place. The balloon pulled up with a jerk. In another moment a score of willing hands were tugging it earthward. At the same instant Bert became aware for the first time of a fresh breeze blowing about him.

For some seconds he stood staggering in the car, which now swayed sickeningly, surveying the exasperated crowd below him, and trying to collect his mind. He was extraordinarily astonished at this run of mishaps. Were the people really so annoyed? Everybody seemed angry with him. No one seemed interested or amused by his arrival. A dispro-portionate amount of the outcry had the quality of imprecation—had, indeed, a strong flavour of riot. Several greatly uniformed officials in cocked hats struggled in vain to control the crowd. Fists and sticks were shaken. And when Bert saw a man on the outskirts of the crowd run to a hay cart and get a brightly pronged pitch-fork, and a blue-clad soldier unbuckle his belt, his doubt whether this little town was after all such a good place for landing became a certainty.

He had clung to the fancy that they would make something of a hero of him. Now he knew that he was mistaken.

He was perhaps ten feet above the people when he made his decision. His paralysis ceased. He leapt up on the seat, and, at imminent risk of falling headlong, disengaged the grapnel-rope from the toggle that held it, sprang on to the trail rope and released that also. A hoarse shout of disgust greeted the descent of the grapnel rope and the swift leap of the balloon, and something—he fancied afterwards it was a turnip—whizzed by his head. The trail-rope followed its fellow. The crowd seemed to jump away from him. With an immense and horrifying rustle the balloon brushed against a telephone pole, and for a tense instant he anticipated either an electric explosion or a bursting of the oiled silk, or both. But fortune was with him.

In another second he was cowering in the bottom of the car, and, released from the weight of the grapnel and the two ropes, rushing up once more through the air. For a time he remained crouching, and when at last he looked out again, the little town was very small and travelling with the rest of lower Germany in a circular orbit round and round the car—or at least it appeared to be doing that.

When he got used to it he found this rotation of the balloon rather convenient; it saved moving about in the car.

5

Late in the afternoon of a pleasant summer day in the year 191–, if one may borrow a mode of phrasing that once found favour with the readers of the late G. P. R. James, a solitary balloonist—replacing the solitary horseman of the classic romances—might have been observed wending his way across Franconia in a north-easterly direction, at a height of about eleven thousand feet above the sea, and still spinning slowly. His head was craned over the side of the car, and he surveyed the country below with an expression of profound perplexity; ever and again his lips shaped inaudible words. "Shootin' at a chap," for example, and "I'll come down right enough soon as I find out 'ow." Over the side of the basket the robe of the Desert Dervish was hanging, an appeal for consideration, an ineffectual white flag.

He was now very distinctly aware that the world below him, so far from being the naïve countryside of his earlier imaginings that day, sleepily unconscious of him and capable of being amazed and nearly reverential at his descent, was acutely irritated by his career, and extremely impatient with the course he was taking. But, indeed, it was not he who took that course, but his masters, the winds of heaven. Mysterious voices spoke to him in his ear, jerking the words up to him by means of megaphones, in a weird and startling manner, in a great variety of languages. Official-looking persons had signalled to him by means of flag flapping and arm waving. On the whole a guttural variant of English prevailed in the sentences that alighted upon the balloon; chiefly he was told to "gome down or you will be shot."

"All very well," said Bert, "but 'OW?"

Then they shot a little wide of the car. Latterly he had been shot at six or seven times, and once the bullet had gone by him with a sound so persuasively like the tearing of silk that he had resigned himself to the prospect of a headlong fall. But either they were aiming near him or they had missed, and as yet nothing was torn but the air about him—and his anxious soul.

He was now enjoying a respite from these attentions, but he felt it was at best an interlude, and he was doing what he could to appreciate his position. Incidentally he was having some hot coffee and pie in an untidy, inadvertent manner with an eye fluttering nervously over the side of the car. At first he had ascribed the growing interest in his career to his ill-conceived attempt to land in the bright little upland town, but now he was beginning to realize that the military rather than the civil arm was concerned about him.

He was quite involuntarily playing that weird mysterious part— the part of an International Spy. He was seeing secret things. He had, in fact, crossed the designs of no less a power than the German Empire, he had blundered into the hot focus of Welt-Politik, he was drifting helplessly towards the great Imperial secret, the immense aeronautic park that had been established at a headlong pace in Franconia to develop silently, swiftly, and on a colossal scale the great discoveries of Hunstedt and Stossel, and so to give Germany before all other nations a fleet of airships, the air power and the Empire of the world.

Later, just before they shot him down altogether, Bert saw that great area of passionate work, warm lit in the evening light, a great area of upland on which the airships lay like a herd of grazing monsters at their feed. It was a vast busy space stretching away northward as far as he could see, methodically cut up into numbered sheds, gasometers, squad encampments, storage areas, interlaced with the omnipresent monorail lines, and altogether free from overhead wires or cables. Everywhere was the white, black, and yellow of Imperial Germany, everywhere the black eagles spread their wings. Even without these indications, the large vigorous neatness of everything would have marked it Germany. Vast multitudes of men went to and fro, many in white and drab fatigue uniforms busy about the balloons, others drilling in sensible drab. Here and there a full uniform glittered.

The airships chiefly engaged his attention, and he knew at once it was three of these he had seen on the previous night, taking advantage of the cloud welkin to manœuvre unobserved.

They were altogether fish-like. For the great airships with which Germany attacked New York in her last gigantic effort for world supremacy—before humanity realized that world supremacy was a dream—were the lineal descendants of the Zeppelin airship that flew over Lake Constance in 1906, and of the Lebaudy navigables that made their memorable excursions over Paris in 1907 and 1908.

These German airships were held together by rib-like skeletons of steel and aluminium and a stout inelastic canvas outer-skin, within which was an impervious rubber gas-bag, cut up by transverse dissepiments into from fifty to a hundred compartments. These were all absolutely gas-tight and filled with hydrogen, and the entire aerostat was kept at any level by means of a long internal balloonette of oiled and toughened silk canvas, into which air could be forced and from which it could be pumped. So the airship could be made either heavier or lighter than air, and losses of weight through the consumption of fuel, the casting of bombs and so forth, could also be compensated by admitting air to sections of the general gas-bag. Ultimately that made a highly explosive mixture; but in all these matters risks must be taken and guarded against. There was a steel axis to the whole affair, a central backbone which terminated in the engine and propeller, and the men and magazines were forward in a series of cabins under the expanded headlike forepart. The engine, which was of the extraordinarily powerful Pforzheim type, that supreme triumph of German invention, was worked by electric controls from this forepart, which was indeed the only really habitable part of the ship. If anything went wrong, the engineers went aft along a rope ladder beneath the frame or along a passage through the gas chambers. The tendency of the whole affair to roll was partly corrected by a horizontal lateral fin on either side, and steering was chiefly effected by two vertical fins, which normally lay back like gill-flaps on either side of the head. It was indeed a most complete adaptation of the fish form to aerial conditions, the position of swimming bladder, eyes, and brain being, however, below instead of above. A striking and unfish-like feature was the apparatus for wireless telegraphy that dangled from the forward cabin—that is to say, under the chin of the fish.

These monsters were capable of ninety miles an hour in a calm, so that they could face and make headway against nearly everything except the fiercest tornado. They varied in length from eight hundred to two thousand feet, and they had a carrying power of from seventy to two hundred tons. How many Germany possessed history does not record, but Bert counted nearly eighty great bulks receding in perspective during his brief inspection. Such were the instruments on which she relied to sustain her in her repudiation of the Monroe doctrine and her bold bid for a share in the Empire of the New World. But not altogether did she rely on these; she had also a one-man bomb-throwing Drachenflieger of unknown value among her resources.

But the Drachenflieger were away in the second great aeronautic park east of Hamburg, and Bert Smallways saw nothing of them in the bird's-eye view he took of the Franconian establishment before they shot him down. For they shot him down very neatly. They used the new bullets with steel trailers that Wolffe of Engelberg had invented for aerial warfare. The bullet tore past him and made a sort of pop as its trailer rent his balloon—a pop that was followed by a rustling sigh and a steady downward movement. And when in the confusion of the moment he dropped a bag of ballast, the Germans very politely but firmly overcame his scruples by shooting his balloon again twice.

FOUR

The German Air Fleet

I

Of all the productions of the human imagination that make the world in which Mr. Bert Smallways lived confusingly wonderful, there was none quite so strange, so headlong and disturbing, so noisy and persuasive and dangerous, as the modernizations of patriotism produced by imperial and international politics. In the soul of all men is a liking for kind, a pride in one's own atmosphere, a tenderness for one's mother speech and one's familiar land. Before the coming of the Scientific Age this group of gentle and noble emotions had been a fine factor in the equipment of every worthy human being, a fine factor that had its less amiable aspect in a usually harmless hostility to strange people, and a usually harmless detraction of strange lands. But with the wild rush of change in the pace, scope, materials, scale, and possibilities of human life that then occurred, the old boundaries, the old seclusions and separations were violently broken down. All the old settled mental habits and traditions of men found themselves not simply confronted by new conditions, but by constantly renewed and changing new conditions. They had no chance of adapting themselves. They were annihilated or perverted or inflamed beyond recognition.

Bert Smallways' grandfather, in the days when Bun Hill was a village under the sway of Sir Peter Bone's parent, had "known his place" to the uttermost farthing, touched his hat to his betters, despised and condescended to his inferiors, and hadn't changed an idea from the cradle to the grave. He was Kentish and English, and that meant hops, beer, dog-roses, and the sort of sunshine that was best in the world. Newspapers and politics and visits to "Lunnon" weren't for the likes of him. Then came the change. These earlier chapters have given an idea of what happened to Bun Hill, and how the flood of novel things had poured over its devoted rusticity. Bert Smallways was only one of countless millions in Europe and America and Asia who, instead of being born rooted in the soil, were born struggling in a torrent they never clearly understood. All the faiths of their fathers had been taken by surprise, and startled into the strangest forms and reactions. Particularly did the fine old tradition of patriotism get perverted and distorted in the rush of the new times. Instead of the sturdy establishment in prejudice of Bert's grandfather, to whom the word "Frenchified" was the ultimate term of contempt, there flowed through Bert's brain a squittering succession of thinly violent ideas about German competition, about the Yellow Danger, about the Black Peril, about the White Man's Burthen— that is to say Bert's preposterous right to muddle further the naturally very muddled politics of the entirely similar little cads to himself (except for a smear of brown) who smoked cigarettes and rode bicycles in Buluwayo, Kingston (Jamaica), or Bombay. These were Bert's "Subject Races," and he was ready to die—by proxy in the person of anyone who cared to enlist—to maintain his hold upon that right. It kept him awake at nights to think that he might lose it.

The essential facts of the politics of the age in which Bert Smallways lived—the age that blundered at last into the catastrophe of the War in the Air—was a very simple one, if only people had had the intelligence to be simple about it. The development of Science had altered the scale of human affairs. By means of rapid mechanical traction it had brought men nearer together, so much nearer socially, economically, physically, that the old separations into nations and kingdoms were no longer possible, a newer, wider synthesis was not only needed but imperatively demanded. Just as the once independent dukedoms of France had to fuse into a nation, so now the nations had to adapt themselves to a wider coalescence, they had to keep what was precious and practicable, and concede what was obsolete and dangerous. A saner world would have perceived this patent need for a reasonable synthesis, would have discussed it temperately, achieved and gone on to organize the great civilization that was manifestly possible to mankind. The world of Bert Smallways did nothing of the sort. Its national governments, its national interests, would not hear of anything so obvious; they were too suspicious of each other, too wanting in generous imagination.

They began to behave like ill-bred people in a crowded public car, to squeeze against one another, elbow, thrust, dispute and quarrel. Vain to point out to them that they had only to rearrange themselves to be comfortable. Everywhere, all over the world, the historian of the early twentieth century finds the same thing, the flow and rearrangement of human affairs inextricably entangled by the old areas, the old prejudices and a sort of heated irascible stupidity; and everywhere congested nations in inconvenient areas, slopping population and produce into each other, annoying each other with tariffs and every possible commercial vexation, and threatening each other with navies and armies that grow every year more portentous.

It is impossible now to estimate how much of the intellectual and physical energy of the world was wasted in military preparation and equipment, but it was an enormous proportion. Great Britain spent upon army and navy money and capacity that, directed into the channels of physical culture and education, would have made the British the aristocracy of the world. Her rulers could have kept the whole population learning and exercising up to the age of eighteen, and made a broad-chested and intelligent man of every Bert Smallways in the islands, had they given the resources they spent in war material to the making of men. Instead of which they waggled flags at him until he was fourteen, incited him to cheer, and then turned him out of school to begin that career of private enterprise we have compactly recorded. France achieved similar imbecilities; Germany was, if possible, worse; Russia under the waste and stresses of militarism festered towards bankruptcy and decay. All Europe was producing big guns and countless swarms of little Smallways. The Asiatic peoples had been forced in self-defence into a like diversion of the new powers science had brought them. On the eve of the outbreak of the war there were six great powers in the world and a cluster of smaller ones, each armed to the teeth and straining every nerve to get ahead of the others in deadliness of equipment and military efficiency. The great powers were first the United States, a nation addicted to commerce, but roused to military necessities by the efforts of Germany to expand into South America, and by the natural consequences of her own, unwary annexations of land in the very teeth of Japan. She maintained two immense fleets east and west, and internally she was in violent conflict between Federal and State governments upon the question of universal service in a defensive militia. Next came the great alliance of Eastern Asia, a close-knit coalescence of China and Japan, advancing with rapid strides year by year to predominance in the world's affairs. Then the German alliance still struggled to achieve its dream of imperial expansion, and its imposition of the German language upon a forcibly united Europe. These were the three most spirited and aggressive powers in the world. Far more pacific was the British Empire, perilously scattered over the globe, and distracted now by insurrectionary movements in Ireland and among all its Subject Races. It had given these Subject Races cigarettes, boots, bowler hats, cricket, race meetings, cheap revolvers, petroleum, the factory system of industry, halfpenny newspapers in both English and the vernacular, inexpensive university degrees, motor-bicycles, and electric trams; it had produced a considerable literature expressing contempt for the Subject Races and rendered it freely accessible to them, and it had been content to believe that nothing would result from these stimulants because somebody once wrote "the immemorial east"; and also, in the inspired words of Kipling—

> East is east and west is west,
> And never the twain shall meet.

Instead of which, Egypt, India, and the subject countries generally had produced new generations in a state of passionate indignation and the utmost energy, activity and modernity. The governing class in Great Britain was slowly adapting itself to a new conception of the Subject Races as waking peoples, and finding its efforts to keep the Empire together under these strains and changing ideas greatly impeded by the entirely sporting spirit with which Bert Smallways at home (by the million) cast his vote, and by the tendency of his more highly coloured equivalents to be disrespectful to irascible officials. Their impertinence was excessive; it was no mere stone throwing and shouting. They would quote Burns at them and Mill and Darwin, and confute them in arguments.

Even more pacific than the British Empire were France and its allies, the Latin powers, heavily armed states indeed but reluctant warriors, and in many ways socially and politically leading western civilization. Russia was a pacific power perforce, divided within itself, torn between revolutionaries and reactionaries who were equally incapable of social reconstruction, and so sinking towards a tragic disorder of chronic political vendetta. Wedged in among these portentous larger bulks, swayed and threatened by them, the smaller states of the world maintained a precarious independence, each keeping itself armed as dangerously as its utmost ability could contrive.

So it came about that in every country a great and growing proportion of its energetic and inventive men was busied either for offensive or defensive ends, in elaborating the apparatus of war, until the accumulating tensions should reach the breaking-point. Each power sought to keep its preparations secret, to hold new weapons in reserve, to anticipate and learn the preparations of its rivals. The feeling of danger from fresh discoveries affected the patriotic imagination of every people in the world. Now it was rumoured the British had an overwhelming gun, now the French an invisible rifle, now the Japanese a new explosive, now the Americans a submarine that would drive every ironclad from the seas. Each time there would be a war panic.

The strength and heart of the nations was given to the thought of war, and yet the mass of their citizens was a teeming democracy as heedless of and unfitted for fighting, mentally, morally, physically, as any population has ever been—or, one ventures to add, could ever be. That was the paradox of the time. It was a period altogether unique in the world's history. The apparatus of warfare, the art and method of fighting, changed absolutely every dozen years in a stupendous progress towards perfection, and people grew less and less warlike, and there was no war.

And then at last it came. It came as a surprise to all the world because its real causes were hidden. Relations were strained between Germany and the United States because of the intense exasperation of tariff conflict and the ambiguous attitude of the former power towards the Monroe Doctrine, and they were strained between the United States and Japan because of the perennial citizenship question. But in both cases these were standing causes of offence. The real deciding cause, it is now known, was the perfecting of the Pforzheim engine by Germany and the consequent possibility of a rapid and entirely practicable airship. At that time Germany was by far the most efficient power in the world, better organized for swift and secret action, better equipped with the resources of modern science, and with her official and administrative classes at a higher level of education and training. These things she knew, and she exaggerated that knowledge to the pitch of contempt for the secret counsels of her neighbours. It may be that with the habit of self-confidence her spying upon them had grown less thorough. Moreover, she had a tradition of unsentimental and unscrupulous action that vitiated her international outlook profoundly. With the coming of these new weapons her collective intelligence thrilled with the sense that now her moment had come. Once again in the history of progress it seemed she held the decisive weapon. Now she might strike and conquer—before the others had anything but experiments in the air.

Particularly she must strike America swiftly, because there, if any-where, lay the chance of an aerial rival. It was known that America possessed a flying-machine of considerable practical value, developed out of the Wright model; but it was not supposed that the Washing-ton War Office had made any wholesale attempts to create an aerial navy. It was necessary to strike before they could do so. France had a fleet of slow navigables, several dating from 1908, that could make no possible headway against the new type. They had been built solely for reconnoitring purposes on the eastern frontier, they were mostly too small to carry more than a couple of dozen men without arms or provisions, and not one could do forty miles an hour. Great Britain, it seemed, in an access of meanness, temporized and wrangled with the imperial-spirited Butteridge and his extraordinary invention. That also was not in play—and could not be so for some months at the earliest. From Asia there came no sign. The Germans explained this by saying the yellow peoples were without invention. No other competitor was worth considering. "Now or never," said the Germans—"now or never we may seize the air—as once the British seized the seas! While all the other powers are still experimenting."

Swift and systematic and secret were their preparations, and their plan most excellent. So far as their knowledge went, America was the only dangerous possibility. America which was also now the leading trade rival of Germany and one of the chief barriers to her Imperial expansion. So at once they would strike at America. They would fling a great force across the Atlantic heavens and bear America down unwarned and unprepared.

Altogether it was a well-imagined and most hopeful and spirited enterprise, having regard to the information in the possession of the German government. The chances of it being a successful surprise were very great. The airship and the flying-machine were very different things from ironclads, which take a couple of years to build. Given hands, given plant, they could be made innumerably in a few weeks. Once the needful parks and foundries were organized, airships and Drachenflieger could be poured into the sky. Indeed when the time came, they did pour into the sky, like, as a bitter French writer put it, flies roused from filth.

The attack upon America was to be the first move in this tremendous game. But no sooner had it started than instantly the aeronautic parks were to proceed to put together and inflate the second fleet which was to dominate Europe and manœuvre significantly over London, Paris, Rome, St. Petersburg, or wherever else its moral effect was required. A World Surprise it was to be—no less, a World Conquest; and it is wonderful how near the calmly adventurous minds that planned it came to succeeding in their colossal design.

Von Sternberg was the Moltke of this War in the Air, but it was the curious hard romanticism of Prince Karl Albert that won over the hesitating Emperor to the scheme. Prince Karl Albert was indeed the central figure of the world drama. He was the darling of the Imperialist spirit in Germany, and the ideal of the new aristocratic feeling—the new Chivalry, as it was called—that followed the overthrow of Socialism through its internal divisions and lack of discipline, and the concentration of wealth in the hands of a few great families. He was compared by obsequious flatterers to the Black Prince, to Alcibiades, to the young Caesar. To many he seemed Nietzsche's Overman revealed. He was big and blond and virile, and splendidly non-moral. The first great feat that startled Europe, and almost brought about a new Trojan war, was his abduction of the Princess Helena of Norway and his blank refusal to marry her. Then followed his marriage with Gretchen Krass, a Swiss girl of peerless beauty. Then came the gallant rescue, which almost cost him his life, of three drowning tailors whose boat had upset in the sea near Heligoland. For that and his victory over the American yacht Defender, C.C.I., the Emperor forgave him and placed him in control of the new aeronautic arm of the German forces. This he developed with marvellous energy and ability, being resolved, as he said, to give to Germany land and sea and sky. The national passion for aggression found in him its extreme exponent, and achieved through him its realization in this astounding war. But his fascination was more than national; all over the world his ruthless strength dominated minds as the Napoleonic legend had dominated minds. Englishmen turned in disgust from the slow, complex, civilized methods of their national politics to this uncompromising forceful figure. Frenchmen believed in him. Poems were written to him in America. He made the war.

Quite equally with the rest of the world, the general German population was taken by surprise by the swift vigour of the Imperial government. A considerable literature of military forecasts beginning as early as 1906, with Rudolf Martin, the author not merely of a brilliant book of anticipations, but of a proverb, "The future of Germany lies in the air," had, however, partially prepared the German imagination for some such enterprise.

2

Of all these world-forces and gigantic designs Bert Smallways knew nothing until he found himself in the very focus of it all and gaped down amazed on the spectacle of that giant herd of airships. Each one seemed as long as the Strand, and about as big as Trafalgar Square. Some must have been a third of a mile in length. He had never before seen anything so vast and disciplined as this tremendous park. For the first time in his life he really had an intimation of the extraordinary and quite important things of which a contemporary may go in ignorance. He had always clung to the illusions that Germans were fat, absurd men, who smoked china pipes, and were addicted to knowledge and horseflesh and sauerkraut and indigestible things generally.

His bird's-eye view was quite transitory. He ducked at the first shot, and directly his balloon began to drop, his mind ran confusedly upon how he might explain himself, and whether he should pretend to be Butteridge or not. "O Lord!" he groaned in an agony of indecision. Then his eye caught his sandals, and he felt a spasm of self-disgust. "They'll think I'm a bloomin' idiot," he said, and then it was he rose up desperately, and threw over the sand-bag and provoked the second and third shots.

It flashed into his head, as he cowered in the bottom of the car, that he might avoid all sorts of disagreeable and complicated explanations by pretending to be mad.

That was his last idea before the airships seemed to rush up about him as if to look at him, and his car hit the ground and bounded and pitched him out on his head. . . .

He awoke to find himself famous, and to hear a voice crying, "Booteraidge! Ja! Ja! Herr Booteraidge! Selbst!"

He was lying on a little patch of grass beside one of the main avenues of the aeronautic park. The airships receded down a great vista, an immense perspective, and the blunt prow of each was adorned with a black eagle of a hundred feet or so spread. Down the other side of the avenue ran a series of gas generators, and big hose-pipes trailed everywhere across the intervening space. Close at hand was his now nearly deflated balloon and the car on its side looking minutely small, a mere broken toy, a shrivelled bubble, in contrast with the gigantic bulk of the nearer airship. This he saw almost end-on, rising like a cliff and sloping forward towards its fellow on the other side so as to overshadow the alley between them. There was a crowd of excited people about him, mostly big men in tight uniforms. Everybody was talking, and several were shouting, in German; be knew that, because they splashed and aspirated sounds like startled kittens. Only one phrase, repeated again and again, could he recognize—the name of "Herr Booteraidge."

"Gollys!" said Bert. "They've spotted it."

"Besser," said someone, and some rapid German followed.

He perceived that close at hand was a field telephone, and that a tall officer in blue was talking thereat about him. Another stood close beside him with the portfolio of drawings and photographs in his hand. They looked round at him.

"Do you spik Cherman, Herr Booteraidge?"

Bert decided that he had better be dazed. He did his best to seem thoroughly dazed. "Where *am* I?" he asked.

Volubility prevailed. "Der Prinz" was mentioned. A bugle sounded far away, and its call was taken up by one nearer, and then by one close at hand. This seemed to increase the excitement greatly. A mono-rail car bumbled past. The telephone bell rang passionately, and the tall officer seemed to engage in a heated altercation. Then he approached the group about Bert, calling out something about "mitbringen."

An earnest-faced, emaciated man with a white moustache appealed to Bert. "Herr Booteraidge, sir, we are chust to start!"

"Where am I?" Bert repeated.

Someone shook him by the other shoulder. "Are you Herr Booteraidge?" he asked.

"Herr Booteraidge, we are chust to start!" repeated the white moustache, and then helplessly, "What is de goot? What can we do?"

The officer from the telephone repeated his sentence about "Der Prinz" and "mitbringen." The man with the moustache stared for a moment, grasped an idea and became violently energetic, stood up and bawled directions at unseen people. Questions were asked, and the doctor at Bert's side answered, "Ja! Ja!" several times, also something about "Kopf." With a certain urgency he got Bert rather unwillingly to his feet. Two huge soldiers in grey advanced upon Bert, and seized hold of him. " 'Ullo!" said Bert, startled. "What's up?"

"It is all right," the doctor explained; "they are to carry you."

"Where?" asked Bert, unanswered.

"Put your arms roundt their—*hals*—round them!"

"Yes! but where?"

"Hold tight!"

Before Bert could decide to say anything more he was whisked up by the two soldiers. They joined hands to seat him, and his arms were put about their necks. "Vorwärts!" Someone ran before him with the portfolio, and he was borne rapidly along the broad avenue between the gas generators and the airships, rapidly and on the whole smoothly except that once or twice his bearers stumbled over hose-pipes and nearly let him down.

He was wearing Mr. Butteridge's Alpine cap, and his little shoulders were in Mr. Butteridge's fur-lined overcoat, and he had responded to Mr. Butteridge's name. The sandals dangled helplessly. Gaw! Everybody seemed in a devil of a hurry. Why? He was carried jaggling and gaping through the twilight, marvelling beyond measure.

The systematic arrangement of wide convenient spaces, the quantities of business-like soldiers everywhere, the occasional neat piles of material, the ubiquitous mono-rail lines, and the towering ship-like hulls about him, reminded him a little of impressions he had got as a boy on a visit to Woolwich Dockyard. The whole camp reflected the colossal power of modern science that had created it. A peculiar strangeness was produced by the lowness of the electric light, which lay upon the ground, casting all shadows upwards, and making a grotesque shadow figure of himself and his bearers on the airship sides, fusing all three of them into a monstrous animal with attenuated legs and an immense fan-like humped body. The lights were on the ground because as far as possible all poles and standards had been dispensed with to prevent complications when the airships arose.

It was deep twilight now, a tranquil blue-skyed evening; everything rose out from the splashes of light upon the ground into dim, translucent, tall masses; within the cavities of the airships small inspecting lamps glowed like cloud-veiled stars, and made them seem marvelously unsubstantial. Each airship had its name in black letters on white on either flank, and forward the Imperial eagle sprawled, an overwhelming bird in the dimness. Bugles sounded, mono-rail cars of quiet soldiers slithered burbling by. The cabins under the heads of the airships were being lit up; doors opened in them, and revealed padded passages. Now and then a voice gave directions to workers indistinctly seen.

There was a matter of sentinels, gangways and a long, narrow passage, a scramble over a disorder of baggage, and then Bert found himself lowered to the ground and standing in the doorway of a spacious cabin—it was perhaps ten feet square and eight high, furnished with crimson padding and aluminium. A tall, bird-like young man with a small head, a long nose, and very pale hair, with his hands full of things like shaving-strops, boot-trees, hair-brushes, and toilet tidies, was saying things about Gott and thunder and Dummer Booteraidge as Bert entered. He was apparently an evicted occupant. Then he vanished, and Bert was lying back on a locker in the corner of the cabin with a pillow under his head and the door of the cabin shut upon him. He was alone. Everybody had hurried out again astonishingly.

"Gollys!" said Bert. "What next?"

He stared about him at the room.

"Butteridge! Shall I try to keep it up, or shan't I?"

The room he was in puzzled him. " 'Tisn't a prison and 'tisn't a norfis?" Then the old trouble came uppermost. "I wish to 'eaven I 'adn't these silly sandals on," he cried querulously to the universe. "They give the whole blessed show away."

3

His door was flung open and a compact young man in uniform appeared, carrying Mr. Butteridge's portfolio, rucksac, and shaving-glass. "I say!" he said, in faultless English, as he entered. He had a beaming face, and a sort of pinkish blond hair. "Fancy you being Butteridge!"

He slapped Bert's meagre luggage down.

"We'd have started," he said, "in another half-hour! You didn't give yourself much time!"

He surveyed Bert curiously. His gaze rested for a fraction of a moment on the sandals. "You ought to have come on your flying-machine, Mr. Butteridge."

He didn't wait for an answer. "The Prince says I've got to look after you. Naturally he can't see you now, but he thinks your coming's providential. Last grace of Heaven. Like a sign. Hullo!"

He stood still and listened.

Outside there was a going to and fro of feet, a sound of distant bugles suddenly taken up and echoed close at hand, men called out in loud tones short, sharp, seemingly vital things, and were answered distantly. A bell jangled, and feet went down the corridor. Then came a stillness more distracting than sound, and then a great gurgling and rushing and splashing of water. The young man's eyebrows lifted. He hesitated, and dashed out of the room. Presently came a stupendous bang to vary the noises without, then a distant cheering. The young man reappeared.

"They're running the water out of the balloonette already."

"What water?" asked Bert.

"The water that anchored us. Artful dodge. Eh?"

Bert tried to take it in.

"Of course!" said the compact young man. "You don't understand."

A gentle quivering crept over Bert's senses. "That's the engine," said the compact young man approvingly. "Now we shan't be long."

Another long listening interval.

The cabin swayed. "By Jove! we're starting already," he cried. "We're starting!"

"Starting!" cried Bert, sitting up. "Where?"

But the young man was out of the room again. There were noises of German in the passage, and other nerve-shaking sounds.

The swaying increased. The young man reappeared. "We're off, right enough!"

"I say!" said Bert, "where are we starting? I wish you'd explain. What's this place? I don't understand."

"What!" cried the young man, "you don't understand?"

"No. I'm all dazed-like from that crack on the nob I got. Where *are* we? *Where* are we starting?"

"Don't you know where you are—what this is?"

"Not a bit of it! What's all the swaying and the row?"

"What a lark!" cried the young man. "I say! What a thundering lark! Don't you know? We're off to America, and you haven't realized. You've just caught us by a neck. You're on the blessed old flagship with the Prince. You won't miss anything. Whatever's on, you bet the Vaterland will be there."

"Us!—off to America?"

"Ra-ther!"

"In an airship?"

"What do *you* think?"

"Me! going to America on an airship! After that balloon! 'Ere! I say— I don't want to go! I want to walk about on my legs. Let me get out! I didn't understand."

He made a dive for the door.

The young man arrested Bert with a gesture, took hold of a strap, lifted up a panel in the padded wall, and a window appeared. "Look!" he said. Side by side they looked out.

"Gaw!" said Bert. "We're going up!"

"We are!" said the young man, cheerfully; "fast."

They were rising in the air smoothly and quietly, and moving slowly to the throb of the engine athwart the aeronautic park. Down below it stretched, dimly geometrical in the darkness, picked out at regular intervals by glow-worm spangles of light. One black gap in the long line of grey, round-backed airships marked the position from which the Vaterland had come. Beside it a second monster now rose softly, released from its bonds and cables, into the air. Then, taking a beautifully exact distance, a third ascended, and then a fourth.

"Too late, Mr. Butteridge!" the young man remarked. "We're off! I daresay it *is* a bit of a shock to you, but there you are! The Prince said you'd have to come."

"Look 'ere," said Bert. "I really *am* dazed. What's this thing? Where are we going?"

"This, Mr. Butteridge," said the young man, taking pains to be explicit, "is an airship. It's the flagship of Prince Karl Albert. This is the German air-fleet, and it is going over to America to give that spirited people 'what for.' The only thing we were at all uneasy about was your invention. And here you are!"

"But!—you a German?" asked Bert.

"Lieutenant Kurt. Luft-lieutenant Kurt, at your service."

"But you speak English!"

"Mother was English—went to school in England. Afterwards, Rhodes scholar. German none the less for that. Detailed for the present, Mr. Butteridge, to look after you. You're shaken by your fall. It's all right, really. They're going to buy your machine and everything. You sit down, and take it quite calmly. You'll soon get the hang of the position."

4

Bert sat down on the locker collecting his mind, and the young man talked to him about the airship.

He was really a very tactful young man indeed, in a natural sort of way. "Daresay all this is new to you," he said; "not your sort of machine. These cabins aren't half bad."

He got up and walked round the little apartment, showing its points.

"Here is the bed," he said, whipping down a couch from the wall and throwing it back again with a click. "Here are toilet things," and he opened a neatly arranged cupboard. "Not much washing. No water we've got; no water at all except for drinking. No baths or anything until we get to America and land. Rub over with loofah. One pint of hot for shaving. That's all. In the locker below you are rugs and blankets; you will need them presently. They say it gets cold. I don't know. Never been up before. Except a little work with gliders—which is mostly going down. Three-quarters of the chaps in the fleet haven't. Here's a folding-chair and table behind the door. Compact, eh?"

He took the chair and balanced it on his little finger. "Pretty light, eh? Aluminium and magnesium alloy and a vacuum inside. All these cushions stuffed with hydrogen. Foxy! The whole ship's like that. And not a man in the fleet, except the Prince and one or two others, over eleven stone. Couldn't sweat the Prince, you know. We'll go all over the thing to-morrow. I'm frightfully keen on it."

He beamed at Bert. "You *do* look young," he remarked. "I always thought you'd be an old man with a beard—a sort of philosopher. I don't know why one should expect clever people always to be old. I do."

Bert parried that compliment a little awkwardly, and then the lieutenant was struck with the riddle why Herr Butteridge had not come in his own flying-machine.

"It's a long story," said Bert. "Look here!" he said abruptly, "I wish you'd lend me a pair of slippers, or something. I'm regular sick of these sandals. They're rotten things. I've been trying them for a friend."

"Right O!"

The ex-Rhodes scholar whisked out of the room and reappeared with a considerable choice of footwear, pumps, cloth bath-slippers, and a purple pair adorned with golden sun-flowers.

But these he repented of at the last moment. "I don't even wear them myself," he said. "Only brought 'em in the zeal of the moment." He laughed confidentially. "Had 'em worked for me—in Oxford. By a friend. Take 'em everywhere."

So Bert chose the pumps.

The lieutenant broke into a cheerful snigger. "Here we are trying on slippers," he said, "and the world going by like a panorama below. Rather a lark, eh? Look!"

Bert peeped with him out of the window, looking from the bright prettiness of the red-and-silver cabin into a dark immensity. The land below, except for a lake, was black and featureless, and the other airships were hidden. "See more outside," said the lieutenant. "Let's go! There's a sort of little gallery."

He led the way into the long passage, which was lit by one small electric light, past some notices in German, to an open balcony and a light ladder and gallery of metal lattice overhanging empty space. Bert followed his leader down to the gallery slowly and cautiously. From it he was able to watch the wonderful spectacle of the first air-fleet flying through the night. They flew in a wedge-shaped formation, the Vaterland highest and leading, the tail receding into the corners of the sky. They flew in long, regular undulations, great dark fish-like shapes, showing hardly any light at all, the engines making a throb-throb-throbbing sound that was very audible out on the gallery. They were going at a level of five or six thousand feet, and rising steadily. Below the country lay silent, a clear darkness dotted and lined out with clusters of furnaces, and the lit streets of a group of big towns. The world seemed to lie in a bowl; the overhanging bulk of the airship above hid all but the lowest levels of the sky.

They watched the landscape for a space.

"Jolly it must be to invent things," said the lieutenant suddenly. "How did you come to think of your machine first?"

"Worked it out," said Bert, after a pause. "Just ground away at it."

"Our people are frightfully keen on you. They thought the British had got you. Weren't the British keen?"

"In a way," said Bert. "Still—it's a long story."

"I think it's an immense thing—to invent. I couldn't invent a thing to save my life."

They both fell silent, watching the darkened world and following their thoughts until a bugle summoned them to a belated dinner. Bert was suddenly alarmed. "Don't you 'ave to dress and things?" he said.

"I've always been too hard at Science and things to go into Society and all that."

"No fear," said Kurt. "Nobody's got more than the clothes they wear. We're travelling light. You might perhaps take your overcoat off. They've an electric radiator each end of the room."

And so presently Bert found himself sitting to eat in the presence of the "German Alexander"—that great and puissant Prince, Prince Karl Albert, the War Lord, the hero of two hemispheres. He was a handsome blond man, with deep-set eyes, a snub nose, upturned moustache, and long white hands. He sat higher than the others, under a black eagle with widespread wings and the German Imperial flags; he was, as it were, enthroned, and it struck Bert greatly that as he ate he did not look at people, but over their heads like one who sees visions. Twenty officers of various ranks stood about the table—and Bert. They all seemed extremely curious to see the famous Butteridge, and their astonishment at his appearance was ill-controlled. The Prince gave him a dignified salutation, to which, by an inspiration, he bowed. Standing next the Prince was a brown-faced, wrinkled man with silver spectacles and fluffy, dingy-grey side-whiskers, who regarded Bert with a peculiar and disconcerting attention. The company sat after ceremonies Bert could not understand. At the other end of the table was the bird-faced officer Bert had dispossessed, still looking hostile and whispering about Bert to his neighbour. Two soldiers waited. The dinner was a plain one—a soup, some fresh mutton, and cheese—and there was very little talk.

A curious solemnity indeed brooded over everyone. Partly this was reaction after the intense toil and restrained excitement of starting; partly it was the overwhelming sense of strange new experiences, of portentous adventure. The Prince was lost in thought. He roused himself to drink to the Emperor in champagne, and the company cried "Hoch!" like men repeating responses in church.

No smoking was permitted, but some of the officers went down to the little open gallery to chew tobacco. No lights whatever were safe amidst that bundle of inflammable things. Bert suddenly fell yawning and shivering. He was overwhelmed by a sense of his own insignificance amidst these great rushing monsters of the air. He felt life was too big for him—too much for him altogether.

He said something to Kurt about his head, went up the steep ladder from the swaying little gallery into the airship again, and so, as if it were a refuge, to bed.

5

Bert slept for a time, and then his sleep was broken by dreams. Mostly he was fleeing from formless terrors down an interminable passage in an airship—a passage paved at first with ravenous trapdoors, and then with openwork canvas of the most careless description.

"Gaw!" said Bert, turning over after his seventh fall through infinite space that night.

He sat up in the darkness and nursed his knees. The progress of the airship was not nearly so smooth as a balloon; he could feel a regular swaying up, up, up and then down, down, down, and the throbbing and tremulous quiver of the engines.

His mind began to teem with memories—more memories and more.

Through them, like a struggling swimmer in broken water, came the perplexing question, What am I to do to-morrow? To-morrow, Kurt had told him, the Prince's secretary, the Graf von Winterfeld, would come to him and discuss his flying-machine, and then he would see the Prince. He would have to stick it out now that he was Butteridge, and sell his invention. And then, if they found him out! He had a vision of infuriated Butteridges. . . . Suppose after all he owned up? Pretended it was their misunderstanding? He began to scheme devices for selling the secret and circumventing Butteridge.

What should he ask for the thing? Somehow twenty thousand pounds struck him as about the sum indicated.

He fell into that despondency that lies in wait in the small hours. He had got too big a job on—too big a job.

Memories swamped his scheming.

"Where was I this time last night?"

He recapitulated his evenings tediously and lengthily. Last night he had been up above the clouds in Butteridge's balloon. He thought of the moment when he dropped through them and saw the cold twilight sea close below. He still remembered that disagreeable incident with a nightmare vividness. And the night before he and Grubb had been looking for cheap lodgings at Littlestone in Kent. How remote that seemed now! It might be years ago. For the first time he thought of his fellow Desert Dervish, left with the two red-painted bicycles on Dymchurch sands. "'E won't make much of a show of it, not without me. Any'ow 'e did 'ave the treasury—such as it was—in his pocket!" . . . The night before that was Bank Holiday night, and they had sat discussing their minstrel enterprise, drawing up a programme and rehearsing steps. And the night before was Whit Sunday.

"Lord!" cried Bert, "what a doing that motor-bicycle give me!" He recalled the empty flapping of the eviscerated cushion, the feeling of impotence as the flames rose again.

From among the confused memories of that tragic flare one little figure emerged very bright and poignantly sweet, Edna, crying back reluctantly from the departing motor-car, "See you to-morrer, Bert?"

Other memories of Edna clustered round that impression. They led Bert's mind step by step to an agreeable state that found expression in, "I'll marry 'er if she don't look out." And then in a flash it followed in his mind that if he sold the Butteridge secret he could! Suppose after all he did get twenty thousand pounds; such sums have been paid! With that he could buy house and garden, buy new clothes beyond dreaming, buy a motor, travel, have every delight of the civilized life as he knew it, for himself and Edna. Of course, risks were involved. "I'll 'ave old Butteridge on my track, I expect!"

He meditated upon that. He declined again to despondency. As yet he was only in the beginning of the adventure. He had still to deliver the goods and draw the cash. And before that   Just now he was by no means on his way home. He was flying off to America to fight there. "Not much fighting," he considered; "all our own way." Still, if a shell did happen to hit the Vaterland on the underside! . . .

"S'pose I ought to make my will."

He lay back for some time composing wills—chiefly in favour of Edna. He had settled now it was to be twenty thousand pounds. He left a number of minor legacies. The wills became more and more meandering and extravagant. . . .

He woke from the eighth repetition of his nightmare fall through space. "This flying gets on one's nerves," he said.

He could feel the airship diving down, down, down, then slowly swinging up, up, up. Throb, throb, throb, throb, quivered the engine. He got up presently and wrapped himself about with Mr. Butteridge's overcoat and all the blankets, for the air was very keen. Then he peeped out of the window to see a grey dawn breaking over clouds, then turned up his light and bolted his door, sat down to the table, and produced his chest-protector.

He smoothed the crumpled plans with his hand, and contemplated them. Then he referred to the other drawings in the portfolio. Twenty thousand pounds, if he worked it right! It was worth trying, anyhow.

Presently he opened the drawer in which Kurt had put paper and writing materials.

Bert Smallways was by no means a stupid person, and up to a certain limit he had not been badly educated. His board-school had taught him to draw up to certain limits, taught him to calculate and understand a specification. If at that point his country had tired of its efforts, and handed him over unfinished to scramble for a living in an atmosphere of advertisements and individual enterprise, that was really not his fault. He was as his State had made him, and the reader must not imagine because he was a little Cockney cad that he was absolutely incapable of grasping the idea of the Butteridge flying-machine. But he found it stiff and perplexing. His motor-bicycle and Grubb's experiments and the "mechanical drawing" he had done in standard seven all helped him out; and, moreover, the maker of these drawings, whoever he was, had been anxious to make his intentions plain. Bert copied sketches, he made notes, he made a quite tolerable and intelligent copy of the essential drawings and sketches of the others. Then he fell into a meditation upon them.

At last he rose with a sigh, folded up the originals that had formerly been in his chest-protector and put them into the breast pocket of his jacket, and then very carefully deposited the copies he had made in the place of the originals. He had no very clear plan in his mind in doing this, except that he hated the idea of altogether parting with the secret. For a long time he meditated profoundly—nodding. Then he turned out his light and went to bed again and schemed himself to sleep.

6

The hochgeborene Graf von Winterfeld was also a light sleeper that night, but then he was one of those people who sleep little and play chess problems in their heads to while away the time—and that night he had a particularly difficult problem to solve.

He came in upon Bert while he was still in bed in the glow of the sunlight reflected from the North Sea below, consuming the rolls and coffee a soldier had brought him. He had a portfolio under his arm, and in the clear, early morning light his dingy grey hair and heavy, silver-rimmed spectacles made him look almost benevolent. He spoke English fluently, but with a strong German flavour. He was particularly bad with his "b's," and his "th's" softened towards weak "z'ds." He called Bert explosively, "Pooterage." He began with some indistinct civilities, bowed, took a folding-table and chair from behind the door, put the former between himself and Bert, sat down on the latter, coughed dryly, and opened his portfolio. Then he put his elbows on the table, pinched his lower lip with his two forefingers, and regarded Bert disconcertingly with magnified eyes. "You came to us, Herr Pooterage, against your will," he said at last.

" 'Ow d'you make that out?" asked Bert, after a pause of astonishment.

"I chuge by ze maps in your car. They were all English. And your provisions. They were all picnic. Also your cords were entangled. You haf been tugging—but no good. You could not manage ze balloon, and anuzzer power than yours prought you to us. Is it not so?"

Bert thought.

"Also—where is ze laty?"

" 'Ere!—what lady?"

"You started with a laty. That is evident. You shtarted for an afternoon excursion—a picnic. A man of your temperament—he would take a laty. She was not wiz you in your balloon when you came down at Dornhof. No! Only her chacket! It is your affair. Still I am curious."

Bert reflected. " 'Ow d'you know that?"

"I chuge by ze nature of your farious provisions. I cannot account, Mr. Pooterage, for ze laty, what you haf done with her. Nor can I tell why you should wear nature-sandals, nor why you should wear such

cheap plue clothes. These are outside my instructions. Trifles, perhaps.
Officially they are to be ignored. Laties come and go—I am a man of ze
worldt. I have known wise men wear sandals and efen practise vegetarian
habits. I haf known men—or at any rate I haf known chemists—who
did not schmoke. You haf, no doubt, put ze laty down somewhere.
Well. Let us get to business. A higher power"—his voice changed its
emotional quality, his magnified eyes seemed to dilate—"has prought
you and your secret straight to us. So!"—he bowed his head—"so pe it.
It is ze Destiny of Chermany and my Prince. I can undershtandt you
always carry zat secret. You are afraidt of roppers and spies. So it comes
wiz you—to us. Mr. Pooterage, Chermany will puy it."

"Will she?"

"She will," said the secretary, looking hard at Bert's abandoned
sandals in the corner of the locker. He roused himself, consulted a
paper of notes for a moment, and Bert eyed his brown and wrinkled
face with expectation and terror. "Chermany, I am instructed to say,"
said the secretary, with his eyes on the table and his notes spread out,
"has always been willing to puy your secret. We haf indeed peen eager
to acquire it—fery eager; and it was only ze fear that you might be, on
patriotic groundts, acting in collusion with your Pritish War Office zat
has made us discreet in offering for your marvellous invention through
intermediaries. We haf no hesitation whatefer now, I am instructed, in
agreeing to your proposal of a hundert tousand poundts."

"Crikey!" said Bert, overwhelmed.

"I peg your pardon?"

"Jest a twinge," said Bert, raising his hand to his bandaged head.

"Ah! Also I am instructed to say that as for that noble, unrightly
accused laty you haf championed so brafely against Pritish hypocrisy
and coldness, all ze chivalry of Chermany is on her site."

"Lady?" said Bert faintly, and then recalled the great Butteridge love
story. Had the old chap also read the letters? He must think him a
scorcher if he had. "Oh! that's aw-right," he said, "about 'er. I 'adn't any
doubts about that. I——"

He stopped. The secretary certainly had a most appalling stare. It
seemed ages before he looked down again. "Well, ze laty as you please.
She is your affair. I haf performt my instructions. And ze title of Paron,

zat also can pe done. It can all pe done, Herr Pooterage." He drummed on the table for a second or so, and resumed. " I haf to tell you, sir, zat you come to us at a crisis in—Welt-Politik. There can be no harm now for me to tell our plans to you. Pefore you leafe this ship again they will be manifest to all ze worldt. War is perhaps already declared. We go—to America. Our fleet will descend out of ze air upon ze United States—it is a country quite unprepared for war eferywhere—eferywhere. Zey have always relied on ze Atlantic. And their navy. We have selected a certain point—it is at present ze secret of our commanders—which we shall seize, and zen we shall establish a depot—a sort of inland Gibraltar. It will be—what will it be?—an eagle's nest. Zere our airships will gazzer and repair, and thence they will fly to and fro ofer ze United States, terrorizing cities, dominating Washington, levying what is necessary, until ze terms we dictate are accepted. You follow me?"

"Go on!" said Bert.

"We could haf done all zis wiz such Luftschiffe and Drachenflieger as we possess, but ze accession of your machine renders our project complete. It not only gifs us a better Drachenflieger, but it remofes our last uneasiness as to Great Pritain. Wizout you, sir, Great Pritain, ze land you lofed so well and zat has requited you so ill, zat land of Pharisees and reptiles, can do nozzing!—nozzing! You see, I am perfectly frank wiz you. Well, I am instructed that Chermany recognizes all this. We want you to blace yourself at our disposal. We want you to become our Chief Head Flight Engineer. We want you to manufacture, we want to equib a swarm of hornets unter your direction. We want you to direct this force. And it is at our depot in America we want you. So we offer you simply, and without haggling, ze full terms you demanded weeks ago—one hundert tousand poundts in cash, a salary of three tousand poundts a year, a pension of one tousand poundts a year, and ze title of Paron as you desired. These are my instructions."

He resumed his scrutiny of Bert's face.

"That's all right, of course," said Bert, a little short of breath, but otherwise resolute and calm; and it seemed to him that now was the time to bring his nocturnal scheming to the issue.

The secretary contemplated Bert's collar with sustained attention. Only for one moment did his gaze move to the sandals and back.

"Jes' lemme think a bit," said Bert, finding the stare debilitating.
"Look 'ere!" he said at last, with an air of great explicitness, "I *got* the
secret."

"Yes."

"But I don't want the name of Butteridge to appear—see? I been
thinking that over."

"A little delicacy?"

"Exactly. You buy the secret—leastways, I give it you—from
Bearer—see?"

His voice failed him a little, and the stare continued. "I want to do
the thing enonymously. See?"

Still staring. Bert drifted on like a swimmer caught by a current.
"Fact is, I'm goin' to edop' the name of Smallways. I don't want no title
of Baron; I've altered my mind. And I want the money quiet-like. I want
the hundred thousand pounds paid into benks—thirty thousand into
the London and County Benk Branch at Bun Hill in Kent directly I
'and over the plans; twenty thousand into the Benk of England; 'arf the
rest into a good French bank, the other 'arf the German National Bank,
see? I want it put there, right away. I don't want it put in the name of
Butteridge. I want it put in the name of Albert Peter Smallways; that's
the name I'm going to edop'. That's condition one."

"Go on!" said the secretary.

"The nex' condition," said Bert, "is that you don't make any inquiries
as to title. I mean what English gentlemen do when they sell or let you
land. You don't arst 'ow I got it. See? 'Ere I am—I deliver you the goods;
that's all right. Some people 'ave the cheek to say this isn't my invention,
see? It is, you know—*that's* all right; but I don't want that gone into. I
want a fair and square agreement saying that's all right. See?"

His "See?" faded into a profound silence.

The secretary sighed at last, leant back in his chair, and produced a
tooth-pick, and used it to assist his meditation on Bert's case. "What
was that name?" he asked at last, putting away the tooth-pick; "I must
write it down."

"Albert Peter Smallways," said Bert, in a mild tone.

The secretary wrote it down, after a little difficulty about the spelling because of the different names of the letters of the alphabet in the two languages.

"And now, Mr. Schmallvays," he said at last, leaning back and resuming the stare, "tell me: how did you ket hold of Mister Pooterage's balloon?"

7

When at last the Graf von Winterfeld left Bert Smallways, he left him in an extremely deflated condition, with all his little story told.

He had, as people say, made a clean breast of it. He had been pursued into details. He had had to explain the blue suit, the sandals, the Desert Dervishes—everything. For a time scientific zeal consumed the secretary, and the question of the plans remained in suspense. He even went into speculation about the previous occupants of the balloon. "I suppose," he said, "the laty *was* the laty. Bot that is not our affair.

"It is fery curious and amusing, yes: but I am afraid the Prince may be annoyt. He acted wiz his usual decision—always he acts wiz wonderful decision. Like Napoleon. Directly he was tolt of your descent into the camp at Dornhof, he said, 'Pring him!—pring him! It is my schtar!' His schtar of Destiny! You see? He will be dthwarted. He directed you to come as Herr Pooterage, and you haf not done so. You haf triet, of course; but it has been a poor try. His chugments of men are fery just and right, and it is better for men to act up to them—gompletely. Especially now. Barticularly now."

He resumed that attitude of his, with his underlip pinched between his forefingers. He spoke almost confidentially. "It will be awkward. I triet to suggest some doubt, but I was overruled. The Prince does not listen. He is impatient in the high air. Perhaps he will think his schtar has been making a fool of him. Perhaps he will think *I* haf been making a fool of him." He wrinkled his forehead, and drew in the corners of his mouth.

"I got the plans," said Bert.

"Yes. There is that! Yes. But you see the Prince was interested in Herr Pooterage because of his romantic seit. Herr Pooterage was so much more—ah!—in the picture. I am afraid you are not equal to controlling the flying machine department of our aerial park as he wished you to do. He hadt promised himself that. . . .

"And der was also the prestige—the worldt prestige of Pooterage with us. . . . Well, we must see what we can do." He held out his hand. "Gif me the plans."

A terrible chill ran through the being of Mr. Smallways. To the end of his life he was never clear in his mind whether he wept or no, but certainly there was weeping in his voice. " 'Ere I say!" he protested. "Ain't I to 'ave—nothin' for 'em?"

The secretary regarded him with benevolent eyes. "You do not deserve anyzing!" he said.

"I might 'ave tore 'em up."

"Zey are not yours!"

"They weren't his, very likely."

"No need to pay anyzing."

Bert's being seemed to tighten towards desperate deeds. "Gaw!" he said, clutching his coat, "*ain't* there?"

"Pe galm," said the secretary. "Listen! You shall haf five hundert poundts. You shall haf it on my promise. I will do that for you, and that is all I can do. Take it from me. Gif me the name of that bank. Write it down. So! I tell you the Prince—is no choke. I do not think he approffed of your appearance last night. No! I can't answer for him. He wanted Pooterage, and you haf spoilt it. The Prince—I do not understandt quite, he is in a strange state. It is the excitement of the starting and this great soaring in the air. I cannot account for what he does. But if all goes well I will see to it—you shall haf five hundert poundts. Will that do? Then gif me the plans."

"Old beggar!" said Bert, as the door clicked. "Gaw!—what an ole beggar!—*Sharp!*"

He sat down in the folding-chair, and whistled noiselessly for a time. "Nice old swindle for 'im if I tore 'em up! I could 'ave."

He rubbed the bridge of his nose thoughtfully. "I gave the whole blessed show away. If I'd jes' kep quiet about being enonymous. . . . Gaw!. . . . Too soon, Bert my boy—too soon and too rushy. I'd like to kick my silly self.

"I couldn't 'ave kep' it up.

"After all, it ain't so very bad," he said.

"After all, five 'undred pounds. . . . It isn't *my* secret, anyhow. It's jes' a pick-up on the road. Five 'undred.

"Wonder what the fare is from America back 'ome?"

8

And later in the day an extremely shattered and disorganised Bert Smallways stood in the presence of the Prince Karl Albert.

The proceedings were in German. The Prince was in his own cabin, the end room of the airship, a charming apartment furnished in wicker-work with a long window across its entire breadth, looking forward. He was sitting at a folding-table of green baize, with Von Winterfeld and two officers sitting beside him, and littered before them was a number of American maps and Mr. Butteridge's letters and his portfolio and a number of loose papers. Bert was not asked to sit down, and remained standing throughout the interview. Von Winterfeld told his story, and every now and then the words Balloon and Pooterage struck on Bert's ears. The Prince's face remained stern and ominous, and the two officers watched it cautiously or glanced at Bert. There was something a little strange in their scrutiny of the Prince—a curiosity, an apprehension. Then presently he was struck by an idea, and they fell discussing the plans. The Prince asked Bert abruptly in English, "Did you ever see this thing go up?"

Bert jumped. "Saw it from Bun 'Ill, your Royal Highness."

Von Winterfeld made some explanation.

"How fast did it go?"

"Couldn't say, your Royal Highness. The papers, leastways the 'Daily Courier,' said eighty miles an hour."

They talked German over that for a time.

"Couldt it standt still? Op in the air? That is what I want to know."

"It could 'ovver, your Royal Highness, like a wasp," said Bert.

"*Viel besser, nicht wahr?*" said the Prince to Von Winterfeld, and then went on in German for a time.

Presently they came to an end, and the two officers looked at Bert.

One rang a bell, and the portfolio was handed to an attendant, who took it away.

Then they reverted to the case of Bert, and it was evident the Prince was inclined to be hard with him. Von Winterfeld protested. Apparently theological considerations came in, for there were several mentions of "Gott!" Some conclusions emerged, and it was apparent that Von Winterfeld was instructed to convey them to Bert.

"Mr. Schmallvays, you haf obtained a footing in this airship," he said, "by disgraceful and systematic lying."

" 'Ardly systematic," said Bert. "I——"

The Prince silenced him with a gesture.

"And it is within the power of his Highness to dispose of you as a spy."

" 'Ere!—I came to sell——"

"Ssh!" said one of the officers.

"However, in consideration of the happy chance that mate you the instrument unter Gott of this Pooterage flying-machine reaching his Highness's hand, you haf been spared. Yes—you were the pearer of goot tidings. You will be allowed to remain on this ship until it is convenient to dispose of you. Do you understandt?"

"We will bring him," said the Prince, and added terribly with a terrible glare, "*als Ballast.*"

"You are to come with us," said Winterfeld, "as—pallast. Do you understandt?"

Bert opened his mouth to ask about the five hundred pounds, and then a saving gleam of wisdom silenced him. He met Von Winterfeld's eye, and it seemed to him the secretary nodded slightly. "Go!" said the Prince, with a sweep of the great arm and hand towards the door. Bert went out like a leaf before a gale.

9

But in between the time when the Graf von Winterfeld had talked to him and this alarming conference with the Prince, Bert had explored the Vaterland from end to end. He had found it interesting in spite of grave preoccupations. Kurt, like the greater number of the men upon the German air-fleet, had known hardly anything of aeronautics before his appointment to the new flagship. But he was extremely keen upon this wonderful new weapon Germany had assumed so suddenly and dramatically. He showed things to Bert with a boyish eagerness and appreciation. It was as if he showed them over again to himself, like a child showing a new toy. "Let's go all over the ship," he said with zest. He pointed out particularly the lightness of everything, the use of exhausted aluminium tubing, of springy cushions inflated with compressed hydrogen; the partitions were hydrogen bags covered with light imitation leather, the very crockery was a light biscuit glazed in a vacuum, and weighed next to nothing. Where strength was needed there was the new Charlottenburg alloy, German steel as it was called, the toughest and most resistent metal in the world.

There was no lack of space. Space did not matter, so long as load did not grow. The habitable part of the ship was two hundred and fifty feet long, and the rooms in two tiers, above these one could go up into remarkable little white-metal turrets with big windows and air-tight double doors that enabled one to inspect the vast cavity of the gas-chambers. This inside view impressed Bert very much. He had never realized before that an airship was not one simple continuous gas-bag containing nothing but gas. Now he saw far above him the backbone of the apparatus and its big ribs, "like the neural and haemal canals," said Kurt, who had dabbled in biology.

"Rather!" said Bert, appreciatively, though he had not the ghost of an idea what these phrases meant.

Little electric lights could be switched on up there if anything went wrong in the night. There were even ladders across the space. "But you can't go into the gas," protested Bert. "You can't breve it."

The lieutenant opened a cupboard door and displayed a diver's suit, only that it was made of oiled silk, and both its compressed air knapsack and its helmet were of an alloy of aluminium and some light metal. "We can go all over the inside netting and stick up bullet holes or leaks," he explained. "There's netting inside and out. The whole outer-case is rope ladder, so to speak."

Aft of the habitable part of the air-ship was the magazine of explosives, coming near the middle of its length. They were all bombs of various types—mostly in glass—none of the German airships carried any guns at all except one small pom-pom (to use the old English nickname dating from the Boer War), which was forward in the gallery upon the shield at the heart of the eagle. From the magazine amidships a covered canvas gallery with aluminium treads on its floor and a hand-rope, ran back underneath the gas-chamber to the engine-room at the tail; but along this Bert did not go, and from first to last he never saw the engines. But he went up a ladder against a gale of ventilation—a ladder that was encased in a kind of gas-tight fire-escape and ran right athwart the great forward air-chamber to the little look-out gallery with a telephone, that gallery that bore the light pom-pom of German steel and its locker of shells. This gallery was all of aluminium-magnesium alloy, the tight front of the airship swelled cliff-like above and below, and the black eagle sprawled everwhelmingly gigantic, its extremities all hidden by the bulge of the gas-bag.

And far down, under the soaring eagles, was England, four thousand feet below perhaps, and looking very small and defenceless indeed in the morning sunlight.

The realization that there was England gave Bert sudden and un-expected qualms of patriotic compunction. He was struck by a quite novel idea. After all, he might have torn up those plans and thrown them away. These people could not have done so very much to him. And even if they did, ought not an Englishman to die for his country? It was an idea that had been hitherto rather smothered up by the cares of a competitive civilization. He became violently depressed. He ought, he perceived, to have seen it in that light before. Why hadn't he seen it in that light before?

Indeed, wasn't he a sort of traitor? . . .

He wondered how the aerial fleet must look from down there. Tremendous, no doubt, and dwarfing all the buildings.

He was passing between Manchester and Liverpool, Kurt told him; a gleaming band across the prospect was the Ship Canal, and a wel-tering ditch of shipping far away ahead, the Mersey estuary. Bert was a southerner; he had never been north of the Midland counties, and the multitude of factories and chimneys—the latter for the most part obsolete and smokeless now—superseded by huge electric generating stations that consumed their own reek—old railway viaducts, mono-rail networks and goods yards, and the vast areas of dingy homes and narrow streets, spreading aimlessly, struck him as though Camberwell and Rotherhithe had run to seed. Here and there, as if caught in a net, were fields and agricultural fragments. It was a sprawl of undistinguished population. There were, no doubt, museums and town halls and even cathedrals of a sort to mark theoretical centres of municipal and religious organization in this confusion; but Bert could not see them, they did not stand out at all in that wide disorderly vision of congested workers' houses and places to work, and shops and meanly conceived chapels and churches. And across this landscape of an industrial civilization swept the shadows of the German airships like a hurrying shoal of fishes. . . .

Kurt and he fell talking of aerial tactics, and presently went down to the under-gallery in order that Bert might see the Drachenflieger that the airships of the right wing had picked up overnight and were towing behind them; each airship towing three or four. They looked like big box-kites of an exaggerated form, soaring at the ends of invisible cords. They had long, square heads and flattened tails, with lateral propellers.

"Much skill is required for those—much skill!"

"Rather!"

Pause.

"Your machine is different from that, Mr. Butteridge?"

"Quite different," said Bert. "More like an insect and less like a bird. And it buzzes, and don't drive about so. What can those things do?"

Kurt was not very clear upon that himself, and was still explaining when Bert was called to the conference we have recorded with the Prince. . . .

And after that was over, the last traces of Butteridge fell from Bert like a garment, and he became Smallways to all on board. The soldiers ceased to salute him, and the officers ceased to seem aware of his existence, except Lieutenant Kurt. He was turned out of his nice cabin, and packed in with his belongings to share that of Lieutenant Kurt, whose luck it was to be a junior, and the bird-headed officer, still swearing slightly and carrying strops and aluminium boot-trees and weightless hair-brushes and hand-mirrors and pomade in his hands, resumed possession. Bert was put in with Kurt because there was nowhere else for him to lay his bandaged head in that close-packed vessel. He was to mess, he was told, with the men.

Kurt came and stood with his legs wide apart, and surveyed him for a moment as he sat despondent in his new quarters.

"What's your real name, then?" said Kurt, who was only imperfectly informed of the new state of affairs.

"Smallways."

"I thought you were a bit of a fraud—even when I thought you were Butteridge. You're jolly lucky the Prince took it calmly. He's a pretty tidy blazer when he's roused. He wouldn't stick a moment at pitching a chap of your sort overboard if he thought fit. No! . . . They've shoved you on to me, but it's my cabin, you know."

"I won't forget," said Bert.

Kurt left him, and when he came to look about him the first thing he saw pasted on the padded wall was a reproduction of the great picture by Siegfried Schmalz of the War God, that terrible, trampling figure with the viking helmet and the scarlet cloak, wading through destruction, sword in hand, which had so strong a resemblance to Karl Albert, the prince it was painted to please.

FIVE

The Battle of the North Atlantic

I

The Prince Karl Albert had made a profound impression upon Bert. He was quite the most terrifying person Bert had ever encountered. He filled the Smallways soul with passionate dread and antipathy. For a long time Bert sat alone in Kurt's cabin, doing nothing and not venturing even to open the door lest he should be by so much nearer that appalling presence.

So it came about that he was probably the last person on board to hear the news that wireless telegraphy was bringing to the airship in throbs and fragments of a great naval battle in progress in mid-Atlantic.

He learnt it at last from Kurt.

Kurt came in with a general air of ignoring Bert, but muttering to himself in English nevertheless. "Stupendous!" Bert heard him say. "Here!" he said, "get off this locker." And he proceeded to rout out two books and a case of maps. He spread them on the folding-table, and stood regarding them. For a time his Germanic discipline struggled with his English informality and his natural kindliness and talkativeness, and at last lost.

"They're at it, Smallways," he said.

"At what, sir?" said Bert, broken and respectful.

"Fighting! The American North Atlantic Squadron and pretty nearly the whole of our fleet. Our Eiserne Kreuz has had a gruelling and is sinking, and their Miles Standish—she's one of their biggest—has sunk with all hands. Torpedoes, I suppose. She was a bigger ship than the

Karl der Grosse, but five or six years older. . . . Gods! I wish we could
see it, Smallways; a square fight in blue water, guns or nothing, and all
of 'em steaming ahead!"

He spread his maps, he had to talk, and so he delivered a lecture on
the naval situation to Bert.

"Here it is," he said, "latitude 30° 50' N., longitude, 30° 50' W. It's a
good day off us anyhow, and they're all going south-west by south full
pelt as hard as they can go. We shan't see a bit of it, worse luck! Not a
sniff we shan't get!"

2

The naval situation in the North Atlantic at that time was a peculiar
one. The United States was by far the stronger of the two powers upon
the sea, but the bulk of the American fleet was still in the Pacific.
It was in the direction of Asia that war had been most feared, for
the situation between Asiatic and white had become unusually violent
and dangerous, and the Japanese Government had shown itself quite
unprecedentedly difficult. The German attack found half the American
strength at Manilla, and what was called the Second Fleet strung out
across the Pacific in wireless contact between the Asiatic station and San
Francisco. The North Atlantic Squadron was the sole American force on
her eastern shore; it was returning from a friendly visit to France and
Spain, and was pumping oil-fuel from tenders in Mid-Atlantic—for
most of its ships were steamships—when the international situation
became acute. It was made up of four battleships and five armoured
cruisers, ranking almost with battleships, not one of which was of a
later date than 1913. The Americans had indeed grown so accustomed
to the idea that Great Britain could be trusted to keep the peace of
the Atlantic that a naval attack on the eastern seaboard found them
unprepared even in their imaginations. But long before the declaration
of war—indeed on Whit Monday—the whole German fleet of eighteen
battleships, with a flotilla of fuel tenders and converted liners containing
stores, to be used in support of the air-fleet, had passed through the
Straits of Dover and headed boldly for New York. Not only did these
German battleships outnumber the Americans two to one, but they
were more heavily armed and more modern in construction—at least

seven of them having high explosive engines built of Charlottenburg steel, and all carrying Charlottenburg steel guns.

The fleets came into contact on Wednesday before any actual declaration of war. The Americans had strung out in the modern fashion at distances of thirty miles or so, and were steaming to keep themselves between the Germans and either the eastern states or Panama; because, vital as it was to defend the seaboard cities, and particularly New York, it was still more vital to save the canal from any attack that might prevent the return of the main fleet from the Pacific. No doubt, said Kurt, this was now making records across that ocean, "unless the Japanese have had the same idea as the Germans." It was obviously beyond human possibility that the American North Atlantic fleet could hope to meet and defeat the German; but, on the other hand, with luck it might fight a delaying action and inflict such damage as to weaken greatly the attack upon the coast defences. Its duty, indeed, was not victory but devotion, the severest task in the world. Meanwhile the submarine defences of New York, Panama, and the other more vital points could be put in some sort of order.

This was the naval situation, and until Wednesday in Whit week it was the only situation the American people had realized. It was then they heard for the first time of the real scale of the Dornhof aeronautic park, and the possibility of an attack coming upon them not only by sea, but by the air. But it is curious that so discredited were the newspapers of that period, that a large majority of New Yorkers, for example, did not believe the most copious and circumstantial accounts of the German air-fleet until it was actually in sight of New York.

Kurt's talk was half soliloquy. He stood with a map on Mercator's projection before him, swaying to the swaying of the ship and talking of guns and tonnage of ships and their build and powers and speed, of strategic points and bases of operation. A certain shyness that reduced him to the status of a listener at the officer's table no longer silenced him.

Bert stood by, saying very little, but watching Kurt's finger on the map. "They've been saying things like this in the papers for a long time," he remarked. "Fancy it coming real!"

Kurt had a detailed knowledge of the Miles Standish. "She used to be a crack ship for gunnery—held the record. I wonder if we beat her shooting or how? I wish I was in it. I wonder which of our ships beat her. Maybe she got a shell in her engines. It's a running fight. I wonder what the Barbarossa is doing," he went on. "She's my old ship. Not a first-rater, but good stuff. I bet she's got a shot or two home by now if old Schneider's up to form. Just think of it! There they are whacking away at each other, great guns going, shells exploding, magazines bursting, ironwork flying about like straw in a gale, all we've been dreaming of for years! I suppose we shall fly right away to New York—just as though it wasn't anything at all. I suppose we shall reckon we aren't wanted down there. It's no more than a covering fight on our side. All those tenders and store-ships of ours are going on south-west by west to New York to make a floating depôt for us. See?" He dabbed his forefinger on the map. "Here we are. Our train of stores goes there, our battleships elbow the Americans out of our way there."

When Bert went down to the men's mess-room to get his evening ration, hardly any one took notice of him, except just to point him out for an instant. Everyone was talking of the battle, suggesting, contradicting—at times, until the petty officers hushed them, it rose to a great uproar. There was a new bulletin, but what it said he did not gather, except that it concerned the Barbarossa. Some of the men stared at him, and he heard the name of "Booteraidge" several times; but no one molested him, and there was no difficulty about his soup and bread when his turn at the end of the queue came. He had feared there might be no ration for him, and if so he did not know what he would have done.

Afterwards he ventured out upon the little hanging gallery with the solitary sentinel. The weather was still fine, but the wind was rising and the rolling swing of the airship increasing. He clutched the rail tightly and felt rather giddy. They were now out of sight of land, and over blue water rising and falling in great masses. A dingy old brigantine under the British flag rose and plunged amid the broad blue waves—the only ship in sight.

3

In the evening it began to blow and the airship to roll like a porpoise as it swung through the air. Kurt said that several of the men were seasick, but the motion did not inconvenience Bert, whose luck it was to be of that mysterious gastric disposition which constitutes a good sailor. He slept well, but in the small hours the light awoke him, and he found Kurt staggering about in search of something. He found it at last in the locker, and held it in his hand unsteadily—a compass. Then he compared his map.

"We've changed our direction," he said, "and come into the wind. I can't make it out. We've turned away from New York to the south. Almost as if we were going to take a hand——"

He continued talking to himself for some time.

Day came, wet and windy. The window was bedewed externally, and they could see nothing through it. It was also very cold, and Bert decided to keep rolled up in his blankets on the locker until the bugle summoned him to his morning ration. That consumed, he went out on the little gallery; but he could see nothing but eddying clouds driving headlong by, and the dim outlines of the nearer airships. Only at rare intervals could he get a glimpse of grey sea through the pouring cloud-drift.

Later in the morning the Vaterland changed altitude, and soared up suddenly in a high, clear sky, going, Kurt said, to a height of nearly thirteen thousand feet.

Bert was in his cabin, and chanced to see the dew vanish from the window and caught the gleam of sunlight outside. He looked out, and saw once more that sunlit cloud floor he had seen first from the balloon, and the ships of the German air-fleet rising one by one from the white, as fish might rise and become visible from deep water. He stared for a moment, and then ran out to the gallery to see this wonder better. Below was cloudland and storm, a great drift of tumbled weather going hard away to the north-east, and the air about him was clear and cold and serene save for the faintest chill breeze and a rare drifting snow-flake. Throb, throb, throb, throb, went the engines in the stillness. That huge herd of airships rising one after another had an effect of strange, portentous monsters breaking into an altogether unfamiliar world. . . .

Either there was no news of the naval battle that morning, or the Prince kept to himself whatever came until past midday. Then the bulletins came with a rush, bulletins that made the lieutenant wild with excitement.

"Barbarossa disabled and sinking," he cried. "Gott im Himmel! *Der alte Barbarossa! Aber welch ein braver Krieger!*"

He walked about the swinging cabin, and for a time he was wholly German.

Then he became English again. "Think of it, Smallways! The old ship we kept so clean and tidy! All smashed about, and the iron flying about in fragments, and the chaps one knew—Gott!—flying about too! Scalding water squirting fire, and the smash, smash of the guns! They smash when you're near! Like everything bursting to pieces! Wool won't stop it—nothing! And me up here—so near and so far! *Der alte Barbarossa!*"

"Any other ships!" asked Smallways presently.

"Gott! Yes! We've lost the Karl der Grosse, our best and biggest. Run down in the night by a British liner that blundered into the fighting—in trying to blunder out. They're fighting in a gale. The liner's afloat with her nose broken, sagging about! There never was such a battle!—never before! Good ships and good men on both sides—and a storm and the night and the dawn and all in the open ocean full steam ahead! No stabbing! No submarines! Guns and shooting! Half our ships we don't hear of any more, because their masts are shot away. Latitude, 30° 38' N.—longitude, 40° 31' W.—where's that?"

He routed out his map again, and stared at it with eyes that did not see.

"*Der alte Barbarossa!* I can't get it out of my head—with shells in her engine-room, and the fires flying out of her furnaces, and the stokers and engineers scalded and dead. Men I've messed with, Smallways— men I've talked to close! And they've had their day at last! And it wasn't all luck for them!

"Disabled and sinking! I suppose everybody can't have all the luck in a battle. Poor old Schneider! I bet he gave 'em something back!"

So it was the news of the battle came filtering through to them all that morning. The Americans had lost a second ship, name unknown; the Hermann had been damaged in covering the Barbarossa. . . . Kurt fretted like an imprisoned animal about the airship, now going up to the forward gallery under the eagle, now down into the swing gallery, now poring over his maps. He infected Smallways with a sense of the immediacy of this battle that was going on just over the curve of the earth. But when Bert went down to the gallery the world was empty and still, a clear inky-blue sky above and a rippled veil of still, thin sunlit cirrus below, through which one saw a racing drift of rain-cloud, and never a glimpse of sea. Throb, throb, throb, throb, went the engines, and the long, undulating wedge of airships hurried after the flagship like a flight of swans after their leader. Save for the quiver of the engines it was as noiseless as a dream. And down there, somewhere in the wind and rain, guns roared, shells crashed home, and after the old manner of warfare, men toiled and died.

4

As the afternoon wore on the lower weather abated, and the sea became intermittently visible again. The air-fleet dropped slowly to the middle air, and towards sunset they had a glimpse of the disabled Barbarossa far away to the east. Smallways heard men hurrying along the passage, and was drawn out to the gallery, where he found nearly a dozen officers collected and scrutinizing the helpless ruins of the battleship through field-glasses. Two other vessels stood by her, one an exhausted petrol tank, very high out of the water, and the other a converted liner. Kurt was at the end of the gallery, a little apart from the others.

"Gott!" he said at last, lowering his binocular, like seeing an old friend with his nose cut off—waiting to be finished. Der Barbarossa!"

With a sudden impulse he handed his glass to Bert, who had peered beneath his hands, ignored by everyone, seeing the three ships merely as three brown-black lines upon the sea.

Never had Bert seen the like of that magnified, slightly hazy image before. It was not simply a battered ironclad that wallowed helpless. It was a mangled ironclad. It seemed wonderful she still floated. Her powerful engines had been her ruin. In the long chase of the night she had got out of line with her consorts, and nipped in between the Susquehanna and the Kansas City. They discovered her proximity, dropped back until she was nearly broadside on to the former battleship, and signalled up the Theodore Roosevelt and the little Monitor. As dawn broke she had found herself hostess of a circle. The fight had not lasted five minutes before the appearance of the Hermann to the east, and immediately after the Fürst Bismarck in the west, forced the Americans to leave her, but in that time they had smashed her iron to rags. They had vented the accumulated tensions of their hard day's retreat upon her. As Bert saw her, she seemed a mere metal-worker's fantasy of frozen metal writhings. He could not tell part from part of her, except by its position.

"Gott!" murmured Kurt, taking the glasses Bert restored to him— "Gott! Da waren Albrecht—der gute Albrecht und der alte Zimmermann—und von Rosen! . . ."

Long after the Barbarossa had been swallowed up in the twilight and distance he remained on the gallery peering through his glasses, and when he came back into his cabin he was unusually silent and thoughtful.

"This is a rough game, Smallways" he said at last—"this war is a rough game. Somehow one sees it different after a thing like that. Many men there were worked to make that Barbarossa, and there were men in it—one does not meet the like of them every day. Albrecht—there was a man named Albrecht—played the zither and improvised; I keep on wondering what has happened to him. He and I—we were very close friends, after the German fashion."

5

Smallways woke the next night to discover the cabin in darkness, a draught blowing through it, and Kurt talking to himself in German. He could see him dimly by the window, which he had unscrewed and opened, peering down. That cold, clear, attenuated light which is not so much light as a going of darkness, which casts inky shadows and so often heralds the dawn in the high air, was on his face.

"What's the row?" said Bert.

"Shut up!" said the lieutenant. "Can't you hear!"

Into the stillness came the repeated heavy thud of guns, one, two, a pause, then three in quick succession.

"Gaw!" said Bert—"guns!" and was instantly at the lieutenant's side. The airship was still very high and the sea below was masked by a thin veil of clouds. The wind had fallen, and Bert, following Kurt's pointing finger, saw dimly through the colourless veil first a red glow, then a quick red flash, and then at a little distance from it another. They were, it seemed for a while, silent flashes, and seconds after, when one had ceased to expect them, came the belated thuds—thud, thud. Kurt spoke in German, very quickly.

A bugle call rang through the airship.

Kurt sprang to his feet, saying something in an excited tone, still using German, and went to the door.

"I say! What's up?" cried Bert. "What's that?"

The lieutenant stopped for an instant in the doorway, dark against the light passage. "You stay where you are, Smallways. You keep there and do nothing. We're going into action," he explained, and vanished.

Bert's heart began to beat rapidly. He felt himself poised over the fighting vessels far below. In a moment, were they to drop like a hawk striking a bird? "Gaw!" he whispered at last, in awe-stricken tones.

Thud! . . . thud! He discovered far away a second ruddy flare flashing back at the first. He perceived some difference in the Vaterland for which he could not account, and then he realized that the engines had slowed to an almost inaudible beat. He stuck his head out of the window and saw in the bleak air the other airships slowed down to a scarcely perceptible motion.

A second bugle sounded, was taken up faintly from ship to ship. Out went the lights; the fleet became dim, dark bulks against an intense blue sky that still retained an occasional star. For a long time they hung, for an interminable time it seemed to him, and then began the sound of air being pumped into the balloonette, and slowly, slowly the Vaterland sank down towards the clouds.

He craned his neck, but he could not see if the rest of the fleet was following them; the overhang of the gas-chambers intervened. There was something that stirred his imagination deeply in that stealthy, noiseless descent.

The obscurity deepened for a time, the last fading star on the horizon vanished, and he felt the cold presence of cloud. Then suddenly the glow beneath assumed distinct outlines, became flames, and the Vaterland ceased to descend and hung observant, and it would seem unobserved just beneath a drifting stratum of cloud a thousand feet, perhaps, over the battle below.

In the night the struggling naval battle and retreat had entered upon a new phase. The Americans had drawn together the ends of the flying line skilfully and dexterously, until at last it was a column and well to the south of the lax sweeping pursuit of the Germans. Then in the darkness before the dawn they had come about and steamed northward in close order with the idea of passing through the German battle-line and falling upon the flotilla that was making for New York in support of the German air-fleet. Much had altered since the first contact of the fleets. By this time the American admiral, O'Connor, was fully informed of the existence of the airships, and he was no longer vitally concerned for Panama, since the submarine flotilla was reported arrived there from Key West, and the Delaware and Abraham Lincoln, two powerful and entirely modern ships, were already at Rio Grande, on the Pacific side of the canal. His manœuvre was, however, delayed by a boiler explosion on board the Susquehanna, and dawn found this ship in sight of and indeed so close to the Bremen and Weimar that they instantly engaged. There was no alternative to her abandonment but a fleet engagement. O'Connor chose the latter course. It was by no means a hopeless fight. The Germans, though much more numerous and powerful than the Americans, were in a dispersed line measuring nearly forty-five miles from end to end, and there were chances that before they could gather in for the fight the column of seven Americans would have ripped them from end to end.

The day broke dim and overcast, and neither the Bremen not the Weimar realized they had to deal with more than the Susquehanna until the whole column drew out from behind her at a distance of a mile or less, and bore down on them. This was the position of affairs when the Vaterland appeared in the sky. The red glow Bert had seen through the column of clouds came from the luckless Susquehanna; she lay almost immediately below, burning fore and aft, but still fighting two of her guns and steaming slowly southward. The Bremen and the Weimar, both hit in several places, were going west by south and away from her. The American fleet, headed by the Theodore Roosevelt, was crossing behind them, pounding them in succession, steaming in between them and the big modern Fürst Bismarck, which was coming up from the west. To Bert, however, the names of all of these ships were unknown, and for a considerable time, indeed, misled by the direction in which the combatants were moving, he imagined the Germans to be Americans and the Americans Germans. He saw what appeared to him to be a column of six battleships pursuing three others, who were supported by a newcomer, until the fact that the Bremen and Weimar were firing into the Susquehanna upset his calculations. Then for a time he was hopelessly at a loss. The noise of the guns, too, confused him, they no longer seemed to boom; they went whack, whack, whack, whack, and each faint flash made his heart leap in anticipation of the instant impact. He saw these ironclads, too, not in profile, as he was accustomed to see ironclads in pictures, but in plan and curiously foreshortened. For the most part they presented empty decks, but here and there little knots of men sheltered behind steel bulwarks. The long, agitated noses of their big guns jetting thin, transparent flashes and the broadside activity of the quick-firers, were the chief facts in this bird's-eye view. The Americans, being steam-turbine ships, had from two to four blast funnels each; the Germans lay lower in the water, having explosive engines which now for some reason made an unwonted muttering roar. Because of their steam propulsion, the American ships were larger and with a more graceful outline. He saw all these foreshortened ships rolling considerably and fighting their guns over a sea of huge low waves and under the cold, explicit light of dawn. The whole spectacle waved slowly with the long, rhythmic rising and beat of the airship.

At first only the Vaterland of all the flying fleet appeared upon the scene below. She hovered high over the Theodore Roosevelt, keeping pace with the full speed of that ship. From that ship she must have been intermittently visible through the drifting clouds. The rest of the German fleet remained above the cloud canopy at a height of six or seven thousand feet, communicating with the flagship by wireless telegraphy, but risking no exposure to the artillery below.

It is doubtful at what particular time the unlucky Americans realized the presence of this new factor in the fight. No account now survives of their experience. We have to imagine as well as we can what it must have been to a battle-strained sailor suddenly glancing upward to discover that long, silent shape overhead, vaster than any battleship, and trailing now from its hinder quarter a big German flag. Presently, as the sky cleared, more of such ships appeared in the blue through the dissolving clouds, and more, all disdainfully free of guns or armour, all flying fast to keep pace with the running fight below.

From first to last no gun whatever was fired at the Vaterland, and only a few rifle shots. It was a mere adverse stroke of chance that she had a man killed aboard her. Nor did she take any direct share in the fight until the end. She flew above the doomed American fleet while the Prince by wireless telegraphy directed the movements of her consorts. Meanwhile the Vogel-stern and Preussen, each with half-a-dozen Drachenflieger in tow, went full speed ahead and then dropped through the clouds, perhaps five miles ahead of the Americans. The Theodore Roosevelt let fly at once with the big guns in her forward barbette, but the shells burst far below the Vogel-stern, and forthwith a dozen single-man Drachenflieger were swooping down to make their attack.

Bert, craning his neck through the cabin port-hole, saw the whole of that incident, that first encounter of aeroplane and ironclad. He saw the queer German Drachenflieger, with their wide flat wings and square, box-shaped heads, their wheeled bodies, and their single-man riders, soar down the air like a flight of birds. "Gaw!" he said. One to the right pitched extravagantly, shot steeply up into the air, burst with a loud report, and flamed down into the sea; another plunged nose forward into the water and seemed to fly to pieces as it hit the waves. He saw little men on the deck of the Theodore Roosevelt below, men foreshortened in plan into mere heads and feet, running out preparing to shoot at the others. Then the foremost flying-machine was rushing between Bert and the American's deck, and then bang! came the thunder of its bomb flung neatly at the forward barbette and a thin little crackling of rifle shots in reply. Whack, whack, whack, went the quick-firing guns of the American's battery and smash came an answering shell from the Fürst Bismarck. Then a second and third flying-machine passed between Bert and the American ironclad, dropping bombs also, and a fourth, its rider hit by a bullet, reeled down and dashed itself to pieces and exploded between the shot-torn funnels, blowing them apart. Bert had a momentary glimpse of a little black creature jumping from the crumpling frame of the flying-machine, hitting the funnel, and falling limply, to be instantly caught and driven to nothingness by the blaze and rush of the explosion.

Smash! came a vast explosion in the forward part of the flagship, and a huge piece of metalwork seemed to lift out of her and dump itself into the sea, dropping men and leaving a gap into which a prompt Drachenflieger planted a flaring bomb. And then for an instant Bert perceived only too clearly in the growing, pitiless light a number of minute, convulsively active animalculæ scorched and struggling in the Theodore Roosevelt's foaming wake. What were they? Not men—surely not men? Those drowning, mangled little creatures tore with their clutching fingers at Bert's soul. "Oh, Gord!" he cried, "Oh, Gord!" almost whimpering. He looked again and they had gone, and the black stem of the Andrew Jackson, a little disfigured by the sinking Bremen's last shot, was parting the water that had swallowed them into two neatly symmetrical waves. For some moments sheer blank horror blinded Bert to the destruction below.

Then, with an immense rushing sound, bearing as were a straggling volley of crashing minor explosions on its back, the Susquehanna, three miles and more now to the east, blew up and vanished abruptly in a boiling, steaming welter. For a moment nothing was to be seen but tumbled water, and then there came belching up from below, with immense gulping noises, eructations of steam and air and petrol and fragments of canvas and woodwork and men.

That made a distinct pause in the fight. It seemed a long pause to Bert. He found himself looking for the Drachenflieger. The flattened ruin of one was floating abeam of the Monitor, the rest had passed, dropping bombs down the American column; several were in the water and apparently uninjured, and three or four were still in the air and coming round now in a wide circle to return to their mother airships. The American ironclads were no longer in column formation; the Theodore Roosevelt, badly damaged, had turned to the south-seat, and the Andrew Jackson, greatly battered but uninjured in any fighting part, was passing between her and the still fresh and vigorous Fürst Bismarck to intercept and meet the latter's fire. Away to the west the

Hermann and the Germanicus had appeared and were coming into action.

In the pause after the Susquehanna's disaster Bert became aware of a trivial sound like the noise of an ill-greased, ill-hung door that falls ajar—the sound of the men in the Fürst Bismarck cheering.

And in that pause in the uproar, too, the sun rose, the darkwaters became luminously blue, and a torrent of golden light irradiated the world. It came like a sudden smile in a scene of hate and terror. The cloud veil had vanished as if by magic, and the whole immensity of the German air-fleet was revealed in the sky; the air-fleet stooping now upon its prey.

"Whack-bang, whack-bang," the guns resumed, but ironclads were not built to fight the zenith, and the only hits the Americans scored were a few lucky chances in a generally ineffectual rifle fire. Their column was now badly broken, the Susquehanna had gone, the Theodore Roosevelt had fallen astern out of the line, with her forward guns disabled, in a heap of wreckage, and the Monitor was in some grave trouble. These two had ceased to fire altogether, and so had the Bremen and Weimar, all four ships lying within shot of each other in an involuntary truce and with their respective flags still displayed. Only four American ships now, with the Andrew Jackson leading, kept to the south-easterly course, and the Fürst Bismarck, the Hermann, and the Germanicus steamed parallel to them and drew ahead of them, fighting heavily. The Vaterland rose slowly in the air in preparation for the concluding act of the drama.

Then falling into place one behind the other, a string of a dozen airships dropped with unhurrying swiftness down the air in pursuit of the American fleet. They kept at a height of two thousand feet or more until they were over and a little in advance of the rearmost ironclad, and then stooped swiftly down into a fountain of bullets, and going just a little faster than the ship below, pelted her thinly protected decks with bombs until they became sheets of detonating flame. So the airships passed one after the other along the American column as it sought to keep up its fight with the Fürst Bismarck, the Hermann, and the Germanicus, and each airship added to the destruction and confusion its predecessor had made. The American gunfire ceased, except for a few heroic shots, but they still steamed on, obstinately unsubdued, bloody, battered, and wrathfully resistent, spitting bullets at the airships and unmercifully pounded by the German ironclads. But now Bert had but intermittent glimpses of them between the rearer bulks of the airships that assailed them. . . .

It struck Bert suddenly that the whole battle was receding and growing small and less thunderously noisy. The Vaterland was rising in the air, steadily and silently, until the impact of the guns no longer smote upon the heart but came to the ear dulled by distance, until the four silenced ships to the eastward were little distant things; but were there four? Bert now could see only three of those, floating, blackened, and smoking rafts of ruin against the sun. But the Bremen had two boats out; the Theodore Roosevelt was also dropping boats to where the drift of minute objects struggled, rising and falling on the big, broad Atlantic waves. . . . The Vaterland was no longer following the fight. The whole of that hurrying tumult drove away to the south-eastward, growing smaller and less audible as it passed. One of the airships lay on the water burning, a remote monstrous fount of flames, and far in the south-west appeared first one and then three other German ironclads hurrying in support of their consorts. . . .

6

Steadily the Vaterland soared, and the air-fleet soared with her and came round to head for New York, and the battle became a little thing far away, an incident before breakfast. It dwindled to a string of dark shapes and one smoking yellow flare that presently became a mere indistinct smear upon the horizon and the bright new day, that was at last altogether lost to sight. . . .

So it was that Bert Smallways saw the first fight of the airship and the final fight of those strangest things in the whole history of war: the ironclad battleships, which began their career with the floating batteries of the Emperor Napoleon III. in the Crimean war, and lasted, with an enormous expenditure of human energy and resources, for seventy years. In that space of time the world produced over twelve thousand five hundred of these strange monsters, in schools, in types, in series, each larger and heavier and more deadly than its predecessors. Each in its turn was hailed as the last birth of time, most in their turn were sold for old iron. Only about five per cent of them ever fought in a battle. Some foundered, some went ashore and broke up, several rammed one another by accident and sank. The lives of countless men were spent in their service, the splendid genius and patience of thousands of engineers and inventors, wealth and material beyond estimating; to their account we must put stunted and starved lives on land, millions of children sent to toil unduly, innumerable opportunities of fine living undeveloped and lost. Money had to be found for them at any cost—that was the law of a nation's existence during that strange time. Surely they were the weirdest, most destructive and wasteful megatheria in the whole history of mechanical invention.

And then cheap things of gas and basket-work made an end of them altogether, smiting out of the sky! . . .

Never before had Bert Smallways seen pure destruction, never had he realized the mischief and waste of war. His startled mind rose to the conception, this also is in life. Out of all this fierce torrent of sensation one impression rose and became cardinal—the impression of the men of the Theodore Roosevelt who had struggled in the water after the explosion of the first bomb. "Gaw!" he said at the memory; "it might 'ave been me and Grubb! . . . I suppose you kick about and get the water in your mouf. I don't suppose it lasts long."

He became anxious to see how Kurt was affected by these things. Also he perceived he was hungry. He hesitated towards the door of the cabin and peeped out into the passage. Down forward, near the gangway to the men's mess, stood a little group of air sailors looking at something that was hidden from him in a recess. One of them was in the light diver's costume Bert had already seen in the gas chamber turret, and he was moved to walk along and look at this person more closely and examine the helmet he carried under his arm. But he forgot about the helmet when he got to the recess, because there he found lying on the floor the dead body of the boy who had been killed by a bullet from the Theodore Roosevelt.

Bert had not observed that any bullets at all had reached the Vaterland, or, indeed, imagined himself under fire. He could not understand for a time what had killed the lad, and no one explained to him.

The boy lay just as he had fallen and died, with his jacket torn and scorched, his shoulder-blade smashed and burst away from his body, and all the left side of his body ripped and rent. There was much blood. The sailors stood listening to the man with the helmet, who made explanations and pointed to the round bullet hole in the floor and the smash in the panel of the passage upon which the still vicious missile had spent the residue of its energy. All the faces were grave and earnest; they were the faces of sober, blond, blue-eyed men accustomed to obedience and an orderly life, to whom this waste, wet, painful thing that had been a comrade came almost as strangely as it did to Bert.

A peal of wild laughter sounded down the passage in the direction of the little gallery and something spoke—almost shouted—in German, in tones of exultation.

Other voices at a lower, more respectful pitch replied.

"Der Prinz," said a voice, and all the men became stiffer and less natural. Down the passage appeared a group of figures, Lieutenant Kurt walking in front carrying a packet of papers.

He stopped point-blank when he saw the thing in the recess, and his ruddy face went white. "So!" said he in surprise.

The Prince was following him, talking over his shoulder to Von Winterfeld and the Kapitän. "Eh?" he said to Kurt, stopping in mid-sentence, and followed the gesture of Kurt's hand. He glared at the crumpled object in the recess and seemed to think for a moment.

He made a slight, careless gesture towards the boy's body, and turned to the Kapitän.

"Dispose of that," he said in German, and passed on, finishing his sentence to Von Winterfeld in the same cheerful tone in which it had begun.

7

The deep impression of helplessly drowning men that Bert had brought from the actual fight in the Atlantic mixed itself up inextricably with that of the lordly figure of Prince Karl Albert gesturing aside the dead body of the Vaterland sailor. Hitherto he had rather liked the idea of war as being a jolly, smashing, exciting affair, something like a Bank Holiday

rag on a large scale, and on the whole agreeable and exhilarating. Now
he knew it a little better.

The next day there was added to his growing disillusionment a third
ugly impression, trivial indeed to describe, a mere necessary everyday
incident of a state of war, but very distressing to his urbanized imagination. One writes "urbanized" to express the distinctive gentleness
of the period. It was quite peculiar to the crowded townsmen of that
time, and different altogether from the normal experience of any preceding age, that they never saw anything killed, never encountered,
save through the mitigating media of book or picture, the fact of
lethal violence that underlies all life. Three times in his existence,
and three times only, had Bert seen a dead human being, and he
had never assisted at the killing of anything bigger than a new-born
kitten.

The incident that gave him his third shock was the execution of one
of the men on the Adler for carrying a box of matches. The case was a
flagrant one. The man had forgotten he had it upon him when coming
aboard. Ample notice had been given to everyone of the gravity of this
offence, and notices appeared at numerous points all over the airships.
The man's defence was that he had grown so used to the notices, and
had been so preoccupied with his work, that he hadn't applied them to
himself; he pleaded, in his defence, what is indeed in military affairs
another serious crime, inadvertency. He was tried by his captain, and
the sentence confirmed by wireless telegraphy by the Prince, and it
was decided to make his death an example to the whole fleet. "The
Germans," the Prince declared, "hadn't crossed the Atlantic to go wool
gathering." And in order that this lesson in discipline and obedience
might be visible to everyone, it was determined not to electrocute or
drown, but hang the offender.

Accordingly the air-fleet came clustering round the flagship like carp
in a pond at feeding-time. The Adler hung at the zenith immediately
alongside the flagship. The whole crew of the Vaterland assembled upon
the hanging gallery; the crews of the other airships manned the air-
chambers, that is to say clambered up the outer netting to the upper
sides. The officers appeared upon the machine-gun platforms. Bert
thought it an altogether stupendous sight, looking down, as he was,

upon the entire fleet. Far off below two steamers on the rippled blue water, one British, and the other flying the American flag, seemed the minutest objects, and marked the scale. They were immensely distant. Bert stood on the gallery, curious to see the execution, but uncomfortable because that terrible blond Prince was within a dozen feet of him, glaring terribly, with his arms folded and his heels together in military fashion.

They hung the man from the Adler. They gave him sixty feet of rope, so that he should hang and dangle in the sight of all evil-doers who might be hiding matches or contemplating any kindred disobedience. Bert saw the man standing, a living, reluctant man, no doubt scared and rebellious enough in his heart, but outwardly erect and obedient, on the lower gallery of the Adler about a hundred yards away. Then they had thrust him overboard. . . .

Down he fell, hands and feet extended, until with a jerk he was at the end of the rope. Then he ought to have died and swung edifyingly, but instead a more terrible thing happened; his head came right off, and down the body went spinning to the sea, feeble, grotesque, fantastic, with the head racing it in its fall.

"Ugh!" said Bert, clutching the rail before him, and a sympathetic grunt came from several of the men beside him.

"So!" said the Prince, stiffer and sterner, glared for some seconds, then turned to the gangway up into the airship.

For a long time Bert remained clinging to the railing of the gallery. He was almost physically sick with the horror of this trifling incident. He found it far more dreadful than the battle. He was indeed a very degenerate, latter-day, civilized person.

Late that afternoon Kurt came into the cabin and found him curled up on his locker, and looking very white and miserable. Kurt had also lost something of his pristine freshness.

"Sea-sick?" he asked.

"No!"

"We ought to reach New York this evening. There's a good breeze coming up under our tails. Then we shall see things."

Bert did not answer.

Kurt opened out folding chair and table, and rustled for a time with his maps. Then he fell to thinking darkly. He roused himself presently, and looked at his companion. "What's the matter?" he said.

"Nothing!"

Kurt stared threateningly. "What's the matter?" he repeated.

"I saw them kill that chap. I saw that flying-machine man hit the funnels of the big ironclad. I saw that dead chap in the passage. I seen too much smashing and killing to-day. That's the matter. I don't like it. I didn't know war was this sort of thing. I'm a civilian. I don't like it."

"*I* don't like it," said Kurt. "By Jove, no!"

"I've read about war, and all that, but when you see it, it's different. And I'm gettin' giddy. I'm gettin' giddy. I didn't mind a bit being up in that balloon at first, but all this looking down and floating over things and smashing up people, it's getting on my nerves. See?"

"It'll have to get off again. . . ."

Kurt thought. "You're not the only one. The men are all getting strung up. The flying—that's just flying. Naturally it makes one a little swimmy in the head at first. As for the killing, we've got to be blooded; that's all. We're tame, civilized men. And we've got to get blooded. I suppose there's not a dozen men on the ship who've really seen bloodshed. Nice, quiet, law-abiding Germans they've been so far. . . . Here they are—in for it. They're a bit squeamy now, but you wait till they've got their hands in."

He reflected. "Everybody's getting a bit strung up," he said.

He turned again to his maps. Bert sat crumpled up in the corner, apparently heedless of him. For some time both kept silence.

"What did the Prince want to go and 'ang that chap for?" asked Bert suddenly.

"That was all right," said Kurt, "that was all right. *Quite* right. Here were the orders, plain as the nose on your face, and here was that fool going about with matches———"

"Gaw! I shan't forget that bit in a 'urry," said Bert irrelevantly.

Kurt did not answer him. He was measuring their distance from New York and speculating. "Wonder what the American aeroplanes are like?" he said. "Something like our Drachenflieger. . . . We shall know by to-morrow at this time. . . . I wonder what we shall know. . . . I wonder. Suppose, after all, they put up a fight. . . . Rum sort of fight!"

He whistled softly and mused. Presently he trotted out of the cabin, and later Bert found him in the twilight upon the swinging platform, staring ahead, and speculating about the things that might happen on the morrow. Clouds veiled the sea again, and the long straggling wedge of airships rising and falling as they flew, seemed like a flock of strange new births in a Chaos that had neither earth nor water, but only mist and sky.

SIX

How War Came to New York

I

The City of New York was in the year of the German attack the largest, richest, in many respects the most splendid, and in some the wickedest, city the world had ever seen. She was the supreme type of the City of the Scientific Commercial Age; she displayed its greatness, its power, its ruthless anarchic enterprise, and its social disorganization most strikingly and completely. She had long ousted London from her pride of place as the modern Babylon, she was the centre of the world's finance, the world's trade, and the world's pleasure; and men likened her to the apocalyptic cities of the ancient prophets. She sat drinking up the wealth of the continent, as Rome once drank the wealth of the Mediterranean, and Babylon the wealth of the East. In her streets one found the extremes of magnificence and misery, of civilization and disorder. In one quarter, palaces of marble, laced and crowned with light and flame and flowers, towered up into her marvellous twilights beautiful beyond description; in another, a black and sinister polyglot population sweltered in indescribable congestion in warrens and excavations beyond the power and knowledge of government. Her vice, her crime, her law alike were inspired by a fierce and terrible energy, and like the great cities of medieval Italy, her ways were dark and adventurous with private war.

It was the peculiar shape of Manhattan Island, pressed in by arms of the sea on either side, and incapable of comfortable expansion except along a narrow northward belt, that first gave New York architects their bias for extreme vertical dimensions. Every need was lavishly supplied them—money, material, labour; only space was restricted. To begin with, therefore, they built high perforce. But to do so was to discover a whole new world of architectural beauty, of exquisite ascendant lines, and long after the central congestion had been relieved by tunnels under the sea, four colossal bridges over the East River, and a dozen mono-rail cables east and west, the upward growth went on. In many ways New York and her gorgeous plutocracy repeated Venice; in the magnificence of her architecture, painting, metal work, and sculpture, for example, in the grim intensity of her political method, in her maritime and commercial ascendancy. But she repeated no previous state at all in the lax disorder of her internal administration, a laxity that made vast sections of her area lawless beyond precedent, so that it was possible for whole districts to be impassable while civil war raged between street and street, and for Alsatians to exist in her midst in which the official police never set foot. She was an ethnic whirlpool. The flags of all nations flew in her harbour, and at the climax the yearly coming and going over-seas numbered together upwards of two million human beings. To Europe she was America, to America she was the gateway of the earth. But to tell the story of New York would be to write a social history of the world; saints and martyrs, dreamers and scoundrels, the traditions of a thousand races and a thousand religions, went to her making and throbbed and jostled in her streets. And over all that torrential confusion of men and purposes fluttered that strange flag, the stars and stripes, that meant at once the noblest thing in life and the least noble, that is to say Liberty on the one hand, and on the other the base jealousy the individual self-seeker feels towards the common purpose in the State.

For many generations New York had taken no heed of war, save as a thing that happened far away, that affected prices and supplied the newspapers with exciting headlines and pictures. The New Yorkers felt perhaps even more certainly than the English had done that war in their own land was an impossible thing. In that they shared the delusion of all North America. They felt as secure as spectators at a bullfight; they risked their money perhaps on the result, but that was all. And such ideas of war as the common Americans possessed were derived from the limited, picturesque, adventurous war of the past. They saw war as they saw history, through an iridescent mist, deodorized, scented indeed, with all its essential cruelties tactfully hidden away. They were inclined to regret it as something ennobling, to sigh that it could no longer come into their own private experience. They read with interest, if not with avidity, of their new guns, of their immense and still more immense ironclads, of their incredible and still more incredible explosives, but just what these tremendous engines of destruction might mean for their personal lives never entered their heads. They did not, so far as one can judge, from their contemporary literature, think that they meant anything to their personal lives at all. They thought America was safe amidst all this piling up of explosives. They cheered the flag by habit and tradition, they despised other nations, and whenever there was an international difficulty they were intensely patriotic; that is to say, they were ardently against any native politician who did not threaten and do harsh and uncompromising things to the antagonist people. They were spirited to Asia, spirited to Germany, so spirited to Great Britain that the international attitude of the Mother Country to her great daughter was constantly compared in contemporary caricature to that between a henpecked husband and a vicious young wife. For the rest, they all went about their business and pleasure as if war had died out of the megatherium. . . .

And then suddenly, into a world peacefully busied for the most part upon armaments and the perfection of explosives, war came; came the shock of realizing that the guns were going off, that the masses of inflammable material all over the World were at last ablaze.

2

The immediate effect upon New York of the sudden onset of war was merely to intensify her normal vehemence.

The newspapers and magazines that fed the American mind—for books upon this impatient continent had become simply material for the energy of collectors—were instantly a coruscation of war pictures and of headlines that rose like rockets and burst like shells. To the normal high-strung energy of New York streets was added a touch of war-fever. Great crowds assembled, more especially in the dinner-hour, in Madison Square, about the Farragat monument, to listen to and cheer patriotic speeches, and a veritable epidemic of little flags and buttons swept through these great torrents of swiftly moving young people who poured into New York of a morning by car and mono-rail and subway and train, to toil and ebb home again between the hours of five and seven. It was dangerous not to wear a war button. The splendid music halls of the time sank every topic in patriotism, and evolved scenes of wild enthusiasm, strong men wept at the sight of the national banner sustained by the whole strength of the ballet, and special searchlights and illuminations amazed the watching angels. The churches re-echoed the national enthusiasm in graver key and slower measure, and the aerial and naval preparations on the East River were greaty incommoded by the multitude of excursion steamers which thronged, helpfully cheering about them. The trade in small arms was enormously stimulated, and many overwrought citizens found an immediate relief for their emotions in letting off fireworks of a more or less heroic, dangerous, and national character in the public streets. Small children's air-balloons of the latest model attached to string became a serious check to the pedestrian in Central Park. And amidst scenes of indescribable emotion the Albany legislature in permanent session, with a generous suspension of rules and precedents, passed through both Houses the long-disputed Bill for universal military service in New York State.

Critics of the American character are disposed to consider that up to the actual impact of the German attack the people of New York dealt altogether too much with the war as if it was a political demonstration. Little or no damage, they urge, was done to either the German or Japanese forces by the wearing of buttons, the waving of small flags, the fireworks or the songs. They forgot that under the conditions of warfare a century of science had brought about, the non-military section of the population could do no serious damage in any form to their enemies, and that there was no reason, therefore, why they should not do as they did. The balance of military efficiency was shifting back from the many to the few, from the common to the specialized. The days when the emotional infantryman decided battles had passed by for ever. War had become a matter of apparatus, of special training, and skill of the most intricate kind. It had become undemocratic. And

whatever the value of the popular excitement, there can be no denying
that the small regular establishment of the United States Government,
confronted by this totally unexpected emergency of an armed invasion
from Europe, acted with vigour, science, and imagination. They were
taken by surprise so far as the diplomatic situation was concerned,
and their equipment for building either navigables or aeroplanes was
contemptible in comparison with the huge German parks. Still they set
to work at once to prove to the world that the spirit that had created the
Monitor and the Southern submarines of 1864 was not dead. The chief
of the aeronautic establishment near West Point was Cabot Sinclair, and
he allowed himself but one single moment of the posturing that was so
universal in that democratic time. "We have chosen our epitaphs," he
said to a reporter, "and we are going to have, 'They did all they could.'
Now run away!"

The curious thing is that they did do all they could; there is no
exception known. Their only defect indeed was a defect of style.

One of the most striking facts historically about this war, and the
one that makes the complete separation that had arisen between the
methods of warfare and the necessity of democratic support, is the
effectual secrecy of the Washington authorities about their airships.
They did not bother to confide a single fact of their preparations
to the public. They did not even condescend to talk to Congress.
They burked and suppressed every inquiry. The war was fought by the
President and the Secretaries of State in an entirely autocratic manner.
Such publicity as they sought was merely to anticipate and prevent
inconvenient agitation to defend particular points. They realized that
the chief danger in aerial warfare from an excitable and intelligent public
would be a clamour for local airships and aeroplanes to defend local
interests. This, with such resources as they possessed, might lead to a
fatal division and distribution of the national forces. Particularly they
feared that they might be forced into a premature action to defend
New York. They realized with prophetic insight that this would be the
particular advantage the Germans would seek. So they took great pains
to direct the popular mind towards defensive artillery, and to divert it
from any thought of aerial battle. Their real preparations they masked
beneath ostensible ones. There was at Washington a large reserve of

naval guns, and these were distributed rapidly, conspicuously, and with much press attention, among the eastern cities. They were mounted upon rough adaptations of the Doan swivel, which at that time gave the maximum vertical range to a heavy gun. Much of this artillery was still unmounted, and nearly all of it was unprotected when the German air-fleet reached New York. And down in the crowded streets when that occurred, the readers of the New York papers were regaling themselves with wonderful and wonderfully illustrated acounts of such matters as:

THE SECRET OF THE THUNDERBOLT.

AGED SCIENTIST PERFECTS ELECTRIC GUN TO ELOCTROCUTE AIR-SHIP CREWS BY UPWARD LIGHTNING.

WASHINGTON ORDERS FIVE HUNDRED.

WAR SECRETARY LODGE DELIGHTED.

SAYS THEY WILL SUIT THE GERMANS DOWN TO THE GROUND.

PRESIDENT PUBLICLY APPLAUDS THIS MERRY QUIP.

3

The German fleet reached New York in advance of the news of the American naval disaster. It reached New York in the late afternoon, and was first seen by watchers at Ocean Grove and Long Branch coming swiftly out of the southward sea and going away to the north-west. The flagship passed almost vertically over the Sandy Hook observation station, rising rapidly as it did so, and in a few minutes all New York was vibrating to the Staten Island guns.

Several of these guns, and especially that at Giffords and the one on Beacon Hill above Matawan, were remarkably well handled. The former, at a distance of five miles, and with an elevation of six thousand feet, sent a shell to burst so close to the Vaterland that a pane of the Prince's forward window was smashed by a fragment. This sudden explosion made Bert tuck in his head with the celerity of a startled tortoise. The whole air-fleet immediately went up steeply to a height of about twelve thousand feet, and at that level passed unscathed over the ineffectual guns. The airships lined out as they moved forward into the form of a flattened V, with its apex towards the city, and with the flagship going highest at the apex. The two ends of the V passed over Plumfield and Jamaica Bay respectively, and the Prince directed his course a little to the east of the Narrows, soared over the Upper Bay, and came to rest above Jersey city in a position that dominated lower New York. There the monsters hung, large and wonderful in the evening light, serenely regardless of the occasional rocket explosions and flashing shell-bursts in the lower air.

It was a pause of mutual inspection. For a time naïve humanity swamped the conventions of warfare altogether; the interest of the millions below and of the thousands above alike was spectacular. The evening was unexpectedly fine—only a few thin level bands of clouds at seven or eight thousand feet broke its luminous clarity. The wind had dropped; it was an evening infinitely peaceful and still. The heavy concussions of the distant guns and those incidental harmless pyrotechnics at the level of the clouds seemed to have as little to do with killing and force, terror and submission, as a salute at a naval review. Below, every point of vantage bristled with spectators, the roofs of the towering buildings, the public squares, the active ferry boats, and every favourable street intersection had its crowds: all the river piers were dense with people, the Battery Park was solid black with east-side population, and every position of advantage in Central Park and along Riverside Drive had its peculiar and characteristic assembly from the adjacent streets. The footways of the great bridges over the East River were also closely packed and blocked. Everywhere shopkeepers had left their shops, men their work, and women and children their homes, to come out and see the marvel.

"It beat," they declared, "the newspapers."

And from above, many of the occupants of the airships stared with an equal curiosity. No city in the world was ever so finely placed as New York, so magnificently cut up by sea and bluff and river, so admirably disposed to display the tall effects of buildings, the complex immensities of bridges and mono-railways and feats of engineering. London, Paris,

Berlin, were shapeless, low agglomerations beside it. Its port reached to its heart like Venice, and, like Venice, it was obvious, dramatic, and proud. Seen from above it was alive with crawling trains and cars, and at a thousand points it was already breaking into quivering light. New York was altogether at its best that evening, its splendid best.

"Gaw! *What* a place!" said Bert.

It was so great, and in its collective effect so pacifically magnificent, that to make war upon it seemed incongruous beyond measure, like laying siege to the National Gallery or attacking respectable people in an hotel dining-room with battle-axe and mail. It was in its entirety so large, so complex, so delicately immense, that to bring it to the issue of warfare was like driving a crowbar into the mechanism of a clock. And the fish-like shoal of great airships hovering light and sunlit above, filling the sky, seemed equally remote from the ugly forcefulness of war. To Kurt, to Smallways, to I know not how many more of the people in the air-fleet came the distinctest apprehension of these incompatibilities. But in the head of the Prince Karl Albert were the vapours of romance: he was a conqueror, and this was the enemy's city. The greater the city, the greater the triumph. No doubt he had a time of tremendous exultation and sensed beyond all precedent the joys of power that night.

There came an end at last to that pause. Some wireless communications had failed of a satisfactory ending, and fleet and city remembered they were hostile powers. "Look!" cried the multitude; "Look!"

"What are they doing?"

"What?" . . . Down through the twilight sank five attacking airships, one to the Navy Yard on East River, one to City Hall, two over the great business buildings of Wall Street and Lower Broadway, one to the Brooklyn Bridge, dropping from among their fellows through the danger zone from the distant guns smoothly and rapidly to a safe proximity to the city masses. At that descent all the cars in the streets stopped with dramatic suddenness, and all the lights that had been coming on in the streets and houses went out again. For the City Hall had awakened and was conferring by telephone with the Federal command and taking measures for defence. The City Hall was asking for airships, refusing to surrender as Washington advised, and developing into a centre of intense emotion, of hectic activity. Everywhere and hastily the police began to clear the assembled crowds. "Go to your homes," they said; and the word was passed from mouth to mouth, "There's going to be trouble." A chill of apprehension ran through the city, and men hurrying in the unwonted darkness across City Hill Park and Union Square came upon the dim forms of soldiers and guns, and were challenged and sent back. In half an hour New York had passed from serene sunset and gaping admiration to a troubled and threatening twilight.

The first loss of life occurred in the panic rush from Brooklyn Bridge as the airship approached it.

With the cessation of the traffic an unusual stillness came upon New York, and the disturbing concussions of the futile defending guns on the hills about grew more and more audible. At last these ceased also. A pause of further negotiation followed. People sat in darkness, sought counsel from telephones that were dumb. Then into the expectant hush came a great crash and uproar, the breaking down of the Brooklyn Bridge, the rifle fire from the Navy Yard, and the bursting of bombs in Wall Street and the City Hall. New York as a whole could do nothing, could understand nothing. New York in the darkness peered and listened to these distant sounds until presently they died away as suddenly as they had begun. "What could be happening?" They asked it in vain.

A long vague period intervened, and people looking out of the windows of upper rooms discovered the dark hulls of German airships, gliding slowly and noiselessly, quite close at hand. Then quietly the electric lights came on again, and an uproar of nocturnal newsvendors began in the streets.

The units of that vast and varied population bought and learnt what had happened; there had been a fight, and New York had hoisted the white flag. . . .

4

The lamentable incidents that followed the surrender of New York seem now in the retrospect to be but the necessary and inevitable consequence of the clash of modern appliances and social conditions produced by the scientific century on the one hand, and the tradition of a crude, romantic patriotism on the other. At first people received the fact with an irresponsible detachment, much as they would have received the slowing down of the train in which they were travelling or the erection of a public monument by the city to which they belonged.

"We have surrendered. Dear me! *have* we?" was rather the manner in which the first news was met. They took it in the same spectacular spirit they had displayed at the first apparition of the air-fleet. Only slowly was this realization of a capitulation suffused with the flush of patriotic passion, only with reflection did they make any personal application. "*We* have surrendered!" came later; "in us America is defeated." Then they began to burn and tingle.

The newspapers which were issued about one in the morning contained no particulars of the terms upon which New York had yielded— nor did they give any intimation of the quality of the brief conflict that had preceded the capitulation. The later issues remedied these deficiencies. There came the explicit statement of the agreement to victual the German airships, to supply the complement of explosives to replace those employed in the fight and in the destruction of the North Atlantic fleet, to pay the enormous ransom of forty million dollars, and to surrender the flotilla in the East River. There came, too, longer and longer descriptions of the smashing up of the City Hall and the Navy Yard, and people began to realize faintly what those brief minutes of uproar had meant. They read the tale of men blown to bits, of futile soldiers in that localized battle fighting against hope amidst an indescribable wreckage, of flags hauled down by weeping men. And these strange nocturnal editions contained also the first brief cables from Europe of the fleet disaster, the North Atlantic fleet for which New York had always felt an especial pride and solicitude. Slowly, hour by hour, the collective consciousness woke up, the tide of patriotic astonishment and humiliation came flowing in. America had come upon disaster; suddenly New York discovered herself, with amazement giving place to wrath unspeakable, a conquered city under the hand of her conqueror.

As that fact shaped itself in the public mind, there sprang up, as flames spring up, an angry repudiation. "No!" cried New York, waking in the dawn. "No! I am not defeated. This is a dream."

Before day broke the swift American anger was running through all the city, through every soul in those contagious millions. Before it took action, before it took shape, the men in the airships could feel the gigantic insurgence of emotion, as cattle and natural creatures feel, it is said, the coming of an earthquake. The newspapers of the Knype group first gave the thing words and a formula. "We do not agree," they said simply. "We have been betrayed!" Men took that up everywhere, it passed from mouth to mouth, at every street corner under the paling lights of dawn orators stood unchecked, calling upon the spirit of America to arise, making the shame a personal reality to everyone who heard. To Bert, listening five hundred feet above, it seemed that the city which had at first produced only confused noises, was now humming like a hive of bees—of very angry bees.

After the smashing of the City Hall and Post-Office, the white flag had been hoisted from a tower of the old Park Row Building, and thither had gone Mayor O'Hagan, urged thither indeed by the terror-stricken property owners of lower New York, to negotiate the capitulation with Von Winterfeld. The Vaterland having dropped the secretary by a rope ladder, remained hovering, circling very slowly above the great buildings, old and new, that clustered round City Hall Park, while the Helmholz, which had done the fighting there, rose overhead to a height of perhaps two thousand feet. So Bert had a near view of all that occurred in that central place. The City Hall and Court House, the Post-Office and a mass of buildings on the west side of Broadway, had been badly damaged, and the three former were a heap of blackened ruins. In the case of the first two the loss of life had not been considerable, but a great multitude of workers, including many girls and women, had been caught in the destruction of the Post-Office, and a little army of volunteers with white badges entered behind the firemen, bringing out the often still living bodies, for the most part frightfully charred, and carrying them into the big Monson building close at hand. Everywhere the busy firemen were directing their bright streams of water upon the smouldering masses: their hose lay about the square, and long cordons of police held back the gathering black masses of people, chiefly from the east side, from these central activities.

In violent and extraordinary contrast with this scene of destruction, close at hand were the huge newspaper establishments of Park Row. They were all alight and working; they had not been abandoned even while the actual bomb throwing was going on, and now staff and presses were vehemently active, getting out the story, the immense and dreadful story of the night, developing comment and, in most cases, spreading the idea of resistance under the very noses of the airships. For a long time Bert could not imagine what these callously active offices could be, then he detected the noise of the presses and emitted his "Gaw!"

Beyond these newspaper buildings again, and partially hidden by the arches of the old Elevated Railway of New York (long since converted into a mono-rail), there was another cordon of police and a sort of encampment of ambulances and doctors, busy with the dead and wounded who had been killed early in the night by the panic upon Brooklyn Bridge. All this he saw in the perspectives of a bird's-eye view, as things happening in a big, irregular-shaped pit below him, between cliffs of high building. Northward he looked along the steep cañon of Broadway, down whose length at intervals crowds were assembling about excited speakers; and when he lifted his eyes he saw the chimneys and cable-stacks and roof spaces of New York, and everywhere now over these the watching, debating people clustered, except where the fires raged and the jets of water flew. Everywhere, too, were flagstaffs devoid of flags; one white sheet drooped and flapped and drooped again over the Park Row buildings. And upon the lurid lights, the festering movement and intense shadows of this strange scene, there was breaking now the cold, impartial dawn.

For Bert Smallways all this was framed in the frame of the open port-hole. It was a pale, dim world outside that dark and tangible rim. All night he had clutched at that rim, jumped and quivered at explosions, and watched phantom events. Now he had been high and now low; now almost beyond hearing, now flying close to crashings and shouts and outcries. He had seen airships flying low and swift over darkened and groaning streets; watched great buildings, suddenly red-lit amidst the shadows, crumple at the smashing impacts of bombs; witnessed for the first time in his life the grotesque, swift onset of insatiable conflagrations. From it all he felt detached, disembodied. The Vaterland did not even fling a bomb; she watched and. ruled. Then down they had come at last to hover over City Hall Park, and it had crept in upon his mind, chillingly, terrifying, that these illuminated black masses were great offices afire, and that the going to and fro of minute dim spectres of lantern-lit grey and white was a harvesting of the wounded and the dead. As the light grew clearer he began to understand more and more what these crumpled black things signified.

He had watched hour after hour since first New York had risen out of the blue indistinctness of the landfall. With the daylight he experienced an intolerable fatigue.

He lifted weary eyes to the pink flush in the sky, yawned immensely, and crawled back whispering to himself across the cabin to the locker. He did not so much lie down upon that as fall upon it and instantly become asleep.

There, hours after, sprawling undignified and sleeping profoundly, Kurt found him, a very image of the democratic mind confronted with the problems of a time too complex for its apprehension. His face was pale and indifferent, his mouth wide open, and he snored. He snored disagreeably.

Kurt regarded him for a moment with a mild distaste. Then he kicked his ankle.

"Wake up!" he said to Smallways' stare, "and lie down decent."

Bert sat up and rubbed his eyes.

"Any more fightin' yet?" he asked.

"No," said Kurt, and sat down, a tired man.

"Gott!" he cried presently, rubbing his hands over his face, "but I'd like a cold bath! I've been looking for stray bullet holes in the air-chambers all night until now." He yawned. "I must sleep. You'd better clear out, Smallways. I can't stand you here this morning. You're so infernally ugly and useless. Have you had your rations? No! Well, go in and get 'em, and don't come back, Stick in the gallery. . . ."

5

So Bert, slightly refreshed by coffee and sleep, resumed his helpless co-operation in the War in the Air. He went down into the little gallery as the lieutenant had directed, and clung to the rail at the extreme end beyond the lookout man, trying to seem as inconspicuous and harmless a fragment of life as possible.

A wind was rising rather strongly from the southeast. It obliged the Vaterland to come about in that direction, and made her roll a great deal as she went to and from over Manhattan Island. Away in the north-west clouds gathered. The throb-throb of her slow screw working against the breeze was much more perceptible than when she was going full speed ahead; and the friction of the wind against the underside of the gas-chamber drove a series of shallow ripples along it and made a faint flapping sound like, but fainter than, the beating of ripples under the stem of a boat. She was stationed over the temporary City Hall in the Park Row building, and every now and then she would descend to resume communication with the mayor and with Washington. But the restlessness of the Prince would not suffer him to remain for long in any one place. Now he would circle over the Hudson and East River; now he would go up high, as if to peer away into the blue distances; once he ascended so swiftly and so far that mountain sickness overtook him and the crew and forced him down again; and Bert shared the dizziness and nausea.

The swaying view varied with these changes of altitude. Now they would be low and close, and he would distinguish in that steep, unusual perspective, windows, doors, street and sky signs, people and the minutest details, and watch the enigmatical behaviour of crowds and clusters upon the roofs and in the streets; then as they soared the details would shrink, the sides of streets draw together, the view widen, the people cease to be significant. At the highest the effect was that of a concave relief map; Bert saw the dark and crowded land everywhere intersected by shining waters, saw the Hudson River like a spear of silver, and Lower Island Sound like a shield. Even to Bert's unphilosophical mind the contrast of city below and fleet above pointed an opposition, the opposition of the adventurous American's tradition and character with German order and discipline. Below, the immense buildings, tremendous and fine as they were, seemed like the giant trees of a jungle fighting for life; their picturesque magnificence was as planless as the chances of crag and gorge, their casualty enhanced by the smoke and confusion of still unsubdued and spreading conflagrations. In the sky

soared the German airships like beings in a different, entirely more
orderly world, all oriented to the same angle of the horizon, uniform
in build and appearance, moving accurately with one purpose as a pack
of wolves will move, distributed with the most precise and effectual
co-operation.

It dawned upon Bert that hardly a third of the fleet was visible.
The others had gone upon errands he could not imagine, beyond the
compass of that great circle of earth and sky. He wondered, but there
was no one to ask. As the day wore on, about a dozen reappeared in
the east with their stores replenished from the flotilla and towing a
number of Drachenflieger. Towards afternoon the weather thickened,
driving clouds appeared in the south-west and ran together and seemed
to engender more clouds, and the wind came round into that quarter
and blew stronger. Towards the evening the wind became a gale into
which the now tossing airships had to beat.

All that day the Prince was negotiating with Washington, while his
detached scouts sought far and wide over the Eastern States for anything
resembling an aeronautic park. A squadron of twenty airships detached
overnight had dropped out of the air upon Niagara and was holding
the town and power works.

Meanwhile the insurrectionary movement in the giant city grew
uncontrollable. In spite of five great fires already involving many acres,
and spreading steadily, New York was still not satisfied that she was
beaten.

At first the rebellious spirit below found vent only in isolated shouts,
street-crowd speeches, and newspaper suggestions; then it found much
more definite expression in the appearance in the morning sunlight
of American flags at point after point above the architectural cliffs of
the city. It is quite possible that in many cases this spirited display of
bunting by a city already surrendered was the outcome of the innocent
informality of the American mind, but it is also undeniable that in
many it was a deliberate indication that the people "felt wicked."

The German sense of correctitude was deeply shocked by this outbreak. The Graf von Winterfeld immediately communicated with the
mayor, and pointed out the irregularity, and the fire look-out stations
were instructed in the matter. The New York police was speedily hard

at work, and a foolish contest in full swing between impassioned citizens resolved to keep the flag flying and irritated and worried officers instructed to pull it down.

The trouble became acute at last in the streets above Columbia University. The captain of the airship watching this quarter seems to have stooped to lasso and drag from its staff a flag hoisted upon Morgan Hall. As he did so a volley of rifle and revolver shots was fired from the upper windows of the huge apartment building that stands between the University and Riverside Drive.

Most of these were ineffectual, but two or three perforated gas-chambers, and one smashed the hand and arm of a man upon the forward platform. The sentinel on the lower gallery immediately replied, and the machine gun on the shield of the eagle let fly and promptly stopped any further shots. The airship rose and signalled the flagship and City Hall, police and militiamen were directed at once to the spot, and this particular incident closed.

But hard upon that came the desperate attempt of a party of young clubmen from New York, who, inspired by patriotic and adventurous imaginations, slipped off in half-a-dozen motor-cars to Beacon Hill, and set to work with remarkable vigour to improvise a fort about the Doan swivel gun that had been placed there. They found it still in the hands of the disgusted gunners, who had been ordered to cease fire at the capitulation, and it was easy to infect these men with their own spirit. They declared their gun hadn't had half a chance, and were burning to show what it could do. Directed by the newcomers, they made a trench and bank about the mounting of the piece, and constructed flimsy shelter-pits of corrugated iron.

They were actually loading the gun when they were observed by the airship Preussen, and the shell they succeeded in firing before the bombs of the latter smashed them and their crude defences to fragments, burst over the middle gas-chambers of the Bingen, and brought her to earth, disabled, upon Staten Island. She was badly deflated, and dropped among trees, over which her empty central gas-bags spread in canopies and festoons. Nothing, however, had caught fire, and her men were speedily at work upon her repair. They behaved with a confidence that verged upon indiscretion. While most of them commenced patching the tears of the membrane, half-a-dozen of them started off for the nearest road in search of a gas main, and presently found themselves prisoners in the hands of a hostile crowd. Close at hand was a number of villa residences, whose occupants speedily developed from an unfriendly curiosity to aggression. At that time the police control of the large polyglot population of Staten Island had become very lax, and scarcely a household but had its rifle or pistols and ammunition. These were presently produced, and after two or three misses one of the men at work was hit in the foot. Thereupon the Germans left their sewing and mending, took cover among the trees, and replied.

The crackling of shots speedily brought the Preussen and Kiel on the scene, and with a few hand grenades they made short work of every villa within a mile. A number of non-combatant American men, women and children were killed and the actual assailants driven off. For a time the repairs went on in peace under the immediate protection of these two airships. Then when they returned to their quarters an intermittent sniping and fighting round the stranded Bingen was resumed, and went on all the afternoon, and merged at last in the general combat of the evening. . . .

About eight the Bingen was rushed by an armed mob, and all its defenders killed after a fierce, disorderly struggle.

The difficulty of the Germans in both these cases came from the impossibility of landing any efficient force, or, indeed, any force at all from the air-fleet. The airships were quite unequal to the transport of any adequate landing parties; their complement of men was just sufficient to manœuvre and fight them in the air. From above they could inflict immense damage; they could reduce any organized Government to a capitulation in the briefest space, but they could not disarm, much less could they occupy, the surrendered areas below. They had to trust to the pressure upon the authorities below of a threat to renew the bombardment. It was their sole resource. No doubt, with a highly organized and undamaged Government and a homogeneous and well-disciplined people that would have sufficed to keep the peace. But this was not the American case. Not only was the New York Government a weak one, and insufficiently provided with police, but the destruction of the City Hall and Post-Office and other central ganglia had hopelessly disorganized the co-operation of part with part. The street cars and railways had ceased; the telephone service was out of gear and only worked intermittently. The Germans had struck at the head, and the head was conquered and stunned—only to release the body from its rule. New York had become a headless monster, no longer capable of collective submission. Everywhere it lifted itself rebelliously; everywhere authorities and officials, left to their own initiative, were joining in the arming and flag-hoisting and excitement of that afternoon.

6

The disintegrating truce gave place to a definite general breach with the assassination of the Wetterhorn—for that is the only possible word for the act—above Union Square, and not a mile away from the exemplary ruins of City Hall. This occurred late in the afternoon, between five and six. By that time the weather had changed very much for the worse, and the operations of the airships were embarrassed by the necessity they were under of keeping head on to the gusts. A series of squalls, with hail and thunder, followed one another from the south by south-east, and in order to avoid these as much as possible, the air-fleet came low over the houses, diminishing its range of observation and exposing itself to a rifle attack.

Overnight there had been a gun placed in Union Square. It had never been mounted, much less fired, and in the darkness after the surrender it was taken with its supplies and put out of the way under the arches of the great Dexter building. Here late in the morning it was remarked by a number of patriotic spirits. They set to work to hoist and mount it inside the upper floors of the place. They made, in fact, a masked battery behind the decorous office blinds, and there lay in wait as simply excited as children, until at last the stem of the luckless Wetterhorn appeared, beating and rolling at a quarter speed over the recently constructed pinnacles of Tiffany's. Promptly that one-gun battery unmasked. The airship's look-out man must have seen the whole of the tenth story of the Dexter building crumble out and smash in the street below to discover the black muzzle looking out from the shadows behind. Then perhaps the shell hit him.

The gun fired two shells before the frame of the Dexter building collapsed, and each shell raked the Wetterhorn from stem to stern. They smashed her exhaustively. She crumpled up like a can that has been kicked by a heavy boot, her forepart came down in the square, and the rest of her length, with a great snapping and twisting of shafts and stays, descended, collapsing athwart Tammany Hall and the streets towards Second Avenue. Her gas escaped to mix with the air, and the air of her rent balloonette poured into her deflating gas chambers. Then with an immense impact she exploded. . . .

The Vaterland at that time was beating up to the south of the City Hall from over the ruins of the Brooklyn Bridge, and the reports of the gun, followed by the first crashes of the collapsing Dexter buildings, brought Kurt and Smallways to the cabin porthole. They were in time to see the flash of the exploding gun, and then they were first flattened against the window and then rolled head over heels across the floor of the cabin by the air wave of the explosion. The Vaterland bounded like a football some one has kicked, and when they looked out again Union Square was small and remote and shattered, as though some cosmically vast giant had rolled over it. The buildings to the east of it were ablaze at a dozen points under the flaming tatters and warping skeleton of the airship, and all the roofs and walls were ridiculously askew and crumbling as one looked. "Gaw!" said Bert. "What's happened? Look at the people."

But before Kurt could produce an explanation, the shrill bells of the airship were ringing to quarters, and he had to go. Bert hesitated and stepped thoughtfully into the passage, looking back at the window as he did so. He was knocked off his feet at once by the Prince, who was rushing headlong from his cabin to the central magazine.

Bert had a momentary impression of the great figure of the Prince, white with rage, bristling with gigantic anger, his huge fist swinging. "Blut und Eisen!" cried the Prince as one who swears. "Oh! Blut und Eisen!"

Someone fell over Bert—something in the manner of falling suggested Von Winterfeld—and someone else paused and kicked him spitefully and hard. Then he was sitting up in the passage, rubbing a freshly bruised cheek and readjusting the bandage he still wore on his head. "Dem that Prince," said Bert, indignant beyond measure. " 'E 'asn't the menners of a 'og!"

He stood up, collected his wits for a minute, and then went slowly towards the gangway of the little gallery. As he did so he heard noises suggestive of the return of the Prince. He shot into his cabin like a rabbit into its burrow, just in time to escape that shouting terror.

He shut the door, waited until the passage was still, then went across to the window and looked out. A drift of cloud made the prospect of the streets and squares hazy, and the rolling of the airship swung the picture up and down. A few people were running to and fro, but for the most part the aspect of the district was desertion. The streets seemed to broaden out, they became clearer, and the little dots that were people larger as the Vaterland came down again. Presently she was swaying along above the lower end of Broadway. The dots below, Bert saw, were not running now, but standing and looking up. Then suddenly they were all running again.

Something had dropped from the aeroplane, something that looked small and flimsy. It hit the pavement near a big archway just underneath Bert. A little man was sprinting along the sidewalk within half-a-dozen yards, and two or three others and one woman were bolting across the roadway. They were odd little figures, so very small were they above the heads, so very active about the elbows and legs. It was really funny to see their legs going. Fore-shortened humanity has no dignity. The little man on the pavement jumped comically—no doubt with terror—as the bomb fell beside him.

Then blinding flames squirted out in all directions from the point of impact, and the little man who had jumped became, for an instant, a flash of fire and vanished—vanished absolutely. The people running out into the road took preposterous clumsy leaps, then flopped down and lay still, with their torn clothes smouldering into flame. Then pieces of the archway began to drop, and the lower masonry of the building to fall in with the rumbling sound of coals being shot into a cellar. A faint screaming reached Bert, and then a crowd of people ran out into the street, one man limping and gesticulating awkwardly. He halted, and went back towards the building. A falling mass of brickwork hit him and sent him sprawling to lie still and crumpled where he fell. Dust and black smoke came pouring into the street, and were presently shot with red flame. . . .

In this manner the massacre of New York began. She was the first of the great cities of the Scientific Age to suffer by the enormous powers and grotesque limitations of aerial warfare. She was wrecked as in the previous century endless barbaric cities had been bombarded, because she was at once too strong to be occupied, and too undisciplined and proud to surrender in order to escape destruction. Given the circumstances the thing had to be done. It was impossible for the Prince to desist and own himself defeated, and it was impossible to subdue the city except by largely destroying it. The catastrophe was the logical outcome of the situation created by the application of science to warfare. It was unavoidable that great cities should be destroyed. In spite of his intense exasperation with his dilemma, the Prince sought to be moderate even in massacre. He tried to give a memorable lesson with the minimum waste of life and the minimum expenditure of explosives. For that night he proposed only the wrecking of Broadway. He directed the air-fleet to move in column over the route of this thoroughfare, dropping bombs, the Vaterland leading. And so our Bert Smallways became a participant in one of the most cold-blooded slaughters in the world's history, in which men who were neither excited nor, except for the remotest chance of a bullet, in any danger, poured death and destruction upon homes and crowds below.

He clung to the frame of the porthole as the airship tossed and swayed, and stared down through the light rain that now drove before the wind, into the twilight streets, watching people running out of the houses, watching buildings collapse and fires begin. As the airships sailed along they smashed up the city as a child will shatter its cities of brick and card. Below, they left ruins and blazing conflagrations, and heaped and scattered dead; men, women, and children mixed together as though they had been no more than Moors, or Zulus, or Chinese. Lower New York was soon a furnace of crimson flames, from which there was no escape. Cars, railways, ferries, all had ceased, and never a light led the way of the distracted fugitives in that dusky confusion but the light of burning. He had glimpses of what it must mean to be down there—glimpses. And it came to him suddenly as an incredible discovery, that such disasters were not only possible now in this strange, gigantic, foreign New York, but also in London—in Bun Hill! that the little island in the silver seas was at the end of its immunity, that nowhere in the world any more was there a place left where a Smallways might lift his head proudly and vote for war and a spirited foreign policy, and go secure from such horrible things.

SEVEN

The Vaterland is Disabled

I

And then above the flames of Manhattan Island came a battle, the first battle in the air. The Americans had realized the price their waiting game must cost, and struck with all the strength they had, if haply they might still save New York from this mad Prince of Blood and Iron, and from fire and death.

They came down upon the Germans on the wings of a great gale in the twilight, amidst thunder and rain. They came from the yards of Washington and Philadelphia, full tilt in two squadrons, and but for one sentinel airship hard by Trenton, the surprise would have been complete.

The Germans, sick and weary with destruction, and half empty of ammunition, were facing up into the weather when the news of this on-set reached them. New York they had left behind to the southeastward, a darkened city with one hideous red scar of flames. All the airships rolled and staggered, bursts of hail-storm bore them down and forced them to fight their way up again; the air had become bitterly cold. The Prince was on the point of issuing orders to drop earthward and trail copper lightning chains when the news of the aeroplane attack came to him. He faced his fleet in line abreast south, had the Drachenflieger manned and held ready to cast loose, and ordered a general ascent into the freezing clearness above the wet and darkness.

The news of what was imminent came slowly to Bert's perceptions. He was standing in the mess-room at the time, and the evening rations were being served out. He had resumed Butteridge's coat and gloves, and, in addition, he had wrapped his blanket about him. He was dipping his bread into his soup and biting off big mouthfuls. His legs were wide apart, and he leant against the partition in order to steady himself amidst the pitching and oscillation of the airship. The men about him looked tired and depressed; a few talked, but most were sullen and thoughtful, and one or two were air-sick. They all seemed to share the peculiarly outcast feeling that had followed the murders of the evening, a sense of a land beneath them and an outraged humanity grown more hostile than the sea.

Then the news lit them. A red-faced sturdy man, a man with light eyelashes and a scar, appeared in the doorway and shouted something in German that manifestly startled everyone. Bert felt the shock of the altered tone although he could not understand a word that was said. The announcement was followed by a pause, and then a great outcry of questions and suggestions. Even the air-sick men flushed and spoke. For some minutes the mess-room was Bedlam, and then, as if it were a confirmation of the news, came the shrill ringing of the bells that called the men to their posts.

Bert, with pantomime suddenness, found himself alone.

"What's up?" he said, though he partly guessed.

He stayed only to gulp down the remainder of his soup, and then ran along the swaying passage and, clutching tightly, down the ladder to the little gallery. The weather hit him like cold water squirted from a hose. The airship engaged in some new feat of atmospheric jiu-jitsu. He drew his blanket closer about him, clutching with one straining hand. He found himself tossing in a wet twilight, with nothing to be seen but mist pouring past him. Above him the airship was warm with lights and busy with the movements of men going to their quarters. Then abruptly the lights went out, and the Vaterland with bounds and twists and strange writhings was fighting her way up the air.

He had a glimpse, as the Vaterland rolled over, of some large buildings burning close below them, a quivering acanthus of flames, and then he saw indistinctly through the driving weather another airship wallowing along like a porpoise, and also working up. Presently the clouds swallowed her again for a time, and then she came back to sight as a dark and whale-like monster, amidst streaming weather. The air was full of flappings and pipings, of void, gusty shouts and noises; it buffeted him and confused him; ever and again his attention became rigid—a blind and deafening balancing and clutching.

"Wow!"

Something fell past him out of the vast darknesses above and vanished into the tumults below, going obliquely downward. It was a German Drachenflieger. The thing was going so fast he had but an instant apprehension of the dark figure of the aeronaut crouched together clutching at his wheel. It might be a manœuvre, but it looked like a catasrophe.

"Gaw!" said Bert.

"Pup-pup-pup," went a gun somewhere in the mirk ahead, and suddenly and quite horribly the Vaterland lurched, and Bert and the sentinels were clinging to the rails for dear life. "Bang!" came a vast impact out of the zenith, followed by another huge roll, and all about him the tumbled clouds flashed red and lurid in response to flashes unseen, revealing immense gulfs. The rail went right overhead, and he was hanging loose in the air holding on to it.

For a time Bert's whole mind and being was given to clutching. "I'm going into the cabin," he said, as the airship righted again and brought back the gallery floor to his feet. He began to make his way cautiously towards the ladder. "Whee-wow!" he cried, as the whole gallery reared itself up forward and then plunged down like a desperate horse.

Crack! Bang! Bang! Bang! And then hard upon this little rattle of shots and bombs came, all about him, enveloping him, engulfing him, immense and overwhelming, a quivering white blaze of lightning and a thunder-clap that was like the bursting of a world.

Just for an instant before that explosion, the universe seemed to be standing still in a shadowless glare.

It was then he saw the American aeroplane. He saw it in the light of the flash as a thing altogether motionless. Even its screw appeared still, and its men were rigid dolls. (For it was so near he could see the men upon it quite distinctly.) Its stern was tilting down, and the whole machine was heeling over. It was of the Colt-Coburn-Langley pattern, with double uptilted wings and the screw ahead, and the men were in a boat-like body netted over. From this very light long body, magazine guns projected on either side. One thing that was strikingly odd and wonderful in that moment of revelation was that the upper wing was burning *downward* with a reddish, smoky flame. But this was not the most wonderful thing about this apparition. The most wonderful thing was that it and a German airship five hundred yards below were threaded as it were on the lightning flash, which turned out of its path as if to take them, and that out from the corners and projecting points of its huge wings everywhere, little branching thorn trees of lightning were streaming.

Like a picture Bert saw these things, a picture a little blurred by a thin veil of wind-torn mist.

The crash of the thunder-clap followed the flash and seemed a part of it, so that it is hard to say whether Bert was the rather deafened or blinded in that instant.

And then darkness, utter darkness, and a heavy report and a thin small sound of voices that went wailing downward into the abyss below.

2

There followed upon these things a long, deep swaying of the airship, and then Bert began a struggle to get back to his cabin. He was drenched and cold and terrified beyond measure, and now more than a little air-sick. It seemed to him that the strength had gone out of his knees and hands, and that his feet had become icily slippery over the metal they trod upon. But that was because a thin film of ice had frozen upon the gallery.

He never knew how long his ascent of the ladder back into the airship took him, but in his dreams afterwards, when he recalled it, that experience seemed to last for hours. Below, above, around him were gulfs, monstrous gulfs of howling wind and eddies of dark, whirling snowflakes, and he was protected from it all by a little metal grating and a rail, a grating and rail that seemed madly infuriated with him, passionately eager to wrench him off and toss him into the tumult of space.

Once he had a fancy that a bullet tore by his ear, and that the clouds and snowflakes were lit by a flash, but he never even turned his head to see what new assailant whirled past them in the void. He wanted to get into the passage! Would the arm by which he was clinging hold out, or would it give way and snap? A handful of hail smacked him in the face, so that for a time he was breathless and nearly insensible. Hold tight, Bert! He renewed his efforts.

He found himself, with an enormous sense of relief and warmth, in the passage. The passage was behaving like a dice-box, its disposition was evidently to rattle him about and then throw him out again. He hung on with the convulsive clutch of instinct until the passage lurched down ahead. Then he would make a short run cabin-ward, and clutch again as the fore-end rose.

Behold! He was in the cabin!

He snapped to the door, and for a time he was not a human being, he was a case of air-sickness. He wanted to get somewhere that would fix him, that he needn't clutch. He opened the locker and got inside among the loose articles, and sprawled there helplessly, with his head sometimes bumping one side and sometimes the other. The lid shut upon him with a click. He did not care then what was happening any more. He did not care who fought, or what bullets were fired or explosions occurred. He did not care if presently he was shot or smashed to pieces. He was full of feeble, inarticulate rage and despair. "Foolery!" he said, his one exhaustive comment on human enterprise, adventure, war, and the chapter of accidents that had entangled him. "Foolery! Ugh!" He included the order of the universe in that comprehensive condemnation. He wished he was dead.

He saw nothing of the stars as presently the Vaterland cleared the rush and confusion of the lower weather, nor of the duel she fought with two circling aeroplanes, how they shot her rearmost chambers through, and how she fought them off with explosive bullets and turned, to run as she did so.

The rush and swoop of these wonderful night birds was all lost upon him; their heroic dash and self-sacrifice. The Vaterland was rammed, and for some moments she hung on the verge of destruction, and sinking swiftly, with the American aeroplane entangled with her smashed propeller, and the Americans trying to scramble aboard. It signified nothing to Bert. To him it conveyed itself simply as vehement swaying.

Foolery! When the American airship dropped off at last with most of its crew shot or fallen, Bert in his locker appreciated nothing but that the Vaterland had taken a hideous upward leap.

But then came infinite relief, incredibly blissful relief. The rolling, the pitching, the struggle ceased instantly and absolutely. The Vaterland was no longer fighting the gale; her smashed and exploded engines throbbed no more; she was disabled and driving before the wind as smoothly as a balloon, a huge, wind-spread, tattered cloud of aerial wreckage.

To Bert it was no more than the end of a series of disagreeable sensations. He was not curious to know what had happened to the airship, nor what had happened to the battle. For a long time he lay waiting apprehensively for the pitching and tossing and his qualms to return, and so, lying boxed up in the locker, he presently fell asleep.

3

He awoke tranquil but very stuffy, and at the same time very cold, and quite unable to recollect where he could be. His head ached, and his breath was suffocated. He had been dreaming confusedly of Edna, and Desert-Dervishes, and of riding bicycles in an extremely perilous manner through the upper air amidst a pyrotechnic display of crackers and Bengal lights—to the great annoyance of a sort of composite person made up of the Prince and Mr. Butteridge. Then for some reason Edna and he had begun to cry pitifully for each other, and he woke up with wet eyelashes into this ill-ventilated darkness of the locker. He would never see Edna any more, never see Edna any more.

He thought he must be back in the bedroom behind the cycle shop at the bottom of Bun Hill, and he was sure the vision he had had of the destruction of a magnificent city, a city quite incredibly great and splendid, by means of bombs, was no more than a particularly vivid dream.

"Grubb!" he called, anxious to tell him.

The answering silence, and the dull resonance of the locker to his voice, supplementing the stifling quality of the air, set going a new train of ideas. He lifted up his hands and feet, and met an inflexible resistance. He was in a coffin, he thought! He had been buried alive! He gave way at once to wild panic. " 'Elp!" he screamed. " 'Elp!" and drummed with his feet, and kicked and struggled. "Let me out! Let me out!"

For some seconds he struggled with this intolerable horror, and then the side of his imagined coffin gave way, and he was flying out into daylight. Then he was rolling about on what seemed to be a padded floor with Kurt, and being punched and sworn at lustily.

He sat up. His head bandage had become loose and got over one eye, and he whipped the whole thing off. Kurt was also sitting up, a yard away from him, pink as ever, wrapped in blankets, and with an aluminium diver's helmet over his knee, staring at him with a severe expression, and rubbing his downy, unshaven chin. They were both on a slanting floor of crimson padding, and above them was an opening like a long, low cellar flap that Bert by an effort perceived to be the cabin door in a half-inverted condition. The whole cabin had in fact turned on its side.

"What the deuce do you mean by it, Smallways?" said Kurt, "jumping out of that locker when I was certain you had gone overboard with the rest of them? Where have you been?"

"What's up?" asked Bert.

"This end of the airship is up. Most other things are down."

"Was there a battle?"

"There was."

"Who won?"

"I haven't seen the papers, Smallways. We left before the finish. We got disabled and unmanageable, and our colleagues—consorts I mean—were too busy most of them to trouble about us, and the wind blew us—Heaven knows where the wind *is* blowing us. It blew us right out of action at the rate of eighty miles an hour or so. Gott! what a wind it was! What a fight! And here we are!"

"Where?"

"In the air, Smallways—in the air! When we get down on the earth again we shan't know what to do with our legs."

"But what's below us?"

"Canada, to the best of my knowledge—and a jolly bleak, empty, inhospitable country it looks."

"But why ain't we right ways up?"

Kurt made no answer for a space.

"Last I remember was seeing a sort of flying-machine in a lightning flash," said Bert. "Gaw! that was 'orrible. Guns going off! Things exploding! Clouds and 'ail! Pitching and tossing. I got so scared and desperate—and sick. . . . You don't know how the fight came off?"

"Not a bit of it. I was up with my squad in those divers' dresses, inside the gas-chambers, with sheets of silk for caulking. We couldn't see a thing outside except the lightning flashes. I never saw one of those American aeroplanes. Just saw the shots flicker through the chambers and sent off men for the tears. We caught fire a bit—not much, you know. We were too wet, so the fires spluttered out before we banged. And then one of their infernal things dropped out of the air on us and rammed. Didn't you feel it?"

"I felt everything," said Bert. "I didn't notice any particular smash——"

"They must have been pretty desperate if they meant it. They slashed down on us like a knife; simply ripped the after gas-chamber like gutting herrings, crumpled up the engines and screw. Most of the engines dropped out as they fell off us, or we'd have grounded—but the rest is sort of dangling. We just turned up our nose to the heavens and stayed there. Eleven men rolled off us from various points, and poor old Winterfeld fell through the door of the Prince's cabin into the chart room and broke his ankle. Also we got our electric gear shot or carried away—no one knows how. That's the position, Smallways. We're driving through the air like a common aerostat, at the mercy of the elements, almost due north—probably to the North Pole. We don't know what aeroplanes the Americans have, or anything at all about it. Very likely we have finished 'em up. One fouled us, one was struck by lightning, some of the men saw a third upset, apparently just for fun. They are going cheap, anyhow. Also we've lost our Drachenflieger. They just skated off into the night. No stability in 'em. That's all. We don't know if we've won or lost. We don't know if we're at war with the British Empire yet or at peace. Consequently we daren't get down. We don't know what we are up to or what we are going to do. Our Napoleon is alone forward, and I suppose he's rearranging his plans. Whether New York was our Moscow or not yet remains to be seen.

We've had a high old time and murdered no end of people! War! Noble war! I'm sick of it this morning! I like sitting in rooms right away up and not on slippery partitions. I'm a civilized man. I keep thinking of old Albrecht and the Barbarossa. . . . I feel I want a wash and kind words and a quiet home. When I look at you, I *know* I want a wash. Gott!"—he stifled a vehement yawn—"What a Cockney tadpole of a ruffian you look!"

"Can't we get any grub?" asked Bert.

"Heaven knows!" said Kurt.

He meditated upon Bert for a time. "So far as I can judge, Small-ways," he said, "the Prince will probably want to throw you overboard—next time he thinks of you. . . . He certainly will if he sees you. . . . After all, you know, you came *als Ballast.* . . . And we shall have to lighten the ship extensively pretty soon. Unless I am mistaken, the Prince will wake up presently and start doing things with tremendous vigour. . . . I've taken a fancy to you. It's the English strain in me. You're a rum little chap. I shan't like seeing you whizz down the air. . . . You'd better make yourself useful, Smallways. I think I shall requisition you for my squad. You'll have to work, you know, and be infernally intelligent, and all that. And you'll have to hang about upside down a bit. Still, it's the best chance you have. We shan't carry passengers much farther this trip, I fancy. Ballast goes overboard—if we don't want to ground precious soon and be taken prisoners of war. The Prince won't do that anyhow. He'll be game to the last."

4

By means of a folding chair, which was still in its place behind the door, they got to the window and looked out in turn and contemplated a sparsely wooded country below, with no railways nor roads, and only occasional signs of habitation. Then a bugle sounded, and Kurt interpreted it as a summons to food. They got through the door and clambered with some difficulty up the nearly vertical passage, holding on desperately with toes and finger-tips to the ventilating perforations in its floor. The mess stewards had found their fireless heating arrange-ments intact, and there was hot cocoa for the officers and hot soup for the men.

Bert's sense of the queerness of this experience was so keen that it blotted out any fear he might have felt. Indeed, he was far more interested now than afraid. He seemed to have touched down to the bottom of fear and abandonment overnight. He was growing accustomed to the idea that he would probably be killed presently, that this strange voyage in the air was in all probability his death journey. No human being can keep permanently afraid; fear goes at last to the back of one's mind, accepted and shelved and done with. He squatted over his soup, sopping it up with his bread, and contemplated his comrades. They were all rather yellow and dirty with four-day beards, and they grouped themselves in the tired, unpremeditated manner of men on a wreck. They talked little. The situation perplexed them beyond any suggestion of ideas. Three had been hurt in the pitching up of the ship during the fight, and one had a bandaged bullet wound. It was incredible that this little band of men had committed murder and massacre on a scale beyond precedent. None of them who squatted on the sloping gas-padded partition, soup mug in hand, seemed really guilty of anything of the sort, seemed really capable of hurting a dog wantonly. They were all so manifestly built for homely châlets on the solid earth and carefully tilled fields and blond wives and cheery merrymaking. The red-faced sturdy man with light eye-lashes who had brought the first news of the air battle to the men's mess had finished his soup, and with an expression of maternal solicitude was readjusting the bandages of a youngster whose arm had been sprained.

Bert was crumbling the last of his bread into the last of his soup, eking it out as long as possible, when suddenly he became aware that everyone was looking at a pair of feet that were dangling across the down-turned open doorway. Kurt appeared and squatted across the hinge. In some mysterious way he had shaved his face and smoothed down his light golden hair. He looked extraordinarily cherubic. "Der Prinz," he said.

A second pair of boots followed, making wide and magnificent gestures in their attempts to feel the door frame. Kurt guided them to a foothold, and the Prince, shaved and brushed and beeswaxed and clean and big and terrible, slid down into position astride the door. All the men and Bert also stood up and saluted.

The Prince surveyed them with the gesture of a man who sits a steed. The head of the Kapitän appeared beside him.

Then Bert had a terrible moment. The blue blaze of the Prince's eye fell upon him, the great finger pointed, a question was asked. Kurt intervened with explanations.

"So," said the Prince, and Bert was disposed of.

Then the Prince addressed the men in short, heroic sentences, steadying himself on the hinge with one hand and waving the other in a fine variety of gesture. What he said Bert could not tell, but he perceived that their demeanour changed, their backs stiffened. They began to punctuate the Prince's discourse with cries of approval. At the end their leader burst into song and all the men with him. "Ein feste Burg ist unser Gott" they chanted in deep, strong tones, with an immense moral uplifting. It was glaringly inappropriate in a damaged half-overturned and sinking airship, which had been disabled and blown out of action after inflicting the cruellest bombardment in the world's history; but it was immensely stirring nevertheless. Bert was deeply moved. He could not sing any of the words of Luther's great hymn, but he opened his mouth and emitted loud, deep, and partially harmonious notes. . . .

Far below, this deep chanting struck on the ears of a little camp of Christianized half-breeds, who were lumbering. They were breakfasting, but they rushed out cheerfully, quite prepared for the Second Advent. They stared at the shattered and twisted Vaterland, driving before the gale, amazed beyond words. In so many respects it was like their idea of the Second Advent, and then again in so many respects it wasn't. They stared at its passage, awe-stricken and perplexed beyond their power of words. The hymn ceased. Then after a long interval a voice came out of heaven. "Vat id diss blace here galled itself; vat?"

They made no answer. Indeed, they did not understand, though the question was repeated.

And at last the monster drove away northward over a crest of pine woods and was no more seen. They fell into a hot and long disputation. . . .

The hymn ended. The Prince's legs dangled up the passage again, and everyone was briskly prepared for heroic exertion and triumphant acts. "Smallways!" cried Kurt, "come here!"

5

Then Bert, under Kurt's direction, had his first experience of the work of an air-sailor.

The immediate task before the captain of the Vaterland was a very simple one. He had to keep afloat. The wind, though it had fallen from its earlier violence, was still blowing strongly enough to render the grounding of so clumsy a mass extremely dangerous, even if it had been desirable for the Prince to land in inhabited country, and so risk capture. It was necessary to keep the airship up until the wind fell, and then, if possible, to descend in some lonely district of the Territory where there would be a chance of repair or rescue by some searching consort. In order to do this weight had to be dropped, and Kurt was detailed with a dozen men to climb down among the wreckage of the deflated air-chambers, and cut the stuff clear, portion by portion, as the airship sank. So Bert, armed with a sharp cutlass, found himself clambering about upon netting four thousand feet up in the air, trying to understand Kurt when he spoke in English, and to divine him when he used German.

It was giddy work, but not nearly so giddy as a rather over-nourished reader sitting in a warm room might imagine. Bert found it quite possible to look down and contemplate the wild subarctic landscape below, now devoid of any sign of habitation, a land of rocky cliffs and cascades and broad swirling desolate rivers, and of trees and thickets that grew more stunted and scrubby as the day wore on. Here and there on the hills were patches and pockets of snow. And over all this he worked, hacking away at the tough and slippery oiled silk and clinging stoutly to the netting. Presently they cleared and dropped a tangle of bent steel rods and wires from the frame, and a big chunk of silk bladder. That was trying. The airship flew up at once as this loose hamper parted. It seemed almost as though they were dropping all Canada. The stuff spread out in the air and floated down and hit and twisted up in a nasty fashion on the lip of a gorge. Bert clung like a frozen monkey to his ropes, and did not move a muscle for five minutes.

But there was something very exhilarating, he found, in this dangerous work, and above everything else there was the sense of fellowship. He was no longer an isolated and distrustful stranger among these others, he had now a common object with them, he worked with a friendly rivalry to get through with his share before them. And he developed a great respect and affection for Kurt, which had hitherto been only latent in him. Kurt with a job to direct was altogether admirable; he was resourceful, helpful, considerate, swift. He seemed to be everywhere. One forgot his pinkness, his light cheerfulness of manner. Directly one had trouble he was at hand with sound and confident advice. He was like an elder brother to his men.

Altogether they cleared three considerable chunks of wreckage, and then Bert was glad to clamber up into the cabins again and give place to a second squad. He and his companions were given hot coffee, and, indeed, even gloved as they were, the job had been a cold one. They sat drinking it and regarding each other with satisfaction. One man spoke to Bert amiably in German, and Bert nodded and smiled. Through Kurt, Bert, whose ankles were almost frozen, succeeded in getting a pair of top-boots from one of the disabled men.

In the afternoon the wind abated greatly, and small, infrequent snow-flakes came drifting by. Snow also spread more abundantly below, and the only trees were clumps of pine and spruce in the lower valleys. Kurt went with three men into the still intact gas-chambers, let out a certain quantity of gas from them, and prepared a series of ripping panels for the descent. Also the residue of the bombs and explosives in the magazine were thrown overboard and fell, detonating loudly in the wilderness below. And about four o'clock in the afternoon, upon a wide and rocky plain within sight of snow-crested cliffs, the Vaterland ripped and grounded.

It was necessarily a difficult and violent affair, for the Vaterland had not been planned for the necessities of a balloon. The captain got one panel ripped too soon, and the others not soon enough. She dropped heavily, bounced clumsily, and smashed the hanging gallery into the fore-part, mortally injuring Von Winterfeld, and then came down in a collapsing heap after dragging for some moments. The forward shield and its machine gun tumbled in upon the things below. Two men were hurt badly—one got a broken leg and one was internally injured— by flying rods and wires, and Bert was pinned for a time under the side. When at last he got clear, and could take a view of the situation, the great black eagle that had started so splendidly from Franconia six evenings ago, sprawled deflated over the cabins of the airship and the frost-bitten rocks of this desolate place and looked a most unfortunate bird—as though someone had caught it and wrung its neck and cast it aside. Several of the crew of the airship were standing about in silence, contemplating the wreckage and the empty wilderness into which they had fallen. Others were busy under the impromptu tent made by the empty gas-chambers. The Prince had gone a little way off and was scrutinizing the distant heights through his field glasses. They had the appearance of old sea cliffs; here and there were small clumps of conifers, and in two places tall cascades. The nearer ground was strewn with glaciated boulders and supported nothing but a stunted Alpine vegetation of compact clustering stems and stalkless flowers. No river was visible, but the air was full of the rush and babble of a torrent close at hand. A bleak and biting wind was blowing. Ever and again a snowflake drifted past. The springless frozen earth under Bert's feet felt strangely dead and heavy after the buoyant airship.

6

So it came about that that great and powerful Prince Karl Albert was for a time thrust out of the stupendous conflict he chiefly had been instrumental in provoking. The chances of battle and the weather conspired to maroon him in Labrador, and there he raged for six long days while war and wonder swept the world. Nation rose against nation, and air-fleet grappled air-fleet; cities blazed and men died in multitudes; but in Labrador one might have dreamt that, except for a little noise of hammering, the world was at peace.

There the encampment lay; from a distance the cabins, covered over with the silk of the balloon part, looked like a gipsy's tent on a rather exceptional scale, and all the available hands were busy in building out of the steel of the framework a mast from which the Vaterland's electricians might hang the long conductors of the apparatus for wireless telegraphy that was to link the Prince to the world again. There were times when it seemed they would never rig that mast. From the onset the party suffered hardship. They were not too abundantly provisioned, and they were put on short rations, and for all the thick garments they had, they were but ill-equipped against the piercing wind and inhospitable violence of this wilderness. The first night was spent in darkness and without fires. The engines that had supplied power were smashed and dropped far away to the south, and there was never a match among the company. It had been death to carry matches. All the explosives had been thrown out of the magazine, and it was only towards morning that the bird-faced man whose cabin Bert had taken in the beginning confessed to a brace of duelling pistols and cartridges, with which a fire could be started. Afterwards the lockers of the machine gun were found to contain a supply of unused ammunition.

The night was a distressing one and seemed almost interminable. Hardly anyone slept. There were seven wounded men aboard, and Von Winterfeld's head had been injured and he was shivering and in delirium, struggling with his attendant and shouting strange things about the burning of New York. The men crept together in the mess-room in the darkling, wrapped in what they could find, and drank cocoa from the fireless heaters, and listened to his cries. In the morning the Prince made them a speech about Destiny, and the God of his Fathers, and the pleasure and glory of giving one's life for his dynasty, and a number of similar considerations that might otherwise have been neglected in that bleak wilderness. The men cheered without enthusiasm, and far away a wolf howled.

Then they set to work, and for a week they toiled to put up a mast of steel, and hang it from a gridiron of copper wires two hundred feet by twelve. The theme of all that time was work, work continually, straining and toilsome work, and all the rest was grim hardship and evil chances, save for a certain wild splendour in the sunset and sunrise, in the torrents and drifting weather, in the wilderness about them. They built and tended a ring of perpetual fires, gangs roamed for brushwood and met with wolves, and the wounded men and their beds were brought out from the airship cabins and put in shelters about the fires. There old Von Winterfeld raved and became quiet and presently died, and three of the other wounded sickened for want of good food, while their fellows mended. These things happened, as it were, in the wings; the central facts before Bert's consciousness were always firstly the perpetual toil, the holding and lifting and lugging at heavy and clumsy masses, the tedious filing and winding of wires, and secondly, the Prince, urgent and threatening whenever a man relaxed. He would stand over them and point over their heads, southward into the open sky. "The world there," he said in German, "is waiting for us! Fifty centuries come to their Consummation." Bert did not understand the words, but he read the gesture. Several times the Prince grew angry; once with a man who was working slowly, once with a man who stole a comrade's ration. The first he scolded and set to a more tedious task; the second he struck in the face and ill-used. He did no work himself. There was a clear space near the fires, in which he would walk up and down sometimes for hours together, with arms folded, muttering to himself of Patience and his destiny. At times these mutterings broke out into rhetoric, into shouts and gestures that would arrest the workers; they would stare at him until they perceived that his blue eyes glared and his waving hand addressed itself always to the southward hills. On Sunday the work ceased for half an hour, and the Prince preached on faith and God's friendship for David, and afterwards they all sang: "Ein feste Burg ist unser Gott!"

In an improvised hovel lay Von Winterfeld, and all one morning he raved of the greatness of Germany. "Blut und Eisen!" he shouted, and then, as if in derision, "Welt-Politik—ha, ha!" Then he would explain complicated questions of polity to imaginary hearers, in low, wily tones. The other sick men kept still, listening to him. Bert's distracted attention would be recalled by Kurt. "Smallways, take that end. So!"

Slowly, tediously, the great mast was rigged, and hoisted foot by foot into place. The electricians had contrived a catchment pool and a wheel in the torrent close at hand—for the little Mulhausen dynamo with its turbinal volute used by the telegraphists was quite adaptable to water driving, and on the sixth day in the evening the apparatus was in working order and the Prince was calling—weakly, indeed, but calling—to his air-fleet across the empty spaces of the world. For a time he called unheeded.

The effect of that evening was to linger long in Bert's memory. A red fire spluttered and blazed close by the electricians at their work, and red gleams ran up the vertical steel mast and threads of copper wire towards the zenith. The Prince sat on a rock close by, with his chin on his hand, waiting. Beyond and to the northward was the cairn that covered Von Winterfeld, surmounted by a cross of steel, and from among the tumbled rocks in the distance the eyes of a wolf gleamed redly. On the other hand was the wreckage of the great airship, and the men bivouacked about a second ruddy glare. They were all keeping very still, as if waiting to hear what news might presently be given them. Far away, across many hundreds of miles of desolation, other wireless masts would be clicking and snapping, and waking into responsive vibration. Perhaps they were not. Perhaps these throbs upon the ether wasted themselves upon a regardless world. When the men spoke, they spoke in low tones. Now and then a bird shrieked remotely, and once a wolf howled. All these things were set in the immense cold spaciousness of the wild.

7

Bert got the news at last, and chiefly in broken English, from his mates. It was only far on in the night that the weary telegraphist got an answer to his calls, but then the messages came clear and strong. And such news it was!

"I say," said Bert at his breakfast, amidst a great clamour, "tell us a bit."

"All de vorld is at vor!" said the linguist, waving his cocoa in an illustrative manner, "all de vorld is at vor!"

Bert stared southward into the dawn. It did not seem so.

"All de vorld is at vor! They haf' burn' Berlin; they haf' burn' London; they haf' burn' Hamburg and Paris. Chapan hass burn' San Francisco. We haf' mate a camp at Niagara. Dat is whad they are telling us. China has cot Drachenflieger and Luftschiffe beyond counting. All de vorld is at vor!"

"Gaw!" said Bert.

"Yess," said the linguist, drinking his cocoa.

"Burnt up London, 'ave they? Like we did New York?"

"It wass a bombardment."

"They don't say anything about a place called Clapham, or Bun Hill, do they?"

"I haf' heard noding," said the linguist.

That was all Bert could get for a time. But the excitement of all the men about him was contagious, and presently he saw Kurt standing alone, hands behind him, and looking at one of the distant waterfalls very steadfastly. He went up and saluted, soldier fashion. "Beg pardon, lieutenant," he said.

Kurt turned his face. It was unusually grave that morning. "I was just thinking I would like to see that waterfall closer," he said. "It reminds me—what do you want?"

"I can't make 'ead or tail of what they're saying sir. Would you mind telling me the news?"

"Damn the news," said Kurt. "You'll get news enough before the day's out. It's the end of the world. They're sending the Graf Zeppelin for us. She'll be here by the morning, and we ought to be at Niagara—or eternal smash—within eight-and-forty hours. . . . I want to look at that waterfall. You'd better come with me. Have you had your rations?"

"Yessir."

"Very well. Come."

And musing profoundly, Kurt led the way across the rocks towards the distant waterfall. For a time Bert walked behind him in the character of an escort; then as they passed out of the atmosphere of the encampment, Kurt lagged for him to come alongside.

"We shall be back in it all in two days' time," he said. "And it's a devil of a war to go back to. That's the news. The world's gone mad. Our fleet beat the Americans the night we got disabled, that's clear. We lost eleven—eleven airships certain, and all their aeroplanes got smashed. God knows how much we smashed or how many we killed. But that was only the beginning. Our start's been like firing a magazine. Every country was hiding flying-machines. They're fighting in the air all over Europe—all over the world. The Japanese and Chinese have joined in. That's the great fact. That's the supreme fact. They've pounced into our little quarrels. . . . The Yellow Peril was a peril after all! They've got thousands of airships. They're all over the world. We bombarded London and Paris, and the French and English have smashed up Berlin. And now Asia is at us all, and on the top of us all. . . . It's mania. China

on the top. And they don't know where to stop. It's limitless. It's the last
confusion. They're bombarding capitals, smashing up dockyards and
factories, mines and fleets."

"Did they do much to London, sir?" asked Bert.

"Heaven knows. . . ."

He said no more for a time.

"This Labrador seems a quiet place," he resumed at last. "I've half
a mind to stay here. Can't do that. No! I've got to see it through. I've
got to see it through. You've got to, too. Everyone. . . . But why? . . . I
tell you—our world's gone to pieces. There's no way out of it, no way
back. Here we are. We're like mice caught in a house on fire; we're like
cattle overtaken by a flood. Presently we shall be picked up, and back
we shall go into the fighting. We shall kill and smash again—perhaps.
It's a Chino-Japanese air-fleet this time, and the odds are against us.
Our turn will come. What will happen to you I don't know; but for
myself, I know quite well, I shall be killed."

"You'll be all right," said Bert, after a queer pause.

"No!" said Kurt. "I'm going to be killed. I didn't know it before, but
this morning at dawn I knew it—as though I'd been told."

" 'Ow?"

"I tell you I know."

"But 'ow *could* you know?"

"I know."

"Like being told?"

"Like being certain."

"I know," he repeated, and for a time they walked in silence towards
the waterfall.

Kurt, wrapped in his thoughts, walked heedlessly, and at last broke
out again. "I've always felt young before, Smallways, but this morning
I feel old—old. So old! Nearer to death than old men feel. And I've
always thought life was a lark. It isn't. . . . This sort of thing has always
been happening, I suppose—these things, wars and earthquakes, that
sweep across all the decency of life. It's just as though I had woke up to it
all for the first time. Every night since we were at New York I've dreamt
of it. . . . And it's always been so—it's the way of life. People are torn
away from the people they care for; homes are smashed, creatures full of

life and memories and little peculiar gifts are scalded and smashed and torn to pieces, and starved and spoilt. London! Berlin! San Franscisco! Think of all the human histories we ended in New York! . . . And the others go on again as though such things weren't possible. As I went on! Like animals! Just like animals!"

He said nothing for a long time, and then he dropped out, "The Prince is a lunatic."

They came to a place where they had to climb, and then to a long peat level beside a rivulet. There a quantity of delicate little pink flowers caught Bert's eyes. "Gaw!" he said, and stooped to pick one. "In a place like this."

Kurt stopped and half turned. His face winced.

"I never see such a flower," said Bert. "It's so delicate."

"Pick some more if you want to," said Kurt.

Bert did so, while Kurt stood and watched him. "Funny 'ow one always wants to pick flowers," said Bert.

Kurt had nothing to add to that.

They went on again, without talking, for a long time.

At last they came to a rocky hummock, from which the view of the waterfall opened out. There Kurt stopped and seated himself on a rock. "That's as much as I wanted to see," he explained. "It isn't very like, but it's like enough."

"Like what?"

"Another waterfall I knew."

He asked a question abruptly. "Got a girl, Smallways?"

"Funny thing," said Bert, "those flowers, I suppose—I was jes' thinking of 'er."

"So was I."

"*What!* Edna?"

"No. I was thinking of *my* Edna. We've all got Ednas, I suppose, for our imaginations to play about. This was a girl. But all that's past for ever. It's hard to think I can't see her just for a moment—just let her know I'm thinking of her."

"Very likely," said Bert, "you'll see her all right."

"No," said Kurt, with decision. "I *know.*

"I met her," he went on, "in a place like this—in the Alps—Engstlen
Alp. There's a waterfall rather like this one—a broad waterfall down
towards Innertkirchen. That's why I came here this morning. We slipped
away and had half a day together beside it. And we picked flowers. Just such flowers as you picked. The same, for all I know. And
gentian."

"I know," said Bert, "me and Edna—we done things like that.
Flowers. And all that. Seems years off now."

"She was beautiful and daring and shy. Mein Gott! . . . I can hardly
hold myself for the desire to see her and hear her voice again before
I die. Where is she? . . . Look here, Smallways, I shall write a sort of
letter—And there's her portrait." He touched his breast pocket.

"You'll see 'er again all right," said Bert.

"No! I shall never see her again. . . . I don't understand why people
should meet just to be torn apart. But I know she and I will never
meet again. That I know as surely as that the sun will rise, and that
cascade come shining over the rocks after I am dead and done. . . .
Oh! It's all foolishness and haste and violence and cruel folly, stupidity,
and blundering hate and selfish ambition—all the things that men
have done—all the things they will ever do. Gott! Smallways, what a
muddle and confusion life has always been—the battles and massacres
and disasters, the hates and harsh acts, the murders and sweatings, the
lynchings and cheatings. This morning I am tired of it all, as though
I'd found it out for the first time. I *have* found it out. When a man
is tired of life, I suppose it is time for him to die. I've lost heart, and
death is over me. Death is close to me, and I know I have got to end.
But think of all the hopes I had only a little time ago, the sense of
fine beginnings! . . . It was all a sham. There were no beginnings. . . .
We're just ants in ant-hill cities, in a world that doesn't matter; that goes
on and rambles into nothingness. New York—New York doesn't even
strike me as horrible. New York was nothing but an ant-hill kicked to
pieces by a fool!

"Think of it, Smallways; there's war everywhere! They're smashing up
their civilization before they have made it. The sort of thing the English
did at Alexandria, the Japanese at Port Arthur, the French at Casablanca,
is going on everywhere. Everywhere! Down in South America even they

are fighting among themselves! No place is safe; no place is at peace. There is no place where a woman and her daughter can hide and be at peace. The war comes through the air, bombs drop in the night. Quiet people go out in the morning and see air-fleets passing overhead—dripping death—dripping death!"

EIGHT

A World at War

I

It was only very slowly that Bert got hold of this idea that the whole world was at war, that he formed any image at all of the crowded countries south of these Arctic solitudes stricken with terror and dismay as these new-born aerial navies swept across their skies. He was not used to thinking of the world as a whole, but as a limitless hinterland of happenings beyond the range of his immediate vision. War in his imagination was something, a source of news and emotion, that happened in a restricted area called the Seat of War. But now the whole atmosphere was the Seat of War, and every land a cockpit. So closely had the nations raced along the path of research and invention, so secret and yet so parallel had been their plans and acquisitions, that it was within a few hours of the launching of the first fleet in Franconia that an Asiatic Armada beat its northward way across, high above, the marvelling millions in the plain of the Ganges. But the preparations of the Confederation of Eastern Asia had been on an altogether more colossal scale than the German. "With this step," said Tan Ting-siang, "we overtake and pass the West. We recover the peace of the world that these barbarians have destroyed."

Their secrecy and swiftness and inventions had far surpassed those of the Germans, and where the Germans had had a hundred men at work the Asiatics had ten thousand. There came to their great aeronautic parks at Chinsi-fu and Tsing-yen, by the mono-rails that now laced the whole surface of China, a limitless supply of skilled and able workmen, workmen far above the average European in industrial efficiency. The news of the German World Surprise simply quickened their efforts. At the time of the bombardment of New York it is doubtful if the Germans had three hundred airships altogether in the world; the score of Asiatic fleets flying east and west numbered several thousand. Moreover, the Asiatics had a real fighting flying-machine, the Niaio as it was called, a light but quite efficient weapon, infinitely superior to the German Drachenflieger. Like that, it was a one-man machine, but it was built very lightly of steel and cane and chemical silk, with a transverse engine and a flapping sidewing. The aeronaut carried a gun firing explosive bullets loaded with oxygen, and in addition, and true to the best tradition of Japan, a sword. The riders were Japanese, and it is characteristic that from the first it was contemplated that the aeronaut should be a swordsman. The wings of these fliers had bat-like hooks forward, by which they were to cling to their antagonist's gas-chambers while boarding him. These light flying-machines were carried with the fleets, and also sent overland or by sea to the front with the men. They were capable of flights of from two to five hundred miles according to the wind.

So, hard upon the uprush of the first German air-fleet, these Asiatic swarms took to the atmosphere. Instantly every organized Government in the world was frantically and vehemently building airships and whatever approach to a flying-machine its inventors had discovered. There was no time for diplomacy. Warnings and ultimatums were telegraphed to and fro, and in a few hours all the panic-fierce world was openly at war, and at war in the most complicated way. For Britain and France and Italy had declared war upon Germany and outraged Swiss neutrality; India, at the sight of Asiatic airships, had broken into a Hindoo insurrection in Bengal and a Mohametan revolt hostile to this in the North-West Provinces—the latter spreading like wild-fire from Gobi to the Gold Coast—and the Confederation of Eastern Asia had seized the oil wells of Burmah and was impartially attacking America and Germany. In a week they were building airships in Damascus and Cairo and Johannesburg; Australia and New Zealand were frantically equipping themselves. One unique and terrifying aspect of this development was the swiftness with which these monsters could be produced. To build an ironclad took from two to four years; an airship could be put together in as many weeks. Moreover, compared with even a torpedo boat the airship was remarkably simple to construct: given the air-chamber material, the engines, the gas-plant, and the design, it was really not more complicated and far easier than an ordinary wooden boat had been a hundred years before. And now from Cape Horn to Nova Zembla, and from Canton round to Canton again, there were factories and workshops and industrial resources.

And the German airships were barely in sight of the Atlantic waters, the first Asiatic fleet was scarcely reported from Upper Burmah, before the fantastic fabric of credit and finance that had held the world together economically for a hundred years strained and snapped. A tornado of realization swept through every stock exchange in the world; banks stopped payment, business shrank and ceased, factories ran on for a day or so by a sort of inertia, completing the orders of bankrupt and extinguished customers, then stopped. The New York Bert Smallways saw, for all its glare of light and traffic, was in the pit of an economic and financial collapse unparalleled in history. The flow of the food supply was already a little checked. And before the world-war had lasted two weeks—by the time, that is, that mast was rigged in Labrador—there was not a city or town in the world outside China, however far from the actual centres of destruction, where police and government were not adopting special emergency methods to deal with a want of food and a glut of unemployed people.

The special peculiarities of aerial warfare were of such a nature as to trend, once it had begun, almost inevitably towards social disorganization. The first of these peculiarities was brought home to the Germans in their attack upon New York: the immense power of destruction an airship has over the thing below, and its relative inability to occupy or police or guard or garrison a surrendered position. Necessarily, in the face of urban populations in a state of economic disorganization and infuriated and starving, this led to violent and destructive collisions, and even where the air-fleet floated inactive above, there would be civil conflict and passionate disorder below. Nothing comparable to this state of affairs had been known in the previous history of warfare, unless we take such a case as that of a nineteenth-century warship attacking some large savage or barbaric settlement, or one of those naval bombardments that disfigure the history of Great Britain in the late eighteenth century. Then, indeed, there had been cruelties and destruction that faintly foreshadowed the horrors of the aerial war. Moreover, before the twentieth century the world had had but one experience, and that a comparatively light one, in the Communist insurrrection of Paris, 1871, of the possibilities of a modern urban population under warlike stresses.

A second peculiarity of airship war as it first came to the world that also made for social collapse, was the ineffectiveness of the early airships against each other. Upon anything below they could rain explosives in the most deadly fashion, forts and ships and cities lay at their mercy, but unless they were prepared for a suicidal grapple they could do remarkably little mischief to each other. The armament of the huge German airships, big as the biggest mammoth liners afloat, was one machine gun that could easily have been packed up on a couple of mules. In addition, when it became evident that the air must be fought for, the air-sailors were provided with rifles with explosive bullets of oxygen or inflammable substance, but no airship at any time ever carried as much in the way of guns and armour as the smallest gunboat on the navy list had been accustomed to do. Consequently, when these monsters met in battle they manœuvred for the upper place, or grappled and fought like junks, throwing grenades, fighting hand to hand in an entirely medieval fashion. The risks of a collapse and fall on either side came near to balancing in every case the chances of victory. As a consequence, and after their first experiences of battle, one finds a growing tendency on the part of the air-fleet admirals to evade joining battle and to seek rather the moral advantage of a destructive counterattack.

And if the airships were too ineffective, the early Drachenflieger were either too unstable, like the German, or too light, like the Japanese, to produce immediately decisive results. Later, it is true, the Brazilians launched a flying-machine of a type and scale that was capable of dealing with an airship, but they built only three or four, they operated only in South America, and they vanished from history untraceably in the time when world-bankruptcy put a stop to all further engineering production on any considerable scale.

The third peculiarity of aerial warfare was that it was at once enormously destructive and entirely indecisive. It had this unique feature, that both sides lay open to punitive attack. In all previous forms of war, both by land and sea, the losing side was speedily unable to raid its antagonists' territory and the communications. One fought on a "front," and behind that front the winner's supplies and resources, his towns and factories and capital, the peace of his country, were secure. If the war was a naval one, you destroyed your enemy's battle fleet and then blockaded his ports, secured his coaling stations, and hunted down any stray cruisers that threatened your ports of commerce. But to blockade and watch a coastline is one thing, to blockade and watch the whole surface of a country is another, and cruisers and privateers are things that take long to make, that cannot be packed up and hidden and carried unostentatiously from point to point. In aerial war the stronger side, even supposing it destroyed the main battle fleet of the weaker, had then either to patrol and watch or destroy every possible point at which he might produce another and perhaps novel and more deadly form of flier. It meant darkening his air with airships. It meant building them by the thousand and making aeronauts by the hundred thousand. A small uninflated airship could be hidden in a railway shed, in a village street, in a wood; a flying-machine is even less conspicuous.

And in the air are no streets, no channels, no point where one can say of an antagonist, "If he wants to reach my capital he must come by here." In the air all directions lead everywhere.

Consequently it was impossible to end a war by any of the established methods. A having outnumbered and overwhelmed B, hovers, a thousand airships strong, over his capital, threatening to bombard it unless B submits. B replies by wireless telegraphy that he is now in the act of bombarding the chief manufacturing city of A by means of three raider airships. A denounces B's raiders as pirates and so forth, bombards B's capital and sets off to hunt down B's airships, while B in a state of passionate emotion and heroic unconquerableness, sets to work amidst his ruins, making fresh airships and explosives for the benefit of A. The war became perforce a universal guerilla war, a war inextricably involving civilians and homes and all the apparatus of social life.

These aspects of aerial fighting took the world by surprise. There had been no foresight to deduce these consequences. If there had been the world would have arranged for a Universal Peace Conference in 1900. But mechanical invention had gone faster than intellectual and social organization, and the world, with its silly old flags, its silly unmeaning tradition of nationality, its cheap newspapers and cheaper passions and imperialisms, its base commercial motives and habitual insincerities and vulgarities, its race lies and conflicts, was taken by surprise. Once the war began there was no stopping it. The flimsy fabric of credit that had grown with no man foreseeing, and that had held those hundreds of millions in an economic interdependence that no man clearly understood, dissolved in panic. Everywhere went the airships dropping bombs, destroying any hope of a rally, and everywhere below were economic catastrophe, starving workless people, rioting, and social disorder. Whatever constructive guiding intelligence there had been among the nations vanished in the passionate stresses of the time. Such newspapers and documents and histories as survive from this period all tell one universal story of towns and cities with the food supply interrupted and their streets congested with starving unemployed: of crises in administration and state of siege, of provisional Governments and Councils of Defence, and in the cases of India and Egypt, insurrectionary committees taking charge of the re-arming of the population, of the making of batteries and gun-pits, of the vehement manufacture of airships and flying-machines.

One sees these things in glimpses, in illuminated moments, as if through a driving reek of clouds, going on all over the world. It was the dissolution of an age; it was the collapse of the civilization that had trusted to machinery, and the instruments of its destruction were machines. But while the collapse of the previous great civilization, that of Rome, had been a matter of centuries, had been a thing of phase and phase, like the ageing and dying of a man, this, like his killing by railway or motor-car, was one swift, conclusive smashing and an end.

2

The early battles of the aerial war were no doubt determined by attempts to realize the old naval maxim, to ascertain the position of the enemy's fleet and to destroy it. There was first the battle of the Bernese Oberland, in which the Italian and French navigables in their flank raid upon the Franconian Park were assailed by the Swiss experimental squadron, supported as the day wore on by German airships; and then the encounter of the British Winterhouse-Dunne aeroplanes with three unfortunate Germans.

Then came the battle of North India, in which the entire Anglo-Indian aeronautic settlement establishment fought for three days against overwhelming odds, and was dispersed and destroyed in detail.

And simultaneously with the beginning of that commenced the momentous struggle of the Germans and Asiatics that is usually known as the Battle of Niagara because of the objective of the Asiatic attack. But it passed gradually into a sporadic conflict over half a continent. Such German airships as escaped destruction in battle descended and surrendered to the Americans, and were remanned, and in the end it became a series of pitiless and heroic encounters between the Americans, savagely resolved to exterminate their enemies, and a continually reinforced army of invasion from Asia quartered upon the Pacific slope and supported by an immense fleet. From the first the war in America was fought with implacable bitterness; no quarter was asked, no prisoners were taken. With ferocious and magnificent energy the Americans constructed and launched ship after ship to battle and perish against the Asiatic multitudes. All other affairs were subordinate to this war, the whole population was presently living or dying for it. Presently, as I shall tell, the white men found in the Butteridge machine a weapon that could meet and fight the flying-machines of the Asiatic swordsmen.

The Asiatic invasion of America completely effaced the German-American conflict. It vanishes from history. At first it had seemed to promise quite sufficient tragedy in itself—beginning as it did in unforgettable massacre. After the destruction of central New York all America had risen like one man, resolved to die a thousand deaths rather than submit to Germany. The Germans grimly resolved upon beating the Americans into submission, and, following out the plans developed by the Prince, had seized Niagara—in order to avail themselves of its enormous power works, expelled all its inhabitants, and made a desert of its environs as far as Buffalo. They had also, directly Great Britain and France declared war, wrecked the country upon the Canadian side for nearly ten miles inland. They began to bring up men and material from the fleet off the east coast, stringing out to and fro like bees getting honey. It was then that the Asiatic forces appeared, and it was in their attack upon this German base at Niagara that the air-fleets of East and West first met and the greater issue became clear.

One conspicuous peculiarity of the early aerial fighting arose from the profound secrecy with which the airships had been prepared. Each power had had but the dimmest inkling of the schemes of its rivals, and even experiments with its own devices were limited by the needs of secrecy. None of the designers of airships and aeroplanes had known clearly what their inventions might have to fight; many had not imagined they would have to fight anything whatever in the air, and had planned them only for the dropping of explosives. Such had been the German idea. The only weapon for fighting another airship with which the Franconian fleet had been provided, was the machine gun forward. Only after the fight over New York were the men given short rifles with detonating bullets. Theoretically, the Drachenflieger were to have been the fighting weapon. They were declared to be aerial torpedo-boats, and the aeronaut was supposed to swoop close to his antagonist and cast his bombs as he whirled past. But indeed these contrivances were hopelessly unstable; not one third in any engagement succeeded in getting back to the mother airship. The rest were either smashed up or grounded.

The allied Chino-Japanese fleet made the same distinction as the Germans between airships and fighting machines heavier than air, but the type in both cases was entirely different from the occidental models, and—it is eloquent of the vigour with which these great peoples took up and bettered the European methods of scientific research—in almost every particular the invention of Asiatic engineers. Chief among these, it is worth remarking, was Mohini K. Chatterjee, a political exile who had formerly served in the British-Indian aeronautic park at Lahore.

The German airship was fish-shaped, with a blunted head; the Asiatic airship was also fish-shaped, but not so much on the lines of a cod or goby as of a ray or sole. It had a wide flat underside, unbroken by windows or any opening except along the middle line. Its cabins occupied its axis, with a sort of bridge deck above, and the gas-chambers gave the whole affair the shape of a gipsy's hooped tent, except that it was much flatter. The German airship was essentially a navigable balloon very much lighter than air; the Asiatic airship was very little lighter than air and skimmed through it with much greater velocity if with considerably less stability. They carried fore and aft guns, the latter much the larger, throwing inflammatory shells, and in addition they had nests for riflemen on both the upper and the under side. Light as this armament was in comparison with the smallest gunboat that ever sailed, it was sufficient for them to outfight as well as outfly the German monster airships. In action they flew to get behind or over the Germans; they even dashed underneath, avoiding only passing immediately beneath the magazine, and then as soon as they had crossed let fly with their rear gun, and sent flares or oxygen shells into the antagonist's gas-chambers.

It was not in their airships, but, as I have said, in their flying-machines proper, that the strength of the Asiatics lay. Next only to the Butteridge machine these were certainly the most efficient heavier-than-air fliers that had ever appeared. They were the invention of a Japanese artist, and they differed in type extremely from the box-kite quality of the German Drachenflieger. They had curiously curved, flexible side wings, more like *bent* butterfly's wings than anything else, and made of a substance like celluloid and of brightly painted silk, and they had a long humming-bird tail. At the forward corner of the wings were hooks, rather like the claws of a bat, by which the machine could catch and hang and tear at the walls of an airship's gas-chamber. The solitary rider sat between the wings above a transverse explosive engine, an explosive engine that differed in no essential particular from those in use in the light motor bicycles of the period. Below was a single large wheel. The rider sat astride of a saddle, as in the Butteridge machine, and he carried a large double-edged two-handed sword, in addition to his explosive-bullet firing rifle.

3

One sets down these particulars and compares the points of the American and German pattern of aeroplane and navigable, but none of these facts were clearly known to any of those who fought in this monstrously confused battle above the American great lakes.

Each side went into action against it knew not what, under novel conditions and with apparatus that even without hostile attacks was capable of producing the most disconcerting surprises. Schemes of action, attempts at collective manœuvring necessarily went to pieces directly the fight began, just as they did in almost all the early ironclad battles of the previous century. Each captain then had to fall back upon individual action and his own devices; one would see triumph in what another read as a cue for flight and despair. It is as true of the Battle of Niagara as of the Battle of Lissa that it was not a battle but a bundle of "battlettes!"

To such a spectator as Bert it presented itself as a series of incidents, some immense, some trivial, but collectively incoherent. He never had a sense of any plain issue joined, of any point struggled for and won or lost. He saw tremendous things happen, and in the end his world darkened to disaster and ruin.

He saw the battle from the ground, from Prospect Park and from Goat Island, whither he fled.

But the manner in which he came to be on the ground needs explaining.

The Prince had resumed command of his fleet through wireless telegraphy long before the Zeppelin had located his encampment in Labrador. By his direction the German air-fleet, whose advance scouts had been in contact with the Japanese over the Rocky Mountains, had concentrated upon Niagara and awaited his arrival. He had rejoined his command early in the morning of the twelfth, and Bert had his first prospect of the Gorge of Niagara while he was doing net drill outside the middle gas-chamber at sunrise. The Zeppelin was flying very high at the time, and far below he saw the water in the gorge marbled with froth, and then away to the west the great crescent of the Canadian Fall shining, flickering, and foaming in the level sunlight, and sending up a deep, incessant thudding rumble to the sky. The air-fleet was keeping station in an enormous crescent, with its horns pointing south-westward, a long array of shining monsters with tails rotating slowly, and German ensigns now trailing from their bellies aft of their Marconi pendants.

Niagara city was still largely standing then, albeit its streets were empty of all life. Its bridges were intact, its hotels and restaurants still flying flags and inviting sky-signs, its power-stations running. But about it the country on both sides of the gorge might have been swept by a colossal broom. Everything that could possibly give cover to an attack upon the German position at Niagara had been levelled as ruthlessly as machinery and explosives could contrive; houses blown up and burnt, woods burnt, fences and crops destroyed. The mono-rails had been torn up, and the roads in particular cleared of all possibility of concealment or shelter. Seen from above the effect of this wreckage was grotesque. Young woods had been destroyed wholesale by dragging wires, and the spoilt saplings, smashed or uprooted, lay in swathes like corn after the sickle. Houses had an appearance of being flattened down by the pressure of a gigantic finger. Much burning was still going on, and large areas had been reduced to patches of smouldering and sometimes still glowing blackness. Here and there lay the debris of belated fugitives, carts, and dead bodies of horses and men; and where houses had had water supplies there were pools of water and running springs from the ruptured pipes. In unscorched fields horses and cattle still fed peacefully. Beyond this desolated area the countryside was still standing, but almost all the people had fled. Buffalo was on fire to an enormous extent, and there were no signs of any efforts to grapple with the flames.

Niagara city itself was being rapidly converted to the needs of a military depôt. A large number of skilled engineers had already been brought from the fleet, and were busily at work adapting the exterior industrial apparatus of the place to the purposes of an aeronautic park. They had made a gas recharging station at the corner of the American Fall above the funicular railway, and they were opening up a much larger area to the south for the same purpose. Over the power houses and hotels and suchlike prominent or important points, the German flag was flying.

The Zeppelin circled slowly over this scene twice while the Prince surveyed it from the swinging gallery; it then rose towards the centre of the crescent and transferred the Prince and his suit, Kurt included, to the Hohenzollern, which had been chosen as the flagship during the impending battle. They were swung up on a small cable from the forward gallery, and the men of the Zeppelin manned the outer netting as the Prince and his staff left them. The Zeppelin then came about, circled down and grounded in Prospect Park, in order to land the wounded and take aboard explosives; for she had come to Labrador with her magazines empty, it being uncertain what weight she might need to carry. She also replenished the hydrogen in one of her forward chambers which had leaked.

Bert was detailed as a bearer and helped carry the wounded one by one into the nearest of the large hotels that faced the Canadian shore. The hotel was quite empty except that there were two trained American nurses and a negro porter, and three or four Germans awaiting them. Bert went with the Zeppelin's doctor into the main street of the place, and they broke into a drug shop and obtained various things of which they stood in need. As they returned they found an officer and two men making a rough inventory of the available material in the various stores. Except for them the wide, main street of the town was quite deserted, the people had been given three hours to clear out, and everybody, it seemed, had done so. At one corner a dead man lay against the wall—shot. Two or three dogs were visible up the empty vista, but towards its river end the passage of a string of mono-rail cars broke the stillness and the silence. They were loaded with hose, and were passing to the trainful of workers who were converting Prospect Park into an airship dock.

Bert pushed a case of medicine, balanced on a bicycle taken from an adjacent shop, to the hotel, and then he was sent to load bombs into the Zeppelin magazine, a duty that called for elaborate care. From this job he was presently called off by the captain of the Zeppelin, who sent him with a note to the officer in charge of the Anglo-American Power Company, for the field telephone had still to be adjusted. Bert received his instructions in German, whose meaning he guessed, and saluted and took the note, not caring to betray his ignorance of the language. He started off with a bright air of knowing his way and turned a corner or so and was only beginning to suspect that he did not know where he was going when his attention was recalled to the sky by the report of a gun from the Hohenzollern and celestial cheering.

He looked up and found the view obstructed by the houses on either side of the street. He hesitated, and then curiosity took him back towards the bank of the river. Here his view was inconvenienced by trees, and it was with a start that he discovered the Zeppelin, which he knew had still a quarter of her magazines to fill, was rising over Goat Island. She had not waited for her complement of ammunition. It occurred to him that he was left behind. He ducked back among the trees and bushes until he felt secure from any after-thought on the part of the Zeppelin's captain. Then his curiosity to see what the German air-fleet faced overcame him, and drew him at last halfway across the bridge to Goat Island. From that point he had nearly a hemisphere of sky and got his first glimpse of the Asiatic airships low in the sky above the glittering tumults of the Upper Rapids.

They were far less impressive than the German ships. He could not judge the distance, and they flew edgeways to him, so as to conceal the broader aspect of their bulk.

Bert stood there in the middle of the bridge, in a place that most people who knew it remembered as a place populous with sightseers and excursionists, and he was the only human being in sight there. Above him, very high in the heavens, the contending air-fleets manœuvred; below him the river seethed like a sluice towards the American Fall. He was curiously dressed. His cheap blue serge trousers were thrust into German airship rubber boots, and on his head he wore an aeronaut's white cap that was a trifle too large for him. He thrust that back to reveal his staring little cockney face, still scarred upon the brow. "Gaw!" he whispered.

He stared. He gesticulated. Once or twice he shouted and applauded.

Then a certain terror seized him and he took to his heels in the direction of Goat Island.

4

For a time after they were in sight of each other, neither fleet attempted to engage. The Germans numbered sixty-seven great airships and they maintained the crescent formation at a height of nearly four thousand feet. They kept a distance of about one and a half lengths, so that the horns of the crescent were nearly thirty miles apart. Closely in tow of the airships of the extreme squadrons on either wing were about thirty Drachenflieger ready manned, but these were too small and distant for Bert to distinguish.

At first only what was called the Southern Fleet of the Asiatics was visible to him. It consisted of forty airships, carrying altogether nearly four hundred one-man flying-machines upon their flanks, and for some time it flew slowly and at a minimum distance of perhaps a dozen miles from the Germans, eastward across their front. At first Bert could distinguish only the greater bulks, then he perceived the one-man machines as a multitude of very small objects drifting like motes in the sunshine about and beneath the larger shapes.

Bert saw nothing then of the second fleet of the Asiatics, though probably that was coming into sight of the Germans at the time, in the north-west.

The air was very still, the sky almost without a cloud, and the German fleet had risen to an immense height, so that the airships seemed no longer of any considerable size. Both ends of their crescent showed plainly. As they beat southward they passed slowly between Bert and the sunlight, and became black outlines of themselves. The Drachenflieger appeared as little flecks of black on either wing of this aerial Armada.

The two fleets seemed in no hurry to engage. The Asiatics went far away into the east, quickening their pace and rising as they did so, and then tailed out into a long column and came flying back, rising towards the German left. The squadrons of the latter came about, facing this oblique advance, and suddenly little flickerings and a faint crepitating sound told that they had opened fire. For a time no effect was visible to the watcher on the bridge. Then, like a handful of snowflakes, the Drachenflieger swooped to the attack, and a multitude of red specks whirled up to meet them. It was to Bert's sense not only enormously remote but singularly inhuman. Not four hours since he had been on one of those very airships, and yet they seemed to him now not gas-bags carrying men, but strange sentient creatures that moved about and did things with a purpose of their own. The flight of the Asiatic and

German flying-machines joined and dropped earthward, became like a handful of white and red rose petals flung from a distant window, grew larger, until Bert could see the overturned ones spinning through the air, and were hidden by great volumes of dark smoke that were rising in the direction of Buffalo. For a time they all were hidden, then two or three white and a number of red ones rose again into the sky, like a swarm of big butterflies, and circled fighting and drove away out of sight again towards the east.

A heavy report recalled Bert's eyes to the zenith, and behold the great crescent had lost its dressing and burst into a disorderly long cloud of airships! One had dropped half-way down the sky. It was flaming fore and aft, and even as Bert looked it turned over and fell, spinning over and over itself and vanished into the smoke of Buffalo.

Bert's mouth opened and shut, and he clutched tighter on the rail of the bridge. For some moments—they seemed long moments— the two fleets remained without any further change, flying obliquely towards each other, and making what came to Bert's ears as a midget uproar. Then suddenly from either side airships began dropping out of alignment, smitten by missiles he could neither see nor trace. The string of Asiatic ships swung round and either charged into or over (it was difficult to say from below) the shattered line of the Germans, who seemed to open out to give way to them. Some sort of manœuvring began, but Bert could not grasp its import. The left of the battle became a confused dance of airships. For some minutes up there the two crossing lines of ships looked so close it seemed like a hand-to-hand scuffle in the sky. Then they broke up into groups and duels. The descent of German airships towards the lower sky increased. One of them flared down and vanished far away in the north; two dropped with something twisted and crippled in their movements; then a group of antagonists came down from the zenith in an eddying conflict, two Asiatics against one German, and were presently joined by another, and drove away eastward all together with others dropping out of the German line to join them. One Asiatic rammed or collided with a still more gigantic German, and the two went spinning to destruction together. The northern squadron of Asiatics came into the battle unnoted by Bert, except that the multitude of ships above seemed presently increased.

In a little while the fight was utter confusion, drifting on the whole to the south-west against the wind. It became more and more a series of group encounters. Here a huge German airship flamed earthward with a dozen flat Asiatic craft about her, crushing her every attempt to recover. Here another hung with its crew fighting off the swordsmen from a swarm of flying-machines. Here, again, an Asiatic aflame at either end swooped out of the battle. His attention went from incident to incident in the vast clearness overhead; these conspicuous cases of destruction caught and held his mind; it was only very slowly that any sort of scheme manifested itself between those nearer, more striking episodes.

The mass of the airships that eddied remotely above was, however, neither destroying nor destroyed. The majority of them seemed to be going at full speed and circling upward for position, exchanging ineffectual shots as they did so. Very little ramming was essayed after the first tragic downfall of rammer and rammed, and whatever attempts at boarding were made were invisible to Bert. There seemed, however, a steady endeavour to isolate antagonists, to cut them off from their fellows and bear them down, causing a perpetual sailing back and interlacing of these shoaling bulks. The greater numbers of the Asiatics and their swifter heeling movements gave them the effect of persistently attacking the Germans. Overhead, and evidently endeavouring to keep itself in touch with the works of Niagara, a body of German airships drew itself together into a compact phalanx, and the Asiatics became more and more intent upon breaking this up. He was grotesquely reminded of fish in a fish-pond struggling for crumbs. He could see puny puffs of smoke and the flash of bombs, but never a sound came down to him. . . .

A flapping shadow passed for a moment between Bert and the sun and was followed by another. A whirring of engines, click, clock, clitter clock, smote upon his ears. Instantly he forgot the zenith.

Perhaps a hundred yards above the water, out of the south, riding like Valkyries swiftly through the air on the strange steeds the engineering of Europe had begotten upon the artistic inspiration of Japan, came a long string of Asiatic swordsmen. The wings flapped jerkily, click, clock, clitter clock, and the machines drove up; they spread and ceased, and the apparatus came soaring through the air. So they rose and fell and rose again. They passed so closely overhead that Bert could hear their voices calling to one another. They swooped towards Niagara city and landed one after another in a long line in a clear space before the hotel. But he did not stay to watch them land. One yellow face had craned over and looked at him, and for one enigmatical instant met his eyes. . . .

It was then the idea came to Bert that he was altogether too conspicuous in the middle of the bridge, and that he took to his heels towards Goat Island. Thence, dodging about among the trees, with perhaps an excessive self-consciousness, he watched the rest of the struggle.

5

When Bert's sense of security was sufficiently restored for him to watch the battle again, he perceived that a brisk little fight was in progress between the Asiatic aeronauts and the German engineers for the possession of Niagara city. It was the first time in the whole course of the war that he had seen anything resembling fighting as he had studied it in the illustrated papers of his youth. It seemed to him almost as though things were coming right. He saw men carrying rifles and taking cover and running briskly from point to point in a loose attacking formation. The first batch of aeronauts had probably been under the impression that the city was deserted. They had grounded in the open near Prospect Park and approached the houses towards the power-works before they were disillusioned by a sudden fire. They had scattered back to the cover of a bank near the water—it was too far for them to reach their machines again; they were lying and firing at the men in the hotels and frame-houses about the power-works.

Then to their support came a second string of red flying-machines driving up from the east. They rose up out of the haze above the houses and came round in a long curve as if surveying the position below. The fire of the Germans rose to a roar, and one of those soaring shapes gave an abrupt jerk backwards and fell among the houses. The others swooped down exactly like great birds upon the roof of the power-house. They caught upon it, and from each sprang a nimble little figure and ran towards the parapet.

Other flapping bird-shapes came into this affair, but Bert had not seen their coming. A staccato of shots came over to him, reminding him of army manœuvres, of newspaper descriptions of fights, of all that was entirely correct in his conception of warfare. He saw quite a number of Germans running from the outlying houses towards the power-house. Two fell. One lay still, but the other wriggled and made efforts for a time. The hotel that was used as a hospital, and to which he had helped carry the wounded men from the Zeppelin earlier in the day, suddenly ran up the Geneva flag. The town that had seemed so quiet had evidently been concealing a considerable number of Germans, and they were now concentrating to hold the central power-house. He wondered what ammunition they might have. More and more of the Asiatic flying-machines came into the conflict. They had disposed of the unfortunate German Drachenflieger and were now aiming at the incipient aeronautic park, the electric gas generators and repair stations which formed the German base. Some landed, and their aeronauts took cover and became energetic infantry soldiers. Others hovered above the fight, their men ever and again firing shots down at some chance exposure below. The firing came in paroxysms; now there would be a watchful lull and now a rapid tattoo of shots, rising to a roar. Once or twice flying-machines, as they circled warily, came right overhead, and for a time Bert gave himself body and soul to cowering.

Ever and again a larger thunder mingled with the rattle and reminded him of the grapple of airships far above, but the nearer fight held his attention.

Abruptly something dropped from the zenith; something like a barrel or a huge football.

CRASH! It smashed with an immense report. It had fallen among the grounded Asiatic aeroplanes that lay among the turf and flower-beds near the river. They flew in scraps and fragments, turf, trees, and gravel leapt and fell; the aeronauts still lying along the canal bank were thrown about like sacks, catspaws flew across the foaming water. All the windows of the hotel hospital that had been shiningly reflecting blue sky and airships the moment before became vast black stars. Bang!— a second followed. Bert looked up and was filled with a sense of a number of monstrous bodies swooping down, coming down on the whole affair like a flight of bellying blankets, like a string of vast dish-covers. The central tangle of the battle above was circling down as if to come into touch with the power-house fight. He got a new effect of airships altogether, as vast things coming down upon him, growing swiftly larger and larger and more overwhelming, until the houses over the way seemed small, the American rapids narrow, the bridge flimsy, the combatants infinitesimal. As they came down they became audible as a complex of shoutings and vast creakings and groanings and beatings and throbbings and shouts and shots. The foreshortened black eagles at the fore-ends of the Germans had an effect of actual combat of flying feathers.

Some of these fighting airships came within five hundred feet of the ground. Bert could see men on the lower galleries of the Germans firing rifles; could see Asiatics clinging to the ropes; saw one man in aluminium diver's gear fall flashing headlong into the waters above Goat Island. For the first time he saw the Asiatic airships closely. From this aspect they reminded him more than anything else of colossal snowshoes; they had a curious patterning in black and white, in forms that reminded him of the engine-turned cover of a watch. They had no hanging galleries, but from little openings on the middle line peeped out men and the muzzles of guns. So, driving in long descending and ascending curves, these monsters wrestled and fought. It was like clouds fighting, like puddings trying to assassinate each other. They whirled and circled about each other, and for a time threw Goat Island and Niagara into a smoky twilight, through which the sunlight smote in shafts and beams. They spread and closed and spread and grappled and drove round over the rapids, and two miles away or more into Canada, and back over the Falls again. A German caught fire, and the whole crowd broke away from her flare and rose about her dispersing, leaving her to drop towards Canada and blow up as she dropped. Then with renewed uproar the others closed again. Once from the men in Niagara city came a sound like an ant-hill cheering. Another German burnt, and one badly deflated by the prow of an antagonist, flopped out of action southward.

It became more and more evident that the Germans were getting the worst of the unequal fight. More and more obviously were they being persecuted. Less and less did they seem to fight with any object other than escape. The Asiatics swept by them and above them, ripped their bladders, set them alight, picked off their dimly seen men in diving clothes, who struggled against fire and tear with fire extinguishers and silk ribbons in the inner netting. They answered only with ineffectual shots. Thence the battle circled back over Niagara, and then suddenly the Germans, as if at a preconcerted signal, broke and dispersed, going east, west, north, and south, in open and confused flight. The Asiatics, as they realized this, rose to fly above them and after them. Only one little knot of four German and perhaps a dozen Asiatics remained fighting about the Hohenzollern and the Prince as he circled in a last attempt to save Niagara.

Round they swooped once again over the Canadian Fall, over the waste of waters eastward, until they were distant and small, and then round and back, hurrying, bounding, swooping towards the one gaping spectator.

The whole struggling mass approached very swiftly, growing rapidly larger, and coming out black and featureless against the afternoon sun and above the blinding welter of the Upper Rapids. It grew like a storm cloud until once more it darkened the sky. The flat Asiatic airships kept high above the Germans and behind them, and fired unanswered bullets into their gas-chambers and upon their flanks. The one-man flying-machines hovered and alighted like a swarm of attacking bees. Nearer they came and nearer, filling the lower heaven. Two of the Germans swooped and rose again, but the Hohenzollern had suffered too much for that. She lifted weakly, turned sharply as if to get out of the battle, burst into flames fore and aft, swept down to the water, splashed into it obliquely and rolled over and over and came down stream rolling and smashing and writhing like a thing alive, halting and then coming on again, with her torn and bent pro- peller still beating the air. The bursting flames spluttered out again in clouds of steam. It was a disaster gigantic in its dimensions. She lay across the rapids like an island, like tall cliffs, tall cliffs that came rolling, smoking, and crumpling, and collapsing, advancing with a sort of fluctuating rapidity upon Bert. One Asiatic airship—it looked to Bert from below like three hundred yards of pavement—whirled back and circled two or three times over that great overthrow, and half-a-dozen crimson flying-machines danced for a moment like great midges in the sunlight before they swept on after their fellows. The rest of the fight had already gone over the island, a wild crescendo of shots and yells and smashing uproar. It was hidden from Bert now by the trees of the island, and forgotten by him in the nearer spectacle of the huge advance of the defeated German airship. Something fell with a mighty smashing and splintering of boughs unheeded behind him.

It seemed for a time that the Hohenzollern must needs break her back upon the Parting of the Waters, and then for a time her propeller flopped and frothed in the river and thrust the mass of buckling, crumpled wreckage towards the American shore. Then the sweep of the torrent that foamed down to the American Fall caught her, and in another minute the immense mass of deflating wreckage, with flames spurting out in three new places, had crashed against the bridge that joined Goat Island and Niagara city, and forced a long arm, as it were, in a heaving tangle under the central span. Then the middle chambers blew up with a loud report, and in another moment the bridge had given way and the main bulk of the airship, like some grotesque cripple in rags, staggered, flapping and waving flambeaux, to the crest of the Fall and hesitated there and vanished in a desperate suicidal leap.

Its detached fore-end remained jammed against that little island, Green Island it used to be called, which forms the stepping-stone between the mainland and Goat Island's patch of trees.

Bert followed the disaster from the Parting of the Waters to the bridge head. Then, regardless of cover, regardless of the Asiatic airship hovering like a huge house roof without walls above the Suspension Bridge, he sprinted along towards the north and came out for the first time upon that rocky point by Luna Island that looks sheer down upon the American Fall. There he stood breathless amidst that eternal rush of sound, breathless and staring.

Far below, and travelling rapidly down the gorge, whirled something like a huge empty sack. For him it meant—what did it not mean?—the German air-fleet, Kurt, the Prince, Europe, all things stable and familiar, the forces that had brought him, the forces that had seemed indisputably victorious. And it went down the rapids like an empty sack and left the visible world to Asia, to yellow people beyond Christendom, to all that was terrible and strange!

Remote over Canada receded the rest of that conflict and vanished beyond the range of his vision. . . .

NINE

On Goat Island

I

The whack of a bullet on the rocks beside him reminded him that he was a visible object and wearing at least portions of a German uniform. It drove him into the trees again, and for a time he dodged and dropped and sought cover like a chick hiding among reeds from imaginary hawks. "Beaten," he whispered. "Beaten and done for. . . . Chinese! Yellow chaps chasing 'em!"

At last he came to rest in a clump of bushes near a locked-up and deserted refreshment shed within view of the American side. They made a sort of hole and harbour for him; they met completely overhead. He looked across the rapids, but the firing had ceased now altogether and everything seemed quiet. The Asiatic aeroplane had moved from its former position above the Suspension Bridge, was motionless now above Niagara city, shadowing all that district about the power-house which had been the scene of the land fight. The monster had an air of quiet and assured predominance, and from its stern it trailed, serene and ornamental, a long streaming flag, the red, black, and yellow of the great alliance, the Sunrise and the Dragon. Beyond, to the east, and at a much higher level, hung a second consort, and Bert, presently gathering courage, wriggled out and craned his neck to find another still airship against the sunset in the south.

"Gaw!" he said. "Beaten and chased! My Gawd!"

The fighting, it seemed at first, was quite over in Niagara city, though a German flag was still flying from one shattered house. A white sheet was hoisted above the power-house, and this remained flying all through the events that followed. But presently came a sound of shots and then German soldiers running. They disappeared among the houses, and then came two engineers in blue shirts and trousers hotly pursued by three Japanese swordsmen. The foremost of the two fugitives was a shapely man, and ran lightly and well; the second was a sturdy little man, and rather fat. He ran comically in leaps and bounds, with his plump arms bent up by his side and his head thrown back. The pursuers ran with uniforms and dark, thin metal and leather head-dresses. The little man stumbled, and Bert gasped, realizing a new horror in war.

The foremost swordsman won three strides on him, and was near enough to slash at him and miss as he spurted.

A dozen yards they ran, and then the swordsman slashed again, and Bert could hear across the waters a little sound like the moo of an elfin cow as the fat little man fell forward. Slash went the swordsman and slash at something on the ground that tried to save itself with ineffectual hands. "Oh, I carn't!" cried Bert, near blubbering and staring with starting eyes.

The swordsman slashed a fourth time and went on as his fellows came up after the better runner. The hindmost swordsman stopped and turned back. He had perceived some movement perhaps; but at any-rate he stood, and ever and again slashed at the fallen body.

"Oo-oo!" groaned Bert at every slash, and shrank closer into the bushes and became very still. Presently came a sound of shots from the town, and then everything was quiet, everything, even the hospital.

He saw presently little figures sheathing swords come out from the houses and walk to the debris of the flying-machines the bomb had destroyed. Others appeared wheeling undamaged aeroplanes upon their wheels as men might wheel bicycles, and sprang into the saddles and flapped into the air. A string of three airships appeared far away in the east and flew towards the zenith. The one that hung low above Niagara city came still lower and dropped a rope ladder to pick up men from the power-house.

For a long time he watched the further happenings in Niagara city as a rabbit might watch a meet. He saw men going from building to building to set fire to them, as he presently realized, and he heard a series of dull detonations from the wheel pit of the power-house. Some similar business went on among the works on the Canadian side. Meanwhile more and more airships appeared, and many more flying-machines, until at last it seemed to him nearly a third of the Asiatic fleet had reassembled. He watched them from his bush, cramped but immovable, watched them gather and range themselves and signal and pick up men, until at last they sailed away towards the glowing sunset, going to the great Asiatic rendezvous above the oil wells of Cleveland. They dwindled and passed away, leaving him alone, so far as he could tell, the only living man in a world of ruin and strange loneliness almost beyond describing. He watched them recede and vanish. He stood gaping after them.

"Gaw!" he said at last, like one who rouses himself from a trance.

It was far more than any personal desolation and extremity that flooded his soul. It seemed to him, indeed, that this must be the sunset of his race.

2

He did not at first envisage his own plight in any definite and comprehensible terms. Things had happened to him so much of late, his own efforts had counted for so little, that he had become passive and planless. His last scheme had been to go round the coast of England as a Desert Dervish, giving refined entertainment to his fellow-creatures. Fate had quashed that. Fate had seen fit to direct him to other destinies, had hurried him from point to point, and dropped him at last upon this little wedge of rock between the cataracts. It did not instantly occur to him that now it was his turn to play. He had a singular feeling that all must end as a dream ends, that presently surely he would be back in the world of Grubb and Edna and Bun Hill, that this roar, this glittering presence of incessant water, would be drawn aside as a curtain is drawn aside after a holiday lantern show, and old, familiar customary things reassume their sway. It would be interesting to tell people how he had seen Niagara. And then Kurt's words came into his head: "People torn away from the people they care for; homes smashed, creatures full of life and memories and peculiar little gifts—torn to pieces, starved, and spoilt. . . ."

He wondered, half incredulous, if that was indeed true. It was so hard to realize it. Out beyond there was it possible that Tom and Jessica were also in some dire extremity? That the little greengrocer's shop was no longer standing open, with Jessica serving respectfully, warming Tom's ear in sharp asides, or punctually sending out the goods?

He tried to think what day of the week it was, and found he had lost his reckoning. Perhaps it was Sunday. If so, were they going to Church—or were they hiding, perhaps in bushes? What had happened to the landlord, the butcher, and to Butteridge, and all those people on Dymchurch beach? Something, he knew, had happened to London—a bombardment. But who had bombarded? Were Tom and Jessica, too, being chased by strange brown men with long, bare swords and evil eyes? He thought of various possible aspects of affliction, but presently one phase ousted all the others. Were they getting much to eat? The question haunted him, obsessed him.

If one was very hungry would one eat rats?

It dawned upon him that a peculiar misery that oppressed him was not so much anxiety and patriotic sorrow as hunger. Of course he was hungry!

He reflected and turned his steps towards the little refreshment shed that stood near the end of the ruined bridge. "Ought to be some-thin'——"

He strolled round it once or twice, and then attacked the shutters with his pocket-knife, reinforced presently by a wooden stake he found conveniently near. At last he got a shutter to give, and tore it back and stuck in his head.

"Grub," he remarked, "anyhow. Leastways——"

He got at the inside fastening of the shutter, and had presently this establishment open for his exploration. He found several sealed bottles of sterilized milk, much mineral water, two tins of biscuits, and a crock of very stale cakes, cigarettes in great quantity but very dry, some rather dry oranges, nuts, some tins of canned meat and fruit, and plates and knives and forks and glasses sufficient for several score of people. There was also a zinc locker, but he was unable to negotiate the padlock of this.

"Shan't starve," said Bert, "for a bit, anyhow." He sat on the vendor's seat and regaled himself with biscuits and milk, and felt for a moment quite contented.

"Quite restful," he muttered, munching and glancing about him restlessly, "after what I been through.

"Crikey! *Wot* a day! Oh! *Wot* a day!"

Wonder took possession of him. "Gaw!" he cried. "What a fight it's been! Smashing up the poor fellers. 'Eadlong! The airships—the fliers and all. I wonder what happened to the Zeppelin? . . . And that chap Kurt—I wonder what happened to 'im? 'E was a good sort of chap was Kurt."

Some phantom of imperial solicitude floated through his mind. "Injia," he said. . . .

A more practical interest arose.

"I wonder if there's anything to open one of these tins of corned beef?"

3

After he had feasted, Bert lit a cigarette and sat meditative for a time. "Wonder where Grubb is," he said; "I do wonder that! Wonder if any of 'em wonder about me?"

He reverted to his own circumstances. "Dessay I shall 'ave to stop on this island for some time."

He tried to feel at his ease and secure, but presently the indefinable restlessness of the social animal in solitude distressed him. He began to want to look over his shoulder, and, as a corrective, roused himself to explore the rest of the island.

It was only very slowly that he began to realize the peculiarities of his position, to perceive that the breaking down of the arch between Green Island and the mainland had cut him off completely from the world. Indeed it was only when he came back to where the fore-end of the Hohenzollern lay like a stranded ship, and was contemplating the shattered bridge, that this dawned upon him. Even then it came with no sort of shock to his mind, a fact among a number of other extraordinary and unmanageable facts. He stared at the shattered cabins of the Hohenzollern and its widow's garment of dishevelled silk for a time, but without any idea of its containing any living thing; it was all so twisted and smashed and entirely upside down. Then for a while he gazed at the evening sky. A cloud haze was now appearing, and not an airship was in sight. A swallow flew by and snapped some invisible victim. "Like a dream," he repeated.

Then for a time the rapids held his mind. "Roaring. It keeps on roaring and splashin' always and always. Keeps on. . . ."

At last his interests became personal. "Wonder what I ought to do now?"

He reflected. "Not an idee," he said.

He was chiefly conscious that a fortnight ago he had been in Bun Hill, with no idea of travel in his mind, and that now he was between the Falls of Niagara amidst the devastation and ruins of the greatest air fight in the world, and that in the interval he had been across France, Belgium, Germany, England, Ireland, and a number of other countries. It was an interesting thought and suitable for conversation, but of no great practical utility. "Wonder 'ow I can get orf this?" he said. "Wonder if there is away out? If not . . . rummy!"

Further reflection decided, "I believe I got myself in a bit of a 'ole coming over that bridge. . . ."

"Any'ow—got me out of the way of them Japanesy chaps. Wouldn't 'ave taken 'em long to cut *my* froat. No. Still——"

He resolved to return to the point of Luna Island. For a long time he stood without stirring, scrutinizing the Canadian shore and the wreckage of hotels and houses and the fallen trees of the Victoria Park, pink now in the light of sundown. Not a human being was perceptible in that scene of headlong destruction. Then he came back to the American side of the island, crossed close to the crumpled aluminium wreckage of the Hohenzollern to Green Islet, and scrutinized the hopeless breach in the further bridge and the water that boiled beneath it. Towards Buffalo there was still much smoke, and near the position of the Niagara railway station the houses were burning vigorously. Everything was deserted now, everything was still. One little abandoned thing lay on a transverse path between town and road, a crumpled heap of clothes with sprawling limbs. . . .

" 'Ave a look round," said Bert, and, taking a path that ran through the middle of the island, he presently discovered the wreckage of the two Asiatic aeroplanes that had fallen out of the struggle that ended the Hohenzollern.

With the first he found the wreckage of an aeronaut too.

The machine had evidently dropped vertically, and was badly knocked about amidst a lot of smashed branches in a clump of trees. Its bent
and broken wings and shattered stays sprawled amidst new splintered
wood, and its fore-peak stuck into the ground. The aeronaut dangled
weirdly head downward among the leaves and branches some yards
away, and Bert only discovered him as he turned from the aeroplane.
In the dusky evening light and stillness—for the sun had gone now and
the wind had altogether fallen—this inverted yellow face was anything
but a tranquillizing object to discover suddenly a couple of yards away.
A broken branch had run clean through the man's thorax, and he hung,
so stabbed, looking limp and absurd. In his hand he still clutched, with
the grip of death, a short, light rifle.

For some time Bert stood very still, inspecting this thing.

Then he began to walk away from it, looking constantly back at it.

Presently in an open glade he came to a stop.

"Gaw!' he whispered. "I don' like dead bodies some'ow! I'd almost
rather that chap was alive."

He would not go along the path athwart which the Chinaman hung.
He felt he would rather not have trees round him any more, and that
it would be more comfortable to be quite close to the sociable splash
and uproar of the rapids.

He came upon the second aeroplane in a clear grassy space by the
side of the streaming water, and it seemed scarcely damaged at all. It
looked as though it had floated down into a position of rest. It lay on
its side with one wing in the air. There was no aeronaut near it, dead or
alive. There it lay abandoned, with the water lapping about its long tail.

Bert remained a little aloof from it for a long time, looking into
the gathering shadows among the trees, in the expectation of another
Chinaman alive or dead. Then very cautiously he approached the
machine, and stood regarding its widespread vans, its big steering wheel
and empty saddle. He did not venture to touch it.

"I wish that other chap wasn't there," he said. "I do wish 'e wasn't
there!"

He saw, a few yards away, something bobbing about in an eddy that
spun within a projecting head of rock. As it went round it seemed to
draw him unwillingly towards it. . . .

What could it be?

"Blow," said Bert. "It's another of 'em."

It held him. He told himself that it was the other aeronaut that had been shot in the air and fallen out of the saddle as he strove to land. He tried to go away, and then it occurred to him that he might get a branch or something and push this rotating object out into the stream. That would leave him with one dead body to worry about. Perhaps he might get along with one.

He hesitated, and then with a certain emotion forced himself to do this. He went towards the bushes and cut himself a wand and returned to the rocks, and clambered out to a corner between the eddy and the stream. By that time the sunset was over and the bats were abroad, and he was wet with perspiration.

He prodded the floating blue-clad thing with his wand, failed, tried again successfully as it came round, and as it went out into the stream it turned over, and the light gleamed on golden hair, and—it was Kurt.

It was Kurt, white, and dead, and very calm. There was no mistaking him. There was still plenty of light for that. The stream took him and he seemed to compose himself in its swift grip as one who stretches himself to rest. Whitefaced he was now, and all the colour gone out of him.

A feeling of infinite distress swept over Bert as the body swept out of sight towards the fall.

"Kurt!" he cried. "Kurt! I didn't mean to! Kurt! don' leave me 'ere! Don' leave me!"

Loneliness and desolation overwhelmed him. He gave way. He stood on the rock in the evening light weeping and wailing passionately like a child. It was as though some link that had held him to all these things had broken and gone. He was afraid like a child in a lonely room, shamelessly afraid.

The twilight was closing about him. The trees were full now of strange shadows. All the things about him became strange and unfamiliar with that subtle queerness one feels oftenest in dreams. "O God! I can' stand this," he said, and crept back from the rocks to the grass and crouched down, and suddenly wild sorrow for the death of Kurt, Kurt the brave, Kurt the kindly, came to his help, and he broke from whimpering to weeping. He ceased to crouch; he sprawled upon the grass and clenched an impotent fist.

"This war," he cried, "this blarsted foolery of a war.

"O Kurt! Lieutenant Kurt.

"I done," he said. "I done. I've 'ad all I want, and more than I want. The world's all rot, and there ain't no sense in it. The night's coming. . . . If 'E comes after me—'E can't come after me—'E can't. . . .

"If 'E comes after me, I'll fro' myself into the water. . . .

Presently he was talking again in a low undertone.

"There ain't nothing to be afraid of reely. It's jest imagination. Poor old Kurt—he thought it would happen. Prevision like. 'E never gave me that letter or tole me who the lady was. It's like what 'e said—people tore away from everything they belonged to—everywhere. Exactly like what 'e said. . . . 'Ere I am cast away—thousand of miles from Edna or Grubb or any of my lot—like a plant tore up by the roots. . . . And every war's been like this, only I 'adn't the sense to understand it. Always. All sorts of 'oles and corners chaps 'ave died in. And people 'adn't the sense to understand, 'adn't the sense to feel it and stop it. Thought war was fine. My Gawd! . . .

"Dear old Edna. She was a fair bit of all right—she was. That time we 'ad a boat at Kingston. . . .

"I bet—I'll see 'er again yet. Won't be my fault if I don't. . . ."

4

Suddenly on the very verge of this heroic resolution, Bert became rigid with terror. Something was creeping towards him through the grass. Something was creeping and halting and creeping again towards him through the dim, dark grass. The night was electrical with horror. For a time everything was still. Bert ceased to breathe. It could not be. No, it was too small!

It advanced suddenly upon him with a rush, with a little meawling cry and tail erect. It rubbed its head against him and purred. It was a tiny, skinny little kitten.

"Gaw! Pussy, 'ow you frightened me," said Bert, with drops of perspiration on his brow.

5

He sat with his back to a tree stump all that night, holding the kitten in his arms. His mind was tired, and he talked or thought coherently no longer. Towards dawn he dozed.

When he awoke he was stiff but in better heart, and the kitten slept warmly and reassuringly inside his jacket. And fear, he found, had gone from amidst the trees.

He stroked the kitten, and the little creature woke up to excessive fondness and purring. "You want some milk," said Bert, "that's what you want. And I could do with a bit of brekker, too."

He yawned and stood up, with the kitten on his shoulder, and stared about him, recalling the circumstances of the previous day, the grey, immense happenings.

"Mus' do something," he said.

He turned towards the trees, and was presently standing contemplating the dead aeronaut again. The kitten he held companionably against his neck. The body was horrible, but not nearly so horrible as it had been at twilight, and now the limbs were limper and the gun had slipped to the ground and lay half hidden in the grass.

"I suppose we ought to bury 'im, Kitty," said Bert, and looked helplessly at the rocky soil about him. "We got to stay on the island with 'im."

It was some time before he could turn away and go on towards that provision shed. "Brekker first," he said, "anyhow," stroking the kitten on his shoulder. She rubbed his cheek affectionately with her furry little face and presently nibbled at his ear. "Wan' some milk, eh?" he said, and turned his back on the dead man as though he mattered nothing.

He was puzzled to find the door of the shed open, though he had closed and latched it very carefully overnight, and he found also some dirty plates he had not noticed before on the bench. He discovered that the hinges of the tin locker were unscrewed and that it could be opened. He had not observed this overnight.

"Silly of me!" said Bert. " 'Ere I was puzzlin' and whackin' away at the padlock, never noticing." It had been used apparently as an ice-chest, but it contained nothing now but the remains of half-a-dozen boiled chickens, some ambiguous substance that might once have been butter and a singularly unappetising smell. He closed the lid again carefully.

He gave the kitten some milk in a dirty plate and sat watching its busy little tongue for a time. Then he was moved to make an inventory of the provisions. There were six bottles of milk unopened and one opened, sixty bottles of mineral water and a large stock of syrups, about two thousand cigarettes and upwards of a hundred cigars, nine oranges, two unopened tins of corned beef and one opened, two tins of biscuits and eleven hard cakes, a hatful of nuts and five large tins of Californian peaches. He jotted it down on a piece of paper. "Ain't much solid food," he said, "still—— A fortnight, say!

"Anything might happen in a fortnight."

He gave the kitten a small second helping and a scrap of beef, and then went down with the little creature running after him, tail erect and in high spirits, to look at the remains of the Hohenzollern. It had shifted in the night and seemed on the whole more firmly grounded on Green Island than before. From it his eye went to the shattered bridge and then across to the still desolation of Niagara city. Nothing moved over there but a number of crows. They were busy with the engineer he had seen cut down on the previous day. He saw no dogs, but he heard one howling.

"We got to get out of this some'ow, Kitty," he said. "That milk won't last for ever—not at the rate you lap it."

He regarded the sluice-like flood before him. "Plenty of water," he said. "Won't be drink we shall want."

He decided to make a careful exploration of the island. Presently he came to a locked gate labelled "Biddle Stairs," and clambered over to discover a steep old wooden staircase leading down the face of the cliff amidst a vast and increasing uproar of waters. He left the kitten above and descended these, and discovered with a thrill of hope a path leading among the rocks at the foot of the roaring downrush of the Centre Fall. Perhaps this was a sort of way?

It led him only to the choking and deafening experience of the Cave of the Winds, and after he had spent a quarter of an hour in a partially stupefied condition flattened between solid rock and nearly as solid waterfall, he decided that this was after all no practicable route to Canada, and retraced his steps. As he reascended the Biddle Stairs, he heard what he decided at last must be a sort of echo, a sound of some one walking about on the gravel paths above. When he got to the top the place was as solitary as before.

Thence he made his way, with the kitten skirmishing along beside him in the grass, to a staircase that led to a lump of projecting rock that enfiladed the huge green majesty of the Horseshoe Fall. He stood there for some time in silence.

"You wouldn't think," he said at last, "there was so much water. . . . This roarin' and splashin', it get's on one's nerves at last. . . . Sounds like people talking. . . . Sounds like people going about. . . . Sounds like anything you fancy."

He retired up the staircase again. "I s'pose I shall keep on goin' round this blessed island," he said drearily. "Round and round and round."

He found himself presently beside the less damaged Asiatic aeroplane again. He stared at it and the kitten smelt it. "Broke!" he said.

He looked up with a convulsive start.

Advancing slowly towards him out from among the trees were two tall, gaunt figures. They were blackened and bandaged; the hindmost one limped and had his head swathed in white, but the foremost one still carried himself as a Prince should do, for all that his left arm was in a sling, and one side of his face scalded a livid crimson. He was the Prince Karl Albert, the War Lord, the "German Alexander," and the man behind him was the bird-faced man whose cabin had once been taken from him and given to Bert.

6

With that apparition began a new phase of Goat Island in Bert's experience. He ceased to be a solitary representative of humanity in a vast and violent and incomprehensible universe, and became once more a social creature, a man in a world of other men. For an instant these two were terrible, then they seemed sweet and desirable as brothers. They too were in this scrape with him, marooned and puzzled. He wanted extremely to hear exactly what had happened to them. What mattered it, if one was a prince and both were foreign soldiers, if neither perhaps had adequate English? His native cockney freedom flowed too generously for him to think of that, and surely the Asiatic fleets had purged all such trivial differences. " 'Ul-*lo*" he said; " 'ow did you get 'ere?"

"It is the Englishman who brought us the Butteridge machine," said the bird-faced officer in German, and then in a tone of horror as Bert advanced, "Salute!" and again louder, "*Salute!*"

"Gaw!" said Bert, and stopped with a second comment under his breath. He stared and saluted awkwardly, and became at once a masked defensive thing with whom co-operation was impossible.

For a time these two perfected modern aristocrats stood regarding the difficult problem of the Anglo-Saxon citizen, that ambiguous citizen who, obeying some mysterious law in his blood, would neither drill nor be a democrat. Bert was by no means a beautiful object, but in some inexplicable way he looked resistent. He wore his cheap suit of serge, now showing many signs of wear, and its loose fit made him seem sturdier than he was; above his disengaging face was a white German cap that was altogether too big for him, and his trousers were crumpled up his legs and their ends tucked into the rubber high-lows of a deceased German aeronaut. He looked an inferior though by no means an easy inferior, and instinctively they hated him.

The Prince pointed to the flying-machine and said something in broken English that Bert took for German and failed to understand. He intimated as much.

"Dummer Kerl!" said the bird-faced officer from among his bandages.

The Prince pointed again with his undamaged hand. "You understan' dis Drachenflieger?"

Bert began to comprehend the situation. He regarded the Asiatic machine. The habits of Bun Hill returned to him. "It's a foreign make," he said ambiguously.

The two Germans consulted. "You are—an expert?" said the Prince.

"We reckon to repair," said Bert, in the exact manner of Grubb.

The Prince sought in his vocabulary. "Is dat," he said, "goot to fly?"

Bert reflected, and scratched his chin slowly. "I got to look at it," he replied. . . . "It's 'ad rough usage."

He made a sound with his teeth he had also acquired from Grubb, put his hands in his trouser pockets and strolled back to the machine.

Typically Grubb chewed something, but Bert could chew only imaginatively. "Three days' work in this," he said, teething. For the first time it dawned on him that there were possibilities in this machine. It was evident that the wing that lay on the ground was disabled. Three stays that held it rigid had snapped across a ridge of rock, and there was also a strong possibility of the engine being badly damaged. The wing hook on that side was also askew, but probably that would not affect the flight. Beyond that there probably wasn't much the matter. Bert scratched his cheek again, and contemplated the broad sunlit waste of the Upper Rapids. "We might make a job of this. . . . You leave it to me."

He surveyed it intently again, and the Prince and his officer watched him. In Bun Hill Bert and Grubb had developed to a high pitch among the hiring stock a method of repair by substitution; they substituted bits of other machines. A machine that was too utterly and obviously done for even to proffer for hire had nevertheless still capital value. It became a sort of quarry for nuts and screws and wheels, bars and spokes, chain-links and the like; a mine of ill-fitting "parts" to replace the defects of machines still current. And back among the trees was a second Asiatic aeroplane.

The kitten caressed Bert's airship boots unheeded. "Mend dat Drachenflieger," said the Prince. "If I do mend it," said Bert, struck by a new thought, "none of us ain't to be trusted to fly it."

"*I* vill fly it," said the Prince.

"Very likely break your neck," said Bert, after a pause.

The Prince did not understand him and disregarded what he said. He pointed his gloved finger to the machine and turned to the bird-faced officer with some remark in German. The officer answered and the Prince responded with a sweeping gesture towards the sky. Then he spoke—it seemed eloquently. Bert watched him and guessed his meaning. "Much more likely to break your neck," he said. " 'Owever, 'ere goes."

He began to pry about the saddle and engine of the Drachenflieger in a search for tools. Also he wanted some black oily stuff for his hands and face. For the first rule in the art of repairing, as it was known to the firm of Grubb and Smallways, was to get your hands and face thoroughly and conclusively blackened. Also he took off his jacket and waistcoat and put his cap carefully to the back of his head in order to facilitate scratching.

The Prince and the officer seemed disposed to watch him, but he succeeded in making it clear to them that this would inconvenience him and that he had to "puzzle out a bit" before he could get to work. They thought him over, but his shop experience had given him something of the authoritative way of the expert with common men. And at last they went away. Thereupon he went straight to the second aeroplane, got the aeronaut's gun and ammunition and hid them in a clump of nettles close at hand. "That's all right," said Bert, and then proceeded to a careful inspection of the debris of the wings in the trees. Then he went back to the first aeroplane to compare the two. The Bun Hill method was quite possibly practicable if there was nothing hopeless or incomprehensible in the engine.

The Germans returned presently to find him already generously smutty, and touching and testing knobs and screws and levers with an expression of profound sagacity. When the bird-faced officer addressed a remark to him he waved him aside with "Nong comprong. Shut it! It's no good."

Then he had an idea. "Dead chap back there wants burying," he said, jerking a thumb over his shoulder.

7

With the appearance of these two men Bert's whole universe had changed again. A curtain fell before the immense and terrible desolation that had overwhelmed him. He was in a world of three people, a minute human world that nevertheless filled his brain with eager speculations and schemes and cunning ideas. What were they thinking of? What did they think of him? What did they mean to do? A hundred busy threads interlaced in his mind as he pottered studiously over the Asiatic aeroplane. New ideas came up like bubbles on soda water.

"Gaw!" he said suddenly. He had just appreciated as a special aspect of this irrational injustice of fate that these two men were alive and that Kurt was dead. All the crew of the Hohenzollern were shot or burnt or smashed or drowned, and these two lurking in the padded forward cabin had escaped.

"I suppose 'e thinks it's 'is bloomin' star," he muttered, and found himself uncontrollably exasperated.

He stood up, facing round to the two men. They were standing side by side regarding him. "It's no good," he said, "starin' at me, You only put me out." And then, seeing they did not understand, he advanced towards them, wrench in hand. It occurred to him as he did so that the Prince was really a very big and powerful and serene-looking person. But he said, nevertheless, pointing through the trees, "dead man!"

The bird-faced man intervened with a reply in German.

"Dead man," said Bert, to him. "There."

He had great difficulty in inducing them to inspect the dead China-man, and at last led them to him. Then they made it evident that they proposed that he, as a common person below the rank of officer, should have the sole and undivided privilege of disposing of the body by dragging it to the water's edge. There was some heated gesticulation, and at last the bird-faced officer abased himself to help. Together they dragged the limp and now swollen Asiatic through the trees, and after a rest or so—for he trailed very heavily—dumped him into the westward rapid. Bert returned to his expert investigation of the flying-machine at last with aching arms, and in a state of gloomy rebellion. "Brasted cheek," he said. "One'd think I was one of 'is beastly German slaves!

"Prancing beggar!"

And then he fell speculating what would happen when the flying-machine was repaired—if it could be repaired.

The two Germans went away again, and after some reflection Bert removed several nuts, resumed his jacket and vest, pocketed those nuts and his tools and hid the set of tools from the second aeroplane in the fork of a tree. "Right O!" he said, as he jumped down after the last of these precautions. The Prince and his companion reappeared as he returned to the machine by the water's edge. The Prince surveyed his progress for a time, and then went towards the Parting of the Waters and stood with folded arms gazing up stream in profound thought. The bird-faced officer came up to Bert, heavy with a sentence in English.

"Go," he said, with a helping gesture, "and eat."

When Bert got to the refreshment shed he found all the food had vanished except one measured ration of corned beef and three biscuits. He regarded this with open eyes and mouth. The kitten appeared from under the vendor's seat with an ingratiating purr. "Of course!" said Bert. "Why! Where's your milk?"

He accumulated wrath for a moment or so, then seized the plate in one hand, and the biscuits in another, and went in search of the Prince, breathing vile words anent "grub" and his intimate interior. He approached without saluting.

" 'Ere!" he said fiercely. "What the devil's this?"

An entirely unsatisfactory altercation followed. Bert expounded the Bun Hill theory of the relations of grub to efficiency in English, the bird-faced man replied with points about nations and discipline in German. The Prince having made an estimate of Bert's quality and physique suddenly hectored. He gripped Bert by the shoulder and shook him, making his pockets rattle, shouted something to him, and flung him struggling back. He hit him as though he was a German private. Bert went back, white and scared, but resolved by all his cockney standards upon one thing. He was bound in honour to "go for" the Prince. "Gaw!" he gasped, buttoning his coat.

"Now," cried the Prince, "vill you go!" and then, catching the heroic gleam in Bert's eye, drew his sword.

The bird-faced officer intervened, saying something in German and pointing skyward.

Far away in the south-west appeared a Japanese airship coming fast towards them. Their conflict ended at that. The Prince was first to grasp the situation and lead the retreat. All three scuttled like rabbits for the trees, and ran to and fro for cover until they found a hollow in which the grass grew rank. There they all squatted within six yards of one another. They sat in this place for a long time, up to their necks in the grass and watching through the branches for the airship. Bert had dropped some of his corned beef, but he found the biscuits in his hand and ate them quietly. The monster came nearly overhead and then went away to Niagara and dropped beyond the power works. When it was near they all kept silence, and then presently they fell into an argument that was robbed perhaps of immediate explosive effect only by their failure to understand one another.

It was Bert who began the talking, and he talked on, regardless of what they understood or failed to understand. But his voice must have conveyed his cantankerous intentions.

"You want that machine done," he said first, "you'd better keep your hands off me!"

They disregarded that and be repeated it.

Then he expanded his idea, and the spirit of speech took hold of him. "You think you got 'old of a chap you can kick and 'it like you do your private soldiers—you're jolly well mistaken. See? I've 'ad about enough of you and your antics. I been thinking you over, you and your war and your Empire, and all the rot of it. Rot it is. It's you Germans made all the trouble in Europe first and last. And all for nothin'. Jest silly prancing! Jest because you've got the uniforms and flags! 'Ere I was—I didn't want to 'ave anything to do with you. I jest didn't care a 'eng at all about you. Then you get 'old of me—steal me practically—and 'ere I am, thousands of miles away from home and everything, and all your silly fleet smashed up to rags. And you want to go on prancing *now!* Not if I know it!

"Look at the mischief you done. Look at the way you smashed up New York—the people you killed, the stuff you wasted. Can't you learn?"

"Dummer Kerl!" said the bird-faced man suddenly, in a tone of concentrated malignity, glaring under his bandages. "E sel!"

"That's German for silly ass! I know. But who's the silly ass—'im or me? When I was a kid I used to read penny dreadfuls about 'aving adventures and being a great c'mander and all that rot. I stowed it. But what's 'e got in 'is head? Rot about Napoleon, rot about Alexander, rot about 'is blessed family and 'im and Gawd and David and all that. Anyone who wasn't a dressed-up silly fool of a Prince could 'ave told all this was goin' to 'appen. There was us in Europe all at sixes and sevens with our silly flags and our silly newspapers raggin' us up against each other and keepin' us apart, and there was China as solid as a cheese, with millions and millions of men only wantin' a bit of science, and a bit of enterprise, to be as good as all of us. You thought they couldn't

get at you. And then they got flying-machines. And bif!—'ere we are.
Why, when they didn't go on making guns and armies in China we
went and poked 'em up until they did. They 'ad to give us this lickin'
they've give us. We wouldn't be 'appy till they did. And, as I say, 'ere
we are!"

The bird-faced officer shouted to him to be quiet, and then began
conversation with the Prince.

"British citizen," said Bert. "You ain't obliged to listen, but I ain't
obliged to shut up." And for some time he continued his dissertation
upon Imperialism, militarism, and international politics. But their
talking put him out, and for a time he was certainly merely repeating
abusive terms, "prancin' nincompoops," and the like, old terms and
new.

Then suddenly he remembered his essential grievance. " 'Owever,
look 'ere—'ere! The thing I started this talk about is where's that food
there was in that shed? That's what I want to know. Where you put it?"

He paused. They went on talking in German. He repeated his
question. They disregarded him. He asked a third time in a manner
insupportably aggressive.

There fell a tense silence. For some seconds the three regarded one
another. The Prince eyed Bert steadfastly, and Bert quailed under his
eye. Slowly the Prince rose to his feet and the bird-faced officer jerked
up beside him. Bert remained squatting.

"Be quaiat," said the Prince.

Bert perceived this was no moment for eloquence.

The two Germans regarded him as he crouched there. Death for a
moment seemed near.

Then the Prince turned away and the two of them went towards the
flying-machine.

"Gaw!" whispered Bert, and then uttered under his breath one single
word of abuse. He sat crouched together for perhaps three minutes, then
he sprang to his feet and went off towards the Chinese aeronaut's gun
hidden among the weeds.

8

There was no pretence after that moment that Bert was under the orders
of the Prince or that he was going on with the repairing of the flying-

machine. The two Germans took possession of that and set to work upon it. Bert, with his new weapon, went off to the neighbourhood of Terrapin Rock, and there sat down to examine it. It was a short rifle with a big cartridge and a nearly full magazine. He took out the cartridges carefully and then tried the trigger and fittings until he felt sure he had the use of it. He reloaded carefully. Then he remembered he was hungry and went off, gun under his arm, to hunt in and out about the refreshment shed. He had the sense to perceive that he must not show himself with the gun to the Prince or his companion. So long as they thought him unarmed they would leave him alone, but there was no knowing what the Napoleonic person might do if he saw Bert's weapon. Also he did not go near them because he knew that within himself boiled a reservoir of rage and fear, that he wanted to shoot these two men. He wanted to shoot them, and he thought that to shoot them would be a quite horrible thing to do. The two sides of his inconsistent civilization warred within him.

Near the shed the kitten turned up again, obviously keen for milk. This greatly enhanced his own angry sense of hunger. He began to talk as he hunted about, and presently stood still shouting insults. He talked of war and pride and Imperialism. "Any other Prince but you would have died with his men and his ship!" he cried.

The two Germans at the machine heard his voice going ever and again amidst the clamour of the waters. Their eyes met and they smiled slightly.

He was disposed for a time to sit in the refreshment shed waiting for them, but then it occurred to him that so he might get them both at close quarters. He strolled off presently to the point of Luna Island to think the situation out.

It had seemed a comparatively simple one at first, but as he turned it over in his mind its possibilities increased and multiplied. Both these men had swords—had either a revolver?

Also, if he shot them both he might never find the food!

So far he had been going about with this gun under his arm, and a sense of lordly security in his mind, but what if they saw the gun and decided to ambush him? Goat Island is nearly all cover, trees, rocks, thickets, and irregularities.

Why not go and murder them both now?

"I carn't," said Bert, dismissing that. "I got to be worked up."

But it was a mistake to get right away from them. That suddenly became clear. He ought to keep them under observation, ought to "scout" them. Then he would be able to see what they were doing, whether either of them had a revolver, where they had hidden the food. He would be better able to determine what they meant to do to him. If he didn't "scout" them, presently they would begin to "scout" him. This seemed so eminently reasonable that he acted upon it forthwith. He thought over his costume and threw his collar and the tell-tale aeronaut's white cap into the water far below. He turned his coat collar up to hide any gleam of his dirty shirt. The tools and nuts in his pockets were disposed to clank, but he rearranged them and wrapped some letters and his pocket handkerchief about them. He started off circumspectly and noiselessly, listening and peering at every step. As he drew near his antagonists, much grunting and creaking served to locate them. He discovered them engaged in what looked like a wrestling match with the Asiatic flying-machine. Their coats were off, their swords laid aside, they were working magnificently. Apparently, they were turning it round and were having a good deal of difficulty with the long tail among the trees. He dropped flat at the sight of them and wriggled into a little hollow, and so lay watching their exertions. Ever and again, to pass the time, he would cover one or other of them with his gun.

He found them quite interesting to watch, so interesting that at times he came near to shouting to advise them. He perceived that when they had the machine turned round they would then be in immediate want of the nuts and tools he carried. Then they would come after him. They would certainly conclude he had them or had hidden them. Should he hide his gun and do a deal for food with these tools? He felt he would not be able to part with the gun again now he had once felt its reassuring company. The kitten turned up and made a great fuss with him and licked and bit his ear.

The sun clambered to midday, and once that morning he saw, though the Germans did not, an Asiatic airship very far to the south, going swiftly eastward.

At last the flying-machine was turned and stood poised on its wheel, with its hooks pointing up the Rapids. The two Germans wiped their

faces, resumed jackets and swords, spoke and bore themselves like men
who congratulated themselves on a good laborious morning. Then they
went off briskly towards the refreshment shed, the Prince leading. Bert
became active in pursuit; but he found it impossible to stalk them
quickly enough and silently enough to discover the hiding-place of the
food. He found them when they came into sight again, seated with their
backs against the shed, plates on knee, and a tin of corned beef and a
plateful of biscuits between them. They seemed in fairly good spirits,
and once the Prince laughed. At this vision of eating Bert's plans gave
way. Fierce hunger carried him. He appeared before them suddenly at
a distance of perhaps twenty yards, gun in hand. " 'Ands up!" he said
in a hard, ferocious voice.

The Prince hesitated, and then up went two pairs of hands. The gun
had surprised them both completely.

"Stand up," said Bert. . . . "Drop that fork!"

They obeyed again.

"What nex'?" said Bert to himself. "Orf stage, I suppose. That way,"
he said. "Go!"

The Prince obeyed with remarkable alacrity. When he reached the
head of the clearing he said something quickly to the bird-faced man
and they both, with an entire lack of dignity, *ran!*

Bert was struck with an exasperating after-thought.

"Gord!" he cried with infinite vexation. "Why! I ought to 'ave took
their swords! 'Ere!"

But the Germans were already out of sight, and no doubt taking
cover among the trees. Bert fell back upon imprecations, then he went
up to the shed, cursorily examined the possibility of a flank attack, put
his gun handy and set to work, with a convulsive listening pause before
each mouthful, on the Prince's plate of corned beef. He had finished
that up and handed its gleanings to the kitten and he was falling-to on
the second plateful, when the plate broke in his hand! He stared, with
the fact slowly creeping upon him that an instant before he had heard
a crack among the thickets. Then he sprang to his feet, snatched up his
gun in one hand and the tin of corned beef in the other, and fled round
the shed to the other side of the clearing. As he did so came a second
crack from the thickets, and something went *phwit!* by his ear.

He didn't stop running until he was in what seemed to him a strongly defensible position near Luna Island. Then he took cover, panting, and crouched expectant.

"They got a revolver after all!" he panted. . . . "Wonder if they got two? If they 'ave—Gord!—I'm done!"

"Where's the kitten? Finishin' up that corned beef, I suppose. Little beggar!"

9

So it was that war began on Goat Island. It lasted a day and a night, the longest day and the longest night in Bert's life. He had to lie close and listen and watch. Also he had to scheme what he should do. It was clear now that he had to kill these two men if he could, and that if they could they would kill him. The prize was first food and then the flying-machine and the doubtful privilege of trying to ride it. If one failed one would certainly be killed, if one succeeded one would get away somewhere over there. For a time Bert tried to imagine what it was like over there. His mind ran over possibilities, deserts, angry Americans, Japanese, Chinese—perhaps Red Indians! (Were there still Red Indians?)

"Got to take what comes," said Bert. "No way out of it that I can see."

Was that voices? He realized that his attention was wandering. For a time all his senses were very alert. The uproar of the Falls was very confusing, and it mixed in all sorts of sounds, like feet walking, like voices talking, like shouts and cries.

"Silly great catarac'," said Bert. "There ain't no sense in it, fallin' and fallin'."

Never mind that now! What were the Germans doing?

Would they go back to the flying-machine? They couldn't do anything with it, because he had those nuts and screws and the wrench and other tools. But suppose they found the second set of tools he had hidden in a tree! He had hidden the things well, of course, but they *might* find them. One wasn't sure, of course—one wasn't sure. He tried to remember just exactly how he had hidden those tools. He tried to persuade himself they were certainly and surely hidden, but his memory began to play antics. Had he really left the handle of the wrench sticking out, shining out at the fork of the branch?

Ssh! What was that? Some one stirring in those bushes? Up went an expectant muzzle. No! Where was the kitten? No! It was just imagination, not even the kitten.

The Germans would certainly miss and hunt about for the tools and nuts and screws he carried in his pockets; that was clear. Then they would decide he had them and come for him. He had only to remain still under cover, therefore, and he would get them. Was there any flaw in that? Would they take off more removable parts of the flying-machine and then lie up for him? No, they wouldn't do that, because they were two to one; they would have no apprehension of his getting off in the flying-machine, and no sound reason for supposing he would approach it, and so they would do nothing to damage or disable it. That, he decided, was clear. But suppose they lay up for him by the food. Well, that they wouldn't do, because they would know he had this corned beef; there was enough in this can to last, with moderation, several days. Of course they might try to tire him out instead of attacking him——

He roused himself with a start. He had just grasped the real weakness of his position. He might go to sleep!

It needed but ten minutes under the suggestion of that idea before he realized that he was going to sleep!

He rubbed his eyes and handled his gun. He had never before realized the intensely soporific effect of the American sun, of the American air, the drowsy sleep-compelling uproar of Niagara. Hitherto these things had on the whole seemed stimulating. . . .

If he had not eaten so much and eaten it so fast, he would not be so heavy. Are vegetarians always bright? . . .

He roused himself with a jerk again.

If he didn't do something he would fall asleep, and if he fell asleep it was ten to one they would find him snoring, and finish him forthwith. If he sat motionless and noiseless he would inevitably sleep. It was better, he told himself, to take even the risks of attacking than that. This sleep trouble, he felt, was going to beat him, must beat him in the end. They were all right; one could sleep and the other could watch. That, come to think of it, was what they would always do; one would do anything they wanted done, the other would lie under cover near at hand, ready to shoot. They might even trap him like that. One might act as a decoy.

That set him thinking of decoys. What a fool he had been to throw his cap away. It would have been invaluable on a stick—especially at night.

He found himself wishing for a drink. He settled that for a time by putting a pebble in his mouth. And then the sleep craving returned.

It became clear to him he must attack.

Like so many great generals before him, he found his baggage, that is to say his tin of corned beef, a serious impediment to mobility. At last he decided to put the beef loose in his pocket and abandon the tin. It was not perhaps an ideal arrangement, but one must make sacrifices when one is campaigning. He crawled perhaps ten yards, and then for a time the possibilities of the situation paralyzed him.

The afternoon was still. The roar of the cataract simply threw up that immense stillness in relief. He was doing his best to contrive the deaths of two better men than himself. Also they were doing their best to contrive his. What, behind this silence, were they doing?

Suppose he came upon them suddenly and fired and missed?

10

He crawled, and halted listening, and crawled again until nightfall, and no doubt the German Alexander and his lieutenant did the same. A large scale map of Goat Island marked with red and blue lines, to show these strategic movements would no doubt have displayed much interlacing, but as a matter of fact neither side saw anything of the other throughout that age-long day of tedious alertness. Bert never knew how near he got to them nor how far he kept from them. Night found him no longer sleepy, but athirst, and near the American Fall. He was inspired by the idea that his antagonists might be in the wreckage of the Hohenzollern cabins that was jammed against Green Island. He became enterprising, broke from any attempt to conceal himself, and went across the little bridge at the double. He found nobody. It was his first visit to these huge fragments of airship, and for a time he explored them curiously in the dim light. He discovered the forward cabin was nearly intact,

with its door slanting downward and a corner under water. He crept
in, drank, and then was struck by the brilliant idea of shutting the door
and sleeping on it.

But now he could not sleep at all.

He nodded towards morning and woke up to find it fully day. He
breakfasted on corned beef and water, and sat for a long time apprecia-
tive of the security of his position. At last he became enterprising and
bold. He would, he decided, settle this business forthwith, one way or
the other. He was tired of all this crawling. He set out in the morning
sunshine, gun in hand, scarcely troubling to walk softly. He went round
the refreshment shed without finding any one, and then through the
trees towards the flying-machine. He came upon the bird-faced man
sitting on the ground with his back against a tree, bent up over his
folded arms, sleeping, his bandage very much over one eye.

Bert stopped abruptly and stood perhaps fifteen yards away, gun in
hand ready. Where was the Prince? Then, sticking out at the side of the
tree beyond, he saw a shoulder. Bert took five deliberate paces to the
left. The great man became visible, leaning up against the trunk, pistol
in one hand and sword in the other, and yawning—yawning. You can't
shoot a yawning man, Bert found. He advanced upon his antagonist
with his gun levelled, some foolish fancy of "hands up!" in his mind.
The Prince became aware of him, the yawning mouth shut like a trap,
and he stood stiffly up. Bert stopped, silent. For a moment the two
regarded one another.

Had the Prince been a wise man he would, I suppose, have dodged
behind the tree. Instead, he gave vent to a shout, and raised pistol and
sword. At that, like an automaton, Bert pulled his trigger.

It was his first experience of an oxygen-containing bullet. A great
flame spurted from the middle of the Prince, a blinding flare, and there
came a thud like the firing of a gun. Something hot and wet struck
Bert's face. Then through a whirl of blinding smoke and steam he saw
limbs and a collapsing, burst body fling themselves to earth.

Bert was so astonished that he stood agape, and the bird-faced officer
might have cut him to the earth without a struggle. But instead the bird-
faced officer was running away through the undergrowth, dodging as
he went. Bert roused himself to a brief ineffectual pursuit, but he had no

stomach for further killing. He returned to the mangled, scattered thing that had so recently been the great Prince Karl Albert. He surveyed the scorched and splashed vegetation about it. He made some speculative identifications. He advanced gingerly and picked up the hot revolver, to find all its chambers strained and burst. He became aware of a cheerful and friendly presence. He was greatly shocked that one so young should see so frightful a scene.

" 'Ere, Kitty," he said, "this ain't no place for you."

He made three strides across the devastated area, captured the kitten neatly, and went his way towards the shed, with her purring loudly on his shoulder.

"*You* don't seem to mind," he said.

For a time he fussed about the shed, and at last discovered the rest of the provisions hidden in the roof. "Seems 'ard," he said, as he administered a saucerful of milk, "when you get three men in a 'ole like this, they can't work together. But 'im and 'is princing was jest a bit too thick!

"Gaw!" he reflected, sitting on the counter and eating, "what a thing life is! 'Ere am I; I seen 'is picture, 'eard 'is name since I was a kid in frocks. Prince Karl Albert! And if any one 'ad tole me I was going to blow 'im to smithereens—there! I shouldn't 'ave believed it, Kitty.

"That chap at Margit ought to 'ave tole me about it. All 'e tole me was that I got a weak chess.

"That other chap, 'e ain't going to do much. Wonder what I ought to do about 'im?"

He surveyed the trees with a keen blue eye and fingered the gun on his knee. "I don't like this killing, Kitty," he said. "It's like Kurt said about being blooded. Seems to me you got to be blooded young. . . . If that Prince 'ad come up to me and said, 'Shake 'ands!' I'd 'ave shook 'ands. . . . Now 'ere's that other chap, dodging about! 'E's got 'is 'ead 'urt already, and there's something wrong with his leg. And burns. Golly! it isn't three weeks ago I first set eyes on 'im, and then 'e was smart and set up—'ands full of 'air-brushes and things, and swearin' at me. A regular gentleman! Now 'e's 'arf-way to a wild man. What am I to do with 'im? What the 'ell am I to do with 'im? I can't let 'im 'ave that flying-machine; that's a bit *too* good, and if I don't kill 'im 'e'll jest hang about this island and starve. . . .

"'E's got a sword, of course. . . ."

He resumed his philosophizing after he had lit a cigarette.

"War's a silly gaim, Kitty. It's a silly gaim! We common people—we were fools. We thought those big people knew what they were up to—and they didn't. Look at that chap! 'E 'ad all Germany be'ind 'im, and what 'as 'e made of it? Smeshin' and blunderin' and destroyin', and there 'e 'is! Jest a mess of blood and boots and things. Jest an 'orrid splash! Prince Karl Albert! And all the men 'e led and the ships 'e 'ad, the airships and the dragon-fliers—all scattered like a paperchase between this 'ole and Germany. And fightin' going on and burnin' and killin' that 'e started, war without end all over the world!

"I suppose I shall 'ave to kill that other chap. I suppose I must. But it ain't at all the sort of job I fancy, Kitty!"

For a time he hunted about the island amidst the uproar of the waterfall looking for the wounded officer, and at last he started him out of some bushes near the head of Biddle Stairs. But as he saw the bent and bandaged figure in limping flight before him, he found his Cockney softness too much for him again; he could neither shoot nor pursue. "I carn't," he said, "that's flat. I 'aven't the guts for it! 'Ell 'ave to go."

He turned his steps towards the flying-machine. . . .

He never saw the bird-faced officer again, nor any further evidence of his presence. Towards evening he grew fearful of ambushes and hunted vigorously for an hour or so, but in vain. He slept in a good defensible position at the extremity of the rocky point that runs out to the Canadian Fall, and in the night he woke in panic terror and fired his gun. But it was nothing. He slept no more that night. In the morning he became curiously concerned for the vanished man, and hunted for him as one might for an erring brother. "If I knew some German," he said, "I'd 'oller. It's jest not knowing German does it. You can't explain."

He discovered, later, traces of an attempt to cross the gap in the broken bridge. A rope with a bolt attached had been flung across and had caught in a fenestration of a projecting fragment of railing. The end of the rope trailed in the seething water towards the fall.

But the bird-faced officer was already rubbing shoulders with certain inert matter that had once been Lieutenant Kurt and the Chinese aeronaut and a dead cow, and much other uncongenial company, in the huge circle of the Whirlpool two and a quarter miles away. Never had that great gathering place, that incessant, aimless, unprogressive hurry of waste and battered things, been so crowded with strange and melancholy derelicts. Round they went and round, and every day brought its new contributions, luckless brutes, shattered fragments of boat and flying-machine, endless citizens from the cities upon the shores of the great lakes above. Much came from Cleveland. It all gathered here, and whirled about indefinitely, and over it all gathered daily a greater abundance of birds.

TEN

The World under the War

I

Bert spent two more days upon Goat Island, and finished all his provisions except the cigarettes and mineral water, before he brought himself to try the Asiatic flying-machine.

Even at last he did not so much go off upon it as get carried off. It had taken only an hour or so to substitute wing stays from the second flying-machine and to replace the nuts he had himself removed. The engine was in working order, and differed only very simply and obviously from that of a contemporary motor-bicycle. The rest of the time was taken up by a vast musing and delaying and hesitation. Chiefly he saw himself splashing into the rapids and whirling down them to the Fall, clutching and drowning, but also he had a vision of being hopelessly in the air, going fast and unable to ground. His mind was too concentrated upon the business of flying for him to think very much of what might happen to an indefinite-spirited Cockney without credentials who arrived on an Asiatic flying-machine amidst the war-infuriated population beyond.

He still had a lingering solicitude for the bird-faced officer. He had a haunting fancy he might be lying disabled or badly smashed in some way in some nook or cranny of the Island; and it was only after a most exhaustive search that he abandoned that distressing idea. "If I found 'im," he reasoned the while, "what could I do wiv' 'im? You can't blow a chap's brains out when 'e's down. And I don't see 'ow else I can 'elp 'im."

Then the kitten bothered his highly developed sense of social responsibility. "If I leave 'er she'll starve. . . . Ought to catch mice for 'erself. . . . *Are* there mice? . . . Birds? . . . She's too young. . . . She's like me; she's a bit too civilized."

Finally he stuck her in his side pocket, and she became greatly interested in the memories of corned beef she found there.

With her in his pocket, he seated himself in the saddle of the flying-machine. Big, clumsy thing it was, and not a bit like a bicycle. Still the working of it was fairly plain. You set the engine going, *so;* kicked yourself up until the wheel was vertical, *so;* engaged the gyroscope, *so,* and then—then—you just pulled up this lever.

Rather stiff it was, but suddenly it came over—

The big curbed wings on either side flapped disconcertingly, flapped again, click, clock, click, clock, clitter-clock!

Stop! The thing was heading for the water; its wheel was in the water. Bert groaned from his heart and struggled to restore the lever to its first position. Click, clock, clitter-clock, he was rising! The machine was lifting its dripping wheel out of the eddies, and he was going up! There was no stopping now! No good in stopping now! In another moment Bert, clutching and convulsive and rigid, with staring eyes and a face as pale as death, was flapping up above the Rapids, jerking to every jerk of the wings, and rising, rising.

There was no comparison in dignity and comfort between a flying-machine and a balloon. Except in its moments of descent, the balloon was a vehicle of faultless urbanity; this was a buck-jumping mule, a mule that jumped up and never came down again. Click, clock, click, clock; with each beat of the strangely shaped wings it jumped Bert upward and caught him neatly again half a second later on the saddle. And while in ballooning there is no wind, since the balloon is a part of the wind, flying is a wide perpetual creation of, and plunging into, wind. It was a wind that above all things sought to blind him, to force him to close his eyes. It occurred to him presently to twist his knees and legs inward and grip with them, or surely he would have been bumped into two clumsy halves. And he was going up, a hundred yards high, two hundred, three hundred, over the streaming, frothing wilderness of water below—up, up, up. That was all right, but how presently would one go horizontally. He tried to think if these things did go horizontally.

No! They flapped up and then they flapped down. For a time he would keep on flapping up. Tears streamed from his eyes. He wiped them with one temerariously disengaged hand.

Was it better to risk a fall over land or over water—such water?

He was flapping up above the Upper Rapids towards Buffalo. It was at any rate a comfort that the Falls and the wild swirl of waters below them were behind him. He was flying up straight. That he could see. How did one turn?

He was presently almost cool, and his eyes got more used to the rush of air, but he was getting very high, very high. He tilted his head forwards and surveyed the country, blinking. He could see all over Buffalo, a place with three great blackened scars of ruin, and hills and stretches beyond. He wondered if he were half a mile high, or more. There were some people among some houses near a railway station between Niagara and Buffalo, and then more people. They went like ants busily in and out of the houses. He saw two motor-cars gliding along the road towards Niagara city. Then far away in the south he saw a great Asiatic airship going eastward. "Oh Gord!" he said, and became earnest in his ineffectual attempts to alter his direction. But that airship took no notice of him, and he continued to ascend convulsively. The world got more and more extensive and map-like. Click, clock, clitter-clock. Above him and very near to him now was a hazy stratum of cloud.

He determined to disengage the wing clutch. He did so. The lever resisted his strength for a time, then over it came, and instantly the tail of the machine cocked up and the wings became rigidly spread. Instantly everything was swift and smooth and silent. He was gliding rapidly down the air against a wild gale of wind, his eyes three-quarters shut. . . .

A little lever that had hitherto been obdurate now confessed itself mobile. He turned it over gently to the right, and whiroo!—the left wing had in some mysterious way given at its edge, and he was sweeping round and downward in an immense right-handed spiral. For some moments he experienced all the helpless sensations of catastrophe. He restored the lever to its middle position with some difficulty, and the wings were equalized again.

He turned it to the left and had a sensation of being spun round backwards. "Too much!" he gasped.

He discovered that he was rushing down at a headlong pace towards a railway line and some factory buildings. They appeared to be tearing up to him to devour him. He must have dropped all that height. For a moment he had the ineffectual sensations of one whose bicycle bolts downhill. The ground had almost taken him by surprise. " 'Ere!" he cried; and then with a violent effort of all his being he got the beating engine at work again and set the wings flapping. He swooped down and up and resumed his quivering and pulsating ascent of the air.

He went high again, until he had a wide view of the pleasant upland country of western New York State, and then made a long coast down, and so up again, and then a coast. Then as he came swooping a quarter of a mile above a village he saw people running about, running away— evidently in relation to his hawk-like passage. He got an idea that he had been shot at.

"Up!" he said, and attacked that lever again. It came over with remarkable docility, and suddenly the wings seemed to give way in the middle. But the engine was still! It had stopped. He flung the lever back, rather by instinct than design. What to do?

Much happened in a few seconds, but also his mind was quick, he thought very quickly. He couldn't get up again; he was gliding down the air; he would have to hit something.

He was travelling at the rate of perhaps thirty miles an hour, down, down.

That plantation of larches looked the softest thing—mossy almost!

Could he get it? He gave himself to the steering. Round to the right— left!

Swirroo! Crackle! He was gliding over the tops of the trees, ploughing through them, tumbling into a cloud of green sharp leaves and black twigs. There was a sudden snapping, and he fell off the saddle forward, a thud and a crashing of branches. Some twigs hit him sharply in the face. . . .

He was between a tree-stem and the saddle, with his leg over the steering lever, and, so far as he could realize, not hurt. He tried to alter his position, and free his leg, and found himself slipping and dropping through branches with everything giving way beneath him. He clutched, and found himself in the lower branches of a tree beneath the flying-machine. The air was full of a pleasant resinous smell. He stared for a moment motionless, and then very carefully clambered down branch by branch to the soft needle-covered ground below.

"Good business," he said, looking up at the bent and tilted kite-wings above.

"I dropped soft!"

He rubbed his chin with his hand and meditated. "Blowed if I don't think I'm a rather lucky fellow!" he said, surveying the pleasant, sun-bespattered ground under the trees. Then he became aware of a violent tumult at his side. "Lord!" he said, you must be 'arf smothered." and extracted the kitten from his pocket-handkerchief and pocket. She was twisted and crumpled and extremely glad to see the light again. Her little tongue peeped between her teeth. He put her down, and she ran a dozen paces and shook herself and stretched and sat up and began to wash.

"Nex'?" he said, looking about him, and then with a gesture of vexation, "Desh it! I ought to 'ave brought that gun!"

He had rested it against a tree when he had seated himself in the flying-machine saddle.

He was puzzled for a time by the immense peacefulness in the quality of the world, and then he perceived that the roar of the cataract was no longer in his ears.

2

He had no very clear idea of what sort of people he might come upon in this country. It was, he knew, America. Americans, he had always understood, were the citizens of a great and powerful nation, dry and humorous in their manner, addicted to the use of the bowie-knife and revolver, and in the habit of talking through the nose like Norfolk, and saying "allow" and "reckon" and "calculate," after the manner of the people who live on the New Forest side of Hampshire. Also they were very rich, had rocking chairs, and put their feet at unusual attitudes, and they chewed tobacco, gum and other substances with untiring industry. Commingled with them were cowboys, Red Indians, and

comic, respectful niggers. This he had learnt from the fiction in his
public library. Beyond that he had learnt very little. He was not surprised
therefore when he met armed men.

He decided to abandon the shattered flying-machine. He wandered
through the trees for some time, and then struck a road that seemed to
his urban English eyes to be remarkably wide but not properly "made."
Neither hedge nor ditch nor curbed distinctive footpath separated it
from the woods, and it went in that long easy curve which distinguishes
the tracks of an open continent. Ahead he saw a man carrying a gun
under his arm, a man in a soft black hat, a blue blouse and black trousers,
and with a broad round fat face quiet innocent of goatee. This person
regarded him askance and heard him speak with a start.

"Can you tell me whereabouts I am at all?" asked Bert.

The man regarded him, and more particularly his rubber boots with
sinister suspicion. Then he replied in a strange outlandish tongue that
was, as a matter of fact, Czech. He ended suddenly at the sight of Bert's
blank face with "Don't spik English."

"Oh!" said Bert. He reflected gravely for a moment, and then went
his way.

"Thenks," he said as an afterthought. The man regarded his back for
a moment, was struck with an idea, began an abortive gesture, sighed,
gave it up, and went on also with a depressed countenance.

Presently Bert came to a big wooden house standing casually among
the trees. It looked a bleak, bare box of a house to him, no creeper
grew on it, no hedge nor wall parted it off from the woods about it.
He stopped before the steps that led up to the door, perhaps thirty
yards away. The place seemed deserted. He would have gone up to the
door and rapped, but suddenly a big black dog appeared at the side
and regarded him. It was a huge heavy-jawed dog of some unfamiliar
breed, and it wore a spike-studded collar. It did not bark nor approach
him, it just bristled quietly and emitted a single sound like a short, deep
cough.

Bert hesitated and went on.

He stopped thirty paces away and stood peering about him among
the trees. "If I 'aven't been and lef' that kitten," he said.

Acute sorrow wrenched him for a time. The black dog came through the trees to get a better look at him and coughed that well-bred cough again. Bert resumed the road.

"She'll do all right," he said. . . . "She'll catch things. . . .

"She'll do all right," he said presently, without conviction. But if it had not been for the black dog he would have gone back.

When he was out of sight of the house and the black dog, he went into the woods on the other side of the way and emerged after an interval trimming a very tolerable cudgel with his pocket-knife. Presently he saw an attractive-looking rock by the track and picked it up and put it in his pocket. Then he came to three or four houses, wooden like the last, each with an ill-painted white veranda (that was his name for it) and all standing in the same casual way upon the ground. Behind, through the woods, he saw pigsties and a rooting black sow leading a brisk, adventurous family. A wild-looking woman with sloe black eyes and dishevelled black hair sat upon the steps of one of the houses nursing a baby, but at the sight of Bert she got up and went inside, and he heard her bolting the door. Then a boy appeared among the pigsties, but he would not understand Bert's hail.

"I suppose it is America!" said Bert.

The houses became more frequent down the road, and he passed two other extremely wild and dirty-looking men without addressing them. One carried a gun and the other a hatchet, and they scrutinized him and his cudgel scornfully. Then he struck a cross-road with a mono-rail at its side, and there was a notice board at the corner with "Wait here for the cars." "That's all right, any'ow," said Bert. "Wonder 'ow long I should 'ave to wait?" It occurred to him that in the present disturbed state of the country the service might be interrupted, and as there seemed more houses to the right than the left he turned to the right. He passed an old negro. " 'Ullo!" said Bert. "Goo' morning!"

"Good day, sah!" said the old negro in a voice of almost incredible richness.

"What's the name of this place?" asked Bert.

"Tanooda, sah!" said the negro.

"Thenks," said Bert.

"Thank *you,* sah!" said the negro overwhelmingly. Bert came to houses of the same detached, unwalled, wooden type, but adorned now with enamelled advertisements partly in English and partly in Esperanto. Then he came to what he concluded was a grocer's shop. It was the first house that professed the hospitality of an open door, and from within came a strangely familiar sound.

"Gaw!" he said, searching in his pockets. "Why! I 'aven't wanted money for free weeks! I wonder if I—Grubb 'ad most of it. Ah!" He produced a handful of coins and regarded it; three pennies, sixpence, and a shilling. "That's all right," he said, forgetting a very obvious consideration.

He approached the door, and as he did so a compactly built, grey-faced man in shirt sleeves appeared in it and scrutinized him and his cudgel. "Mornin'," said Bert. "Can I get anything to eat 'r drink in this shop?"

The man in the door replied, thank Heaven, in clear, good American. "This, sir, is not A shop, it is A store."

"Oh!" said Bert, and then, "Well, can I get anything to eat?"

"You can," said the American in a tone of confident encouragement, and led the way inside.

The shop seemed to him by his Bun Hill standards extremely roomy, well lit, and unencumbered. There was a long counter to the left of him, with drawers and miscellaneous commodities ranged behind it, a number of chairs, several tables and two spittoons to the right, various barrels, cheeses and bacon up the vista, and beyond, a large archway leading to more space. A little group of men was assembled round one of the tables, and a woman of perhaps five-and-thirty leant with her elbows on the counter. All the men were armed with rifles, and the barrel of a gun peeped above the counter. They were all listening idly, inattentively, to a cheap, metallic-toned gramophone that occupied a table near at hand. From its brazen throat came words that gave Bert a qualm of home-sickness, that brought back in his memory a sunlit beach, a group of children, red-painted bicycles, Grubb and an approaching balloon:

> Ting-a-ling-a-ting-a-ling-a-ting-a-ling-a-tang
> What price hairpins now?

A heavy-necked man in a straw hat, who was chewing something, stopped the machine with a touch, and they all turned their eyes on Bert. And all their eyes were tired eyes.

"Can we give this gentleman anything to eat, mother, or can we not?" said the proprietor.

"He kin have what he likes," said the woman at the counter, without moving, "right up from a cracker to a square meal." She struggled with a yawn, after the manner of one who has been up all night.

"I want a meal," said Bert, "but I 'aven't very much money. I don't want to give mor'n a shillin'."

"Mor'n a *what?*" said the proprietor sharply.

"Mor'n a shillin'," said Bert, with a sudden disagreeable realization coming into his mind.

"Yes," said the proprietor, startled for a moment from his courtly bearing, "but what in hell *is* a shilling?"

"He means a quarter," said a wise-looking lank young man in riding gaiters.

Bert, trying to conceal his consternation, produced a coin. "That's a shilling," he said.

"He calls A store A shop," said the proprietor, "and he wants A meal for A shilling. May I ask you, sir, what part of America you hail from?"

Bert replaced the shilling in his pocket as he spoke. "Niagara," he said.

"And when did you leave Niagara?"

" 'Bout an hour ago."

"Well," said the proprietor, and turned with a puzzled smile to the others. "Well!"

They asked various questions simultaneously.

Bert selected one or two for reply. "You see," he said, "I been with the German air-fleet. I got caught up by them, sort of by accident, and brought over here."

"From England?"

"Yes—from England. Way of Germany. I was in a great battle with them Asiatics, and I got lef' on a little island between the Falls."

"Goat Island?

"I don' know what it was called. But any'ow I found a flying-machine and made a sort of fly with it and got here."

Two men stood up with incredulous eyes on him. "Where's the flying-machine?" they asked; "outside?"

"It's back in the woods here—'bout 'arf a mile away."

"Is it good?" said a thick-lipped man with a scar.

"I come down rather a smash——"

Everybody got up and stood about him and talked confusingly. They wanted him to take them to the flying-machine at once.

"Look 'ere," said Bert, "I'll show you—only I 'aven't 'ad anything to eat since yestiday—except mineral water."

A gaunt soldierly-looking young man with long lean legs in riding gaiters and a bandolier, who had hitherto not spoken, intervened now on his behalf in a note of confident authority. "That's aw right," he said, "Give him a feed, Mr. Logan—from me. I want to hear more of that story of his. We'll see his machine afterwards. If you ask me, I should say it's a remarkably interesting accident had dropped this gentleman here. I guess we requisition that flying-machine—if we find it—for local defence."

3

So Bert fell on his feet again, and sat eating cold meat and good bread and mustard and drinking very good beer, and telling in the roughest outline and with the omissions and inaccuracies of statement natural to his type of mind, the simple story of his adventures. He told how he and a "gentleman friend" had been visiting the seaside for their health, how a "chep" came along in a balloon and fell out as he fell in, how he had drifted to Franconia, how the Germans had seemed to mistake him for someone and had "took him prisoner" and brought him to New York, how he had been to Labrador and back, how he had got to Goat Island and found himself there alone. He omitted the matter of the Prince and the Butteridge aspect of the affair, not out of any deep deceitfulness, but because he felt the inadequacy of his narrative powers. He wanted everything to seem easy and natural and correct, to present himself as a trustworthy and understandable Englishman in a sound mediocre position, to whom refreshment and accommodation might be given with freedom and confidence.

When his fragmentary story came to New York and the battle of Niagara they suddenly produced newspapers which had been lying about on the table, and began to check him and question him by these vehement accounts. It became evident to him that his descent had revived and roused to flames again a discussion, a topic, that had been burning continuously, that had smouldered only through sheer exhaustion of material during the temporary diversion of the gramophone, a discussion that had drawn these men together, rifle in hand, the one supreme topic of the whole world, the War and the methods of the War. He found any question of his personality and his personal adventures falling into the background, found himself taken for granted, and no more than a source of information. The ordinary affairs of life, the buying and selling of everyday necessities, the cultivation of the ground, the tending of beasts, was going on as it were by force of routine, as the common duties of life go on in a house whose master lies under the knife of some supreme operation. The over-ruling interest was furnished by those great Asiatic airships that went upon incalculable missions across the sky, the crimson-clad swordsmen who might come fluttering down demanding petrol, or food, or news. These men were asking, all the continent was asking, "What are we to do? What can we try? How can we get at them?" Bert fell into his place as an item, ceased even in his own thoughts to be a central and independent thing.

After he had eaten and drunken his fill and sighed and stretched and told them how good the food seemed to him, he lit a cigarette they gave him and led the way, with some doubts and trouble, to the flying-machine amidst the larches. It became manifest that the gaunt young man, whose name, it seemed, was Laurier, was a leader both by position and natural aptitude. He knew the names and characters and capabilities of all the men who were with him, and he set them to work at once with vigour and effect to secure this precious instrument of war. They got the thing down to the ground deliberately and carefully, felling a couple of trees in the process, and they built a wide flat roof of timbers and tree boughs to guard their precious find against its chance of discovery by any passing Asiatics. Long before evening they had an engineer from the next township at work upon it, and they were casting lots among the seventeen picked men who wanted to take it for its first flight. And Bert found his kitten and carried it back to Logan's store and handed it with earnest admonition to Mrs. Logan. And it was reassuringly clear to him that in Mrs. Logan both he and the kitten had found a congenial soul.

Laurier was not only a masterful person and a wealthy property owner and employer—he was president, Bert learnt with awe, of the Tanooda Canning Corporation—but he was popular and skilful in the arts of popularity. In the evening quite a crowd of men gathered in the store and talked of the flying-machine and of the war that was tearing the world to pieces. And presently came a man on a bicycle with ill-printed newspaper of a single sheet which acted like fuel in a blazing furnace of talk. It was nearly all American news; the old-fashioned cables had fallen into disuse for some years, and the Marconi stations across the ocean and along the Atlantic coastline seemed to have furnished particularly tempting points of attack.

But such news it was.

Bert sat in the background—for by this time they had gauged his personal quality pretty completely—listening. Before his staggering mind passed strange vast images as they talked of great issues at a crisis, of nations in tumultuous march, of continents overthrown, of famine and destruction beyond measure. Ever and again, in spite of his efforts to suppress them, certain personal impressions would scamper across the weltering confusion, the horrible mess of the exploded Prince, the Chinese aeronaut upside down, the limping and bandaged bird-faced officer blundering along in miserable and hopeless flight. . . .

They spoke of fire and massacre, of cruelties and counter cruelties, of things that had been done to harmless Asiatics by race-mad men, of the wholesale burning and smashing up of towns, railway junctions, bridges, of whole populations in hiding and exodus. "Every ship they've got is in the Pacific," he heard one man exclaim. "Since the fighting began they can't have landed on the Pacific Slope less than a million men. They've come to stay in these States, and they will—living or dead."

Slowly, broadly, invincibly, there grew upon Bert's mind realization of the immense tragedy of humanity into which his life was flowing; the appalling and universal nature of the epoch that had arrived; the conception of an end to security and order and habit. The whole world was at war and it could not get back to peace, it might never recover peace.

He had thought the things he had seen had been exceptional, conclusive things, that the besieging of New York and the battle of the
Atlantic were epoch-making events between long years of security. And
they had been but the first warning impacts of universal cataclysm. Each
day destruction and hate and disaster grew, the fissures widened between
man and man, new regions of the fabric of civilization crumbled and
gave way. Below, the armies grew and the people perished; above, the
airships and aeroplanes fought and fled, raining destruction.

It is difficult perhaps for the broad-minded and long-perspectived
reader to understand how incredible the breaking down of the scientific
civilization seemed to those who actually lived at this time, who in
their own persons went down in the debacle. Progress had marched
as it seemed invincible about the earth, never now to rest again. For
three hundred years and more the long, steadily accelerated diastole of
Europeanized civilization had been in progress; towns had been multiplying; populations increasing, values rising, new countries developing;
thought, literature, knowledge unfolding and spreading. It seemed but
a part of the process that every year the instruments of war were vaster
and more powerful, and that armies and explosives outgrew all other
growing things. . . .

Three hundred years of diastole, and then came the swift and unexpected systole, like the closing of a fist. They could not understand it
was a systole. They could not think of it as anything but a jolt, a hitch, a
mere oscillatory indication of the swiftness of their progress. Collapse,
though it happened all about them, remained incredible. Presently some
falling mass smote them down, or the ground opened beneath their feet.
They died incredulous. . . .

These men in the store made a minute, remote group under this
immense canopy of disaster. They turned from one little aspect to
another. What chiefly concerned them was defence against Asiatic
raiders swooping for petrol or to destroy weapons or communications.
Everywhere levies were being formed at that time to defend the plant
of the railroads day and night in the hope that communication would
speedily be restored. The land was still far away. A man with a flat
voice distinguished himself by a display of knowledge and cunning.
He told them all with confidence just what had been wrong with

the German Drachenflieger and the American aeroplanes, just what
advantage the Japanese fliers possessed. He launched out into a romantic
description of the Butteridge machine and riveted Bert's attention. "I
see that," said Bert, and was smitten silent by a thought. The man with
the flat voice talked on, without heeding him, of the strange irony of
Butteridge's death. At that Bert had a little twinge of relief—he would
never meet Butteridge again. It appeared Butteridge had died suddenly,
very suddenly.

"And his secret, sir, perished with him! When they came to look for
the parts—none could find them. He had hidden them all too well."

"But couldn't he tell?" asked the man in the straw hat. "Did he die
so suddenly as that?"

"Struck down, sir. Rage and apoplexy. At a place called Dymchurch
in England."

"That's right," said Laurier. "I remember a page about it in the
Sunday 'American.' At the time they said it was a German spy had
stolen his balloon."

"Well, sir," said the flat-voiced man, "that fit of apoplexy at Dymchurch was the worst thing that ever happened to the world. For if it
had not been for the death of Mr. Butteridge——"

"No one knows his secret?"

"Not a soul. It's gone. His balloon, it appears, was lost at sea, with
all the plans. Down it went, and they went with it."

Pause.

With machines such as he made we could fight these Asiatic fliers on
more than equal terms. We could outfly and beat down those scarlet
humming-birds wherever they appeared. But it's gone, it's gone, and
there's no time to reinvent it now. We got to fight with what we got—
and the odds are against us. *That* won't stop us fightin'. No! but just
think of it!"

Bert was trembling violently. He cleared his throat hoarsely.

"I say," he said, "look here, I——"

Nobody regarded him. The man with the flat voice was opening a
new branch of the subject. "I allow——" he began.

Bert became violently excited. He stood up. He made clawing mo-
tions with his hands. "I say!" he exclaimed, "Mr. Laurier. Look 'ere—I
want—about that Butteridge machine——"

Mr. Laurier, sitting on an adjacent table, with a magnificent gesture, arrested the discourse of the flat-voiced man. "What's *he* saying?" said he.

Then the whole company realized that something was happening to Bert; either he was suffocating or going mad. He was spluttering, "Look 'ere! I say! 'Old on a bit!" and trembling and eagerly unbuttoning himself.

He tore open his collar and opened vest and shirt. He plunged into his interior, and for an instant it seemed he was plucking forth his liver. Then as he struggled with buttons on his shoulder they perceived this flattened horror was, in fact, a terribly dirty flannel chest-protector. In another moment Bert, in a state of irregular décolletage, was standing over the table displaying a sheaf of papers.

"These!" he gasped. "These are the plans! . . . You know! Mr. Butteridge—his machine! What died! I was the chap that went off in that balloon!"

For some seconds everyone was silent. They stared from these papers to Bert's white face and blazing eyes, and back to the papers on the table. Nobody moved. Then the man with the flat voice spoke.

"Irony!" he said, with a note of satisfaction. "Real rightdown Irony! *When it's too late to think of making 'em any more!*"

4

They would all, no doubt, have been eager to hear Bert's story over again, but it was at this point that Laurier showed his quality. "No, *sir,*" he said, and slid from off his table.

He impounded the dispersing Butteridge plans with one comprehensive sweep of his arm, rescuing them even from the expository fingermarks of the man with the flat voice, and handed them to Bert. "Put those back," he said, "where you had 'em. We have a journey before us."

Bert took them.

"Whar?" said the man in the straw hat.

"Why, sir, we are going to find the President of these States and give these plans over to him. I decline to believe, sir, we are too late"

"Where is the President?" asked Bert weakly, in the pause that followed.

"Logan," said Laurier, disregarding that feeble inquiry, "you must help us in this."

It seemed only a matter of a few minutes before Bert and Laurier and the storekeeper were examining a number of bicycles that were stowed in the hinder room of the store. Bert didn't like any of them very much. They had wood rims, and an experience of wood rims in the English climate had taught him to hate them. That, however, and one or two other objections to an immediate start were overruled by Laurier. "But where *is* the President?" Bert repeated, as they stood behind Logan while he pumped up a deflated tyre.

Laurier looked down on him. "He is reported in the neighbourhood of Albany—out towards the Berkshire Hills. He is moving from place to place and, as far as he can, organizing the defence by telegraph and telephone. The Asiatic air-fleet is trying to locate him. When they think they have located the seat of government they throw bombs. This inconveniences him, but so far they have not come within ten miles of him. The Asiatic air-fleet is at present scattered all over the Eastern States, seeking out and destroying gas-works and whatever seems conducive to the building of airships or the transport of troops. Our retaliatory measures are slight in the extreme. But with these machines

Sir, this ride of ours will count among the historical rides of the world!"

He came near to striking an attitude.

"We shan't get to him to-night?" asked Bert.

"No, sir!" said Laurier. "We shall have to ride some days, sure!"

"I suppose we can't get a lift on a train—or anything?"

"No, sir! There's been no transit by Tanooda for three days. It is no good waiting. We shall have to get on as well as we can."

"Startin' now?"

"Starting now!"

"But 'ow about——We shan't be able to do much to-night."

"May as well ride till we're fagged and sleep then. So much clear gain. Our road is eastward."

"Of course——" began Bert, with memories of the dawn upon Goat Island, and left his sentence unfinished.

He gave his attention to the more scientific packing of the chest-protector, for several of the plans flapped beyond his vest.

5

For a week Bert led a life of mixed sensations. Amidst these fatigue in the legs predominated. Mostly he rode, rode with Laurier's back inexorably ahead, through a land like a larger England, with bigger hills and wider valleys, larger fields, wider roads, fewer hedges, and wooden houses with commodious piazzas. He rode. Laurier made inquiries, Laurier chose the turnings, Laurier doubted, Laurier decided. Now it seemed they were in telephonic touch with the President; now something had happened and he was lost again. But always they had to go on, and always Bert rode. A tyre was deflated. Still he rode. He grew saddle sore. Laurier declared that unimportant. Asiatic flying-ships passed overhead, the two cyclists made a dash for cover until the sky was clear. Once a red Asiatic flying-machine came fluttering after them, so low they could distinguish the aeronaut's head. He followed them for a mile. Now they came to regions of panic, now to regions of destruction, here people were fighting for food, here they seemed hardly stirred from the countryside routine. They spent a day in a deserted and damaged Albany. The Asiatics had descended and cut every wire and made a cinder heap of the Junction, and our travellers pushed on eastward. They passed a hundred half-heeded incidents, and always Bert was toiling after Laurier's indefatigable back. . . .

Things struck upon Bert's attention and perplexed him, and then he passed on with unanswered questionings fading from his mind.

He saw a large house on fire on a hillside to the right, and no man heeding it.

They came to a narrow railroad bridge, and presently to a monorail train standing in the track on its safety feet. It was a remarkably sumptuous train, the Last Word Trans-Continental Express, and the passengers were all playing cards or sleeping or preparing a picnic meal on a grassy slope near at hand. They had been there six days. . . .

At one point ten dark-complexioned men were hanging in a string from the trees along the roadside. Bert wondered why. . . .

At one peaceful-looking village where they stepped off to get Bert's tyre mended and found beer and biscuits, they were approached by an extremely dirty little boy without boots, who spoke as follows:

"Deyse been hanging a Chink in does woods!"

"Hanging a Chinaman?" said Laurier.

"Sure. Der sleuths got him rubberin' der railroad sheds!"

"Oh!"

"Dose guys done wase cartridges. Deyse hung him and dey pulled his legs. Deyse doin' all der Chinks dey can fine dat weh! Dey ain't takin' no risks. All der Chinks dey can fine."

Neither Bert nor Laurier made any reply, and presently, after a little skilful expectoration, the young gentleman was attracted by the appearance of two of his friends down the road, and shuffled off, whooping weirdly. . . .

That afternoon they almost ran over a man shot through the body, and partly decomposed, lying near the middle of the road, just outside Albany. He must have been lying there for some days. . . .

Beyond Albany they came upon a motor-car with a tyre burst and a young woman sitting absolutely passive beside the driver's seat. An old man was under the car trying to effect some impossible repairs. Beyond, sitting with a rifle across his knees, with his back to the car, and staring into the woods, was a young man. The old man crawled out at their approach, and, still on all fours, accosted Bert and Laurier. The car had broken down overnight. The old man said he could not understand what was wrong, but he was trying to puzzle it out. Neither he nor his son-in-law had any mechanical aptitude. They had been assured this was a fool-proof car. It was dangerous to have to stop in this place. His party had been attacked by tramps and had had to fight. It was known they had provisions. He mentioned a great name in the world of finance. Would Laurier and Bert stop and help him? He proposed it first hopefully, then urgently, at last in tears and terror.

"No!" said Laurier inexorably. "We must go on! We have something more than a woman to save. We have to save America!"

The girl never stirred. . . .

Once they passed a madman singing. . . .

At last they found the President hiding in a small saloon upon the outskirts of a place called Pinkerville on the Hudson, and gave the plans of the Butteridge machine into his hands.

ELEVEN

The Great Collapse

I

And now the whole fabric of civilization was bending and giving, and dropping to pieces and melting in the furnace of war. The stages of the swift and universal collapse of the fianancial and scientific civilization with which the twentieth century opened followed each other very swiftly, so swiftly that upon the foreshortened page of history they seem altogether to overlap. To begin with, one sees the world nearly at a maximum of wealth and prosperity. To its inhabitants indeed it seemed also at a maximum of security. When now in retrospect the thoughtful observer surveys the intellectual history of this time, when one reads its surviving fragments of literature, its scraps of political oratory, the few small voices that chance has selected out of a thousand million utterances to speak to later days, the most striking thing of all this web of wisdom and error is surely that hallucination of security. To men living in our present world state, orderly, scientific, and secured, nothing seemed so precarious, so giddily dangerous as the fabric of the social order with which the men of the opening of the twentieth century were content. To us it seems that every institution and relationship was the result of haphazard and tradition and the manifest sport of chance, their laws each made for some separate occasion and having no relation to any further needs, their customs illogical, their education aimless and wasteful. Their method of economic exploitation indeed impresses a trained and informed mind as the most frantic and desperate scramble it is possible to conceive; their credit and monetary system resting on an unsubstantial tradition of the worthiness of gold, seems a thing almost fantastically unstable. And they lived in planless cities, for the most part dangerously congested, their rails and roads and population were distributed over the earth in the wanton confusion ten thousand irrelevant considerations had made. Yet they thought confidently that this was a secure and permanent progressive system, and on the strength of some three hundred years of chancy and irregular improvement, they answered the doubter with, "Things always *have* gone well. We'll worry through!"

But when we contrast the state of man in the opening of the twentieth century with the condition of any previous period in his history, then perhaps we may begin to understand something of that blind confidence. It was not so much a reasoned confidence as the inevitable consequence of sustained good fortune. By such standards as they possessed, things *had* gone amazingly well for them. It is scarcely an exaggeration to say that for the first time in history whole populations found themselves regularly supplied with more than enough to eat, and the vital statistics of the time witness to an amelioration of hygienic conditions rapid beyond all precedent, and to a vast development of intelligence and ability in all the arts that make life wholesome. The level and quality of the average education had risen tremendously; and at the dawn of the twentieth century comparatively few people in Western Europe or America were unable to read or write. Never before had there been such reading masses. There was wide social security. A common man might travel safely over three-quarters of the habitable globe, could go round the earth at the cost of less than the annual earnings of a skilled artisan. Compared with the liberality and comfort of the ordinary life of the time, the order of the Roman Empire under the Antonines was local and limited. And every year, every month, came some new increment to human achievement, a new country opened up, new mines, new scientific discoveries, a new machine!

For those three hundred years, indeed, the movement of the world seemed wholly beneficial to mankind. Men said, indeed, that moral organization was not keeping pace with physical progress, but few attached any meaning to these phrases, the understanding of which lies at the basis of our present safety. Sustaining and constructive forces did indeed for a time more than balance the malign drift of chance and the natural ignorance, prejudice, blind passion, and wasteful self-seeking of mankind.

The accidental balance on the side of Progress was far slighter and infinitely more complex and delicate in its adjustments than the people of that time suspected; but that did not alter the fact that it was an effective balance. They did not realize that this age of relative good fortune was an age of immense but temporary opportunity for their kind. They complacently assumed a necessary progress towards which they had no moral responsibility. They did not realize that this security of progress was a thing still to be won or lost, and that the time to win it was a time that passed. They went about their affairs energetically enough, and yet with a curious idleness towards those threatening things. No one troubled over the real dangers of mankind. They saw their armies and navies grow larger and more portentous; some of their ironclads at the last cost as much as their whole annual expenditure upon advanced education; they accumulated explosives and the machinery of destruction; they allowed their national traditions and jealousies to accumulate; they contemplated a steady enhancement of race hostility as the races drew closer without concern or understanding, and they permitted the growth in their midst of an evil-spirited press, mercenary and unscrupulous, incapable of good and powerful for evil. Their State had practically no control over the press at all. Quite heedlessly they allowed this touch-paper to lie at the door of their war magazine for any spark to fire. The precedents of history were all one tale of the collapse of civilizations—the dangers of the time were manifest. One is incredulous now to believe they could not see.

Could mankind have prevented this disaster of the War in the Air? An idle question that, as idle as to ask could mankind have prevented the decay that turned Assyria and Babylon to empty deserts or the slow decline and fall, the gradual social disorganization, phrase by phrase, that closed the chapter of the Empire of the West! They could not, because they did not, they had not the will to arrest it. What mankind could achieve with a different will is a speculation as idle as it is magnificent. And this was no slow decadence that came to the Europeanized world; those other civilizations rotted and crumbled down, the Europeanized civilization was, as it were, blown up. Within the space of five years it was altogether disintegrated and destroyed. Up to the very eve of the War in the Air one sees a spacious spectacle of incessant advance, a world-wide security, enormous areas with highly organized industry and settled populations, gigantic cities spreading gigantically, the seas and oceans dotted with shipping, the land netted with rails and open ways. Then suddenly the German air-fleets sweep across the scene, and we are in the beginning of the end.

2

This story has already told of the swift rush upon New York of the first German air-fleet and of the wild, inevitable orgy of inconclusive destruction that ensued. Behind it a second air-fleet was already swelling at its gasometers when England and France and Spain and Italy showed their hands. None of these countries had prepared for aeronautic warfare on the magnificent scale of the Germans, but each guarded secrets, each in a measure was making ready, and a common dread of German vigour, and that aggressive spirit Prince Karl Albert embodied, had long been drawing these powers together in secret anticipation of some such attack. This rendered their prompt co-operation possible, and they certainly co-operated promptly. The second aerial power in Europe at this time was France; the British, nervous for their Asiatic empire, and sensible of the immense moral effect of the airship upon half-educated populations, had placed their aeronautic parks in North India, and were able to play but a subordinate part in the European conflict. Still, even in England, they had nine or ten big navigables, twenty or thirty smaller ones, and a variety of experimental aeroplanes. Before the fleet of Prince Karl Albert had crossed England, while Bert was still surveying Manchester in bird's eye view, the diplomatic changes were going on that led to an attack upon Germany. A heterogeneous collection of navigable balloons of all sizes and types gathered over the Bernese Oberland, crushed and burnt the twenty-five Swiss airships that unexpectedly resisted this concentration in the battle of the Alps, and then, leaving the Alpine glaciers and valleys strewn with strange wreckage, divided into two fleets and set itself to terrorize Berlin and destroy the Franconian Park, seeking to do this before the second air-fleet could be inflated.

Both over Berlin and Franconia the assailants with their modern explosives effected great damage before they were driven off. In Franconia twelve fully distended and five partially filled and manned giants were able to make head against, and at last, with the help of a squadron of Drachenflieger from Hamburg, defeat and pursue the attack and to relieve Berlin; and the Germans were straining every nerve to get an overwhelming fleet in the air, and were already raiding London and Paris when the advance fleets from the Asiatic air-parks, the first intimation of a new factor in the conflict, were reported from Burmah and Armenia.

Already the whole financial fabric of the world was staggering when that occurred. With the destruction of the American fleet in the North Atlantic, and the smashing conflict that ended the naval existence of Germany in the North Sea, with the burning and wrecking of billions of pounds' worth of property in the four cardinal cities of the world, the fact of the hopeless costliness of war came home for the first time, came like a blow in the face, to the consciousness of mankind. Credit went down in a wild whirl of selling. Everywhere appeared a phenomenon that had already in a mild degree manifested itself in preceding periods of panic; a desire to *secure and hoard gold* before prices reached bottom. But now it spread like wild-fire, it became universal. Above was visible conflict and destruction; below something was happening far more deadly and incurable to the flimsy fabric of finance and commercialism in which men had so blindly put their trust. As the airships fought above, the visible gold supply of the world vanished below. An epidemic of private cornering and universal distrust swept the world. In a few weeks, money, except for depreciated paper, vanished into vaults, into holes, into the walls of houses, into ten million hiding-places. Money vanished, and at its disappearance trade and industry came to an end. The economic world staggered and fell dead. It was like the stroke of some disease; it was like the water vanishing out of the blood of a living creature; it was a sudden, universal coagulation of intercourse. . . .

And as the credit system that had been the living fortress of the scientific civilization, reeled and fell upon the millions it had held together in economic relationship, as these people, perplexed and help-less, faced this marvel of credit utterly destroyed, the airships of Asia, countless and relentless, poured across the heavens, swooped eastward to America and westward to Europe. The page of history becomes a long crescendo of battle. The main body of the British Indian air-fleet perished upon a pyre of blazing antagonists in Burmah; the Germans were scattered in the great battle of the Carpathians; the vast peninsula of India burst into insurrection and civil war from end to end, and from Gobi to Morocco rose the standards of the "Jehad." For some weeks of warfare and destruction it seemed as though the Confederation of Eastern Asia must needs conquer the world, and then the jerry-built "modern" civilization of China too gave way under the strain. The teeming and peaceful population of China had been "westernized" during the opening years of the twentieth century with the deepest resentment and reluctance; they had been dragooned and disciplined under Japanese and European influence into an acquiescence with sanitary methods, police controls, military service, and a wholesale process of exploitation against which their whole tradition rebelled. Under the stresses of the war their endurance reached the breaking point. China rose in incoherent revolt, and the practical destruction of the central government at Pekin by a handful of British and Ger-man airships that had escaped from the main battles rendered that revolt invincible. In Yokohama appeared barricades, the black flag, and the social revolution. With that the whole world became a welter of conflict.

So that a universal social collapse followed, as it were a logical conse-quence, upon world-wide war. Wherever there were great populations, great masses of people found themselves without work, without money, and unable to get food. Famine was in every working-class quarter in the world, within three weeks of the beginning of the war. Within a month there was not a city anywhere in which the ordinary law and social procedure had not been replaced by some form of emergency control, in which firearms and military executions were not being used to keep order and prevent violence. And still in the poorer quarters, and in the populous districts, and even here and there already among those who had been wealthy, famine spread.

3

So what historians have come to call the Phase of the Emergency Committees sprang from the opening phase and from the phase of social collapse. Then followed a period of vehement and passionate conflict against disintegration; everywhere the struggle to keep order and to keep fighting went on. And at the same time the character of the war altered through the replacement of the huge gas-filled airships by flying-machines as the instruments of war. So soon as the big fleet engagements were over, the Asiatics endeavoured to establish in close proximity to the more vulnerable points of the countries against which they were acting, fortified centres from which flying-machine raids could be made. For a time they had everything their own way in this, and then, as this story has told, the lost secret of the Butteridge machine came to light, and the conflict became equalized and less conclusive than ever. For these small flying-machines, ineffectual for any large expedition or conclusive attack, were horribly convenient for guerilla warfare, rapidly and cheaply made, easily used, easily hidden. The design of them was hastily copied and printed in Pinkerville, and scattered broadcast over the United States, and copies were sent to Europe, and there reproduced. Every man, every town, every parish that could, was exhorted to make and use them. In a little while they were being constructed not only by governments and local authorities, but by robber bands, by insurgent committees, by every type of private person. The peculiar social destructiveness of the Butteridge machine lay in its complete simplicity. It was nearly as simple as a motor-bicycle. The broad outlines of the earlier stages of the war disappeared under its influence, the spacious antagonism of nations and empires and races vanished in a seething mass of detailed conflict. The world passed at a stride from a unity and simplicity broader than that of the Roman Empire at its best to a social fragmentation as complete as the robber-baron period of the Middle Ages. But this time, for a long descent down gradual slopes of disintegration, comes a fall like a fall over a cliff. Everywhere were men and women perceiving this, and struggling desperately to keep, as it were, a hold upon the edge of the cliff.

A fourth phase follows. Through the struggle against Chaos, in the wake of the Famine, came now another old enemy of humanity—the Pestilence, the Purple Death. But the war does not pause. The flags still fly. Fresh air-fleets rise, new forms of airship, and beneath their swooping struggles the world darkens—scarcely heeded by history.

It is not within the design of this book to tell that further story, to tell how the War in the Air kept on through the sheer inability of any authorities to meet and agree and end it, until every organized government in the world was as shattered and broken as a heap of china beaten with a stick. With every week of those terrible years history becomes more detailed and confused, more crowded and uncertain. Not without great and heroic resistance was civilization borne down. Out of the bitter social conflict below rose patriotic associations, brotherhoods of order, city mayors, princes, provisional committees, trying to establish an order below and to keep the sky above. The double effort destroyed them. And as the exhaustion of the mechanical resources of civilization clears the heavens of airships at last altogether, Anarchy, Famine, and Pestilence are discovered triumphant below. The great nations and empires have become but names in the mouths of men. Everywhere there are ruins and unburied dead, and shrunken, yellow-faced survivors in a mortal apathy. Here there are robbers, here vigilance committees, and here guerilla bands ruling patches of exhausted territory, strange federations and brotherhoods, form and dissolve, and religious fanaticisms begotten of despair gleam in famine-bright eyes. It is a universal dissolution. The fine order and welfare of the earth have crumpled like an exploded bladder. In five short years the world and the scope of human life have undergone a retrogressive change as great as that between the age of the Antonines and the Europe of the ninth century. . . .

4

Across this sombre spectacle of disaster goes a minute and insignificant person for whom perhaps the readers of this story have now some slight solicitude. Of him there remains to be told just one single miraculous thing. Through a world darkened and lost, through a civilization in its death agony, our little Cockney errant went and found his Edna! He found his Edna!

He got back across the Atlantic partly by means of an order from the President and partly through his own good luck. He contrived to get himself aboard a British brig in the timber trade that put out from Boston without cargo, chiefly, it would seem, because its captain had a vague idea of "getting home" to South Shields. Bert was able to ship himself upon her mainly because of the seamanship of his rubber boots. They had a long, eventful voyage, they were chased, or imagined themselves to be chased, for some hours by an Asiatic ironclad, which was presently engaged by a British cruiser. The two ships fought for three hours, circling and driving southward as they fought, until the twilight and the cloud-rift of a rising gale swallowed them up. A few days later Bert's ship lost her rudder and mainmast in a gale. The crew ran out of food and subsisted on fish. They saw strange airships going eastward near the Azores, and landed to get provisions and repair the rudder at Teneriffe. There they found the town destroyed, and two big liners, with dead still aboard, sunken in the harbour. From there they got canned food and material for repairs, but their operations were greatly impeded by the hostility of a band of men amidst the ruins of the town who sniped them and tried to drive them away.

At Mogador they stayed and sent a boat ashore for water, and were nearly captured by an Arab ruse. Here, too, they got the Purple Death aboard, and sailed with it incubating in their blood. The cook sickened first, and then the mate, and presently everyone was down and three in the forecastle were dead. It chanced to be calm weather, and they drifted helplessly and indeed careless of their fate backwards towards the Equator. The captain doctored them all with rum. Nine died altogether, and of the four survivors none understood navigation; when at last they took heart again and could handle a sail they made a course by the stars roughly northward and were already short of food once more when they fell in with a petrol-driven ship from Rio to Cardiff, shorthanded by reason of the Purple death, and glad to take them aboard. So, at last, after a year of wandering, Bert reached England. He landed in bright June weather, and found the Purple Death was there just beginning its ravages.

The people were in a state of panic in Cardiff and many had fled
to the hills, and directly the steamer came to the harbour she was
boarded and her residue of food impounded by some unauthenticated
Provisional Committee. Bert tramped through a country disorganized
by pestilence, foodless, and shaken to the very base of its immemorial
order. He came near death and starvation many times, and once he was
drawn into scenes of violence that might have ended his career. But the
Bert Smallways who tramped from Cardiff to London, vaguely "going
home," vaguely seeking something of his own that had no tangible form
but Edna, was a very different person from the Desert Dervish who
was swept out of England in Mr. Butteridge's balloon a year before. He
was brown and lean and enduring, steady-eyed and pestilence-salted,
and his mouth, which had once hung open, shut now like a steel trap.
Across his brow ran a white scar that he had got in a fight on the brig. In
Cardiff he had felt the need of new clothes and a weapon, and had, by
means that would have shocked him a year ago, secured a flannel shirt,
a corduroy suit, and a revolver and fifty cartridges, from an abandoned
pawnbroker's. He also got some soap and had his first real wash for
thirteen months in a stream outside the town. The Vigilance bands
that had at first shot plunderers very freely were now either entirely
dispersed by the plague, or busy between town and cemetery in a vain
attempt to keep pace with it. He prowled on the outskirts of the town
for three or four days, starving, and then went back to join the Hospital
Corps for a week, and so fortified himself with a few square meals before
he started eastward.

The Welsh and English countryside at that time presented the
strangest mingling of the assurance and wealth, a sort of Düreresque
mediævalism. All the gear, the houses and mono-rails, the farm hedges
and power cables, the roads and pavements, the signposts and advertisements of the former order were still for the most part intact. Bankruptcy,
social collapse, famine and pestilence, had done nothing to damage
these; it was only to the great capitals and ganglionic centres, as it
were, of the State, that positive destruction had come. Anyone dropped
suddenly into the country would have noticed very little difference. He
would have remarked first, perhaps, that all the hedges needed clipping,
that the roadside grass grew rank, that the road-tracks were unusually

rainworn, and that the cottages by the wayside seemed in many cases shut up, that a telephone wire had dropped here, and that a cart stood abandoned by the wayside. But he would still find his hunger whetted by the bright assurance that Wilder's Canned Peaches were excellent, or that there was nothing so good for the breakfast table as Gobble's Sausages. And then suddenly would come the Düreresque element; the skeleton of a horse, or some crumpled mass of rags in the ditch, with gaunt extended feet and a yellow, purple-blotched skin and face, or what had been a face, gaunt and glaring and devastated. Then here would be a field that had been ploughed and not sown, and here a field of corn carelessly trampled by beasts, and here a hoarding torn down across the road to make a fire.

Then presently he would meet a man or a woman, yellow-faced and probably negligently dressed and armed—prowling for food. These people would have the complexions and eyes and expressions of tramps and criminals, and often the clothing of prosperous middle-class or upper-class people. Many of these would be eager for news, and willing to give help and even scraps of queer meat, or crusts of grey and doughy bread in return for it. They would listen to Bert's story with avidity, and attempt to keep him with them for a day or so. The virtual cessation of postal distribution and the collapse of all newspaper enterprise had left an immense and aching gap in the mental life of this time. Men had suddenly lost sight of the ends of the earth and had still to recover the rumour-spreading habits of the Middle Ages. In their eyes, in their bearing, in their talk, was the quality of lost and deoriented souls.

As Bert travelled from parish to parish and from district to district, avoiding as far as possible those festering centres of violence and despair, the larger towns, he found the condition of affairs varying widely. In one parish he would find the large house burnt, the vicarage wrecked, evidently in violent conflict for some suspected and perhaps imaginary store of food, unburied dead everywhere, and the whole mechanism of the community at a standstill. In another he would find organizing forces' stoutly at work, newly-painted notice boards warning off vagrants, the roads and still cultivated fields policed by armed men, the pestilence under control, even nursing going on, a store of food husbanded, the cattle and sheep well guarded, and a group of two or three justices, the village doctor or a farmer, dominating the whole place; a reversion, in fact, to the autonomous community of the fifteenth century. But at any time such a village would be liable to a raid of Asiatics or Africans or such-like air-pirates, demanding petrol and alcohol or provisions. The price of its order was an almost intolerable watchfulness and tension. Then the approach to the confused problems of some larger centre of population and the presence of a more intricate conflict would be marked by roughly smeared notices of "Quarantine" or "Strangers Shot," or by a string of decaying plunderers dangling from the telephone poles at the roadside. About Oxford big boards were put on the roofs warning all air wanderers off with the single word, "Guns."

Taking their risks amidst these things, cyclists still kept abroad, and once or twice during Bert's long tramp powerful motor-cars containing masked and goggled figures went tearing past him. There were few police in evidence, but ever and again squads of gaunt and tattered soldier-cyclists would come drifting along, and such encounters became more frequent as he got out of Wales into England. Amidst all this wreckage they were still campaigning. He had some idea of resorting to the workhouses for the night if hunger pressed him too closely, but some of these were closed and others converted into temporary hospitals, and one he came up to at twilight near a village in Gloucestershire stood with all its doors and windows open, silent as the grave, and, as he found to his horror by stumbling along evil-smelling corridors, full of unburied dead.

From Gloucestershire Bert went northward to the British aeronautic park outside Birmingham, in the hope that he might be taken on and given food, for there the Government, or at any rate the War Office, still existed as an energetic fact, concentrated amidst collapse and social disaster upon the effort to keep the British flag still flying in the air, and trying to brisk up mayor and mayor and magistrate and magistrate in a new effort of organization. They had brought together all the best of the surviving artisans from that region, they had provisioned the park for a siege, and they were urgently building a larger type of the Butteridge machine. Bert could get no footing at this work, he was not sufficiently skilled, and he had drifted to Oxford when the great fight occurred in which these works were finally wrecked. He saw something,

but not very much, of the battle from a place called Boar Hill. He saw
the Asiatic squadron coming up across the hills to the south-west, and
he saw one of their airships circling southward again chased by two
aeroplanes, the one that was ultimately overtaken, wrecked and burnt
at Edge Hill. But he never learnt the issue of the combat as a whole.

He crossed the Thames from Eton to Windsor and made his way
round the south of London to Bun Hill, and there he found his brother
Tom, looking like some dark, defensive animal in the old shop, just
recovering from the Purple Death, and Jessica upstairs delirious, and,
as it seemed to him, dying grimly. She raved of sending out orders to
customers, and scolded Tom perpetually lest he should be late with
Mrs. Thompson's potatoes and Mrs. Hopkins' cauliflower, though all
business had long since ceased, and Tom had developed a quite un-
canny skill in the snaring of rats and sparrows and the concealment
of certain stores of cereals and biscuits from plundered grocers' shops.
Tom received his brother with a sort of guarded warmth.

"Lor!" he said, "it's Bert. I thought you'd be coming back some day,
and I'm glad to see you. But I carn't arst you to eat anything, because I
'aven't got anything to eat. . . . Where you been, Bert, all this time?"

Bert reassured his brother by a glimpse of a partly-eaten swede,
and was still telling his story in fragments and parentheses, when he
discovered behind the counter a yellow and forgotten note addressed
to himself. "What's this?" he said, and found it was a year-old note from
Edna. "She came 'ere," said Tom, like one who recalls a trivial thing,
"arstin' for you and arstin' us to take 'er in. That was after the battle and
settin' Clapham Rise afire. I was for takin' 'er in, but Jessica wouldn't
'ave it—and so she borrowed five shillings of me quiet like and went
on. I dessay she's tole you——"

She had, Bert found. She had gone on, she said in her note, to an
aunt and uncle who had a brick-field near Horsham. And there at last,
after another fortnight of adventurous journeying, Bert found her.

5

When Bert and Edna set eyes on one another, they stared and laughed
foolishly, so changed they were, and so ragged and surprised. And then
they both fell weeping.

"Oh! Bertie boy!" she cried. "You've come—you've come!" and put out her arms and staggered. "I told 'im. He said he'd kill me if I didn't marry him."

But Edna was not married, and when presently Bert could get talk from her, she explained the task before him. That little patch of lonely agricultural country had fallen under the power of a band of bullies led by a chief called Bill Gore, who had begun life as a butcher boy and developed into a prizefighter and a professional "sport." They had been organized by a local nobleman of former eminence upon the turf, but after a time he had disappeared, no one quite knew how, and Bill had succeeded to the leadership of the countryside, and had developed his teacher's methods with considerable vigour. There had been a strain of advanced philosophy about the local nobleman, and his mind ran to "improving the race" and producing the Over-Man, which in practice took the form of himself especially, and his little band in moderation, marrying with some frequency. Bill followed up this idea with an enthusiasm that even trenched upon his popularity with his followers. One day he had happened upon Edna tending her pigs, and had at once fallen a-wooing with great urgency among the troughs of slush. Edna had made a gallant resistance, but he was still vigorously about and extraordinarily impatient. He might, she said, come at any time; and she looked Bert in the eyes. They were back already in the barbaric stage when a man must fight for his love.

And here one deplores the conflicts of truth with the chivalrous tradition. One would like to tell of Bert sallying forth to challenge his rival, of a ring formed and a spirited encounter, and Bert by some miracle of pluck and love and good fortune winning. But indeed nothing of the sort occurred. Instead, he reloaded his revolver carefully, and then sat in the best room of the cottage by the derelict brickfield, looking anxious and perplexed, and listening to talk about Bill and his ways, and thinking, thinking. Then suddenly Edna's aunt, with a thrill in her voice, announced the appearance of that individual. He was coming with two others of his gang through the garden gate. Bert got up, put the woman aside, and looked out. They presented remarkable figures. They wore a sort of uniform of red golfing jackets and white sweaters, football singlets and stockings and boots, and each had let his fancy play about his headdress. Bill had a woman's hat full of cock's feathers, and all had wild, slouching cowboy brims.

Bert sighed and stood up, deeply thoughtful, and Edna watched him, marvelling. The women stood quite still. He left the window, and went out into the passage rather slowly, and with the careworn expression of a man who gives his mind to a complex and uncertain business. "Edna!" he called, and when she came he opened the front door.

He asked very simply, and pointing to the foremost of the three, "That 'im? . . . Sure? . . ." and being told that it was, shot his rival instantly and very accurately through the chest. He then shot Bill's best man much less tidily in the head, and then shot at and winged the third man as he fled. The third gentleman yelped, and continued running with a comical end-on twist.

Then Bert stood still meditating with the pistol in his hand, and quite regardless of the women behind him.

So far things had gone well.

It became evident to him that if he did not go into politics at once he would be hanged as an assassin, and accordingly, without a word to the women, he went down to the village public-house he had passed an hour before on his way to Edna, entered it from the rear, and confronted the little band of ambiguous roughs, who were drinking in the tap-room and discussing matrimony and Bill's affections in a facetious but envious manner, with a casually held but carefully loaded revolver, and an invitation to join what he called, I regret to say, a "Viligance Committee" under his direction. "It's wanted about 'ere, and some of us are gettin' it up." He presented himself as one having friends outside, though indeed he had no friends at all in the world but Edna and her aunt and two female cousins.

There was a quick but entirely respectful discussion of the situation. They thought him a lunatic who had tramped into this neighbourhood ignorant of Bill. They desired to temporize until their leader came. Bill would settle him. Someone spoke of Bill.

"Bill's dead," said Bert. "I jest shot 'im. We don't need reckon with 'im. 'E's shot, and a red 'aired chap with a squint, 'e's shot. We've settled up all that. There ain't going to be no more Bill, ever. 'E'd got wrong ideas about marriage and things. It's 'is sort of chap we're after."

That carried the meeting.

Bill was perfunctorily buried, and Bert's Viligance Committee (for so it continued to be called) reigned in his stead.

That is the end of this story so far as Bert Smallways is concerned. We leave him with his Edna to become squatters among the clay and oak thickets of the Weald, far away from the stream of events. From that time forth life became a succession of peasant's encounters, an affair of pigs and hens and small needs and little economies and children, until Clapham and Bun Hill and all the life of the Scientific Age became to Bert no more than the fading memory of a dream. He never knew how the War in the Air went on, or whether it still went on. There were rumours of airships going and coming, and of happenings Londonward. Once or twice their shadows fell on him as he worked, but whence they came or whither they went he could not tell. Even his desire to tell died out for want of food. At times came robbers and thieves, at times came diseases among the beasts and shortness of food, once the country was worried by a pack of boarhounds he helped to kill; he went through many inconsecutive, irrelevant adventures. He survived them all.

Accident and death came near them both ever and again, and passed them by; and they loved and suffered and were happy, and she bore him many children—eleven children—one after the other, of whom only four succumbed to the necessary hardships of their simple life. They lived and did well, as well was understood in those days. They went the way of all flesh, year by year.

The Epilogue

It happened that one bright summer's morning exactly thirty years after the launching of the first German air-fleet, an old man took a small boy to look for a missing hen through the ruins of Bun Hill and out towards the splintered pinnacles of the Crystal Palace. He was not a very old man; he was, as a matter of fact, still within a few weeks of sixty-three, but constant stooping over spades and forks and the carrying of roots and manure, and exposure to the damps of life in the open air without a change of clothing, had bent him into the form of a sickle. Moreover, he had lost most of his teeth, and that had affected his digestion and through that his skin and temper. In face and expression he was curiously like that old Thomas Smallways who had once been coachman to Sir Peter Bone, and this was just as it should be, for he was Tom Smallways the son, who formerly kept the little greengrocer's shop under the straddle of the mono-rail viaduct in the High Street of Bun Hill. But now there were no greengrocers' shops, and Tom was living in one of the derelict villas hard by that unoccupied building site that had been and was still the scene of his daily horticulture. He and his wife lived upstairs, and in the drawing and dining-rooms, which had each French windows opening on the lawn, and all about the ground floor generally, Jessica, who was now a lean and lined and baldish but still very efficient and energetic old woman, kept her three cows and a multitude of gawky hens.

These two were part of a little community of stragglers and returned fugitives, perhaps a hundred and fifty souls of them altogether, that had settled down to the new condition of things after the Panic and Famine and Pestilence that followed in the wake of the War. They had come back from strange refuges and hiding-places, and had squatted down among the familiar houses and begun that hard struggle against nature for food which was now the chief interest of their lives. They were by sheer preoccupation with that a peaceful people, more particularly after Wilkes, the house agent, driven by some obsolete dream of acquisition, had been drowned in a pool by the mined gasworks for making inquiries into title and displaying a litigious turn of mind. (He had not been murdered, you understand, but the people had carried an exemplary ducking ten minutes or so beyond its healthy limits.)

This little community had returned from its original habits of suburban parasitism to what no doubt had been the normal life of humanity for nearly immemorial years, a life of homely economies in the most intimate contact with cows and hens and patches of ground, a life that breathes and exhales the scent of cows and finds the need for stimulants satisfied by the activity of the bacteria and vermin it engenders. Such had been the life of the European peasant from the dawn of history to the beginning of the Scientific Era, so it was the large majority of the people of Asia and Africa had always been wont to live. For a time it had seemed that by virtue of machines and scientific civilization, Europe was to be lifted out of this perpetual round of animal drudgery, and that America was to evade it very largely from the outset. And with the smash of the high and dangerous and splendid edifice of mechanical civilization that had arisen so marvelously, back to the land came the common man, back to the manure.

The little commodities, still haunted by ten thousand memories of a greater state, gathered and developed almost tacitly a customary law and fell under the guidance of a man of medicine or a priest. The world rediscovered religion and the need of something to hold its communities together. At Bun Hill this function was entrusted to an old Baptist minister. He taught a simple but adequate faith. In his teaching a good principle called the Word fought perpetually against a diabolical female influence called the Scarlet Woman and an evil being called Alcohol. This Alcohol had long since become a purely spiritualized conception

deprived of any element of material application; it had no relation to
the occasional finds of whisky and wine in Londoners' cellars that gave
Bun Hill its only holidays. He taught this doctrine on Sundays, and
on week-days he was an amiable and kindly old man, distinguished
by his quaint disposition to wash his hands, and if possible his face,
daily, and with a wonderful genius for cutting up pigs. He held his
Sunday services in the old church in the Beckenham Road, and then
the countryside came out in a curious reminiscence of the urban dress of
Edwardian times. All the men without exception wore frock coats, top
hats and white shirts, though many had no boots. Tom was particularly
distinguished on these occasions because he wore a top hat with gold
lace about it and a green coat and trousers that he had found upon a
skeleton in the basement of the Urban and District Bank. The women,
even Jessica, came in jackets and immense hats extravagantly trimmed
with artificial flowers and exotic birds' feathers—of which there were
abundant supplies in the shops to the north—and the children (there
were not many children, because a large proportion of the babies born
in Bun Hill died in a few days' time of inexplicable maladies) had similar
clothes cut down to accommodate them; even Stringer's little grandson
of four wore a large top hat.

That was the Sunday costume of the Bun Hill district, a curious and
interesting survival of the genteel traditions of the Scientific Age. On a
weekday the folk were dingily and curiously hung about with dirty rags
of housecloth and scarlet flannel, sacking, curtain serge and patches of
old carpet, and went either bare-footed or on rude wooden sandals.
These people, the reader must understand, were an urban population
sunken back to the state of a barbaric peasantry, and so without any of
the simple arts a barbaric-peasantry would possess. In many ways they
were curiously degenerate and incompetent. They had lost any idea
of making textiles, they could hardly make up clothes when they had
material, and they were forced to plunder the continually dwindling
supplies of the ruins about them for cover. All the simple arts they had
ever known they had lost, and with the breakdown of modern drainage,
modern water supply, shopping, and the like, their civilized methods
were useless. Their cooking was worse than primitive. It was a feeble
muddling with food over wood fires in rusty drawing-room fire-places;

for the kitcheners burnt too much. Among them all no sense of baking or brewing or metal-working was to be found.

Their employment of sacking and suchlike coarse material for work-a-day clothing, and their habit of tying it on with string and of thrusting wadding and straw inside it for warmth, gave these people an odd, "packed" appearance, and as it was a week-day when Tom took his little nephew for the hen-seeking excursion, so it was they were attired.

"So you've really got to Bun Hill at last, Teddy," said old Tom, beginning to talk and slackening his pace so soon as they were out of range of old Jessica. "You're the last of Bert's boys for me to see. Wat I've seen, young Bert, I've seen, Sissie and Matt, Tom what's called after me, and Peter. The traveller people brought you along all right, eh?"

"I managed," said Teddy, who was a dry little boy.

"Didn't want to eat you on the way?"

"They was all right," said Teddy. "And on the way near Leatherhead we saw a man riding on a bicycle."

"My word!" said Tom, "there ain't many of those about nowadays. Where was he going?"

"Said he was going to Dorking if the High Road was good enough. But I doubt if he got there. All about Burford it was flooded. We came over the hill, uncle—what they call the Roman Road. That's high and safe."

"Don't know it," said old Tom. "But a bicycle! You're sure it was a bicycle! Had two wheels?"

"It was a bicycle right enough."

"Why! I remember a time, Teddy, when there was bicycles no end, when you could stand just here—the road was as smooth as a board then—and see twenty or thirty coming and going at the same time, bicycles and moty bicycles, moty cars, all sorts of whirly things."

"No!" said Teddy.

"I do. They'd keep on going by all day—'undreds and 'undreds."

"But where was they all going?" asked Teddy.

"Tearin' off to Brighton—you never seen Brighton, I expect—it's down by the sea, used to be a moce 'mazing place—and coming and going from London."

"Why?"

"They did."

"But why?"

"Lord knows why, Teddy. They did. Then you see that great thing there like a great big rusty nail sticking up higher than all the houses, and that one yonder, and that, and how something's fell in between 'em among the houses. They was parts of the mono-rail. They went down to Brighton, too, and all day and night there was people going, great cars as big as 'ouses full of people."

The little boy regarded the rusty evidences across the narrow muddy ditch of cow-droppings that had once been a High Street. He was clearly disposed to be sceptical, and yet there the ruins were! He grappled with ideas beyond the strength of his imagination.

"What did they go for?" he asked; "all of 'em?"

"They 'ad to. Everything was on the go those days—everything."

"Yes, but where did they come from?"

"All round 'ere, Teddy, there was people living in those 'ouses, and up the road more 'ouses and more people. You'd hardly believe me, Teddy, but it's Bible truth. You can go on that way for ever and ever, and keep on coming on 'ouses, more 'ouses, and more. There's no end to 'em. No end. They get bigger and bigger." His voice dropped as though he named strange names. "It's *London*," he said.

"And it's all empty now and left alone. All day it's left alone. You don't find 'ardly a man, you won't find nothing but dogs and cats after the rats until you get round by Bromley and Beckenham, and there you find the Kentish men herding swine. (Nice rough lot they are too!) I tell you that so long as the sun is up it's as still as the grave. I been about by day—orfen and orfen." He paused.

"And all those 'ouses and streets and ways used to be full of people before the War in the Air and the Famine and the Purple Death. They used to be full of people, Teddy, and then came a time when they was full of corpses, when you couldn't go a mile that way before the stink of 'em drove you back. It was the Purple Death 'ad killed 'em every one. The cats and dogs and 'ens and vermin caught it. Everything and everyone 'ad it. Jest a few of us 'appened to live. I pulled through and your aunt, though it made 'er lose 'er 'air. Why, you find the skeletons in the 'ouses now. This way we been into all the 'ouses and took what we wanted and buried moce of the people, but up that way, Norwood way, there's 'ouses with the glass in the windows still, and the furniture not touched—all dusty and falling to pieces—and the bones of the people lying, some in bed, some about the 'ouse, jest as the Purple Death left 'em five-and-twenty years ago. I went into one—me and old Higgins las' year—and there was a room with books, Teddy—you know what I mean by books, Teddy?"

"I seen 'em. I seen 'em with pictures."

"Well, books all round, Teddy, 'undreds of books, beyond rhyme or reason, as the saying goes, green-mouldy and dry. I was for leavin' 'em alone—I was never much for reading—but ole Higgins he must touch 'em. 'I believe I could read one of 'em *now*,' 'e says.

" 'Not I,' I says.

" 'I could,' 'e says, laughing, and takes one out and opens it.

"I looked, and there, Teddy, was a cullud picture, oh, so lovely! It was a picture of women and serpents in a garden. I never see anything like it.

" 'This suits me,' said old Higgins, 'to rights.'

"And then kind of friendly he gave the book a pat——"

Old Tom Smallways paused impressively.

"And then?" said Teddy.

"It all fell to dus'. White dus'!" . . . He became still more impressive. "We didn't touch no more of them books that day. Not after that."

For a long time both were silent. Then Tom, playing with a subject that attracted him with a fatal fascination, repeated, "All day long they lie—still as the grave."

Teddy took the point at last. "Don't they lie o' nights?" he asked.

Old Tom shook his head. "Nobody knows, boy, nobody knows."

"But what could they do?"

"Nobody knows. Nobody ain't seen to tell—not nobody."

"Nobody?"

"They tell tales," said old Tom. "They tell tales, but there ain't no believing 'em. I gets 'ome about sundown, and keeps indoors, so I can't say nothing, can I? But there's them that thinks some things and them as thinks others. I've 'eard it's unlucky to take clo'es off of 'em unless they got white bones. There's stories——"

The boy watched his uncle sharply. "*Wot* stories?" he said.

"Stories of moonlight nights and things walking about. But I take no stock in 'em. I keeps in bed. If you listen to stories—Lord! you'll get afraid of yourself in a field at midday."

The little boy looked round and ceased his questions for a space.

"They say there's a 'og man in Beek'n'am what was lost in London three days and three nights. 'E went up after whisky to Cheapside, and lorst 'is way among the ruins and wandered. Three days and three nights 'e wandered about and the streets kep' changing so's 'e couldn't get 'ome. If 'e 'adn't remembered some words out of the Bible 'e might 'ave been there now. All day 'e went and all night—and all day long it was still. It was as still as death all day long, until the sunset came and the twilight thickened, and then it began to rustle and whisper and go pit-a-pat with a sound like 'urrying feet."

He paused.

"Yes," said the little boy breathlessly. "Go on. What then?"

"A sound of carts and 'orses there was, and a sound of cabs and omnibuses, and then a lot of whistling, shrill whistles, whistles that froze 'is marrer. And directly the whistles began things begun to show, people in the streets 'urrying, people in the 'ouses and shops busying themselves, moty cars in the streets, a sort of moonlight in all the lamps and winders. People, I say, Teddy, but they wasn't people. They was the ghosts of them that was overtook, the ghosts of them that used to crowd those streets. And they went past 'im and through 'im and never 'eeded 'im, went by like fogs and vapours, Teddy. And sometimes they was cheerful and sometimes they was 'orrible, 'orrible beyond words. And once 'e come to a place called Piccadilly, Teddy, and there was lights blazing like daylight and ladies and gentlemen in splendid clo'es crowding the pavement, and taxi-cabs follering along the road. And as he looked they all went evil—evil in the face, Teddy. And it seemed to 'im suddenly *they saw 'im*, and the women began to look at 'im and say things to 'im—'orrible—wicked things. One come very near 'im, Teddy, right up to 'im, and looked into 'is face—close. And she 'adn't got a face to look with, only a painted skull, and then 'e see they was all painted skulls. And one after another they crowded on 'im saying 'orrible things, and catchin 'at 'im and threatenin' and coaxin' 'im, so that 'is 'eart near left 'is body for fear. . . ."

"Yes," gasped Teddy in an unendurable pause.

"Then it was he remembered the words of Scripture and saved himself alive. 'The Lord is my 'Elper,' 'e says, 'therefore I will fear nothing,' and straight away there came a cock-crowing and the street was empty from end to end. And after that the Lord was good to 'im and guided 'im 'ome."

Teddy stared and caught at another question. "But who was the people," he asked, "who lived in all these 'ouses? What was they?"

"Gent'men in business, people with money—leastways we thought it was money till everything smashed up, and then seemingly it was jes' paper—all sorts. Why, there was 'undreds of thousands of them. There was millions. I've seen that 'I Street there regular so's you couldn't walk along the pavements, shoppin' time, with women and people shoppin'."

"But where'd they get their food and things?"

"Bort 'em in shops like I used to 'ave. I'll show you the place, Teddy, as we go back. People nowadays 'aven't no idee of a shop—no idee. Plateglass winders—it's all Greek to them. 'Why, I've 'ad as much as a ton and a 'arf of petaties to 'andle all at one time. You'd open your eyes till they dropped out to see jest what I used to 'ave in my shop. Baskets of pears 'eaped up, marrers, apples and pears, d'licious great nuts." His voice became luscious—"Benanas, oranges."

"What's Benanas?" asked the boy, "and Oranges?"

"Fruits they was. Sweet, juicy, d'licious fruits. Foreign fruits. They brought 'em from Spain and N'York and places. In ships and things. They brought 'em to me from all over the world, and I sold 'em in my shop. *I* sold 'em, Teddy! Me what goes about now with you, dressed up in old sacks and looking for lost 'ens. People used to come into my shop, great beautiful ladies like you'd 'ardly dream of now, dressed up to the nines, and say, 'Well, Mr. Smallways, what you got 'smorning?' and I'd say, 'Well, I got some very nice C'nadian apples,' or p'raps I got custed marrers. See? And they'd buy 'em. Right off they'd say, 'Send me some up. Lord! what a life that was. The business of it, the bussel, the smart things you saw, moty-cars going by, kerridges, people, organ-grinders,

German bands. Always something going past—always. If it wasn't for those empty 'ouses I'd think it all a dream."

"But what killed all the people, uncle?" asked Teddy.

"It was a smash up," said old Tom. "Everything was going right until they started that War. Everything was going like clockwork. Everybody was busy and everybody was 'appy and everybody got a good square meal every day." He met incredulous eyes. "Everybody," he said firmly. "If you couldn't get it anywhere else, you could get it in the workhuss, a nice 'ot bowl of soup called skilly, and bread better'n anyone knows 'ow to make now, reg'lar *white* bread, gov'ment bread."

Teddy marvelled but said nothing. It made him feel deep longings that he found it wisest to fight down.

For a time the old man resigned himself to the pleasures of gustatory reminiscence. His lips moved. "Pickled Sammin!" he whispered, "an' vinegar. . . . Dutch cheese, *Beer!* A pipe of terbakker."

"But *'ow* did the people get killed?" asked Teddy presently.

"There was the War. The War was the beginning of it. The War banged and flummocked about, but it didn't really *kill* many people. But it upset things. They came and set fire to London and burnt and sank all the ships there used to be in the Thames—we could see the smoke and steam for weeks—and they threw a bomb into the Crystal Palace and made a bust-up, and broke down the rail lines and things like that. But as for killin' people, it was just accidental if they did. They killed each other more. There was a great fight all hereabout one day, Teddy—up in the air. Great things bigger than fifty 'ouses, bigger than the Crystal Palace—bigger, bigger than anything, flying about up in the air and whacking at each other and dead men fallin' off 'em. T'riffic! But it wasn't so much the people they killed as the business they stopped. There wasn't any business doin', Teddy; there wasn't any money about, and nothin' to buy if you 'ad it."

"But 'ow did the people get *killed?*" said the little boy in the pause.

"I'm tellin' you, Teddy," said the old man. "It was the stoppin' of business come nex'. Sudden, some'ow, there didn't seem to be any money. There was cheques—they was a bit of paper written on, and they was jes' as good as money—jes' as good if they come from customers you knew. Then all of a sudden they wasn't. I was lef' with three of 'em and two I'd given change. Then it got about that five-pun' notes were no good, and then the silver sort of went off. Gold you couldn't get for love or—anything. The banks in London 'ad got it, and the banks was all smashed up. Everybody went bankrup'. Everybody was thrown out of work. Everybody!"

He paused, and scrutinized his hearer. The small boy's intelligent face expressed hopeless perplexity.

"That's 'ow it 'appened," said old Tom. He sought for some means of expression. "It was like stoppin' a clock," he said. "Things were quiet for a bit, deadly quiet, except for the airships fighting about in the sky, and then people begun to get excited. I remember my lars' customer, the very lars' customer that ever I 'ad. He was a Mr. Moses Gluckstein, a city gent and very pleasant and fond of sparrowgrass and chokes, and 'e cut in—there 'adn't been no customers for days—and began to talk very fast, offerin' me for anything I 'ad, anything, petaties or anything, its weight in gold. 'E said it was a little speculation 'e wanted to try. 'E said it was a sort of bet reely, and very likely 'e'd lose; but never mind that, 'e wanted to try. 'E always 'ad been a gambler, 'e said. 'E said I'd only got to weigh it out and 'e'd give me 'is cheque right away. Well, that led to a bit of a argument, perfectly respectful it was, but a argument about whether a cheque was still good, and while 'e was explaining there come by a lot of these here unemployed with a great banner they 'ad for everyone to read—everyone could read those days—'We Want Food.' Three or four of 'em suddenly turns and comes into my shop.

" 'Got any food?' says one.

" 'No,' I says, 'not to sell. I wish I 'ad. But if I 'ad I'm afraid I couldn't let you have it. This gent, 'e's been offerin' me——'

"Mr. Gluckstein 'e tried to stop me, but it was too late.

" 'What's 'e been offerin' you?' says a great big chap with a 'atchet; 'what's 'e been offerin' you?' I 'ad to tell.

" 'Boys,' 'e said, ' 'ere's another feenancier!' and they took 'im out there and then, and 'ung 'im on a lam'pose down the street. 'E never lifted a finger to resist. After I tole on 'im 'e never said a word. . . ."

Tom meditated for a space. "First chap I ever sin 'ung!" he said.

" 'Ow old was you?" asked Teddy.

" 'Bout thirty," said old Tom.

"Why! I saw free pig-stealers 'ung before I was six," said Teddy. "Father took me because of my birfday being near. Said I ought to be blooded. . . ."

"Well, you never saw no-one killed by a moty car, any'ow," said old Tom, after a moment of chagrin. "And you never saw no dead men carried into a chemis' shop."

Teddy's momentary triumph faded. "No," he said, "I 'aven't."

"Nor won't. Nor won't. You'll never see the things I've seen, never. Not if you live to be a 'undred. . . . Well, as I was saying, that's how the Famine and Riotin' began. Then there was strikes and Socialism, things I never did 'old with, worse and worse. There was fightin' and shootin' down, and burnin' and plunderin'. They broke up the banks up in London and got the gold. But they couldn't make food out of gold. 'Ow did *we* get on? Well, we kep' quiet. We didn't interfere with no-one and no-one didn't interfere with us. We 'ad some old 'tatoes about, but mocely we lived on rats. Ours was a ole 'ouse full of rats, and the famine never seemed to bother 'em. Orfen we got a rat. Orfen. But moce of the people who lived hereabouts was too tender stummicked for rats. Didn't seem to fancy 'em. They'd been used to all sorts of fallals, and they didn't take to 'onest feeding, not till it was too late. Died rather.

"It was the famine began to kill people. Even before the Purple Death come along they was dying like flies at the end of the summer. 'Ow I remember it all! I was one of the first to 'ave it. I was out seein' if I mightn't get 'old of a cat or somethin', and then I went round to my bit of ground to see whether I couldn't get up some young turnips I'd forgot, and I was took something awful. You've no idee the pain, Teddy—it doubled me up pretty near. I jes' lay down by that there corner, and your aunt come along to look for me and dragged me 'ome like a sack.

"I'd never 'ave got better if it 'adn't been for your aunt. 'Tom,' she says to me, 'you got to get well,' and I 'ad to. Then *she* sickened. She sickened, but there ain't much dyin' about your aunt. 'Lor!' she says, 'as if I'd leave you to go muddlin' along alone!' That's what she says. She's got a tongue 'as your aunt. But it took 'er 'air off—and arst though I might, she's never cared for the wig I got 'er—orf the old lady what was in the vicarage garden.

"Well, this 'ere Purple Death—it jes' wiped people out, Teddy. You couldn't bury 'em. And it took the dogs and the cats too, and the rats and 'orses. At last every 'ouse and garden was full of dead bodies. London way you couldn't go for the smell of them, and we 'ad to move out of the 'I Street into that villa we got. And all the water run short that way. The drains and underground tunnels took it. Gor' knows where the Purple Death come from; some say one thing and some another. Some said it come from eatin' rats and some from eatin' nothin'. Some say the Asiatics brought it from some 'I place, Thibet, I think, where it never did nobody much 'arm. All I know is it come after the Famine. And the Famine come after the Penic, and the Penic come after the War."

Teddy thought. "What made the Purple Death?" he asked.

" 'Aven't I tole you?"

"But why did they 'ave a Penic?"

"They 'ad it."

"But why did they start the War?"

"They couldn't stop theirselves. 'Aving them airships made 'em."

"And 'ow did the War end?"

"Lord knows if it's ended, boy," said old Tom. "Lord knows if it's ended. There's been travellers through 'ere—there was a chap only two summers ago—say it's goin' on still. They say there's bands of people up north who keep on with it, and people in Germany and China and 'Merica and places. 'E said they still got flying-machines and gas and things. But we 'aven't seen nothin' in the air now for seven years, and nobody 'asn't come nigh of us. Last we saw was a crumpled sort of airship going away—over there. It was a littleish-sized thing and lop-sided, as though it 'ad something the matter with it."

He pointed, and came to a stop at a gap in the fence, the vestiges of the old fence from which, in the company of his neighbour, Mr. Stringer the milkman, he had once watched the South of England Aero Club's Saturday afternoon ascents. Dim memories, it may be, of that particular afternoon returned to him.

"There, down there, where all that rus' looks so red and bright, that's the gasworks."

"What's gas?" asked the little boy.

"Oh, a hairy sort of nothin' what you put in balloons to make 'em go up. And you used to burn it till the 'lectricity come."

The little boy tried vainly to imagine gas on the basis of these particulars. Then his thoughts reverted to a previous topic.

"But why didn't they end the War?"

"Obstinacy. Everybody was getting 'urt, but everybody was 'urtin', and everybody was 'ighspirited and patriotic, and so they smeshed up things instead. They jes' went on smeshin'. And afterwards they jes' got desp'rite and savige."

"It ought to 'ave ended," said the little boy.

"It didn't ought to 'ave begun," said old Tom. "But people was proud. People was la-dy-ish and uppish and proud. Too much meat and drink they 'ad. Give in—not them! And after a bit nobody arst 'em to give in. Nobody arst 'em. . . ."

He sucked his old gums thoughtfully, and his gaze strayed away across the valley to where the shattered glass of the Crystal Palace glittered in the sun. A dim, large sense of waste and irrevocably lost opportunities pervaded his mind. He repeated his ultimate judgment upon all these things, obstinately, slowly, and conclusively, his final saying upon the matter.

"You can say what you like," he said. "It didn't ought ever to 'ave begun."

He said it simply—somebody somewhere ought to have stopped something, but who or how or why were all beyond his ken.

In the Bison Frontiers of Imagination series

CPSIA information can be obtained at www.ICGtesting.com
Printed in the USA
LVOW01s2022130815

450018LV00007B/104/P